THE PROPOSAL PLAY

LAUREN BLAKELY

COPYRIGHT

ABOUT THE BOOK

My plan when I win a date in Vegas with my brother's hockey-star best friend? Play poker and get to bed early. Instead, I wake up with a ring on my finger and a naked, sexy athlete beside me.

But Asher's my best friend too, so we'll get this annulled and laugh about this secret for years.

Trouble is, our wedding pics went viral overnight.

Now everyone thinks we're really married. We race home, where I've just landed the art commission of my dreams, and he's launching a sports charity so we need to look like we meant to tie the knot.

Easy enough. We'll claim we've been secretly in love, all while staying in separate rooms for the rest of hockey season.

The last thing either of us wants is to risk our friendship by falling into bed again.

But at home, I experience a new side of my husband. He cooks for me, encourages me...and buys me so many toys.

And, it's more fun to share your toys with a friend.

We're just enjoying a few temporary marital benefits. Except, the more he calls me his wife, the more I wonder if Asher was ever pretending?

And if my heart's ready to take the biggest risk of all.

DID YOU KNOW?

To be the first to find out when all of my upcoming books go live click here!

PRO TIP: Add lauren@laurenblakely.com to your contacts before signing up to make sure the emails go to your inbox!

Did you know this book is also available in audio and paperback on all major retailers? Go to my website for links!

For content warnings for this title, go to my site.

THE PROPOSAL PLAY

By Lauren Blakely
Love and Hockey #3

This book is dedicated to anyone whoever wondered, "Do I have too many toys?" The answer is you can't have too many toys.

PROLOGUE
THE MARRIAGE PACT

Asher

Two Years Ago

"The thing about bad ideas is they usually seem like good ideas at the time."

I take a planned pause from my best man speech to survey the sea of wedding guests. They're relaxed here under the white tent, rumpled suit jackets and little purses slung over their chair backs as the sun dips below the Golden Gate Bridge behind us.

With a glass of award-winning champagne in hand, I stroll around the head table, flash a *we knew better* glance at the groom, then shoot a winning smile for the hundred-strong crowd. Time to bring this speech home for Beckett. He deserves the best toast ever, and I'm the one who can give it to him.

"Like, say, that final shot of tequila," I say, with a curve in my lips. "Always seems like a good idea. But it's pretty much the opposite."

A collective groan echoes through the room. Yup. We've all been there and done that.

"Or, for instance, a homemade zip line," I add, shaking my head in disbelief at the antics of our younger selves. I stage whisper into the mic, "College. The genesis of nearly all bad ideas."

At the head table, the maid of honor—also known as the sister of the groom—laughs, then lifts a manicured hand in solidarity, her sparkly silver nail polish glinting in the soft light. "Can confirm it was the worst idea."

"We were lucky you were there." I nod toward the sometimes blonde, sometimes brunette. Maeve's hair color seems to change with her mood. Tonight at her brother's wedding, it's chestnut brown and twisted in, well, some kind of twist, with golden-streaked tendrils framing her face. "After all, she's the one who took us to the ER the night Beckett and I made a backyard ride out of rope eight years ago." A handful of guests laugh lightly, and I add, "But the shoulder injury—so worth it."

"Better your shoulder than mine," the groom shouts.

"My coach disagreed, but I digress," I say, then turn back to the audience, which is made up mostly of friends, but some family. Beckett's family primarily consists of him and his sister, and it's been that way since we met. I clear my throat, heading into the home stretch. "But luckily, it goes the other way, too, with good ideas. Like when Maeve said she wanted to set up her brother with a gallery manager she knew." I gesture toward the bride, Reina, who smiles dotingly at my friend. "I thought it was a terrible plan. Especially since there was that little matter of Beckett *refusing* to go on a setup."

Maeve smiles faux demurely, maybe a little wickedly.

Kind of her specialty. "But we knew better," she says proudly.

I shoot her a pointed look. "*You* knew better. Me? I told you setups *never* work." I turn back to the guests. "But Maeve insisted, and I went along with her. She's very clever. Very creative."

"Very tricky," Beckett says with a fake cough.

"You benefited from it," Maeve says and gestures grandly to the evidence—the damn wedding.

"So we organized a game night. Invited...*a bunch of friends*." I sketch air quotes since we invited exactly no one. "When Beckett arrived at my place, he looked around and asked where everyone else was. I said they were coming but we could get started, just the four of us. Spoiler alert: No one showed up but Reina, and during a vicious game of trivia where those two tried to one-up each other, Maeve and I slipped into the kitchen to refresh the snacks. And..." I gesture proudly to the newlyweds. "Here we are. Thanks to a fake-out from the maid of honor and the best man."

"It was the best idea," Beckett says genuinely, then drops a quick kiss to his bride's cheek, before turning to his sister and giving her a grateful hug. "Can't thank you enough, Maeve," he says, his voice choked with obvious emotion. She hugs him back, holding on before letting go.

The emotional moment between the two of them makes me look away. It feels private, personal. But then, it's not a secret they're all each other has.

When Maeve blows out a clearing breath and adopts a smile, I take that as my cue to restore the levity.

I lift a glass. "But don't worry about me, Beckett. I've still got a partner in crime the next time I want to make a homemade zip line." I look to the new second-in-command in troublemaking, Maeve, then once more to the guy who's been my best friend for almost a decade. "To finding the love of your life and keeping her close every day."

The crowd toasts with a *hear, hear*, while Maeve's big hazel eyes capture mine for a long beat, and then she mouths, *"Good job."*

And I...blink.

Because wow...

Look at her lips.

They're awfully pouty tonight. Terribly glossy. And strangely, incredibly tempting. They're shiny and the color of a raspberry—a ripe, red raspberry I want to taste.

What. The. Hell?

I jerk my gaze away as I try to shake off the fog of lust that rolls in like unexpected weather. Maybe it's the wedding makeup. Because *something* has to be messing with my head.

I clear my throat. Fucking raspberries.

"So," I say to the crowd once more, "let's get this party started!"

I set down the mic and try to dismiss these new thoughts about Maeve. I've known her for eight years. Met her in grief counseling. She's not only my best friend's sister—she's my *other* best friend.

In all that time, I've never thought of her lips. I mean, not much. No more than the average number of lip-related thoughts a straight guy would have about a straight woman.

This is just a passing thought. And passing thoughts... pass.

Bet it goes away right now as the bride and groom hit

the dance floor, urging everyone to join them while the upbeat pop song plays.

Maeve's heading toward me in a black dress that hits right below her knees and hugs her hips. "Want to know what's never a bad idea?" she asks when she reaches me.

"What's that?"

"A dance," she says, and yes, of course. That's a perfect reminder of our long-standing friendship.

We dance to a few tunes, all fun and friendly. It's enough to erase those errant thoughts from before. We roll into the cake-cutting and then the toasts from the bride's relatives. Then another slow song begins, and Beckett grabs the mic and points to us. "And now it's time for the traditional best-man and maid-of-honor dance."

"That's not a thing," I say.

Maeve rolls her eyes at my retort. "I don't bite," she says as she nears me.

But *does* she bite? In bed? Does she like to be bitten?

Ah, fuck.

What is happening to me? I could blame Frank Sinatra, singing about foolish hearts. Or maybe it's the wedding messing with my head. I'm a big fan of weddings —my dads took me to a million of them when I was growing up. In the years since, the dates were always plentiful, the times were always good. I'm simply a wedding kind of guy.

That's all.

Relieved that I finally get what's going on in my brain, I take Maeve into my arms, my hands curling around her soft waist.

That's nice.

A friendly kind of nice though.

The way my palms fit around her figure is very, *very*

friendly, I'm sure. I'm not distracted by her bare shoulders and the freckles dotting her fair skin. Besides, we're a respectable distance away from each other. Several inches, probably. Studies have shown that several inches is a platonic amount of space.

"Question for you," Maeve says, pulling me out of my thoughts and back to the speech.

"Hit me," I say.

"Do you remember something else that seemed like a good idea? Like the morning you thought it'd be a good idea to do a Zoom interview with The Sports Network while *not* wearing pants?"

"The team publicist almost didn't forgive me," I say, laughing as I recall the *are you kidding me* shock on the publicity director's face when I showed up at the arena later that day.

"But of course, you had to get the Pop-Tart out of the toaster in the middle of the interview."

"It would have burned," I say with zero sarcasm. No remorse either.

"Thank god you saved that Pop-Tart. If not, the whole world wouldn't have seen your...wait for it...*best hockey butt ever.*"

I'm not even embarrassed that I'm known for having a great ass. "I had on compression shorts—"

"Tight, nearly see-through, white compression shorts," she corrects.

"That made my ass famous," I counter. "And now I have a great underwear sponsor. So really, the ass paid off."

It pays handsomely every day. The top three search results for me are Asher Callahan stats (they're awesome), Asher Callahan girlfriend (the answer is none), and Asher

Callahan ass (it's even more awesome than my stats, and that's saying something).

"I stand corrected," Maeve admits. "In *hindsight* it was a good idea to get the Pop-Tart out in the middle of an on-air interview."

"It was brown sugar cinnamon."

"Ah, that makes perfect sense now," she deadpans, but then her brow cinches like she's considering something. "I was always curious what kind it was. I tried to figure it out from the video. I watched it so many times," she muses.

"So it was *you* that drove up the view count. How many times? 'Fess up," I say, but the second the taunt breaks free from my lips, my head spins. *Why* did she watch it so many times? Did she like it?

Why do I care?

But Maeve simply shrugs innocently. "A lady never tells. But maybe I'll tell the story at your wedding someday when I give a toast," she says as we sway, then she slows her pace, asking with a soft laugh, "wait, am I going to be your best woman when you get hitched?"

"Only if I'm your man of honor," I fire back. My toasting her at her nuptials feels distinctly possible. More likely than my learning if she likes biting.

But Maeve simply scoffs. "You know my track record. No one wants to marry a broke artist who's bad at romance."

"You're not bad at romance," I say gently. *You just pick dickheads who don't appreciate you.* She looks to her brother and Reina with a happy sigh, then turns back to me with a helpless little shrug—like she wants what they have but doesn't think she'll ever have it.

Something comes over me—maybe it's the champagne, or maybe it's just that weddings make you think about, well, weddings. Whatever it is, I say casually, "Don't worry. If it comes down to it, I'll marry you."

She pauses, then arches a skeptical brow. "You're suggesting a marriage pact, Callahan?"

Seems I am.

I don't back down from a challenge—not one thrown at me or one *I* throw down. Besides, she seems to need certainty right now. "Sure," I say. "If you ever need a husband, I'm your guy."

A laugh bursts from her, but then she schools her expression. "Fine," she says primly, adopting a regal air. "Since you made such a heartfelt proposal, I accept your marriage pact."

"I'll hold you to it," I say.

"You do that."

Then I dip the fuck out of her here on the dance floor. Her back bows and her foot pops up, but she holds on tight, laughing brightly. The sound of her laughter knocks something else loose inside my head as I tug her back to standing. Possibly a few brain cells that slept through the last eight years of friendship. Because...Maeve is pretty and charming and fucking adorable. How did I miss what's been right in front of me?

Her laugh, like wind chimes, sounds prettier than it has before. Her perfume, like wildflowers on a sultry summer day, hits differently now. Her lush lips are suddenly impossible to look away from. How much champagne did I have tonight? A couple of glasses? But even so, I'm not a lightweight. I'm more than six feet tall, and I'm sturdy as fuck.

As I try to count my cocktails, I glimpse one of the bride's uncles dancing near the band. He's cutting the rug,

twirling his wife, but when he pulls her back into his arms
—*bam.*

He bumps right into Maeve's back. She pitches
forward in my arms, slamming against my chest, her chin
tipped up, her eyes wide. "Oh!"

She's breathless.

And she's also suddenly a very dangerous four inches
closer to me. I'm barely aware of anyone else on the dance
floor, under the tent, in the whole damn city. I look down
at my best friend's sister, mesmerized without warning. It's
like I've never quite seen her clearly until tonight—from
the hair to the lips to the laughter to the dance, to her *this*
close to me. "I've got you," I say softly, holding her hips
tighter, keeping her near.

She glances down, too, but doesn't pull away. "You...do
have me, Asher."

She sounds surprised. Maybe confused. That makes
two of us. I swallow roughly and simply echo, "I do."

I don't move.

She doesn't either.

Her body fits mine in a whole new way. Our hips flush,
her breasts pressed to me—everything temptingly
aligned. Her raspberry lips are so close that I can tell it's
not the makeup making her look so pretty tonight.

She *is* pretty.

Did it take me crossing these final four inches to
notice Maeve *like this*?

No idea, but I'm noticing Maeve like this now. Oh hell,
am I noticing my friend. My chest is crackling. My skin,
hot. My pulse, spiking. Everything inside me turns electric, and I know the meaning of the term insta-lust.

It's my goddamn life right now.

For several seconds that go by too fast we sway together as the song inevitably ends.

When a fast song blasts brightly under the tent, we wrench apart. In a heartbeat, that shuddery sensation vanishes like it didn't even happen. Like it was just a very vivid dream.

A passing thought doing what it does—passing.

My skin's no longer hot. My chest isn't tingly. Whatever dirty spell I was under is broken.

I can breathe again. I inhale and exhale a few quick times. And yup, order is restored to my universe.

What a close call. I can't believe for a second there—okay, for several seconds—I thought I was into my best friend.

Good thing I'm not.

Because falling for your best friend would be a very bad idea. Especially if you just made a marriage pact with her.

1

A PRETTY PINK DICK

Maeve

Present day

Does this clutch look like a dick?

When I grabbed it from the back of my closet of thrift shop wonders this evening before racing out the door, it looked innocent enough for a fancy pants event. But now that I'm sitting demurely under a chandelier in an upscale ballroom in a historic mansion, I'm having second thoughts about my choice of accessory.

I want to ask Asher what he thinks of it—one of our regular *questions for you*—but he's getting ready to parade around on stage so someone here can bid on a date with him.

Pretty sure I can make an executive call, though, about the clutch. It's pink, shiny, and about seven inches long.

Yup. It's definitely got dick energy, and I don't want to look like I'm fondling it as I sneak another peek at my phone during this charity fundraising auction.

In my reserved seat in the front row, I surreptitiously slide my index finger along the sparkly satin material and snap it open in slow-mo, hoping no one notices me checking my phone *again*. There's room for lipstick, too, in the clutch and a couple credit cards, so maybe people will think I'm just making sure my makeup is safe and my accounts are in good standing.

No one will see me sneaking a peek. No one, like, oh say, my big brother next to me. Or his wife next to him. Or, really, anyone at all.

Because...rude.

But in my defense, I'm waiting for an email about a life-changing job, and it's supposed to arrive tonight. I peer around the packed ballroom. Every seat is taken this Thursday night in January, filled with perfumed, groomed, and coiffed humans eager to bid for dates with all the eligible hockey bachelors in the city.

Asher's not due to strut his stuff yet. Miles Falcon is up next, so I can get away with one more look before it's my best friend's turn.

As Erin—the color commentator for the team's games on The Sports Network—regales the audience on stage, I slowly slide out the corner of my phone. My agent told me she'd email this evening about a huge mural project she submitted my portfolio for weeks ago. I made it past the first round. She assured me the decision was coming tonight, and I was among the top three candidates.

"And now we have Miles Falcon, the accomplished center for the San Francisco Sea Dogs who dominates the faceoff," Erin says into the mic, her confident and playful voice filling the room as she reads from an index card touting Miles's hobbies like hiking mountain trails and playing a mean game of pool. "He also enjoys the thrill of urban treasure hunts. Get ready to bid high when it's time —because a date with Miles Falcon will be an adventure!"

Well, with that kind of setup, no one is going to be looking at little old me.

As Miles crosses the stage, I slide a thumb over the screen and pray to the universe to deliver me my dream job at last. I've spent the last few years cobbling odd jobs together, trying desperately to make a living as an artist. Mostly, though, I've been making a living as a server at some high-end events, which thrills my aunt, who owns the catering company I work for, but it doesn't thrill me.

When I glance at the screen, it mocks me with its nothingness, and the empty bars in the corner where my cell reception should be.

Who invented phones?

Shoulders slumping, I snap the clutch closed as my brother nudges me.

"Maeve. You can swipe right later," Beckett whispers in my ear.

I shoot him a look. "I was not checking a dating app. Those things are dead to me," I hiss.

They are so dead that I hosted a party with my girl-friends the other month to delete the hell out of the latest and last dating app I'd tried. It had delivered nothing but bad matches, like men who claimed dumpster dinners were a new life hack, or guys who asked me for pictures of my feet.

Screw apps. I'm a goddamn goddess. I deserve only top-tier matches.

Beckett glances down at the phone peeking out of the

little purse, then back to my face, his gaze just shy of disappointed. He's such a big brother. "Asher's next," he reminds me in case I forgot.

Which I didn't.

"I know," I say out of the corner of my mouth. "He's the reason I'm here."

My brother arches a brow. "Oh, so you *are* going to bid on him?"

I stare him down. "Yes, Beckett. *I'm* going to bid on a star athlete. With all my spare change. There's actually a piggy bank inside here," I say, patting the clutch. "Can't wait to break it open."

The coin in it, plus my catering gigs at my aunt Vivian's company, add up to almost, maybe, possibly just enough to cover the rent each month.

I'm not here to bid. I'm here for one reason only— Asher Callahan worships at the altar of superstitions. He's gone for the highest bid at the last two of these auctions while I've cheered him on from the front row, and he hasn't missed a single hockey game in all that time. Now he claims I am the key, somehow, to his fundraising success and injury-free status on the ice.

Who am I to argue with someone's quirks? I've got a suitcase full of my own. So here I am in the same chair, rooting for my bestie to go for top bucks.

As I set my hands on the clutch, I spot Asher offstage in the wings, looking polished in a three-piece, sapphire-blue suit I picked for him to wear tonight from his closet of custom clothes. The man makes this tailored choice look stunning. It hugs his muscles in all the right ways. Plus, that vest looks as good as I'd predicted.

Asher runs a hand through his thick, slightly unruly

brown hair. His green eyes are movie-star-level mesmerizing. He spots me as he smooths his lapels, and he smirks, lifts a brow, then mouths, *"Hey, good luck charm."*

I roll my eyes. *"You're ridiculous,"* I mouth back.

But I'm ridiculous, too, since I'm here, showing up for him as requested.

As Miles leaves the stage, Erin flips to the next card—this one for the final hockey star in this year's auction. "Ladies and gentlemen, prepare to meet the player who's as golden as his stats! It's our fan-favorite left winger—the fiery *Asher Callahan!*"

The crowd goes even wilder than before as Asher strides across the stage. Whispers of *I'm going to bid so hard on him,* and *OMG, I want him* land on my ears. A few seats away, a woman with jet-black hair and a spray tan points at him. She looks familiar. Maybe she's the daughter of some San Francisco rich dude? Oh! I think she's the one who's launching a new beauty line. With a cool, confident air, she says something to the friend next to her.

Probably, *I'll win him, hands down.*

More power to you, babe.

Erin introduces him. "When Asher's not leading the charge on the rink, he's a dedicated supporter of mental health initiatives, using his platform to make a positive impact." Erin sings his praises, encouraging big bidding for charity. "But do you know why we call Asher fiery? The Vancouver-born winger is a hot sauce aficionado, constantly hunting for the hottest, most daring flavors to challenge his taste buds. So, if you're up for an evening full of spice and excitement, raise a paddle for Asher when it's time to place your bids...because a date with him is sure to sizzle!"

Pride floods me at the intro—not the hot sauce part because whatever. The *other* part. With his megawatt smile and high profile, he'll have no problem going for top dollar, with or without me.

Erin finishes Asher's intro and says, "We'll take a fifteen-minute break for you to prepare your bids now that you've seen all the entrants. Then, get ready to break the bank to support a good cause."

I get ready to support a good cause too—my self-esteem. It's time to find somewhere in this historic mansion with cell service. "Be right back," I tell Beckett, gripping the clutch tightly.

"Good luck checking your matches. But remember, just because *you* think napping is an Olympic sport, it's a bad idea to pick a guy who lists sleeping in as a hobby."

"I told you," I say, "I am not trolling for dates right now. Also, napping *is* an Olympic sport, and I am a gold medalist."

Whirling away, I hustle my ass toward the door, weaving through the guests who pop up from their seats as they plan their bids. Women with cut-crease eyeshadow and glittery dresses. Men with sharp suits and fresh haircuts. The team raises a ton of money for charity at this annual event, with its eligible players entering each season.

I dart through the pretty crowd, the scent of seductive colognes and alluring body sprays nearly cloying—everyone is dressed to win a date with a pro athlete tonight.

My focus, though, is singular, and it has been for a long time.

Follow your dreams.

Those words are tattooed on my heart, and I'm putting

them into action. After I escape the ballroom, I extract my phone and scurry down an opulent hallway, holding the device out in front of me like an offering to the technology gods.

Still no signal.

What about the ladies' room? I pop inside, where a throng of women check their reflections. It's a dead zone in here, too, so I retrace my steps and then march farther down the hall.

Don't rich people need to communicate like the rest of us? Actually, come to think of it, they probably clap, and the universe delivers whatever they need on silver serving platters.

Frustration bubbles up inside me as I search for a room that'll lead to, I dunno, maybe a window?

That's it! All I need is a window.

I'm almost at the last door in the hallway when my phone flickers with a hint of a bar.

The door's closed, which *probably* means I shouldn't go in. There's also a reserved sign hanging on it. Which is *possibly* a nice way of saying *stay the hell out.*

But reserved doesn't necessarily mean *off-limits.* There's room for interpretation, so I interpret.

Holding my breath, I gently push open the door that leads into...a library.

And it's empty.

Well, it's clearly not reserved now.

I shut the door most of the way, just in case anyone comes by, and take in the towering mahogany book-shelves filled to the brim with leather-bound tomes. They're beautiful enough, but the real prize is in the corner.

"Come to me, you sexy window. Wait, no. I'll go to

you," I say to the glass panes since now I evidently talk to windows.

I race across the library and stand under the towering window, phone held aloft. The first bar fills in. Hope floods my cells. Except...that's barely enough service to send a text, let alone receive an email.

But if I were *at* the window level...

There's a ladder positioned against the bookshelf right next to the window, and a grin takes over my face. That has to be a sign. I'm a painter, so ladders and I are tight.

I set the dick clutch on the marble floor, then give a quick glance at my vintage, rose-gold dress—1920s style but without the flapper fringe. I need a little more wiggle room, so I kick off my shoes, hike up the skirt, and climb the ladder attached to one of the bookshelves. I angle my phone toward the source of that elusive signal, trying to balance myself on the ladder rungs while holding the phone high.

The window is a foot or so away. If I can just stretch out my arm, my phone will receive emails like coins pouring into a leprechaun's pot at the end of the rainbow. And I can surely reach a little farther. I'm limber. Hell, I'm almost a cat, thanks to the pole classes I take with my friends. This ladder's practically a pole.

Like Belle in *Beauty and the Beast*, I lift my left foot up to get a little more reach, then stretch on my right.

A faint chime echoes through the library, breaking the silence with its sweet sound. That has to be my inbox.

My heart! It foxtrots.

My future is landing. I just know it. But right as I'm about to climb down, my heart tugs.

Only...that's not my heart.

That's the delicate lace bodice of this vintage dress caught on one of the protruding hooks on the ladder.

No, no, no, no.

I try to free the dress, but the hook stubbornly refuses to release its grip on the fabric.

Holding on tight to the ladder with one hand, I try to wiggle the lace with the hand that's holding my phone. But footsteps creak in the hallway, growing louder. My heart speeds. Shit. I can't be caught like this by mansion security. It might be embarrassing for Asher if his plus-one is discovered climbing ladders she shouldn't be climbing, in libraries she shouldn't be frequenting.

Are the owners going to slap me with a trespassing fine? Is that even a thing?

I don't know, but my phone's dangling from my fingertips in its protective case. I make a split-second decision and let it go. Right as it clatters to the marble floor, I hoist my boobs up, freeing the dress from the hook.

I am a superhero! I saved the dress and the phone and my ass.

I swing around the ladder like it's a pole. It'll be faster to jump than to climb down. I let go, bracing myself to land on my feet, when...

Oof!

My head snaps back as my dress snags on another hook. My feet hit the floor, and just as a loud rip echoes through the air, the door swings open and Asher walks in.

"I was looking for you. I'm almost up. I need my good luck charm."

He stops, his smile vanishing when he sees me crouched on the marble floor, my pink zebra-print bra on full display thanks to my first-ever ripped bodice. This didn't come in a fit of passion but rather a fit of desperation.

Asher's green eyes widen, as if he's never seen a person who's been stripped by a ladder before and he doesn't know what to say. But he has an auction to do, and I don't want him to feel off-kilter.

I glance down at the phone case and back up at Asher. "Question for you—does this clutch look like a dick?"

2

MY ACTIVE IMAGINATION

Asher

I've found Maeve in some unusual places over the years. At my door, dressed as a coquettish French maid, holding a butler costume and asking me to a last-minute costume party. In an empty lecture hall on her college campus, crying on the anniversary of her mother's death. Stuck in a roadside gas station restroom after a concert one night. (Her hairpin came in handy to free her that time.) But this is tops.

Still, I didn't think when I spotted her darting into this room that I'd find her on the floor...like *this*.

Maybe I *should* have, but this is fucking distracting. Because there's...cleavage and kissable flesh on display. There's a sexy bra in my line of sight and wildly inappropriate ideas forming in my head. Disheveled is a surprisingly good look on Maeve.

I never knew zebra print was hot.

Except...she's Beckett's sister and she's *my* best friend.

Best to banish those dirty thoughts to a faraway land because there's no place for them in our friendship. Or in my life, frankly. I have plans and shit.

But before I can even ask what the hell happened, she pops up, hastily grabbing at the tattered top of her dress, trying to jam the fabric back together with sheer will. "So much for being a good luck charm," she says, her voice trembling. "I can't go back in there looking like a bad omen."

She's right. She *can't* go back in there looking like this. Because nearly every man will stare at her hungrily, and I'm not okay with that.

But first things first. "You're not a bad omen," I reassure her.

"I am. I'm the worst, Asher. I'm so sorry," she says as she tries to tie the tops of the ripped sides together with her talented fingers. She's good at all things creative, but I'm pretty sure fixing a torn dress without a needle and thread is out of her wheelhouse. "I ruined your night. I came in here looking for a cell signal, and instead, I turned into..." She flaps her hands, letting go of the bodice. "A fucking agent of chaos."

Well, she *is* an agent of chaos and it's one of her many endearing qualities. But now probably isn't the right time to point out that Maeve is simply being Maeve. I have to go back on stage for the bidding in seven minutes, and I need her in the audience. I went looking for her to make sure she hadn't lost track of time or, I dunno, discovered a stray dog or cat or duck that she needed to take home tonight. All viable possibilities.

This is potentially a big night for a lot of reasons, and not simply because I *want* to keep up the tradition—

though, of course, I do. The exposure that comes with winning big will help the plans Beckett and I have to launch a new charity. It's not necessarily difficult to get people to pitch in for stray dogs and cats; it's harder to know how to help underprivileged kids. Our charity can bridge that gap... *if* I can get their attention in this media-saturated world.

But that's a few weeks down the road. *This* is now. Like we're on the ice, behind in the third period, and it's up to me to send the puck to the net, I say, matter-of-factly, "Let's fix it."

That's what I do best. Solve problems for people. Help my friends.

Shutting the library door, I advance into the room.

"How?" she asks, plucking at the lace in a way I can't let distract me. "I don't have a sewing kit with me." A moment later, she brightens. "Do you think somebody does? Reina? Maybe Everly? She's backstage, right?"

Everly is both the team publicist and Maeve's good friend. But who carries a sewing kit in their pocket? Even if she did, that rip is inches long and would take more than a few minutes to fix. "There's not enough time. We need a fix in this room," I say.

Maeve bites the corner of her lips. "Will you forgive me? I'm such an idiot. I should never have climbed that ladder."

"Forgiveness?" I laugh; this is nowhere near the unforgivable zone, and she should know that. "On one condition."

"Name it."

"I have to know—what made you climb it? Was it because it was there? Because honestly, that's reason enough." Every moment with her is a delightfully unpredictable show, and this one might just be the most Maeve thing yet.

As she fiddles with the pieces of the dress, trying vainly once more to fix it somehow, she confesses, "Angelina said she'd email me tonight." Angelina is Maeve's agent, and Maeve has been waiting to hear about a particularly coveted commission that could be a big break for her.

"Did you get the gig?"

She shrugs. "No idea. *This* sort of took precedent," she says, gesturing to her ripped bodice. She spins around, searching the library. "Wait! What if I carry a bunch of books in front of me? I can hold them like a prop!"

"That might be a little obvious." But that word—*obvious*—presents the solution. For fuck's sake, how did I miss this?

I shed my suit jacket and thrust it at her. "Here."

"You're brilliant," she says as she slides her arms into it, the cuffs hitting the tips of her fingers. A laugh bursts from her. "Why do you have to be so big?"

But that's not really the problem. The problem is the button in the middle, since that's where jacket buttons live. When she fastens it, the jacket doesn't even begin to cover up the top of her breasts, which, *wow,* look particularly lush and tempting right now.

Get it together.

"It looks better on you anyway," she adds, shrugging off the jacket and handing it to me. I set it on the ornate arm of the forest-green couch.

"Not sure I agree. Looked pretty good on you." Though I'd never admit just how good.

Maeve, ever the optimist, scans the room. "Think

there's a wrap or something lying around? Maybe a fancy scarf or a throw forgotten by some posh guest?"

Her suggestion is cute, but I have another plan. It just requires a little ingenuity. "I've got a better idea," I say, brushing my fingers over the fabric of my vest, then glancing at her elegantly twisted hair. The solution is right there. "But I'm going to need your help. Can you hand me one of those hairpins?"

"Sure thing." Always game, she reaches up to pull one out, and as she does, the bodice of her dress slips lower.

Her dress was already hanging by a thread. Now, gravity tugs down, leaving nothing but the barest of barriers between us and something far more dangerous. Rogue thoughts conjure scenarios I've no business entertaining—her dress torn away, her body laid bare, her lips daring me to do something reckless.

I fight to clear my head, but my imagination has always been a double-edged sword. As a kid, I was always pretending I was someone else—a superhero, a spy, a pirate, a fireman, and sometimes even a professional hockey player.

Okay, that last one came true. But that doesn't mean this push-Maeve-up-against-the-wall one will. Because it'd be a very bad idea. Our lives are too tangled together. Something might go wrong. I hate when things go wrong.

Focus—fix the dress, help her out, get your head back in the game. But damn, if it isn't a struggle when Maeve is this close, this vulnerable—a temptation I never expected I'd struggle to resist.

Focusing on things I can control, I take the hairpin and blow out a steadying breath.

"Question for you," she begins.

"Yeah?"

"What's the plan?"

Wresting control of my thoughts, I give her a *don't you worry* grin. "Do you trust me?"

Her head tilts. "You know I do." It comes out soft and true. A promise made again and again over the years.

A promise kept.

"I've got this, then." I tuck the hairpin in my pocket then make quick work of the buttons on my vest. Good thing there are more of them. Good thing they go higher than the one on my jacket did. Maeve's eyes widen with intrigue and then with understanding.

"Are you MacGyvering me an outfit?" There's excitement in her voice now. Maybe even a thrill.

I don't say a word. I answer with actions, sliding the vest onto her. One side, then around her, then the other side. My hands feel a little buzzy as they touch her arms.

"Good thing I told you to wear a vest," she says.

"And I resisted. But you knew best."

She rolls her eyes. "Don't give me too much credit tonight. You're the one fixing my dress without a sewing kit."

But I'm giving her all the credit because, so far, she looks extraordinary in my clothes.

She slips on the dark blue vest, and I do the buttons up. Her scent tickles my nose. At her brother's wedding it was wildflowers. Now it's like sweet plums, something I'd pick from a tree in the summer and sink my teeth into. My pulse surges as my fingers skate over her soft skin. This is ridiculous, these reactions to her. She's a friend—that's all.

I slide the final button in, a vein throbbing in my neck.

Or something is throbbing, and it's not in my neck.

This moment is dangerously close to that wedding two years ago all over again. I remind myself I have an active imagination, and thoughts are not actions. Wild scenarios don't need to come true.

I step back.

She looks down at her new ensemble, her smile spreading fast.

"It hits just right," she says, choosing the words she'd said to me when I tried the vest on at her suggestion.

"A little loose, though," I say, my voice gravelly. I move behind her, grabbing the hairpin from my pocket. Quickly, I gather the silky fabric at the back of the vest and fold it over, tightening it, then sliding the hairpin over it to hold it in place. "How's that?"

"You're a tailor," she says, tucking the pieces of lacy fabric out of sight under the front of the vest while I adjust the back. I smooth a hand over it, making sure the pin will stay.

"Everything good back there?" she asks.

I roam my eyes up and down her. *You have no idea how good.*

"It's great," I say as evenly as I can. I move around her, and holy fuck...

That vest does unfair things to her tits. It boosts them up, but not too much, she's not too risqué. Just right.

She offers a hopeful smile as she makes a few final adjustments to the ripped fabric. "Do I look good in your clothes?"

The question echoes through my head. *Does she look good in my clothes?* She looks fucking incredible, and I don't know what to make of that. "You look like..."

Mine.

The word forms on my tongue. How could she look like anything else but mine when she's wearing my vest?

Instead, I amend my statement to, "You look like the best lucky charm. Now, go check your phone."

"You know me too well."

"Yeah, I do," I say.

She flicks open the case. A few scrolls and her shoulders slump. She groans when she meets my eyes. "Angelina says they haven't decided and they're putting it off for another week or two."

She swallows hard, gulping down her disappointment, I'm sure. I wish I could make things easier for her. She's made inroads in her career for sure, nabbing opportunities here and there, chances to paint some murals on buildings, and to showcase some of her more unusual pieces of art—bedazzled lamps made from liquor bottles —at a night market. But it hasn't been easy. It's been years of desperately trying to make it. Years of yearning.

"Who's the job with?" I ask, wondering if it's one of the galleries or gigs she's mentioned to me. If I know more, I can give her a pep talk. Keep her spirits up.

She shakes her head. "Doesn't matter."

"It does to me," I say.

She smiles faintly and pats my shoulder. "It's your night. You're the ultimate prize. Let's get in there."

We leave with two minutes to spare. When we pass the restroom on the way back, Maeve nods to it and says tightly that she'll pop in there for a second. "I promise I'll be out in thirty."

I gesture to the ballroom at the end of the hall. "I'll meet you inside," I say.

"I'll be there," she adds quietly.

"I know," I say, a little like Han Solo, but I can be cocky for a moment. It's a good feeling to know she'll be there.

It's a feeling I don't want to ever lose.

3

SNAKE GIRL

Maeve

How stupid am I? I can't believe I did that. I can't believe I nearly ruined his night, and for what?

For nothing.

I shut the door to a stall. I don't have to pee, but I need to get myself together before I go back in there. I yank off some toilet paper and daub under my eyes as Angelina's words replay in my mind.

They received an influx of portfolios at the last minute, so they won't be making their decision yet.

But I submitted mine early, so that means it wasn't good enough to make it to the final round. If it were, they wouldn't care about the last-minute submissions.

Story of my adult life. I can't catch a break. Maybe the universe is trying to give me a sign—*give up painting. Toss the towel in on making art. No one makes a living as an artist anyway. You're not special.*

That's certainly the message I get from my aunt

Vivian, though hers is coated in honey and laced with a little vested interest. She says things like, "Oh, sweetie, it's too hard to make it as an artist. Just work with me instead."

I try to shut out both voices with a few deep breaths as the main door to the ladies' room swings open. The clock is ticking. Wallow time is over. But shoes click, and a voice carries.

"I'm so ready. Daddy upped the limit on my card, so I got an advance to bid on Asher," a soprano voice says gleefully.

Hand on the latch, I tip my head closer, straining to catch every word.

"And when people think I'm dating him, I'll get soooo many new followers for the brand," she adds. "I've laid all the groundwork by wearing his jersey in videos. One date, and it'll be catnip for clicks."

My skin crawls, and I gasp silently, but I don't move.

The other woman's voice is softer, almost cautious. "It sounds like a great plan, but...are you sure this is the best way to go about it? What if it backfires?"

"Backfire? No way. He's dating someone new every few months. It'll be easy to pull off."

"People might see through it," the careful one says.

"Ever heard of Photoshop? I'll take so many pics of us, change my outfits in them, and then I can just dole them out like we're totally a thing. The timing will be perf. People believe what you tell them."

My temperature shoots through the roof as I peer through the slat, glimpsing jet-black hair and a spray tan.

Her. The one launching a new beauty line. And she's planning to use Asher to do it.

I burn, then I break, fumbling with the latch as I push

open the door to give her a piece of my mind. "Are you for real?" I bite out. But the liar-to-be is already scurrying out of the restroom, ready to spin fables about my friend.

I beeline for the ballroom, debating tactics on the way and not sure confronting her will do a thing. Instead, I try to devise a more clever solution to her kind of trickery. It's not like I can dramatically shout, *Stop, thief!* from the doorway. She'd laugh it off and call me crazy. I could race backstage and tell Everly, but what could she do? Disqualify a bidder on account of me overhearing a ladies' room convo?

I certainly can't outbid an heiress and her daddy's money. I'm...nobody.

Pissed off and penniless, I join my brother, slumping into the cushioned chair with a *harrumph*.

"In the nick of time," Beckett says, then eyes me suspiciously, arching a brow. "Are you wearing Asher's vest?"

"Vests are totally in, babe," Reina tells him, like it's the moment for a gentle fashion correction. "And you look hot," she tells me.

"Thank you." But I don't care about me right now. I care about Snake Girl with the credit card. "Listen to this."

I spill everything I overheard.

Reina's nose twitches, and then she nods to my new nemesis a row over. "That's Miranda Blush. Her dad owns a shipping business. I heard she claimed her new beauty line is cruelty-free, but a research lab discovered it's not."

"It's cruelty-full? Ugh, I hate her even more," I seethe.

"How do you know all this?" Beckett asks his wife, eyebrows raised in amazement.

"I like knowing things. It's an Akiyama thing," she says, using her maiden name, which she kept because she wanted to keep her Japanese heritage alive.

"And you're damn good at it," he agrees. He hums thoughtfully like he's weighing all this intel. Beckett's more measured than I am. I got all the impulsive genes, and he got the strategic ones. Maybe that's why he owns a small chain of gyms, and I climb ladders that rip my dress. But a moment later, his eyes narrow, and he says darkly, "No one fucks with my guy."

Reina squeezes his arm. "Protective Beckett is in the house. But what are you going to do?"

Before Beckett can answer, Everly's voice echoes bright and loud as she strides on stage with the mic.

"Thank you so much for coming back with full wallets and big hearts. Let's have a round of applause for Erin and her intros," she says to the buzzing audience. The color commentator started the auction. Now it's the team publicist's turn to finish the night. Everly looks sleek and stylish in a blue dress and black heels with her signature blonde ponytail. "We are so excited that all the money raised this evening will go to San Francisco-based non-profits, including animal rescues, food drives, housing initiatives, and efforts to combat homelessness, as well as our ongoing support for local libraries. So get ready, Sea Dogs fans! Now is your chance to win a date with a hockey star. I'll tell you a little more about what each date package with each guy looks like."

As she dives into the details, I huddle with my brother and his wife again. Reina whispers a warning, "It's going to be bad if Miranda claims she's dating Asher."

"She might make up all sorts of things about him for her own purposes," I second.

Asher's on the brink of launching a new charity he's been building over the last year with my brother—they're calling it Total Teamwork. Asher's reputation matters to him. He's earned it with focus and dedication throughout his entire career. He's known as one of the most accessible, friendly, outgoing guys on the team for a reason—that's who he legit is. He's the guy who has his teammates' backs and who cares about his city in a deep and real way.

On the eve of the Total Teamwork debut, it'd be a terrible stain on Asher's rep if he was embroiled in a messy lie of a fake romance with someone who's only using him for clout—especially since that *someone* has a dubious history of her own. With animals, no less!

"I can already see the posts spinning out of control before we have a chance to stop them," I say.

"It could be a real mess," Beckett agrees. He lets out a long, annoyed breath as Everly talks up date packages that include concerts, cooking classes with gourmet chefs, and an art and culture day touring the best museums and galleries in San Francisco.

I picture Snake Girl gallivanting around the city with *my* friend, then tossing photos online, claiming they're together. Then Asher would have to say they're not together, and she would no doubt throw some sort of online fit.

Frustration boils up inside me. I have to do something. There are still a few more minutes for me to pull Everly aside somehow. Tell her what I heard. Ask her to refuse Snake Girl's bid, maybe.

It could work. Stranger things have happened.

"Next up, we have a date with the formidable and fun Alexei Volkov," Everly says, as Beckett whispers something to Reina only. "Who's ready to take a shot at an unforgettable evening? The bidding begins at twenty thousand dollars."

When the first paddle lifts, I don't wait another

second. "I'm going to find someone backstage. Maybe Everly's assistant," I tell Beckett, pushing up in my chair, ready to jet off, to fly past my friend Leighton, who's freelancing here tonight, snapping pictures of the event for the team.

Setting a hand on my shoulder, he keeps me in place. "No, you're not."

"Why not? We can't let this happen. How else can I stop it?" I implore him.

If I can go hunting in libraries for cell service *for me*, I will damn well finagle my way backstage for *my friend*.

But as a pair of women vie for Alexei, a clever smile spreads across my brother's face. He strokes his chin, looking like he's got the world at his fingertips. "The money does go to a good cause. These are all causes that I support, anyway. My accountant said it was time to make a charitable donation."

"But you're launching your own charity," I point out.

"Yeah, and I like *these* causes too."

I connect the dots and breathe the biggest sigh of relief, wrapping an arm around him. "I knew you'd come through and do it."

But he shakes his head, his smile turning downright wicked. "I'm not going to outbid her," he says. "You are."

4

MY BROTHER'S MONEY

Maeve

Fifteen minutes later, I'm on the edge of my seat as Everly begins the bidding on the last man standing.

"And now, for our final hockey player of the evening, we have a date with none other than Asher Callahan. You've heard all about our auction superstar. He's gone for the highest amount the last two years. Let's see if he can make it a hat trick."

Asher grins, then leans closer to her mic, his trademark charm radiating across the whole ballroom as he says, "And I've already had two on the ice this season."

Everly laughs. "Then this ought to be easy. Like a straight shot to the net." She pauses and turns back to the audience, all business. "Bidding starts at fifty thousand dollars. Who's ready to take home the night of a lifetime?"

Snake Girl doesn't bat an eye. From her seat, a row over, she casually lifts her paddle like it's nothing. She's seated next to a freckled redhead. Must be the woman she was talking to in the ladies' room.

My stomach churns with nerves but also excitement. Playing with Monopoly money is like riding a death-defying, daring roller coaster. It's terrifying and thrilling all at once.

"Are you sure?" I ask Beckett one more time.

"Save our friend," he says with a crisp nod.

Doesn't have to tell me twice.

I lift the paddle I never thought I would lift. But I am not cool. I am not calm. I have zero chill as I shout, "Fifty-five thousand."

On stage, Asher blinks. It's the play he didn't see coming. His green eyes lock with mine and questions flash across them. Like *where did you get fifty-five thousand dollars?* And *aren't you the girl with the ripped bodice who can barely make her rent?*

I flash a knowing smile his way, then a *take that* one in the direction of my competition.

Buckle up, Snake Girl. This woman does not back down.

Without missing a beat, Miranda raises her paddle again, her voice dripping with smugness. "Sixty thousand."

My heart pounds, but I refuse to let anyone see me sweat. I glance at Beckett, who gives me a subtle nod. I lift the paddle higher, my voice steady now, but my insides shaking. "Seventy thousand."

There's a collective gasp in the room.

Everly looks around, searching the audience, shooting a concerned glance my way, cautious for me. "Seventy thousand. Anyone want to bid more than seventy thousand for a date with Asher Callahan?"

Snake Girl shoots me a scathing look, then flicks her black hair over her shoulder, sneering in my direction before she ups the ante. "Eighty-five thousand."

For a moment, the air has been sucked out of the room. Then, whispers begin, and in seconds they turn louder. "*What are you doing?*" Asher mouths to me.

I don't answer him. I can't back down now. Not when I've come this far. I lift my hand one more time, my voice loud and clear. "One hundred thousand."

Beckett wheezes out a shocked, "Holy fuck."

Like he's not okay that I've gone that high. But...I guess I don't fuck around with my brother's money.

Everly blinks, her surprised smile taking over her face. "We've never had a bid that high. Does anybody want to counter the bid?"

Even Snake Girl hesitates, her confidence faltering for the first time. She looks at me, eyes narrowing into slits as if sizing me up, but there's a flicker of doubt in her gaze.

How much is a beauty line worth? *I guess we'll find out, folks.*

"Going once, going twice," Everly says.

A few tense seconds that extend longer than my last relationship tick by. Snake Girl lingers, tapping her long, fuchsia fingernails against the wooden paddle before she reluctantly lowers it.

The victory is mine. *Yes!* I punch the air.

Everly's voice cuts through the tension, triumphant. "Sold! One hundred thousand to the woman in the vest! Congratulations, Maeve! You've just won a date with Asher Callahan!"

A wild laugh bursts from me, adrenaline still pumping through my veins. Next to me, my brother's face is pale and he's clutching his stomach like he can't quite believe he gave the go-ahead on that.

Reina is rubbing his back.

And Asher looks equal parts impressed...and bewildered.

5

THE ICE STREAKER SCALE

Asher

I'm not usually thrown for a loop. But consider me officially loop-thrown here on stage. It's like that time last season when some dude jumped over the glass and onto the ice during a break in game action. Wearing only a bathing suit, a sandwich board, and skates, he flew down the ice toward the tunnel, advertising his new adventure tour business. Talk about a stunt.

And on a scale of one to ice streaker, I'm definitely off-the-charts surprised right now. Because I'm going on a hundred-thousand-dollar date with my best friend. Why would she do that? It can't be a real date she wants. She wouldn't need to throw down money for a real date since, well, we hang out all the time.

Then, like a puck slamming into the boards, it hits me. She wanted to drive up the price to make sure I didn't break my streak. She did it for me because I wouldn't have gone for the top amount if she hadn't started a bidding war with Miranda Blush.

She did it because, well, I asked her to be my good luck charm.

Did I...overplay my hand? Force my luck? Shit. Tinkering with chance can be a big mistake. I don't even want to think about what *could* go wrong.

Everly's voice breaks through my spiraling thoughts. "And there you go," she announces, turning the mic toward me. "For the third year in a row, you've gone for the highest amount in our Win a Date Auction. What's the secret?"

I push aside the unease gnawing at my gut and take the mic with a practiced grin. *Think fast. Don't be the buzzkill.* I'm the guy who keeps the party going, not the one who kills the vibe.

"It must be my good luck charm," I say, shrugging like it's no big deal.

"Do you have a rabbit's foot in your pocket? Or maybe a lucky puck?"

I shake my head and nod to Maeve, who's sitting in the front row wearing an outfit that matches mine perfectly. "My friend Maeve's my good luck charm. She's been here for the last couple years, but tonight she decided to surprise me with a date," I say easily.

"Did it work?" Maeve chimes in, as if this is another of our big adventures.

"Sure did but you know what I like," I say, up for the challenge too.

"Are you a big fan of Outrageous Record?" Everly asks, cutting in.

That must be the date package we're going on—a concert. I didn't pay close attention to the details. But no harm, no foul. "Love that band," I reply, smoothing over my earlier distraction. A concert will be easy enough to attend with Maeve. Just like every other time we've hung out. It'll be like old times—bonfires, amusement parks, spelunking, cake-making. "I've always wanted to see them in concert," I add, keeping control of the situation.

Maeve grins, victorious. "That's why I wanted to surprise you."

"It seems it worked," Everly says, wrapping up the auction. "Thank you again to everyone who came out tonight. We raised more than half a million dollars for some great causes and on behalf of everyone at the Sea Dogs, we are so grateful to all of you. And here's hoping the winners post pics of their dates—we'll be sure to reshare. Thank you again."

As the crowd begins to disperse, Everly nods to me as we head backstage. "Stay with me while we finalize the details. We need to record everything formally."

"Absolutely," I say.

A few seconds later, the winners of the dates are ushered into a room backstage. I cut through the crowd, making a beeline for Maeve. I need to know what she was thinking.

I pull her aside. "What was that all about? And where are you hiding one hundred grand? You know you could get a *date* with me for less than a dime," I say, sketching air quotes as I try to keep the moment light, even though the truth of that statement unnerves me in a way I don't want to deal with right now.

Or ever, to be honest.

"To protect you," she replies, her expression serious. "I'll explain more later." She pauses, a playful smirk crossing her face. "But it's a good story. There's always a story with me."

Truer words. But this is a Maeve plot twist I didn't see coming. And it's driving me a little batty. "Give me a hint," I whisper.

She rises on tiptoes, cups my ear, and whispers, "Miranda Blush was going to bid on you and claim she was your girlfriend. Use you to build up her new beauty line. Probably spin a ton of lies. I couldn't let that happen. That would be bad luck. So, I told Beckett, and he put up the money. And I saved you from her." She steps back, meeting my gaze after serving up well more than a hint. "Just like you saved me earlier."

"That was hardly an even trade," I say, but holy fuck. Maeve has quite the protective side. It's...sexy. But I shouldn't find it sexy. Maybe it's just...captivating? Yeah, that's it.

And sure, it was nice of my friend. I'll need to pay Beckett back. He shouldn't be putting up that kind of money.

Either way, maybe there's no forced luck after all. Just quick thinking from both of them. I let out a relieved breath, glad that debate is resolved.

Everly finishes taking down the details of Maeve's bid then gives her friend a pointed look. "Girls' breakfast soon —I'm going to need all of the details of your big surprise," she says.

"And you'll get them," Maeve says, her voice brimming with mischief.

Everly looks to both of us. "That is, if you can fit me in before you guys take off for Vegas next weekend."

Wait, what? "We don't play the Sabers till next month," I point out, reminding Everly of the hockey schedule that she usually has memorized. Our game against the Vegas team isn't till February.

"I know. I mean the date package we assigned to you, Asher," Everly continues with a professional smile. "It was donated by Outrageous Record. They have a week-long stint in Vegas, so there's a whole package—flight, a night at a hotel, dinner on the Strip. It's next weekend, which is perfect since you have two nights off from hockey. Have fun."

She spins around and heads to Miles's highest bidder to handle the details of his date, leaving me standing there, trying to wrap my head around this new wrinkle.

I look back at Maeve, and my thoughts feel like they're tangled up in knots even though a quick trip with her should be no big deal. We've taken lots of trips—it's kind of our thing. So why does this feel different?

It shouldn't feel any different simply because my best friend looks ludicrously sexy wearing my vest. It shouldn't be any different no matter how good it feels when I wrap my arm around her and Leighton snaps a picture for the team's social feed.

But Vegas?

Vegas *is* different. It's like walking into a carnival and getting swept up in the crowd right away. It's a vortex for all varieties of luck, good and bad, forced and natural.

And for troublemaking.

We've never needed help finding trouble—but in Vegas, trouble usually finds you.

6

NO HARD FEELINGS

Asher

I seriously appreciate Maeve playing the role of goalie tonight. But now I've got to handle the fallout. She takes off, and as the crowd thins out, I grab my phone from the back pocket of my pants and toggle over to my banking app. I don't think twice. I tap a few keys, setting up the transfer. Then I cut through the lingering groups and make my way to the front entrance of the Cartwright Mansion, where Beckett's picking up a pair of jackets from coat check.

Reina's probably in the ladies' room, so I stride over, determination in my step. "Hey, Beck. About that bid—thanks, but I can't let you drop that kind of cash just to save my streak."

Beckett looks up from tipping the woman behind the counter, one eyebrow quirked. "It wasn't about the streak."

"Fine, you were looking out for me, which is

awesome." I clap his shoulder. "I appreciate it, man. But I can't let you cover that. I'm going to pay you back."

Well, I already did, but he'll find out soon enough. Semantics and all.

Beckett laughs, low and easy. "You don't owe me anything, Ash," he says, thanking the woman and stepping away from the counter and next to a scalloped mirror that looks like it costs five figures. "And I'm not taking your money."

I give him a stern look. "You can't just drop that kind of cash and brush it off. I can cover it."

"And so can I," he says. "Look, that situation was going to be messy, and neither one of us needs that right now, but especially you. You're the face of Total Teamwork, man. Maeve came to me with the situation, and Reina and I made the decision to put up the money. It was for a good cause, and we're always happy to give to charity. Besides, I didn't want Miranda Blush anywhere near you. That woman's trouble."

"I appreciate that," I admit, but I can't let this go. "And yet...I still felt like I owe you something."

My best friend's a smart man. He shoots me a searing stare. "No, you don't. We're all good. We're in this together. You hear me?"

He makes a fair point, but sometimes I just like to get my way. Fine, fine. Most of the time. "I do. But sometimes a man's got to do what a man's got to do."

He shoots me a searing stare. "No, you didn't."

I flash a big grin. "Yes. I did. Have fun with the wife tonight. Catch you later."

I don't even give him the chance to protest. I take off, heading into the cool San Francisco night. Once outside, as the fog curls its arms around me, I open an app to grab a ride home when a hand comes down on my shoulder. I don't flinch since it's my job to handle surprises.

I turn around to see...Miranda. Her smile is as sleek as her hair. Her eyes glint with opportunity.

"We could still go out. Maybe it's even better this way," she says, her voice a purr, her hand curling tighter around me. I hear a rustle nearby. Someone else, maybe? Who knows?

"Thanks, but I'm busy," I say coolly. It's not the first time a woman has sashayed over and put her hands on me without asking. I'd be naive to think it'll be the last.

"You can't be busy every night though," she says, inching closer, hand gripping tighter.

I reach for her hand and peel it off me. And I do mean peel, because holy hell, this woman has claws, and they are digging in. I'm well aware that eyes are always on pro athletes. That rustle could be someone, and *someones* have cameras. One wrong move can lead to a scandal. So I'm careful as I let Miranda's hand fall, then step back from her.

"Thanks again for coming tonight. Really appreciate your support," I say as shoes click toward me on the sidewalk, coming from the other direction.

I turn to the sound.

A vision emerges in the foggy night. A woman sporting a vest, a trench coat, and an attitude.

I fight off a smile.

"Hey, babe," she says, then flashes a saccharin smile at Miranda. "And hey, no hard feelings about that whole thing in there, right?" Maeve waves a hand airily at the mansion. "I just couldn't let anyone else get their hands on this man."

She slides right up to me, wraps an arm around my neck, the other around my waist, and drops a kiss on my cheek, like the date she won is real.

Right now, with her wedged against me, the date *feels* real.

That's my excuse at least. Since this might seem like a bad idea later, but right now, I have zero regrets as I make a game-day decision, turn my face, and impulsively capture her lips with mine.

A soft brush. An almost-chaste touch. But I smell sweet plums, and I taste raspberry lipstick. Most of all, I *feel* Maeve's mouth as she kisses me back. Brushing her lips against mine. Parting them the slightest bit.

An invitation, perhaps, for more?

Like I could say no. I coast my lips across hers. In no time, her fingers curl tighter around my neck. Her other hand presses more firmly on my waist. The tiniest gust of breath from her sweet mouth has my chest overheating. I cup her cheek, and my head pings with wild possibilities. What if this kiss became more real? What if it was a prelude to something else entirely?

In a few terribly short seconds, I already want to toss her over my shoulder and take her home. See if she looks as good in my ties, bound to her wrists, as she does in that vest.

But just as quickly as it started, the kiss ends. Over after it barely began. I don't know if she wrenches apart first or if I do. Maybe we both knew we needed to stop. I swallow roughly. She catches her breath.

My brain comes back online, and I reconnect to the fog, the night, the rustle of people, the birds, a car nearby.

And, most of all, the onlooker.

Right...Miranda.

The kiss lasted less than ten seconds. It was a kiss for an audience. A kiss for a cause. But mostly, it was a stolen kiss for me.

Miranda rolls her eyes, then says to me, "You're not even that hot."

Maeve scoffs and tugs me harder against her. "My date is the hottest, and you know it."

"Whatever." Miranda lifts a dismissive hand, wheels around, and marches back into the mansion.

Maeve looks at me, affection in her eyes. "You're totally hot. Don't let her get you down," she says, patting my chest in a friendly way.

Friendly.

The kiss wasn't friendly, but we are.

And if I needed a better reason to get this lust for Maeve out of my system, she just gave it to me—the reminder that we're friends. That the kiss didn't rattle her. That gust of breath or not, parted lips or not, that stolen kiss is barely a blip on her radar.

Maybe that's what I really needed tonight—a sign, rather than some luck. And I got it—a sign that we're just friends.

Still, when I'm home alone that night, I'm stupidly replaying a ten-second kiss.

* * *

A couple days later, as I'm tugging on a hoodie so I can head to morning skate with my teammate Max, my phone pings with a notification. It's a reversal of the transfer I made to Beckett. I roll my eyes. Ever since I met him in a grief support group ten years ago, he's always been the stubborn one, nearly impossible to sway once his mind's made up.

But I don't back down easily either. I take his hundred grand and send it back through the banking channels one more time – this time funneling it to Total Teamwork.

> Asher: Have it your way. A hundred thousand dollars to the new charity we're launching instead.

> Beckett: Always have to have the last word, don't you?

> Asher: Yes, I do. I'm stubborn like that.

A note from Maeve pops up too.

> Maeve: Evidently, I am a vest thief. Obviously, I wore it home and now it's trying to move into my apartment. Sneaky little thing. But I should probably, I don't know, dry clean it? Does anyone use dry cleaning anymore? Does dry cleaning even exist? Does it only exist for lawyers, bankers and athletes who wear suits? What even is dry cleaning?

I chuckle at how very Maeve she is as I head to the door. Max will be here any minute to pick me up. But I dictate a reply.

> Asher: No, you don't need to dry clean it. Also, it looked good on you. You should just keep it. Make vests a thing.

> Maeve: I think they're already a thing.

> Asher: Well, then. They're your thing.

> Maeve: Really?

> Asher: Yes. Keep it. I mean it.

Truth is, I'd probably sniff it for a hint of her if she returned it. It's better she doesn't give it back.

* * *

That night, I'm on the ice, determined to demolish Phoenix. The crowd roars as I battle against the boards, trying to shake off a defender who's hellbent on stripping the puck from me.

Not going to happen. This puck is mine. We're in the third period, tied up, and every second counts.

I knock my shoulder into him, spinning free. I hoard the puck as I slip behind the net, then fly around it. When I spot an opening I cut across the ice, aiming for the top corner of the posts. I wind up and send the puck flying— but the goalie deflects it.

I curse, but then move the hell on when Falcon nabs the rebound and feeds it right back to me.

I don't hesitate. I fake left, then snap a shot right, the puck sailing past the goalie's glove this time, lodging in the twine.

The lamp lights, and everything feels right in the world. Adrenaline surges through me, the rush unmatched by anything else. Hockey has always been the greatest high. Even when it hurts, it feels good. Even when it's tough, I'm in control. There's nothing else in the world that gives itself to me the way this sport does.

I hop over the boards and grab some water during the line change, but my thoughts drift back to the night of the auction. To that moment when Maeve wrapped her arms around me and I stole a kiss—one she seemed to sink into.

But I've got a charity to launch with my best friend, a hockey season to dominate, and my dads' thirty-fifth wedding anniversary coming up, though I like to tease them that their life together didn't really start till they adopted me as a newborn. Point being, I'm too busy to get caught up in fantasies that are going exactly nowhere.

I know where I stand. Maeve's my friend, and I'm not going to mess that up by entertaining more stolen kisses.

The game's not over yet, but I've already made my decision. No matter what happened the other night, Maeve and I are just friends. And that's how it's going to stay.

When it's time for another line shift, I jump over the boards and get back into the game. I'm here to win, on and off the ice, and that means sticking to what I know—friendship with Maeve. Nothing more, nothing less.

I'm all focus and power for the rest of the game as our goalie—Max Lambert—shuts down the other team.

When the final buzzer sounds, signaling our win, I skate off the ice with a clear head and a renewed focus. Maeve and I are going to Vegas next weekend as friends, and that's how it's going to stay.

I'm recommitting my mind to only friendly thoughts of Maeve.

7

A POP ART KISS

Maeve

A funny thing happens on Monday morning as I head into the studio space in the Mission District that I share with a handful of other artists in the city. Sometimes I paint here, but I also work on my side hustle—decorative art like lamps, mirrors, and vases—since, well, it's at least steady. While I'm refurbishing some antique mirrors by adding rhinestones and gems to sparkle them up, I replay that kiss from the other night.

Again.

What is wrong with my brain? It wasn't even a real kiss. We were like two actors on stage.

Actors don't linger over stage kisses, I suspect. I shouldn't either.

And yet as I affix tiny pink rhinestones to an art deco mirror that I'll sell at the night market, the kiss plays on repeat. His lips were soft but confident. He smelled like soap and maybe oak, clean and woodsy. It felt a little like a kiss in a painting. Like the kind I secretly paint when I get extra studio time and when I have the space to myself. Like the kind I want to sell someday because of the way they make me feel. Warm, heady, like honey. Like I'm the woman in a Roy Lichtenstein painting, kissed in that pop art style, living my life in bold lines and bright colors.

But kisses in paintings aren't real.

So why am I binging on it? Maybe because it was empirically a good kiss? Yeah, that makes sense. That's why it's looping in my brain. Good kisses are like chocolates, poems, and songs. They stay with you.

I set down the mirror on a workbench and pick up a brush instead. Maybe if I paint the kiss, I'll get it out of my head.

Trouble is, I think about the kiss again the next day, and the next, and by Friday morning, it's a little overwhelming in my head. I should not be thinking too long on one single, short kiss. I can't cling to Asher like this, even in my head, so I vow to shake off the kiss once and for all as I pack for Vegas, and head out to see my friends before I catch the flight.

"Guess who still hasn't heard about the super-secret awesome job?" I announce when I reach their table at Moon Over Milkshakes, our favorite retro-themed diner buzzing with the morning crowd. Setting my overnight bag down on the pink tiled floor, I slide into the mint green booth where my friends are already gathered, the air rich with the scent of freshly brewed coffee and sizzling bacon. Josie and Fable are draining big coffee mugs. Everly's cup likely contains a London fog latte. She's as loyal to that drink as she is to her friends. Leighton's here, too, with a green tea. She's a friend of Everly's, and when Everly introduced us to her a couple months ago, we all hit it off. Immediately, we annexed her into our friend group late last year.

Before we dive into conversation though, I wave over the server, admiring the intricate ink of flowers on her arms. "First, those are some gorgeous dahlias. Second, can I get the overnight oats and the biggest chai latte in the city?"

She smiles. "Thank you. And not only is our chai latte the biggest, it's the best."

"Good. Maeve likes her chai lattes big," Josie puts in.

"And other things big too," Fable adds under her breath.

"Of course I do," I say, unapologetic about my preferences.

The server laughs. "Understandable."

My friends throw in their breakfast orders. We thank the server and when she leaves, Josie sets down her mug, her blue eyes kind behind her glasses as she meets my gaze. "How are you holding up, friend? I know you were eager to hear about the job."

I shrug, trying to hide my disappointment about the delay in the mural decision. "I'm thinking of starting a YouTube channel—'How to Arrange Hors d'Oeuvres Like an Artist.' Maybe it'll be my big break. I can make art with mushroom canapés and bacon-wrapped shrimp! Munch on Masterpieces by Maeve. Can you imagine how happy Aunt Vivian would be?" My friends know my mom's sister wants me to come on board full-time. And then maybe run her catering company someday. She has a good business, but it's just not my dream.

Fable gives a sympathetic smile from across the table. "Just because you haven't heard yet about the mural doesn't mean it's not happening."

She's sweet to say that, but the writing's on the wall. When we talked on the phone yesterday Angelina said no news is good news, but she *also* urged me to focus on other options, so I'm thinking that's her agent-y way of softening the eventual blow. I ought to try harder to mask my disappointment when I'm with my friends. I don't really want to be the downer of the group, especially when they're all thriving in their careers. Everly's the publicist for the Sea Dogs, recently promoted. Josie's the most amazing digital librarian. And Fable is the lead merch designer for the Renegades, one of the city's football teams, while also running a growing Etsy shop for her jewelry designs. Leighton's a freelance photographer, and even though she's the youngest of us, she's already making some inroads with boudoir sessions, lifestyle, and sports photography. I'm the only one of us floundering.

After my mom died, the royalties from her books went to my dad, then to my brother and me, and now, ten years later, they go toward renting my shared studio space, which feels like exactly what my mother would have wanted for me.

And yet, the money won't last forever, and soon, I might have to make some tough choices.

"It's fine," I say, waving away the pesky idea of a viable career. "If the YouTube thing doesn't work out, I'll learn how to grow money trees. I have a green thumb. How hard can it be to plant a few coins in the soil and watch them bloom into big bills?"

"Sign me up," Leighton quips. After a chuckle, she shifts to a more serious tone. "Who is the mural job with?"

"You did one for the Noe Valley Business Association just the other month, right?" Everly puts in.

"Yes!" I say, touched Everly remembered that recent

assignment. "I did a design stretching across a brick building in that neighborhood representing the small businesses in the area, from glasses shops to restaurants to toy stores. That was the lead submission in the portfolio Angelina submitted for me."

As we chat, the server arrives with my chai latte. She sets down plates, too—the overnight oats, omelets, and pancakes. "The biggest and the best. Let me know if you need anything else," she says.

"The chance to paint a huge coffee cup and a plate of eggs and bacon on the wall," I offer with a bright smile.

The server shoots me a bemused look. "I'll, um, keep that in mind."

"Thanks," I say, since I am not above begging. You never know who's hiring.

Once the server heads to another table, Everly turns to me. "Is this super-secret job something like the neighborhood association one?"

I hesitate because I haven't told them who the potential job is with. There's a reason I've been vague—I don't want to be handed anything. I don't want them to try to intervene, and they might. It's one thing for me to drop a mention of my art to a server—it's another to canvas all my friends and family for a boost.

My mother was a writer, and she taught me both the value of art and the value of self-worth. "If you love what you do, then chase it with all your heart, even when it feels like chasing the hem of a cloud," she'd said. "Chances are, it'll feed your artist's soul. And the artist's soul is very, very hungry."

Most days, my artist's soul is a ravenous beast. I chase my dreams with running shoes on, not jumping the line like a nepo baby. I want to be good enough on my own. I want it so badly it hurts sometimes. The waiting has been dragging me down for more than a week, and if I don't share this longing, it'll weigh me down too.

"I'll tell you," I say, warning them, "but you can't tell your guys."

Josie lifts a hand in an oath. "Girls only."

Everly nods solemnly. "It won't leave this booth."

Fable says, "Padlocker promise."

I smile at the name. It started as a joke last fall when we promised we'd be Everly's padlock when she was tempted by the team's goalie, now her boyfriend. The name stuck, though, because we look out for each other.

"It's with the Sea Dogs," I whisper.

Everly gasps. "You're being considered for that mural project? I wrote the press release announcing our search for local artists."

She showed it to me last month and suggested I submit my portfolio. The team is commissioning a fun, cartoon-y mural of San Francisco for the inside of its arena to celebrate its partnerships with the city. One side of the arena's concessions area is closed for renovations right now, and the team is hoping to reopen it with some city-centric new art. "Yes, you did. And when you mentioned it to me, I immediately told Angelina, and she said I'm already on the list."

"You didn't tell me," Everly admonishes me playfully.

"I know," I admit. "I didn't want you to feel like you had to put in a word for me. Also, I wanted to get through the first round on my own merits."

"That's understandable," Josie says.

"So what's next then?" Fable asks.

"More waiting." I sigh. I made it through the first

round, but then they cast a wider net. "But it's fine. I've resigned myself to the fact that I'm not getting it."

"Why?" Leighton asks with genuine curiosity. "Why does this mean it won't be you? Maybe they're just doing their due diligence."

"I second that," Josie says with an *I'm with her* nod. "Besides, aren't you the closet optimist? You once told me I shouldn't be afraid to say my dreams out loud."

I narrow my eyes at her. "You and your iron trap of a memory."

My longtime friend stares me down. "Well...?"

"Yes," I say heavily. "I did say that. I do believe that. It's just...harder to believe it some days than others. And I don't want to walk around with my hopes up all the time. So I didn't say anything. But you can't tell Wes," I tell Josie and turn to Everly next. "Or Max." Then to Leighton, whose father is the coach. "Or your dad."

She scoff-laughs. "Trust me, I'm not going to tell my dad."

"Good. I haven't even told Asher."

"Why not?" Fable asks with a tilt of her head.

Because I know Asher. "If I tell him, he'll march up to whoever's in charge of hiring and demand they give me the assignment." I turn to Josie. "And I didn't tell you at first because I didn't want you to have to keep it from Wes. He might try to help too."

"He would," Josie concedes. "He can't help himself from helping."

I laugh. "Truer words." I let the laughter fade and share more. "I wanted to get it on my own. I don't want to paint the walls of the arena knowing I wasn't truly the artist who deserved it. I want to earn it," I admit, my throat catching.

Sometimes, it's hard to mask my feelings. Fine, most of the time. It sucks wearing your heart on your sleeve. Which is why most of my exes are, well, exes.

If you ask Gideon, the hedge fund manager I dated last year, he'll say I'm too emotional, too interested, too clingy. "I wish I had time for you, Maeve. But I don't think any man can meet your needs," he'd said. Ironic because he loved being the center of attention when we went out. Loved when I told him how handsome he was, how good he looked, and how fascinating he made the topic of finance this and ROI that. But in the end, I was too much for him. Story of my dating life.

I don't want the Sea Dogs to pick me because I'm too needy, too desperate for the commission, which is how it might seem if everyone I know in the organization pitched me to management. I want them to hire me because they've fallen in love with my sketches or they can't resist my paintbrush.

Except, clearly, they can.

I shrug, then paste on my best "moving on" smile. "Anyway, it looks unlikely, and that's fine. When I return from Vegas, I'll be back hustling in the art world. Angelina snagged me another live painting gig—"

"What's live painting?" Josie, always curious, leans closer. "And why have you never told me about it before?"

"It's becoming more popular, actually. Some people hire painters to 'live paint' a wedding, a party, a celebration."

"Sounds fun," Fable chimes in, "and also nerve-racking."

"It is!" I say. "Sometimes people set up camp and watch you paint the whole time. Angelina scheduled one for me tomorrow night, right after I return. A fashion designer is hosting an event at his home in Cow Hollow. It should be pretty fancy, with all sorts of art world types."

"So, it's a networking opportunity?" Everly asks.

I shake my head. "That's frowned upon at events like this. But that's okay. Angelina's lining up new gallery appointments." With stubborn optimism, I tick them off on my fingers. "The Julien Aldridge Gallery, the Freida Claiborne Gallery...I catered for both of them. So, fingers crossed. Angelina's also talking to all sorts of brands that are using public art. Yoga studios, dance studios, boutiques, restaurants..."

I want to be hopeful even with the Sea Dogs job falling through. But I feel my career teetering on the precipice of disaster. Like soon I'll have to decide if I should throw in the towel.

But that's too heavy a topic for today, and I focus on the positive. "Plus, Leighton is going to take pics of some of my mirrors and vases for my site and my social." I give Leighton a one-armed hug. It's awkward with her next to me in the booth, but I don't mind.

"I can photograph you live painting, too, if you want," Leighton suggests ever the savvy young businesswoman. "You can put that on your site."

I let out a low whistle. "You're good. You're very good."

"See?" Everly says brightly. "Even if the mural doesn't happen, you're working all the angles. And it's wise to look for ways to expand your opportunities. You never know where the next gig will come from."

"Sounds like the date in Vegas is coming at a good time," Fable puts in. "You can get away for the night and then come back refreshed and ready to jump right back into it at the party."

Or I'll dive into some serious self-talk about whether

or not my painting dreams are circling the drain. But I don't mention that here.

"Exactly," I say. "Flight's early this afternoon. I've got my playlist for the plane to get in an Outrageous Record state of mind. I've got my favorite little skirt and a pair of cute pink boots for the show. And then I plan to enjoy a fantastic night's sleep at The Extravagant Hotel. The band put together a nice package. I'm a big fan of hotel beds. I might even start a fan club."

Fable's hazel eyes widen. "You're sharing a room with Asher?"

Laughing, I shake my head. "No. The package is for two rooms."

"We have to request that," Everly explains, all business. "When companies donate date packages to our player auctions, there can't be any expectations of a romantic date at all."

Fable's brow furrows like she's remembering something. "But a Renegades quarterback once fell in love with his best friend after one of these auctions. Wilder was telling me about it." Wilder's both her boss and boyfriend. "Cooper Armstrong, I think. But that was a while back. And back when the winning bids were twenty thousand dollars."

Her tone's hopeful and her glance speculative. My friends all have romance on their minds. No surprise—nearly all of them are happily paired up.

I can't even imagine what a fulfilling partnership would be like in my life. How could I?

My mother always said, *"Fulfill yourself first before you try to fulfill a partner."* Wise advice. My father was the opposite. All his happiness came from the way he worshiped my mother. Where did that blind adoration get him though, after her death?

His own end.

I breathe past the empty ache in my chest and focus on refuting Fable's example. "Just because it happened to Cooper after a player auction doesn't mean it'll happen to us."

Josie smiles impishly. "I don't think we said anything would happen. But maybe it's on your mind?"

I give her a pointed look. "It's not," I say. I'd be terrible for Asher for so many reasons. Hell, I'm terrible for me when it comes to romance. I'm terrified of losing people, so I hold on too tightly. And that painting kiss aside, our friendship works beautifully as is. I don't want to risk anything more.

Fable hums, then tucks a strand of red hair behind her ear. "Seems like he likes putting up with you."

"Well, we are friends," I point out.

She laughs, shaking her head. "That's not what I mean. I've seen the way you two are together."

I frown, genuinely puzzled. "And?"

"And you kind of flirt with Asher," she says with a knowing smile.

A flash of guilt lances through me. Like, wrapping my arms around him in public? Like, pretending he's mine in front of that woman? Like, kissing him on the sidewalk? But that wasn't even a real kiss. I can't get caught up in it any more than I already did earlier in the week. "Fine, we like to tease each other," I concede. "But it's not really flirting. We're just comfortable."

Everly chuckles, taking a sip of her latte. "If that's what you want to call it."

"That's what it is," I say firmly.

Josie narrows her eyes at me. "But you did kiss him last week."

I sit up straighter, caught off guard. I didn't tell them about the kiss on the street. There wasn't anything to tell, really. That kiss was to get Miranda off his back. "How did you know about that?"

Leighton seems to fight off a smile. "The Internet."

Josie lifts a playful brow. "You know, that thing where people post pictures of other people?" She pulls out her phone and shows me a picture on the social media feed of someone with the handle SeaDogsfangirl. It must be someone who was at the auction. The picture is taken from a distance, and it's dark, but there it is—Asher kissing me.

My chest goes a little tingly as I look at it. A fizzy feeling spreads briefly under my skin, and I'm reliving that kiss once more.

But I've been accused of being the world's clingiest girlfriend, so I'm definitely not clinging to this—a kiss with my brother's best friend. A kiss with *my* friend. A fake kiss, for all intents and purposes.

Even though, as I look at the picture, I feel that kiss in every cell in my body.

8

A SEND-OFF GIFT

Asher

I'm lacing up my skates in the locker room before practice Friday morning when Wesley clears his throat from the stall next to mine.

"Callahan," he says, his tone serious.

I grab my helmet. "What's up, Bryant?"

His dark eyes are unreadable. "We have something for your trip to Sin City."

I'm heading to the airport right after practice, which is no secret...obviously.

From across the room, Miles chimes in as he tugs on his jersey. "We figured you could use a...getaway gift."

Their tag-teaming is making me suspicious. "Why am I getting the feeling this is going to be like the fake tooth kit we got Hugo last year?"

I glance at the defenseman. Hugo Bergstrand is known for both his solid defending and occasional stints in the penalty box. The bearded brute just smiles. "It's better than fake teeth."

From across the room, Max reaches into his stall and pulls out...an erasable marker? What the hell?

"Guys, appreciate the send-off," I say, "but Coach will have our heads if we're late hitting the ice." I'm antsy to get out there. If we're tardy, he'll make us practice longer.

"We'll be fast, Callahan," Max says. "Something you should be familiar with...in bed?"

I flip him the bird as he goes to the whiteboard hanging in the corner of the locker room. Technically, it's for last-minute strategy discussions before practice. Mostly we use it to draw stick figures with dick noses because we're mature like that.

Curious but wary, I follow Max to the DickNose board, then stop and groan as I get a look at what's waiting for me. There are no rudimentary sketches of phallic noses— it's a list titled *Top Five Times Asher Has Said Something Cute About Maeve.*

Using a hockey stick as a pointer, Wesley adopts a lawyerly voice, tapping the board. "Exhibit A. The time you mentioned her love of the night market and said we should all go there and buy her lamps and mirrors and stuff."

I cross my arms. "Which you did because she's fucking talented."

"True, but not the point," Wesley says, handing the stick to Max.

The goalie points to the next item. "The time you said how fucking cute it was that she watches time-lapse videos of people painting."

I did say that, and I stand by it. Hell, she even got me hooked on those videos. They're relaxing.

I gesture for them to hurry this along. Clearly, they're not going to let up until they review the whole list, which only has four items, despite the title. I'd roast them back for their inability to count, but I want to get this over with.

Miles grabs the stick, tapping the third item on the whiteboard. "The time you wanted to check on her after a game because she'd been under the weather."

"That's just being nice, you fuckheads," I say, grumbling.

Hugo claps me on the back. "Nothing to be ashamed of, man. I do that for Melissa all the time. After she stayed up late baking jersey cookies for the cart five nights in a row, I rubbed her neck when I got home after a game." His wife is a cookie-baking and decorating maven who sells her goodies here at the arena. But instead of regaling us with tales of her cookie artistry—as he often does—he taps the board. "Back to you, Callahan." He reads item four. "Don't forget the time you were so excited Maeve came to a game."

I furrow my brow. "She comes to a lot of games."

With a satisfied grin, Max uncaps the erasable pen and adds the missing item five. *She comes to a lot of games.*

"How is that cute?" I ask.

He claps my shoulder. "Tone, Callahan. It's your tone."

I hold my hands out wide. "Well, this was a great gift. Truly."

"I knew he'd love it. Let's frame it for him, guys," Hugo says, snapping a pic of the board—because of course he does. These assholes will never let me live this down.

"I'll blow that up poster-size and hang it tonight. And listen, can't wait to return the favor with gifts for all of you. Let's hit the ice," I say, turning around.

Wesley whistles loudly for attention, and I turn back. "That wasn't your gift."

"You found another way to give me a hard time?" I ask.

"That was the setup," Wesley says, then reaches into his stall and tosses me—a box of condoms.

I catch it and immediately toss it back. "With friends like you..." I mutter, then head straight out to the ice for practice.

I am *not* going to think about the intended use of their gift. Not. At. All.

The moment practice is over, I'm the first one off the ice. Back in the locker room, I shower and change at lightning speed, avoiding my friends as best as I can when I grab my bag and go.

I don't need their comments in my head. Because those assholes are annoyingly right. But the thing is— Maeve *is* awesome. That's a fact. She's funny, bold, and wild, and she's faced pain no one should ever have to face. But she's on the other side, strong and gutsy, and she'd fight off a nest of vipers for anyone she loves.

I'm one of those *anyones*. And I'm not stupid enough to risk losing that.

Doesn't matter that I liked kissing her.

Doesn't matter that I have dirty dreams about her.

Doesn't even matter that I loved the way she looked in my clothes.

Nothing can ever come of this *friendly affection* I feel for her, and it's not simply because of my friendship with her brother. I'm damaged goods when it comes to romance. I'm radioactive, and I guess I've accepted it as part of who I am.

Nora died when I was twenty-two, and since then, I've

had nothing but a series of short-term relationships that never make it past the six-month mark. They're broken-down cars sputtering, running out of gas at the end of a deserted highway with nowhere to go.

Somewhere inside my heart, there's an expiration date for some damn reason. Even if I tried with Maeve, we'd inevitably end. And no fucking way am I risking losing her. She means too much to me and so does her brother.

In the back of the Lyft headed to the airport, I power through some emails from Soraya, the executive Beckett and I hired to run day-to-day operations for Total Team-work. She's an Iranian-born former competitive ice skater who grew up in Portland, and she's experienced firsthand the benefits of what we're trying to build.

Total Teamwork focuses on underprivileged kids. It's about sports and support. The clinics and camps we're launching will have counselors available and offer peer support through group sessions. Our goal? To teach kids that problems are best solved together.

We have a ton of events planned for the project's kick-off, so Soraya is checking with me on details. Am I ready for the board meeting next week? Then, we'll focus on the launch picnic after that and then the glow-in-the-dark fun run.

I fire off responses to her emails, but then, when the car nears the exit for San Bruno Avenue, a message pops up from one of my dads and then the other.

> Carlos: Is Vegas tonight? Beware the blackjack tables. You know your track record.

John: And the house always wins. So try not to lose your shirt.

My jaw drops at the suggestion I'm bad at gambling.

Asher: I believe you sent your message to the wrong person.

John: Nope. I meant it for you.

Asher: Mean!

Carlos: Mean and honest. A winning combo.

Asher: And you're giving me a hard time, too? Great. Just great.

John: Someone has to keep you humble. It's a parent's job.

Asher: And you two excel at that. I'll have you know I am as awesome at blackjack as I am at managing a baseball team.

Carlos: You don't manage a baseball team.

Asher: Yet. I don't yet.

John: Right. And someday, I'll be good at pickleball.

I grin at their banter, but seeing Carlos's name reminds me of something I wanted to tell him. It's too much for a text, so I hit dial.

He answers quickly with a curious, "Hey, what's going on?"

"Good news. Just wanted to let you know I looked into that elbow pain J-Dad was having," I say, turning toward the window.

There's a pause, and then he says, "Oh, you did?"

"Yeah. Remember after my game last week, his arm was kind of sore?"

"Sure," he says, sounding tentative.

"I checked online, and I don't think it's radiculopathy, where one of the nerve roots is irritated. There would be tingling and numbness in the arm if it was. More likely, it's just regular muscle pain." Passing that on rekindles the relief I felt that weekend after looking up arm pain symptoms and their probable causes.

Carlos answers, "I wasn't really worried." His tone is just shy of paternalistic, but he *is* a dad.

"Oh good."

"We've been playing pickleball. So it was probably that," he adds.

"Good, good. Just wanted to be sure." The car is nearing the terminal. "Carry on with the pickleball."

He laughs lightly, pauses, then says, "We will. And... thanks, kid."

"Anytime."

When I hang up, I switch over to my camera app and hit record, still in the Lyft's back seat.

"If you don't hear from me, assume I won big at the tables and bought a baseball team, proving you both wrong. But I'm not as mean as you two, so I'll get you good seats to all the games." I pause and lower my voice in case the driver's listening in. "Love you two."

I hit end, watch it, then roll my eyes. Fuck, that's cheesy, but it's on brand for us—full of sarcasm and love. And, really, you should tell the people in your life that you love them.

Because you never know.

9

THE WARM NUT CONSPIRACY

Maeve

"Question for you," I begin as our short flight to Vegas hits cruising altitude.

"Hit me," Asher says, stretching his long legs out in front of him in first class. He always upgrades us whenever I travel with him—an extravagance he waves off, saying he has points or that he fits better in this row. The luxury, which I eat up while I can, is the opposite of my life. I live in a tiny apartment with a shower that's too short, a toilet that faces the wall, and a couch with a broken spring.

When I fly solo, it's all cramped seats and rude people clipping their toenails, so I try not to get too spoiled on our trips. But still, I like Asher's world better—a world of warm nuts and champagne.

I nod toward the flight attendant in the nearby galley, prepping beverages and snacks for our short ride across the California sky. "Day drinking—yes or no?"

A smile coasts across Asher's lips, and the thought that pops into my head is *I kissed those full lips, and they tasted good.*

Pretend it didn't happen, girl.

"Yes," he answers. "Because don't you know? There's no alcohol in champagne when you're flying."

"The nuts are calorie-free, too, right?"

"Obviously."

"Maybe I can get two of each," I whisper.

"Go for it," he urges.

But when the attendant comes by with a tray of both, I behave myself and only take one flute and one tiny dish of warm, salted nuts. I pop a cashew into my mouth and sigh happily as I chew, enjoying this respite from my normal life where I don't know if I'll ever catch a big break. "Why are warm cashews better on planes? Are they this good on land?"

"No one knows. No one serves them on land."

"Why not?" I demand.

"It's one of the great mysteries of the universe, Maeve," he says.

I playfully bang my fist on the armrest. "We need to solve that mystery, Asher."

"How about this? When we return, we'll get to the bottom of the warm nut conspiracy."

That's what friends do—tackle silly adventures together. "I'm in," I say, snagging an almond.

Asher holds up a finger to catch the flight attendant's attention. "Hey, Ginger. Thanks for these, but it seems mine disappeared into my stomach already. Any chance I can have another dish of warm nuts?"

"Of course, sir."

"See? You're an addict, too," I tease.

Teasing him will remind us both that the kiss last week was just for show, and that's all. I can't risk being too much for Asher. What would I do without these moments with him?

When Ginger hands Asher a white ceramic dish, he thanks her and then slides it onto my tray. "Here you go," he says.

Oh. "I thought you were getting that for yourself. You said—"

My eye falls on his full dish. The nuts *didn't* disappear into his belly. He got the extra...for me. It's a small but completely Asher gesture. A *friendly* gesture.

"You enabler," I say with a smile. Clearly, he wants to stay in the friend zone too.

"What can I say? I aim to please," he says, lifting his glass of champagne.

He's resetting. This is good. This is exactly what I need. What we both need—a reminder that the kiss didn't mean anything more for either of us. I know a good way to recalibrate too.

"Plane selfie," I declare, whipping out my phone. "Speaking of, we still need to plan our big adventure this year."

He gives me a look like I didn't just say that. "I told you that last month."

Oops. "I can't help it if you're more on top of things than I am," I joke.

"I even gave you suggestions."

Hmm. Maybe he did. "This is sounding vaguely familiar."

He rolls his eyes. "Airstream glamping. Yoga with pigs. Or visiting the new hot pepper truck in Darling Springs."

I tap my chin. "Those are all tempting."

He laughs, shaking his head. "That's what you said when I texted them to you."

"I'm nothing if not consistent, then."

"Take the pic, Maeve."

"I am definitely on top of our photo album though," I point out.

"You are," he concedes.

I'm the keeper of our never-ending pictorial record. I add to it all year long with snaps like this of daily life and then show it to him on our annual Big Adventure trip.

I hold up the camera and lean next to him, my shoulder bumping his. A spark skitters down my chest.

That's odd.

I don't think I've felt a spark like this with Asher before. Not one that traveled between my thighs. Except... maybe I did after the auction? When we kissed on the street?

But that was a normal byproduct of a kiss. That's all.

Perhaps this spark is a side effect of selfie-taking? That has to be it. I angle the phone and snap a shot of us in first class, relaxing in cushy seats, enjoying champagne and extra warm nuts.

Our heads touch, and that spark rekindles. But I don't analyze it this time.

When I put down the phone, I raise my glass to offer a toast. "To this year's Big Adventure, whatever it might be."

Lifting his glass, he laughs. "I'll drink to that. How about we pick when we get back? While we're tackling the warm nut conspiracy?"

"Deal," I say, a cozy, safe feeling spreading inside me as we clink glasses.

We started what we call our annual Big Adventure several years ago. It was a "death-iversary" of sorts, which sounds morbid, but it's not. Maybe because grief isn't entirely morbid for someone who's lost both their parents —it's a part of life. For different reasons, the two of us have been trying to move through grief for the last decade. Or really swim through it—it's an ocean, that bitch. And it's best to ride the waves.

Asher and I met in grief counseling ten years ago, when I was nineteen, he was twenty-two, and my brother was twenty-three. I took my brother along to a local support group since it had been a hell of a year—our mom had died, and six months later our dad died too. The meetings were held in the basement of a small community center, where the beige walls and creaky folding chairs felt as heavy as the sadness we carried. It was a place of hushed voices and tissues passed from hand to hand, a sanctuary for our pain.

Asher was leading the group, and that surprised me. I'd have expected a therapist type—a cuddly aunt or the classic sensitive, nice guy in khakis and a V-neck sweater. Not an athlete in a hoodie with wild hair and a crooked grin. But his humor helped us both cope with the twin losses of our parents, and we helped him too—I think—to deal with the loss of his longtime girlfriend. The three of us became fast friends.

A few years later, though, when my brother was working in Los Angeles and the anniversary of our mom's death rolled around, the thought of visiting the lighthouse where we'd scattered her ashes was too heavy. I wanted to do something different to remember her and my sad, devastated father.

I wanted to celebrate...living.

"Let's have an adventure instead," Asher had said.

The annual Big Adventure was born. Some were in

town; some were road trips. Some were hours away by plane or train. One time, we spent the day on a lavender farm in a small artsy town called Darling Springs; another time, we went camping in a tree tent near Evergreen Falls in the mountains of Northern California. The next year, we hopped on a plane and visited an ice hotel near Quebec City, with warm nuts along the way.

Maybe that's what this trip to Vegas is—another adventure tale told in pictures. I drink the champagne, feeling more settled now than I've felt all week while replaying that kiss.

I know what this trip is—the next stop in our shenanigans.

I know what it's not, too—a real date.

That's for the best. There's too much I need to deal with on the other side of today. There's the live painting party and the search for a commission. The endless, ravenous search.

I sigh, a little content but mostly wistful. Life might be unpredictable back home. My work situation is anything but reliable. But here with Asher? Life feels steady and certain. Like the earth's not about to rumble under my feet.

Who else would give me his extra warm nuts? I pop a cashew into my mouth and rest my head on his shoulder.

10

NO GOOD DEED

Asher

As the afternoon draws to a close, our black town car cruises along the Strip, nearing The Extravagant, when a billboard of me looms overhead.

Maeve points and grins. "Hello, sir!"

I roll my eyes. I had no idea CheekyBeast had rolled out a new billboard of me cooking eggs and bacon in nothing but giraffe boxer briefs. The slogan *Elevate Your Breakfast Game* stretches across the bottom of the sign. That photo shoot was months ago, but the new campaign is running all year—online and, apparently, in front of the entire city. "The slogan's not bad, but they should have gone with *Go Pants-Less at Breakfast*," I quip.

"And all day long," she adds, giving me a playful once-over. "Are you wearing giraffes now?"

"Wouldn't you like to know?" I tease.

I hope so.

Nope. Don't go there. Don't think about that.

"Actually, I would like to know," Maeve says, her eyes wide with curiosity.

The words *find out* hover on my tongue, but I bite them back. "No," I murmur, leaning in closer to her, unable to resist teasing. "That's not what I'm wearing right now."

I don't say anything more because the car has just pulled up to the entrance of The Extravagant. I step out first then hold the door for her. The late-January air of Vegas greets us with a crisp, refreshing chill as the sun dips low in the sky. The city's lights flicker on, the bright neon summoning the night.

After the driver pops the trunk, I sling my duffel over my shoulder and reach for Maeve's bag too.

"I can carry it," she says.

"I know, but I want to," I say, taking her small roller bag.

"Do you always get what you want?" It's asked playfully. Teasingly.

But as I look at her, an unexpected pang lodges in my chest—a pang that feels like it's trying to tell me something I don't want to hear. I quickly look away, trying to dismiss this irritating emotion as best I can. "No. But maybe I'll win at blackjack tonight," I say, hoping to cover up the ache I've no business feeling.

We head inside.

The hotel's jewel-themed lobby is over the top, even for Vegas, with ruby-red velvet couches and an emerald-green carpet. A huge chandelier dripping with faux gemstones hangs from the ceiling.

"This place looks like a jewelry box. Good thing I brought something nice to wear," Maeve muses as we weave past the Friday sleek and stylish crowd on our way to the check-in desk. "Or they'd kick me out."

"Why do I feel like you'd enjoy being kicked out?" I joke.

"Because I would. It'd be another adventure."

"You'd get your 'Kicked out of a Vegas hotel' badge," I say, grateful for the levity.

Her eyes widen. "Yes!"

"I suspect I'd be picking you up at the police station," I tell her.

"And you'd love every second of it," she says.

The thing is, I would, a thought I don't want to examine too closely right now.

We reach the long, shiny brass check-in desk. The first available clerk, a young man with a sharp suit and perfectly gelled black hair, greets us with a practiced smile. "Welcome to The Extravagant. How was your flight?"

"I have zero complaints because my best friend upgraded me to first class," Maeve says, looking my way with a smile.

"Well, he's a keeper, then," the clerk responds with a wink.

"Don't I know it," Maeve replies.

As the polished clerk takes our IDs, a harried sigh draws my attention to a couple checking in with the next clerk. A man and woman stand at the counter with three kids circling the luggage at their ankles. One child is maybe in middle school, but the other two are younger, the girl tugging relentlessly on her mother's sleeve while the younger boy darts around the adults, making airplane noises.

The woman looks at the older man behind the desk

with an exhausted plea. "Is there any way we can get an extra room? For the kids?"

"I'm sorry, ma'am." The clerk glances at his screen through gold-rimmed glasses. "We're fully booked tonight."

Her shoulders slump. "Thanks for trying."

The husband, judging by his wedding ring, rubs her shoulders. "We'll make the best of it, honey."

"I know," she murmurs. It sounds like an attempt to stay upbeat, but both their expressions say sleep is the new sex.

Ouch. I've had some sleepless nights myself. More than I'd like, so I feel for them. Maeve and I exchange a quick glance of sympathy, then she mouths, *"We should share."*

For a couple of seconds, I don't move. I picture her and me in one room together. Navigating showers, and bedtime, and changing into going-out clothes. That sounds fuck-all hard. No way will that help me stay on the friendship path. After these *passing thoughts* I've had, I don't need temptation.

But I'm a grown-ass adult. I can handle a hotel room, no problem. This family has a problem we can fix, and it'd be the right thing to do.

I give Maeve a nod that says, *Go for it*, and she claps in excitement. Her delight in helping someone is worth my discomfort.

Maeve lifts a hand to catch the tired mom's attention. "Hey," she says with a cheery smile. "I couldn't help but hear that you were looking for an extra room. We happen to have two. They're both on the eleventh floor—pretty close to each other too. East Tower. Would you like to trade?"

The mom's jaw falls open. "Oh my god. We're on the twelfth floor. Are you sure?"

"Absolutely," Maeve says.

"It's not a problem at all," I agree, then turn back to the slick guy checking us in. "We'll take their room and give our two to this family."

"How kind of you," he says, then quickly makes the adjustment in conjunction with the other clerk.

"Thank you," the mother says with visible relief as she pulls her kids closer.

"We seriously appreciate it," the man with her says. Then he peers at me more closely, as if my face is a math problem to solve. "This might be weird. But you look familiar."

I hadn't thought about people recognizing me here. It happens more in San Francisco than in other cities, but it still occurs. Maybe he's seen the billboard on the drive in, but asking a strange guy if he remembers seeing me in my briefs probably isn't the conversation starter his wife wants to hear.

I offer a fan-friendly smile. "I play hockey."

He scratches his jaw, admitting, "I'm more of a baseball guy."

"Can't fault you for that. I'm counting the days till spring training myself."

"Me too," he says.

Before I can ask what team he roots for, Maeve slides next to me and clears her throat. "Baseball is fine, but may I suggest you try the hockey entree from the sports menu this season? Studies show hockey is a more satisfying sport." Maeve flashes a smile my way. "Plus, I'm pretty sure all those Canadians can't be wrong."

The man laughs. "Sold. I'm Hal, by the way. Otherwise known as *New Hockey Fan*."

It's my turn to introduce myself, but their son tugs on his mom's hand. "Can we go play in the pool?"

"Once we check in, sweetheart. If you can just let Mommy finish this." She turns back to me with a glint in her eyes now. "I'm Jen. And *I know* you're having a great season."

Hal jerks his gaze to his wife, questions flashing in his eyes. "You follow hockey?"

"I know his stats are good," she tells her husband.

More like excellent, but I don't correct her. Besides, maybe Jen's just being nice. Even so, I rap on the counter for luck, though it's not wood. "That's all her doing—my season," I say, curling a hand over Maeve's shoulder. I don't want to leave my companion in the dust. I'm here with Maeve, and I want to include her. "She's my good luck charm."

"Clearly," Jen says. "She brought us good luck tonight too. Thank you again. This is exactly how I want to get lucky in Vegas."

Laughing, Hal nuzzles his wife. He might have other luck in mind. And yeah, maybe the extra room is exactly what this couple needs. Maybe sex is the new sleep.

Their clerk continues with their check-in while ours hands us our key cards. We thank him, then say goodbye to the family.

But Jen whispers something to her husband, then is looking a little sheepishly at me as he fiddles with his phone. And I know that look. I see it in the fans who wait by the players' parking lot after games for photos, where I happily stop and take them. He nudges her, whispering something like *go ahead.*

"Did you want a pic?" I ask helpfully, to make it easier for them.

Her eyes widen. "If it's not a problem."

"Not at all," I say.

She beams, then points to her husband, blurting out, "I bought him the fire-breathing dragon ones for our anniversary after seeing an online ad."

Oh. It all makes sense now. She doesn't know me from the sport. She knows me from the CheekyBeast campaign.

"Go pants-less," Maeve snickers, then clears her amusement and says, "I can take a pic of both of you with the world's hottest underwear model. Would you like that, Jen?"

"Oh yes," Jen says, right as I say to Maeve in a stern tone, "Hockey player."

Maeve parts her lips in an O. "Oops. My bad. I meant... pants-less hockey player."

Hal nods to Maeve. "But we need you in it, since you bring all the good luck, I hear."

"I also take great selfies," Maeve says, then takes Hal's offered phone, snapping a shot of the four of us as the kids wait patiently. That'll be up on social soon enough, I bet, which will probably make Everly happy since she did say she hoped the winners would post pics of their dates.

And we're on it.

"Will you tag me?" I ask. I can reshare it then.

"Definitely," Hal says, then squeezes his wife's shoulder. "And thanks again. It's the little surprises, like dragon underwear, that keep the spark alive."

"Glad to hear," I say.

Jen gives a soft smile, gratitude in her eyes. "And seriously, this was amazing. Is there anything we can do for you?"

It's sweet they asked, really. But I just wave a hand and say, "Enjoy yourselves tonight."

"We will," Jen says. "We'll pay it forward."

"Sounds great."

Maeve and I head toward the elevator. Along the way, I shake off the bit of unease I felt walking into the hotel. There's really no need for it. This room switch is more proof of how seamlessly Maeve and I can slide from a smoldering kiss last week right back into friendship this week. More proof of how necessary our friendship is too. We've handled the flight, the room, the whole damn trip so far like pros. And when it comes to the room, who cares if we're sharing one? We had an extra, after all.

I step into the elevator. Right foot first.

The doors close and Maeve asks, "Was that your first sighting as an underwear model?"

"No."

She shoves my shoulder playfully. "You never told me you've been spotted in the wild in your underwear."

"Because I haven't been spotted *in them*."

Maeve holds up one finger. "Your honor, I object. Some might say that underwear in a Zoom call is indeed in the wild."

"It was in my home, and they weren't sponsorship boxers anyway," I wave her objection off.

"It's even more impressive that she recognized you *before* you started walking away."

Groaning, I drag a hand down my face. "I can't take you anywhere."

"True. But back to these sightings. Do they come up to you and say Google is right. *You have the best ass ever?*"

Wait. She knows the Internet says that about me? I raise my face. "Been googling me, Maeve?"

"Sometimes I do," she says.

I shouldn't like that so much. I really shouldn't. And yet...I do. "Well, don't believe everything you read online." Then I shrug casually. "But this one is true."

"I know," she says with a smirk, then nods toward me, like she's checking out my backside. "Do you have fire-breathing dragon boxer briefs with you?"

"Maybe I'm wearing them right now."

"Did CheekyBeast give you all its styles?"

"That is one of the perks," I say.

I'm poised for her to let loose a sassy response, but her gaze goes thoughtful. "I know I tease you all the time, but that was seriously cute—how she knew you. How she'd given them to her husband. This might sound kind of out there...but it's almost like they needed that in that moment. It's like, I could feel them reconnecting right in front of us," she says, her eyes lively.

I nod. "I could too."

"Maybe it was all meant to be—us having two rooms in the date package from the auction."

"Yeah, maybe it was meant to be," I say, agreeing as I linger on those three words—*meant to be.*

Some things do feel that way. But if I believe in meant to be, then aren't bad things meant to be too?

I shake off the darker thoughts. There's no place for them. Not in this city where a good time is the only item on the menu. Where good times are meant to be.

The elevator shoots up twelve floors, then dings. We walk down the hallway to our room. I unlock the door, and we step inside. It's a large room, with a king-sized bed and floor-to-ceiling windows offering a sweeping view of the Vegas Strip. Not ideal for a family of five. The room is decked out in luxurious shades of sapphire and silver, with plush furniture and a marble-topped bar in one corner. A bucket with a split of champagne sits in it. The hotel must have brought that up when we switched rooms with Jen and Hal.

Maeve drops her bag on the chair by the window and stretches. "Yep. This is what I need tonight," she says, sounding relieved, but also a bit melancholy as she gazes at the view of the neon-lit Strip below.

Something in her voice catches my attention. "Did something happen earlier? Did you hear from your agent?" Last I heard Maeve was still waiting on that job.

She snaps her gaze back to me, her expression clearing. "No. Just that I have a lot to do when I get back to town. But I'm sure you do too. I mean, you do have a game in two nights' time, and you'd better not miss it," she says, waggling a finger at me.

But her tone's too bright, too cheery. "I won't. But is everything okay with you?" I ask, sensing that she's holding back in some way.

Ah, fuck.

Is she holding back now because of the kiss last week? We never talked about it. We just went our separate ways. A knot tightens in my chest, and along with it comes a familiar twinge of worry. A twinge that rears its head every now and then and has ever since Nora died when I was twenty-two, a few weeks after I'd broken up with her since I'd fallen out of love. I'd tried to do it gently, to say I wanted to be *just friends*, which was true. She said she didn't know if she could be friends with me since I'd broken her heart. But then, a few weeks later, she said she wanted to try. We were supposed to meet for lunch one Sunday—in an attempt to truly *stay* friends post-breakup. But before I even left my home to meet her, I learned that, during a regular training ride down through the Marin Headlands on her new road-racing bicycle, she'd been hit by a car.

Becoming friends with Nora was never going to happen.

A reminder that you never know what's coming. And it's important to talk through things, to listen to people, to hear what's going on with them. When you don't, you might regret it.

No, you *will* regret it.

With tightness in my muscles but a determination to fix whatever's wrong powering me, I walk over to Maeve where she's standing by the window. "Hey," I say, setting a hand on her shoulder. "What's going on?"

She turns to me, wearing a sad smile. "It's silly," she says with a sigh. "Sometimes I get down about work. You know? Sometimes it just seems like...things aren't going to happen for me."

My heart squeezes for her. "I'm sorry you're feeling that way. I'm sure they will though."

"Maybe. Who knows? I'm trying to be hopeful. But at some point, am I just chasing something I can never catch, Asher?" Her throat hitches.

Heart lurching, I reach for her, pulling her into a hug. "You're going through self-doubt. That's normal. For any artist."

"I wonder if my mom ever did," she whispers into my chest.

I run my hand down her back. "I'm sure she did."

"I don't know. I think she was always successful," Maeve says, her voice...small. Her usual bravado is noticeably absent.

I pull back and tuck a finger under her chin. "You *are* successful. You're always working."

Rolling her eyes, she scoffs. "Always hustling."

"And the hustle pays off," I say.

She shoots me a look like I've gone mad. "I don't know about that." She sighs heavily, like she's resigning herself to finally sharing since she adds, "Not everyone makes it. Not everyone pulls it off. What if it's time to throw in the towel when it comes to painting? You know that's what Vivian wants. She wants me to go full-time with her. And then maybe to take things over when she retires. Like me running a catering business is a good idea," she says with an eye roll.

But it's a real pressure she feels from her aunt, who's tried in her own, sometimes misguided, way to look out for Maeve.

I want to tell Maeve not to worry about her aunt, but family is complicated. Mine seems easy on the surface, but we've had our exhausting years.

I want to tell Maeve, too, that the decorative art she makes is great, but that's not what she wants to hear right now, I suspect. "You know I don't think it's towel-throwing-in time, now or ever. You know I think you're amazing at what you do. But I hear you that it's hard, and I'm sorry you're feeling that right now," I say.

"I hate to admit it, but I guess I've kind of been in a... spiral this past week."

Well, that's no good, but she came to the right guy. "What can we do about it?" I ask, cupping her shoulders, rising to the occasion. "How can we un-spiral you?"

She peers around the room, then to the windows over-looking the glittering streets below, then back to me. "I just want to have fun tonight, okay? How does that sound?"

"Well, it's what I was planning on too," I say dryly.

"I know," she says, tone playful again, and that's a promising step in the un-spiraling. "I just mean—let's have a great time. Let's not think about anything else. Just...this night."

I know just what the doctor ordered. "One second," I say, then hustle over to the bar, grab the champagne split and loosen the cage. I hold the bottle at an angle, then pop open the cork.

Maeve joins me, her hazel eyes twinkling with mischief. "Do not even bother with a glass. Let's drink it just like that."

I lift the open bottle. "To fun. Just fun. Nothing else is allowed tonight. Got that?"

"Just fun," she echoes, then snags the bottle from me, lifts it, and brings it to her lips. I don't stare, I swear I don't stare, I seriously promise I don't stare.

Ah, fuck it.

I stare unabashedly as her lush lips meet the green glass and she tips some bubbly down her throat. Then she lowers the bottle, and hands it to me. "Your turn."

"To just fun," I say, then knock some back. I'm not thinking of where her lips were. I'm not tasting her raspberry lipstick.

News flash: I fucking am.

But I set down the bottle like a good friend. Not a dirty fucker. "It's my personal mission to make sure you have fun tonight. Think of me as your fun guide."

And failure is not an option.

Her smile is buoyant, and it feels like old times

between us. "We're going to have the best time at the concert tonight," she says, patting my chest. It's a friendly gesture, like she did after the kiss that we don't speak of.

Her hand on me feels annoyingly good—so good I want to cover it, press her palm closer to my pecs, kiss that lush mouth one more time, and tell her to sink to her knees.

And that inappropriate thought was brought to you by Las Vegas.

I shake it off as I check my watch. We should get a move on. "I'd better shower before we head out."

Then I picture stepping under the water and great. Fucking great. That won't be awkward at all with her in the next room. I guess I didn't think this one-room thing through clearly. But there's a door in the bathroom. It's no big deal. It's fine. It's totally fine.

"Good idea. You shower first, and then I'll go," she says with a dash of awkwardness in her tone. Or maybe it's me hearing things.

"Sounds like a plan," I say, doing my best to keep an even tone, already unzipping my bag to unpack. This is supposed to be a night of no complications, an evening of fun with my best friend. And dammit I will make it fun. I will make it easy. I will make it care-fucking-free.

That's what she needs, and that's what I can do. But as I unload the contents of my bag onto the bed, something black and shiny catches my eye. Nestled between my clothes is a box of condoms. I freeze, staring at the black box as the pieces fall into place. Those assholes in the locker room must have slipped it in after practice.

Before I can shove it back into the bag, Maeve pads across the carpet. Her eyes go wide, and then, with a smirk, she says, "Got a hot date tonight after the concert?"

For a split second, I wonder if she's joking or if she actually thinks I'm planning to hook up with someone here. The idea leaves me momentarily speechless. "No," I say quickly, irked. "I'd never do that while I'm with you. This is just a locker room prank."

But saying it's a locker room prank raises the question of why this would *be* a locker room prank. I'm definitely not telling her a thing about the whiteboard.

Maeve raises an eyebrow, her smirk deepening. "Sure, sure," she teases lightly, but there's an edge of curiosity in her voice. "You can if you want to. *Just fun* and all."

I quickly shove the box back into my bag, trying to recover. "First off, I didn't come to Vegas with you to hook up with someone else. Second, the guys were being dickheads."

"For suggesting you might need condoms for—?" But she stops before finishing the question, maybe exactly aware of where that sentence was going—that I'd need condoms for her. "For Vegas," she course-corrects with a strangled sound.

"Yes. Exactly," I grit out, and I need some space right now. I need hot water and a moment to clear my head. But right when I'm about to claim the shower, I realize how selfish that'd be—showering before her when she probably needs more time to get ready. "Do you want to shower first after all?"

"Sure," she says and grabs some items from her bag, then turns back to the window. But there's a new tension in the air, something unspoken lingering between us. So much for the *just fun* toast. The easygoing vibe from earlier has shifted.

What seemed like an easy solution to someone else's

problem—giving up our second room—now seems like a dicey solution to *my* problem.

Actually, it seems like it's a whole new problem for me. Because once she's in the shower, I can't stop thinking about her naked.

11

GIRL SORCERY

Asher

After I've showered, Maeve is back in the bathroom, curling her hair, or straightening it, or rolling it. Who even knows? She's working some kind of girl sorcery in the bathroom while I'm sitting on the couch, reading up on off-season baseball trades.

My nose twitches. Sweet plum. Well, fuck me. She must be spritzing something on herself in the next room. The scent of her body spray floats out here, and it's definitely time to go.

That's entirely too tempting for a man tasked with pulling off *just fun*. "I'll meet you in the casino. I'm going to play a round," I call out.

"Don't do anything I wouldn't do," she shouts back.

"I guess I won't try to pull off a casino heist tonight," I say as I head to the door, tucking a key card into my pocket.

As I walk down the hall, I pull out my phone. A couple

replies have popped up from my parents since I sent that video.

> Carlos: It's been a few hours. Do we need to bail you out yet?

> John: Our bags are packed. Just say the word.

Asher: If it's true I suck at cards, and I categorically deny that accusation, then it's YOUR fault. You guys taught me to play.

> Carlos: You mean we tried to teach you to play, Ash. We tried.

Asher: I can't wait to prove you wrong when I win big tonight. Also, is this why I'm so good at hockey? Because you two negative reinforced me the whole time?

> John: Yes. You're welcome. It's all part of our master plan.

> Carlos: We can't help it if you loved a challenge. If someone said you couldn't do something, that only made you want it more.

I grumble as I walk. Damn them. They're right. I fucking love proving people wrong. Not sure what that says about me. But it is what it is.

Asher: Just you wait then.

Carlos: Holding my breath. Well, figuratively. I've seen you try blackjack.

John: Bating mine. BTW, what is bated breath? It sounds like bad breath with a fishy aftertaste.

Carlos: It's breath you hold when you're waiting, babe.

John: Ah, good to know. And here I thought I needed mints.

I laugh at the way they rib each other, the way they always have, even when times were hard when John was sick for a while back when I was thirteen and fourteen. But we made it through.

We banter like that as I make my way to the casino floor. Once I'm there I put the phone away, buy some chips, then beeline for a table. I'm eager to play a round before dinner and the show and try to clear my head with some straightforward decisions that I am damn fucking good at, no matter what they say, before I begin my official mission.

Fun. Only fun.

Fifteen minutes later, I'm nursing a glass of scotch, contemplating my cards, deciding if I want to stay in or hit. The dealer is waiting, the other players at the table glancing my way as I weigh my chances. I've got a sixteen, and the dealer's showing a seven. Risk it or play it safe? The usual tension of blackjack—knowing the odds, yet still gambling against them—tightens in my chest.

But before I can make a call, a charge slides down my

spine. It's like my body feels her before my eyes see her. When I look up from my cards a second later, my mouth goes dry.

Maeve's weaving through the blackjack tables, a jean skirt brushing mid-thigh, short pink cowboy boots padding softly on the carpet, and...my vest snug on her body.

That's it. Just the vest. She's all bare arms and cleavage, and I can hardly handle how good my friend looks.

In. My. Clothes.

My fingers tighten on the edges of the cards, my brain fogging as I try to focus on the decision in front of me. Sixteen against a seven. My gut screams to hit, but with Maeve in my line of sight coming, I can't think.

With her easy smile, she's oblivious to the effect her girl sorcery is having as she walks closer. That's good. I really don't want to let on that she's cast a spell on me, and that I've got a bad case of lust for my best friend.

She's your best friend's sister too.

The dealer clears his throat. "What's it gonna be?" His expression is neutral, but there's a hint of impatience in his eyes. I can't find it in me to care, though, since all I see is Maeve and the way the vest dips in all the right places. She must have taken it in since she last wore it, because it's so goddamn snug right now it should be illegal.

Still, I manage to tear my gaze back to the cards. Normally, I'd play this hand safe, maybe even fold, like I'd do if I were playing on the team jet with the guys. But here tonight, I want to win. No, I'm compelled to win.

Possibly because there's a reckless edge to my thoughts right now, spurred on by the mission of the evening. Or maybe it's driven by the sight of her in that vest.

Yes, Maeve can definitely make vests a thing.

"Hit me," I say, my voice rougher than intended.

The dealer nods, sliding a card my way. I flip it over and want to pump a fist. A five. I've got twenty-one.

Yep, luck is on our side tonight.

Maeve sidles up to me, her bare arm brushing mine as she leans in, just close enough that her scent—like a fruit I want to bite into—invades my senses. "Nice hand," she murmurs.

Electricity shoots through me, from her voice, her words, her scent. "Nice vest," I reply, my voice equally low, matching her tone.

"Oh, this thing? It's a hand-me-down," she says, fingering the top of it, drawing my attention to the pale, freckled flesh of her chest, covered in layers of silver chains, to the column of her throat, to her face. Heart-shaped with a spray of freckles across her nose and mischievous hazel eyes, with wild curls framing her face.

And I know I got lucky that round. I want to keep that luck for the rest of the night, so it's time to walk away from the table. "Let's get some food, and then see the show."

"Let's do it," she says as I take my chips and follow her, snapping a pic as I go. Feeling a little smug, I send it to my dads.

Asher: Oh, ye of little faith.

Carlos: Yes! I always believed in you.

John: We knew you could do it.

Laughing, I shake my head as I dictate a final reply for now.

> Asher: Lies, sweet little lies.

Then, I tuck my phone away so I can focus on Maeve for the rest of the night.

* * *

After we eat, we head to the theater in the heart of The Extravagant, walking through a glitzy concourse, flanked by high-end boutiques and bustling cafés. Along the way, Maeve pinwheels her arms, pointing frantically up ahead.

I groan when I see another ad for CheekyBeast. Damn, the brand really went all out here in Vegas—but then again, this is the kind of city where you bring your best drawers. Several feet away a glossy image of me is plastered to the wall. In it, I'm striding to a work-at-home-style desk, dressed in a crisp button-down and a pair of monkey-print briefs, with the slogan *Monkey Around at the Home Office* across the bottom of the image.

Maeve grabs my arm, tugging me to a stop. "We need a selfie with the real thing and the image. I'll call it—Seeing Double."

Even I have limits when it comes to this woman. "That'd be a hard no."

"Why not?"

I scoff, then spin around, arms out. The concourse is packed. "If I'm spotted taking a selfie with an ad of me in boxer briefs, how long do you think the guys will give me hell for?"

She taps her chin. "Forever?"

"And then some," I add, and we move on past the image, but not before Maeve waves to it, saying, "Bye, Asher's ass."

As we continue down the hall, she shoots me a quizzical look. "So you're wearing monkeys tonight?"

"A gentleman doesn't tell," I say.

"Are you a gentleman?"

Not in bed. "Sometimes," I say, holding her gaze for a beat before we reach the venue. The Sapphire Theater holds around five thousand, and the place is packed as we head toward our VIP seats in the front.

As we make our way through the crowd, I reach for her hand, then position myself slightly ahead of Maeve, clearing a path through the boisterous throng. The scent of beer, sweat, and perfume mingles in the air, blending with the riotous sounds of laughter and cheers. The party atmosphere is in full swing, and the anticipation for the show builds with each step. The crush of bodies is intense, so I grip her hand tighter, keeping her close to my side.

"Aren't you possessive," she says.

"Don't want anyone touching my date," I joke, only it's not a joke.

I fucking don't.

I scan the theater, making sure no one is getting too close to her.

No one but me.

By the time we reach the front of the room, I'm all too aware of her warmth beside me. But as she slips into her seat, flashing me that carefree smile, I remind myself to keep it cool. Tonight's about fun—just fun. And I'm going to do whatever it takes to make that happen.

I can't find her a job or line up clients, but there's one thing I know I can do—make her smile. And when she does, it lights up her whole face. That makes everything worth it.

When she turns to me, she flashes it full wattage, and says, "Let's see if you're a hundred-thousand-dollar date, Callahan."

I crack up but quickly school my expression. "Is that a challenge?"

"I believe it is," she teases. "I paid a lot for you."

I toss my head back, laughing. I'm about to point out the obvious—that she paid nothing—but stop myself. That's poor sportsmanship. It's also untrue. She might not have paid in dollars, but she paid in chutzpah, in guts, and in fucking loyalty, wanting to save me from someone I didn't even know wanted to use me as a pawn. I think back to the mom and dad in the lobby, to their happiness and relief at getting a break tonight. I think, too, of how easily we made that happen for them.

I loop back to the auction, when Maeve saved me from what could've been a sticky situation with Miranda. So yeah, Maeve definitely threw down for me. And I'm going to show her what a great date I can be.

"You sure did. And I'm going to make it worth every single cent," I say.

When the band comes on, I don't hold back. I cheer, I shout, I grab her hand, and the crowd around us gets to their feet too. We sing along, voices getting hoarse, but I don't care. I don't play hockey with my voice. I play it with my body, and I use it tonight, dancing with a friend, showing her the time of her life.

When servers come by, trying to get our attention above the noise, I scan the menu and ask for a Lemonade Affair. It's rosemary, lemonade, and gin. Maeve's eyes light up, so I amend the order to make it two. When the drinks arrive, I toast to us.

"You are a good time. I should bid on you every year," she says, and the thought of that goes straight to my head, making it crackle with ideas—some I shouldn't be entertaining. Blame the Lemonade Affair.

"I'll keep making it worth your while," I say.

"Oh, I know you will. I'm jealous of every woman you've ever had a date with," she says, and damn, she's saying things that are making my mind race way too far ahead. But the way she's having fun, singing along, is all I care about.

When the lead singer finishes their hit song "Blown Away" with an epic strum of his guitar, Maeve turns to me, her face flushed, her eyes bright. "I love that song. I just do."

"I know," I say.

She blushes. "I've said that before?"

I hold up my thumb and forefinger to show a sliver of space. "A few times. You said it makes you happy." I have to cup my hand around her ear because it's loud.

She shivers as I touch her. At least I think she does. And that reaction goes south of the pants border. Good thing it's dark.

"Well, it still makes me happy. This whole night is making me happy. So whatever you're doing tonight, Callahan, it's working."

A surge of satisfaction spreads warmth through my chest. Mission accomplished. I can't help the grin that stretches across my face, wide and sure. This is what I set out to do—to make her forget everything else, if only for tonight. Her happiness is my win, and knowing I'm the reason for it makes me feel like I'm on top of the world.

The singer clears his throat, his deep, raspy baritone booming across the theater. "I've got a new song for you tonight. Something I've been working on for a while. A little number about promises. Promises made, and promises kept."

Maeve's eyes widen. "Did you know he was going to premiere a new song?"

As if I have that kind of sway with the band. Still, I play along. "One hundred thousand dollars? Of course it comes with a brand-new tune from your favorite band."

"Best date ever," she shouts.

With a drink in her hand and her arms in the air, Maeve cheers as the opening notes fill the theater. Then he leads into the song, and the lyrics hit me like an arrow to the heart: *Remember that promise we made? When I was little and thought I'd marry you? Now that we're all grown up, I know just what I wanna do...*

The words strike me, like a brilliant idea. Like a goddamn roadmap for the best night ever. For a second, or maybe more, I'm back in time to a night I don't like to dwell on. To a night that made me feel things I shouldn't really feel. But thanks to a Lemonade Affair and a brand-new song, I'm not holding back. I'm remembering a promise made at a wedding two years ago.

Maeve doesn't need a husband. But she needs a big adventure.

"Remember how we haven't planned our Big Adventure yet? Well, I've got an idea..."

12

ARE FLAMINGOS SULTRY?

Maeve

Never let it be said that I back down from a dare. And no one can, because a couple of hours later, I've got a marriage license in my hand, a daisy tucked behind my ear, and a white satin cami underneath Asher's vest—now mine. Well, a bride's got to wear white, so we grabbed one from an all-night lingerie shop. Because of course Vegas has a twenty-four-hour lingerie shop.

"It's my bridal flair," I declare, then glance at Asher, my eyes widening as a thought suddenly hits me. "What are you going to wear?"

Or maybe I shout it. It's possible those Lemonade Affairs were stronger than I'd realized. It's also possible I had more of them than I'd thought. Hard to say at this point in the night. All I know is everything feels warm and fizzy, inside and out. The lights are festive, the neon is blindingly bright, and the energy pulses through me as the car zips us back from the Clark County Marriage

License Bureau to our hotel, where we booked a wedding in its little chapel.

"We have to get him a tuxedo!" I shout to the Lyft driver.

The driver chuckles. "Let me know if you want to stop at an all-night tux shop. We have those too."

Asher sets a calming hand on my arm. "Let me point out the obvious—you're not wearing a dress."

"Oh! I bet they'll have something at the chapel," I say confidently, then turn to my best friend. "They have clothes to rent usually. One time, we were all at Elodie's Chocolates, and the owner told us about when she got married in Vegas. At the same place! She said she rented a burgundy dress at the chapel they used, and her hubs got a velvet jacket, and they walked down the aisle to 'It Had to Be You,' and..."

Wow. Asher's green eyes never stray from me as I babble. He really is good-looking. Like, ridiculously good-looking. Actually, he's so good-looking it's like looking at the sun. "You know what? You're the hottest groom ever. Nobody has ever looked better in jeans and a Henley. In fact, you don't need a tux. Wear that."

He laughs dryly. "Thanks. I am wearing it. And I will."

But then a thought occurs to me, and I lean in conspiratorially. "Wait, what color is your underwear? Are you wearing monkeys or dragons? Why won't you tell me? Or do I just have to find out for myself?"

His clever eyes darken for a second. Turning smoldering. Flickering with heat. I like that too. I definitely like that. Like, ridiculously like it. I like it also when he smirks, leaning in close, his breath tickling my ear as he whispers, "Flamingos."

I like it so much my breath catches. A shiver runs

through me. From the closeness of him. From the way that word sounds strangely sultry. Are flamingos sultry? It takes me several seconds—maybe a minute—to process what he just shared because all I want to process is how good he smells after dancing. There's a faint lingering scent of sweat, but even that smells fresh, mingling with the clean, oaky aftershave he always uses.

My best friend is really hot.

I mean, of course, he's hot. I've always known this. How could you not know when your best friend is a sexy hockey player that women throw themselves at? But then I blink, realizing what he's just said. "You're wearing flamingo underwear?"

He shoots me a playful look. "It's CheekyBeast's newest style. But don't tell a soul. That campaign hasn't rolled out yet."

"I'll keep your secret," I say.

"Good girl," he says, lighting an unexpected spark in my chest from those two words. Words I wouldn't mind hearing again.

As we pull up to the hotel, which has a chapel inside, I'm struck with the strangest thought—I want to see my best friend's flamingo underwear.

But you know what? That's probably totally normal when you're getting married as part of your annual Big Adventure, fulfilling a marriage pact made for fun one night at your brother's wedding. A pact we'll undo when we're back in San Francisco. On the way over, we briefly talked about getting an annulment when we're back home. But for tonight? I'm absolutely getting my money's worth from the date I won.

The car stops at The Extravagant, and we tumble out. Asher holds my elbow, steadying me, and while I don't feel stumbling-drunk, I do feel like the world is tilted in our favor tonight. We walk into the hotel, under the chandelier, across the casino, through the concourse, past the CheekyBeast ad, and right into the chapel, where we've reserved the one-thirty a.m. slot.

As you do when you make marriage pacts.

Once we're in the foyer, we sign papers with the couple who runs it—a sturdy, bald man named Hitch Malone and his busty wife, Mrs. Matrimony. When she tells me they have a Marilyn Monroe-style dress that would look fabulous on me, and a tuxedo with ruffles that would suit Asher perfectly, I revise my decision on a tux and a dress.

"Pictures," I tell Asher, breathlessly. "We're going to need photos for the album. I don't want to be in a jean skirt. This is like a costume party. We need to do ourselves up in full regalia."

His smile is a little wicked, a lot pleased. "When in Rome, Maeve."

I sigh, feeling bubbly and electric, and alive in a way I haven't felt in a long time. "I could kiss you."

For a second, his smile fades, replaced by something deeper, more intense, that flickers in his eyes—a look I can't quite place. Even as the warmth from the Lemonade Affairs starts to fade, that look makes my heart skip a beat. I push the thought aside, focusing on the fun of this. "You'll look good in ruffles," I tease.

"No one looks good in ruffles," he counters, shaking his head.

"No," I say, stepping closer, insisting, "A man who can pull off flamingo underwear will look good in ruffles."

Asher laughs, but there's something tender in his eyes, something that makes me feel invincible, like I'm not teetering on the edge of a career disaster. Like anything is possible tonight.

Thanks to him. He knew I needed this.

He turns to the couple in charge. "I'll take one tux with ruffles," he says, his voice steady.

Hitch chuckles and claps him on the back. "Good man. It's wise to listen to your soon-to-be wife. And I've got one just your size."

Mrs. Matrimony turns to me, her eyes sparkling with mischief. "Let me take you to the bridal suite. I can fix your makeup a little bit, sweetheart. You're going to want the pictures with your new hubs to look fabulous, aren't you?"

"He's actually my best friend," I say, the correction slipping out before I can stop it. But when I glance at Asher, other words slip out too. "Isn't he hot?"

Mrs. Matrimony smiles knowingly. "It's a good thing you feel that way about your soon-to-be husband—we all need a hot friend in our bed, don't we?"

Marital advice from Mrs. Matrimony, but I don't bother to correct her this time. There's no point. Asher and I are here, honoring our playful marriage pact and having the biggest adventure of our lives. Besides, people seem to like to give us life tips. Me, I understand. I scream *hot mess*. But he's got his act together, so who knows why we're a magnet for it?

Before she takes me away though, Hitch calls out, "You got a special song, lovebirds? If not, I can play my cover of 'Can't Help Falling In Love.'"

It's adorable that Hitch has recorded the Elvis tune, but that song feels like it belongs to other couples. To couples who spend a year planning a wedding, to men who drop down on one knee in Paris, to women who cry real tears at a proposal—not to partners in crime having an adventure just for one night.

I've got some more playful options on the tip of my tongue, like "Accidentally in Love" or "We've got Tonight," so I turn to Asher to toss them his way. He looks so good, in his jeans and Henley, that my pulse kicks a little faster. But he'll look good in a tux too, and that's when I know our song isn't either of those.

I know what our song is. "'The Way You Look Tonight,'" I say.

His lips quirk up in a grin. "Perfect."

And briefly, I wonder why it's so perfect to him, but the thought falls from my head when Mrs. Matrimony leads me to a mirrored door that opens into a large wardrobe. This must be the bridal suite. It's full of gowns with sequins, satin, and swishy fabrics, and behind the closed door Hitch calls Asher away to another part of the chapel. I take a deep breath, running my fingers over the clothes, letting the messy joy of the moment wash over me.

Fifteen minutes later, I feel kind of beautiful in this soft white dress that clings to my curves and my pink boots, but I stop at the chapel door as my thoughts start to clear. Am I drunk? No. I'm definitely not. But I'm tipsy still. Definitely.

And even so, I want to do this. Life is for the living. I've been chasing my dreams ever since my mother shared her dying wish with me: *Follow your dreams.*

I don't know if I ever dreamed of getting married, but I've always dreamed of squeezing every drop of richness and sweetness out of life, every single day.

This has to count, right?

As "The Way You Look Tonight" plays over the sound

system I tell myself it doesn't matter that I'm blurring the line between best friend and husband. The song is both perfect and perfectly ephemeral. Like tonight.

This is a moment that will inspire a painting, a story, a memory I can call upon later when I'm feeling blue and need to believe in hope again. I can capture the way I feel on a canvas when I return home. That's what Asher gave me so many years ago when we became friends, and that's what he gives me every day.

With my heart full, I step down the aisle toward my temporary husband, letting myself soak in the joy of this moment—nothing more, nothing less.

13

WAIT FOR IT

Asher

Standing in front of the gleaming white altar, I'd like to say I can't believe we're actually doing this.

But I can. This feels like an inevitable adventure for us. Like that marriage pact was never merely an offhand comment made at her brother's wedding. It was a real promise that if she ever needed a husband, I'd step up.

But she wanted an escape from the frustrations of her career, if only for a night.

And this wedding is just that. The chapel is a blend of old Vegas glamor and kitschy charm. Red velvet drapes frame the walls, and gold accents shimmer in every corner. It's the kind of place where anything can happen, and probably often does.

Mrs. Matrimony fusses over Maeve one last time, making sure the Marilyn Monroe-style dress is perfect on her. Spoiler alert: It is. Maeve looks stunning. Better than she did in the vest, and that's saying something.

"You'll look fabulous in those pictures, doll," Mrs. Matrimony whispers to my temporary bride before stepping back to join Hitch.

Now dressed in an Elvis jumpsuit because, of course, it's Vegas, Hitch adjusts his oversized sunglasses. "Ready to make it official, lovebirds?" he asks, sounding like the King as Frank Sinatra plays softly in the background.

I answer with a confident, "We are."

"Let's do this," Maeve echoes.

"How about we kick this ceremony off with some vows? What do you say there?" Hitch asks.

Maeve's eyes widen, but then she seems to go with it, tossing the question to me. "Where did you put the vows, honey?"

She's such a troublemaker. But I know a thing or two about thinking on my feet.

I tap my temple. "Right here."

"I can't wait," she says, in a challenge.

I step closer to Maeve, my hand slipping into hers. "Maeve," I begin, ready to dive into something that'll make her laugh—like *I pledge to be the best husband for one night*, since we'll unwind the clock on this marriage tomorrow. But I flash back to earlier in the hotel room, when she opened her heart and shared her fears. While I can't commission a big painting for her, or land her a coveted gallery spot, I absolutely can let her know that I'll be by her side through those ups and downs. So with more gravitas than I'd expected, I say, "You've been my best friend for years, the person who shows up when I need it, who asks no questions, and who's always up for the wildest adventures—like this one."

She smiles so big, so beautifully, that my heart tugs.

Maybe even aches a bit. A reminder that I best not stay in this zone too long.

I steer the vows into lighter territory. "I can't promise I'll be a perfect husband," I say, then cough subtly, leaning into the *Just Fun* order from the menu at last, adding, "*tonight*. But I can promise I'll always be there for you."

Maeve's eyes sparkle playfully as she takes a breath, her grip on my hand tightening. "Asher," she begins, and there's a tenderness in her expression that catches me off guard. "You've been the constant in my life when everything else felt like chaos. For years, you've been my rock, my partner in crime, and my biggest supporter."

And...she's following my lead. Speaking from the heart. Like we're renewing our vows—of friendship. My chest warms a little unexpectedly.

"I don't deserve you, but somehow you're still here, hanging out with me."

"You do," I assure her. She gives more than she realizes.

Her smile returns, and with it, a hint of mischief. "I can't promise I won't drag you into more schemes, but I promise I'll always have your back..." She takes a moment, then mimics me as she adds, "tonight."

Right as Frank hits that word in the song too.

That last word lingers—*tonight*—a reminder of the sheer temporariness of this union. But so do the others—words like *rock*, and *supporter*, words like *constant* and *for years*. And as they hang in the air, everything else fades away. It's just us, standing in this chapel, making promises that feel entirely true.

I kind of don't want to move. I sort of want to stop time. I know we should exchange rings, since the clock is ticking. I bet there's another wedding scheduled any minute, but I'm enjoying the view of Maeve too much right now, especially when she finishes her vows with, "Also, I told you you'd look hot in ruffles. And I was right."

It's the strangest compliment I've ever gotten, and it makes my skin sizzle. My pulse surges. And my thoughts tumble free before I even want to stop them. "And you're stunning," I rasp out, heat in my voice. I wonder if she notices the bedroom tone. I wonder, too, if I care that I'm a little see-through right now.

I don't get an answer since Hitch clears his throat, bringing us back to the practical details. "And now the rings," he says.

Mrs. Matrimony offers a satin pillow that holds two shiny gold bands. We take them, and I hold Maeve's gaze once again as I slide the ring onto her finger. Probably best for my control—frayed a little thin as it is—to return to the style of the vows, so I say, "Maeve, with this ring, I promise to get to the bottom of the warm nut conspiracy."

She snorts. She actually snorts, clutching her stomach briefly. Then she turns almost serious as she takes my hand. "Asher," she deadpans, "I promise I'll always be ready to start and end a bidding war for you."

"It's a deal," I say, grateful for the levity, but when I stare at the metal on Maeve's finger, I feel a little like I'm floating above this scene. How the hell can my ring look that good on her finger?

Must be the fading remnants of my buzz, that's all.

"By the power vested in me by the state of Nevada, I now pronounce you husband and wife," Hitch declares, utter delight in his voice. "You may kiss the bride."

Maeve looks to me, eyes bright, lips parted, zero reticence. Then, she lifts her chin.

Holy fuck.

She's asking for a kiss.

Which means...I wouldn't be stealing it this time since she's giving it.

I'm not a professional athlete for nothing. When I spot an opening, I go for it. I close the distance between us, cup her cheek, hold her face. I pause, but not because I'm hesitating—because I want her to feel the anticipation. To crave my kiss.

Maybe even to beg for it.

I slide my thumb along her cheekbone, stroking her soft skin. Her eyes pop. I run my thumb back down, along her chin. When her breath catches, I wait a little longer, then murmur in a low, but commanding tone, "Ask for it."

She shudders. "Kiss me," she pants out, desperate, needy.

I brush my lips to hers, but the instant we touch, I can't hold back. I clasp her face in both hands, taste her mouth, and kiss my best friend in a whole new way.

It's a soulful, lingering kiss that thrums deep in my bones. She's soft in my arms, her breath gusting across her lips. A whimper crosses them too, and it sounds like a plea for more.

I want to swallow all her sounds, let them lead me on into the night.

Because they are *not* platonic.

They are *not* friendly.

They *are* unbearably sexy and needy.

Maeve Hartley tastes incredible, and this kiss rattles through my entire body, touching every damn corner of me. I don't let go. As I kiss her more deeply, I'm struck with a cold, new clarity. It wasn't merely affection I felt all along. It wasn't simply lust either. It's a whole lot more than basic attraction.

I'm wildly, annoyingly obsessed with my best friend. Otherwise known as...*my wife*.

14

BET IT ALL ON RED

Maeve

What even was that? Have I ever been kissed like that? Is that what epic kisses are like?

For a while, I thought I had studied too many kisses in paintings. I figured I'd put too much stock in Francesco Hayez's seminal work—*The Kiss*, where an unknown Italian man in a cape kisses a woman in a silvery-gray dress so passionately, I feel the kiss in my bones whenever I look at a reproduction of it. Or I assumed Roy Lichtenstein's pop art depictions of women looking lost in deeply intimate kisses had cast a spell on me.

Now, I think I've had one of those kisses. And I don't know how to go back.

As we head to the door of our chapel, dressed in our clothes again, Mrs. Matrimony gives me a motherly hug. "I'll send you those pics soon, doll. You looked beautiful. And don't ever forget—the key to a happy marriage is forgiveness and selective hearing," she says.

"Thanks. I'll keep that in mind," I say, but it's hard to think about anything except the way my husband kissed me.

Once we exit the chapel though, the warm, heady atmosphere vanishes like smoke. We're thrust into the chaotic night again, and I don't know what to say. Seems he doesn't either. We pass through the concourse quietly, then step into the bright casino, and the neon lights, the clinking of slot machines, and the hum of conversation try to slingshot me back into reality.

But I'm still several steps behind, caught up in my own painting kind of kiss. Has anyone ever consumed me like Asher? Has anyone ever wanted to? Not until tonight after I said *I do.*

Now, Asher's hand is pressed on the small of my back, guiding me through the late-night crowds. Like he touched me when he led me to the front of the concert venue. He's...touchy in a way that sends a message to others—a *do not touch her* message. I try to understand why by sneaking glances at him, like I can read what's going on in his head. Was the kiss as good for him? Was it a Lichtenstein kiss? A Hayez kiss? I search his eyes, but instead of answers, I find more questions. It's like he's at war with himself. Or maybe frustrated? Annoyed with me?

My heart races with worry. He's arranged this whole night for me—to give me a great time since I was feeling down. But the possibility that he's annoyed or frustrated sends a twinge of guilt through my body.

The casino is alive, the noise and energy pulling us into its midnight embrace. But I'm not entirely comfortable with that look in his eyes, so I stop walking and turn to him.

"You okay?" I ask, trying to keep my voice casual, to mask my worry.

"I'm great," he says, stopping too, his tone...even. That's all. Just even.

"Are you sure?" I press, needing to know.

"Yes," he replies, but his expression almost seems resigned, like he's wishing he didn't feel whatever it is he's feeling. Or perhaps he's wondering what happens next too. Is there a guidebook for what's to come after you temporarily marry your best friend as part of a pact? Do we sit down and work out the specific details of our annulment?

But talking about the necessary end of this union feels too businesslike. I don't want to tackle that right now. Do we go back to the room? What will happen if we walk through that door while I'm still feeling this kiss in every cell in my body?

That feels too dangerous. Like walking into a fire.

I scan the casino, searching for a distraction. That's it! Vegas itself is the perfect solution. The roulette table ahead catches my attention. "Let's play a round," I suggest, leading the way to the table. "It's on me."

"You had me at let's play, and it's definitely on me," Asher says, like he's shedding whatever his frustrations were.

"I know better than to fight you on this."

"Good," he says as I grab his hand, catching a glimpse of the gold on his ring finger. What a strange sight. But it'll be gone tomorrow.

The roulette table is buzzing with excitement as we approach, a mix of high rollers and tourists surrounding the table. The croupier, a sharp-looking man in a tailored suit, calls for final bets.

Asher and I join the crowd of eager gamblers, sliding in next to a man with ginger hair sticking straight up and a Hawaiian shirt. Asher tugs me a little closer, then hands me a chip from earlier. I place a small bet on black. The croupier nods, spinning the wheel with a practiced flick of his wrist. The ball clatters around the edge and the crowd leans in, all eyes on the spinning wheel.

As the ball bounces between the numbers, a woman in a fuchsia pink jumpsuit and gold hoop earrings lifts a tall glass of something toward our side of the table. "When in Vegas," she says to the crowd, lifting her arm in a rocker salute, then toasting.

"When in Vegas," I shout back in good times solidarity.

Then, I turn to watch the wheel too, with a mix of focus and distraction, still feeling the heat of Asher's kiss. Absently, I lift my fingers to my lips to relive it once more. When I touch my lower lip, a spark kindles. Like my body's remembering his mouth on me. So much for the game distracting me.

I'm distracting me.

I try to escape my thoughts, homing in on the ball as it clatters around the wheel, finally landing on red.

My shoulders slump.

"Guess luck's not on our side tonight," I say, but the joke doesn't quite land, and I don't want Asher to think for a second that I'm not having a great time. I want him to feel all the brightness, all the joy, all the exuberance of a Big Adventure. So I try again. I flash Asher a flirty grin. Maybe it's because I can't stop thinking about that kiss, or maybe it's because tonight feels like the ultimate "When in Vegas" kind of night. Whatever it is, I don't analyze it too much as I say, "How about we make a bet?"

He raises an eyebrow. "What kind?"

"If it lands on red this time," I say, leaning in closer, some new desire, some shimmery curiosity driving me on. "I get another kiss."

A slow, knowing smile spreads across his face. "You're betting for a kiss, wife?"

When he says it like that...

Impulsively, I add, "It's been so long since I had a good kiss, I wasn't sure I remembered how to do it."

His clever eyes glimmer, then briefly flick behind me, maybe to the man standing on my other side. "Is that so?" Asher asks, focusing solely on me again.

"Yes."

"And you want your husband to help you remember how?" he asks, his voice gravelly as he loops an arm around me, his hand curling around my waist.

Possessively, once more.

Moving me a little farther away from the redheaded man. For a few heavy seconds, he stares at the man with a *get the fuck away from my woman* look in his eyes.

My pulse shoots to the moon.

When Asher's gaze returns to me, I answer him.

"Yes," I say, and I sound breathless. I feel breathless. Maybe it's because tonight, the usual friendship rules don't apply. Maybe we can break them this once and return to normal tomorrow.

When we leave Vegas, we'll leave this all behind.

He glances around the table, as if he's sizing up the crowd, and then takes his time tucking a curl of hair behind my ear, like he's wanted to do that for some time. And like he wants them to know I'm with him. Right now, I am.

"Let's bet on tonight," Asher echoes, then plunks

down some chips. In the tone of a man determined to get what he wants, he says to the croupier, "Red." He turns back to me, staring at my mouth, his voice deep, commanding as he says, "Like your lips after you've been kissed."

Pretty sure my panties melt off.

"Red it is," the croupier says.

The ball spins, my heart pounding as I watch it circle the wheel. It bounces once, twice, and then lands...

On red.

15

IT'S ALL COMING BACK TO ME

Maeve

When the door to our room shuts, my nerves gallop, but so does my excitement. I catch a glimpse of his duffel bag, with the box of condoms poking out. Kissing is one thing, but sex is entirely another. I don't think I can have forget-about-it-tomorrow sex with Asher. It's too intimate. And I'm too needy.

I need boundaries for my own emotional health. I place a hand on his chest. "Just kissing. That's all."

"Don't worry. I won't let you see the flamingos," he says.

I laugh, and his comment erases my nerves. He knew what to say. Asher always knows what to say to settle my wild thoughts and my racing heart.

"Besides, there's a marriage pact loophole where you get free kissing practice on your wedding night," he adds.

"I had no idea. You're quite the expert on marriage pacts," I tease.

"Well, I did strike ours, and look—it paid off. You're having fun."

"I am," I say, but then my nerves resurface. Where do we go? The bed? The couch? Here? Do we stand and make out?

Before I even have time to analyze all the logistics, Asher takes my hand and leads me to the couch. He sinks down on it, and I follow, sitting next to him. Closer than I usually do.

But now what? "This is awkward," I observe, looking at my hands.

"Doesn't have to be," he replies, sounding relaxed, confident. Maybe I need that.

"Yeah?" Is it obvious how eager I am?

Of course it is. I bet him for a kiss.

He takes a beat, his gaze thoughtful, then asks, "Do you trust me?"

He said those words at the auction, and my answer came easily. It flies off my tongue tonight too. "Yes."

"Then let me help you remember," he says. I expect him to come in for a kiss, but instead, he takes his time, lifting a hand and running a finger across my lower lip.

Like I did moments ago at the table. I tremble. He knew what I was doing then—recalling the kiss.

But the other thing I realize is...*he noticed.*

Does Asher watch me?

The bold part of me wants to ask him that question—when in Vegas, after all. But the part of me that likes how he's setting the pace waits for him to go next.

He lowers his hand, meets my eyes with his darkened ones. "Does that help you remember how I turned you on so much with our wedding kiss that you bet on another one at the roulette table?"

I'm so obvious, and he likes it. "Is that what you think happened?" I ask coyly, testing him. I've never known what Asher's like after dark, of course. Haven't really thought about it much either. Now, my curious mind is buzzing with questions.

His gaze locks on mine. "I don't *think* it. I know that's what happened."

My heart stutters. Is my life-of-the-party, emotionally astute, shoulder-to-lean-on friend a bossy man in the bedroom?

Please say yes, universe.

Wait. I can't think that. I really can't. Except, I am. And I want more of it, so I tease him with a bob of my shoulder and a flirty, "Maybe."

There's a rumble in his throat. Then, he says, "Pretty sure it is...*wife.*"

My breath hitches from the thoroughly possessive way he uttered one word. "Okay. You're right," I murmur.

"I know," he says, and he cups my jaw, stroking it slowly.

Is my jaw an erogenous zone? Well, it sure seems it is, since I feel like a cat, purring, leaning into his hand, moving with him as his thumb explores the line of my jaw. I'm shivery from what he's doing. He slides the pad of his thumb up to my ear, tracing the shell with a light caress. He hasn't even dropped his mouth to mine again. He hasn't even dipped his face near me.

And yet, I'm melting inside.

"We're not practicing kissing," I whisper, but my eyes are fluttering closed and I'm not sure my thoughts are truly coherent. I feel like a chocolate bar in the sun right now, and it's all from his fingers on my face.

He tips my chin up, forcing me to look at him. My eyes

float open. Asher's green irises are usually clever, inviting. Now they're mesmerizing, glimmering. They're...a little filthy too.

"We are, Maeve," he says, firm, commanding. "We are practicing kissing."

My brow knits. I'm a little confused. "But—"

Then, he shuts me up by pressing a finger to my lips. "Do you think a good kiss only involves lips?"

"Well..."

He shakes his head. "A kiss doesn't start with lips. It starts with want. With desire. With anticipation," he says, and I whimper from his words and the way they're tugging low in my belly. Then, he slides a hand down my bare arm, watching as the little hairs on my arm rise up. "It starts with other people looking at you. Thinking they have a chance with you. And being so fucking wrong."

My chest burns from his seductive words. "Why are they wrong?"

He dusts a thumb across my lower lip. "Because this pretty mouth? It belongs to me tonight."

My breath hitches. "It does."

"There's one more thing I want you to remember about kissing," he says, like a professor.

"What is it?"

"A good kiss starts with me getting you so wound up, you're..." He stops, dips his face to my ear, then whispers, "wet before I even kiss you."

The sound I make—it's needy.

It's feral.

It's not at all friendly.

I swallow roughly, then say in a feathery voice, "I'm starting to remember."

"Good. Let's see if it all comes back to you."

His fingers glide down my cheekbones to my chin, skimming the bare skin at the top of the vest. Then he stops, respecting my limits—which is so damn hot—even as I wonder how far I want to stretch them tonight.

He brackets my face with his hands, and I feel... controlled, but in a way I didn't know I wanted. Until now. I feel almost blindfolded, with no idea what he has in store for me—where his hands, his mouth, his plans will take me as he shows me how to kiss again.

He sweeps my hair aside, then with a firm hand on my face, he tilts my head, exposing the side of my neck. He lays open-mouthed caresses along my throat, from shoulder to hairline, and I'm sighing, murmuring, gasping.

"You're still not kissing me," I pant out.

"Got a problem with that?" he taunts.

I smile as I lean my head back, inviting more of his prelude to a kiss. "I don't know. Maybe you should keep *not* kissing me. I mean, that sounds like a good idea to me."

He laughs softly, maybe remembering his toast about good ideas and bad ones once upon a time.

"Teasing is a good idea. And you like it. Seems you like the anticipation too," he says as he presses a hot kiss to the hollow of my throat.

It's not a question, so I don't answer with words. I answer with touch, looping my arms around his neck.

For a second, he freezes, like my touch is too much. He squeezes his eyes closed. Shudders.

Wow.

Watching that tremble move through him like he has to fight it might be the sexiest thing I've ever seen. Come to think of it, Asher kissing me like he wants me to remember it for all time is the most electrifying thing I've ever felt.

But when he opens his eyes, both those things are wrong.

The look in his green irises right now—darkened, almost tormented, but determined—is the hottest thing ever.

"You were saying?" he asks, then he crushes his lips to mine.

Oh, god.

The sound that comes from my mouth is embarrassing—it's a needy whimper.

I part my mouth, asking for more.

He slides his tongue between my lips, holding my face, exploring me. It's a hard kiss. Different from the one at the chapel. That was a sultry kiss on a beach under the shimmering sun. It's different, too, from the one on the street after the auction. That was a simple tease, a sip of whiskey, a little heat.

This is something else entirely.

This is devouring. His thumb presses under my jaw, tilting my head back so he can kiss me deeply.

His kisses are hungry. They're greedy. They're demanding. Asher doesn't kiss me like we're best friends. He kisses me like he met me tonight and wants to put me on my hands and knees and fuck me into next week.

That image lodges in my brain and won't budge. With each sweep of his tongue, I picture him throwing me down. Every press of his lips makes me imagine him grabbing my wrists, binding them in his hands. As fingers sweep over my face, I feel myself surrendering to whatever he'd ask me to do.

I sink into his kiss on the couch, taking everything he gives, until I'm aching not merely between my thighs.

But I'm craving him in every damn cell in my body.

I break apart for a second, just to catch my breath, maybe to get my bearings, and he looks wild.

I feel wild. "I think I *almost* remember now," I say.

"Better make sure," he taunts.

"Yeah, I better." I take his taunt and turn it up a notch. I climb onto his lap, bracketing his face with my hands, and kiss him—a deep, passionate kiss that makes me feel out of control. That makes me feel free.

Before I know it, I'm straddling him, my short skirt hiked up as I rock against the outline of his hard cock. And wow—what an outline it is. Thick and pulsing, and I should not know that about Asher. I really shouldn't. This is a bad idea. Such a bad idea. We're friends. We're just playing around. This is just a practice kiss.

I have to say that. I have to make some boundaries clear. I wrench away. "This is just kissing. Nothing more."

His lips quirk into a grin. "I know. Don't worry—I'm not going to try anything."

"I know," I say, but a nagging voice in the back of my mind wants to ask why he seemed tense earlier, what that emotion was. But then he curves a palm around the back of my thigh, tugging me closer, and my questions scatter like alphabet soup. "Is this...part of how to kiss?" I ask.

He slides his palm higher, dangerously close to my ass. "A good kiss includes hands, Maeve."

"Well then," I say, then curl my hands around his shoulders and cover his lips with mine.

"Good girl," he encourages, and fuck me.

He gives praise so confidently that my head swims

with his woodsy scent, with the sound of his breath, with the feel of his strong hands.

Impulsively, I rock against the ridge of his erection.

He tenses for a second or two, like he's battling with himself, but then I can feel a *fuck it* move through his body as he tugs a little harder on the back of my thighs.

Boundaries. What even are they? I'm off and running. With barely a thought. With only this ache between my thighs, this need in my body.

I kiss and grind, and it vaguely occurs to me I'm dry-humping my best friend.

But I don't want to think too hard about what that means, because it feels so good, my belly is tightening, coiling, then...

Out of nowhere, an orgasm slams into me.

It grips my whole body, and I'm gasping, tensing, and then shuddering on my best friend's lap.

I've gone off in less than a minute.

My mind crackles. My body turns white-hot and electric as I fall apart on my friend. My hundred-thousand-dollar date. My temporary husband.

When I pull away, I'm shocked. And honestly, embarrassed.

Asher looks stunned. In his wide eyes, his slightly parted lips.

I am too. "I didn't see that coming," I say, pun not intended.

After a surprised second or two, he says, "I didn't either."

My lips part. "Was that like a premature orgasm?" I ask, a little horrified, a lot embarrassed.

He grins. He can't seem to stop smiling. It's a very

satisfied smile. "I didn't even know that was a thing for a woman."

"Me neither," I squeak, and scurry off him.

I didn't mean for this remember-how-to-kiss session to turn into how-to-come-in-under-sixty-seconds.

I cover my mouth with my hand, mortified that I shot off like that. I have no idea what to do.

"I'm going to shower," I squeak, sounding like Minnie Mouse as I bolt.

16

QUICK-DRAW MAEVE

Asher

Not gonna lie—I feel like a king.

But a very confused king since I'm sitting here on the couch, brow scrunched, dick deflating, wondering what the hell just happened. Besides the obvious—Maeve used my hard-on as a fast-acting sex toy, and that was outrageously awesome.

But...what's next?

I glance around the room, searching for answers in our open suitcases, or maybe in the empty champagne bottle from earlier. I peer out the floor-to-ceiling windows at the lights streaking by below, the city still buzzing at—what time is it? I check my watch. Holy shit. It's three. A yawn hits me, along with the reminder that I've got a game on Sunday night back home. I need to head to San Francisco in several hours, then gear up to crush our opponents a day later. Which means it's time for some shut-eye, but my brain's too busy cycling through shouldn'ts.

I shouldn't have kissed her.

I shouldn't have played roulette.

I shouldn't have...married her.

But strangely, I don't feel regret for any of those. I don't feel as frustrated as I did when we left the chapel. I feel good.

Of course you do, asshole. You gave the woman a screaming orgasm in world record time.

Well, great nights often end with orgasms.

Trouble is now I'm left sorting through the mess of my emotions. Part of me feels like I've won something, some secret, fleeting victory. But there's also that nagging voice reminding me I've crossed a line I swore I wouldn't.

But what happens in Vegas stays in Vegas, right? She wanted to kiss, and we did. Now it's time to move on.

I push up from the couch as the sound of the shower patters in the background. I tug off my Henley, strip out of my jeans, and run a hand through my hair. I plug my phone into the nightstand and drop onto the bed. A yawn threatens to pull me under, but I resist. I need to be awake when she comes out. We need to talk, clear the air, and maybe, just maybe, figure out where to go from here.

Hey Maeve, you cool with coming like a teenager on my denim-clad dick?

Because I was. And...do you want to ride my dick like a wild cowgirl again?

"Fuck," I mutter, because I don't know what the hell to do next. But the water shuts off, so I'll have to figure it out, stat.

A few minutes later, Maeve emerges from the bathroom, looking flustered and undeniably sexy in a cami and sleep shorts, her makeup scrubbed off, her skin dewy, and her hair tugged back in a pink fluffy headband.

She winces. "You were supposed to be asleep."

Well, that probably won't happen anytime soon. I shove my messy emotions aside as I sit up in bed. "Why did you want me to be asleep?"

She blinks, then waves a hand at my boxer briefs. They're white and covered in pink birds. "You're just in your flamingo underwear," she says, her voice breathy.

"Do my flamingos tempt you?" I ask jokingly, when what I really want to ask is *do I tempt you,* even though the evidence seems clear—see Exhibit O. But it's such a foreign thought that she might feel the same way I do, especially when I've been wrestling with my own temptations on and off for the last two years.

She holds out her hands in surrender. "Clearly."

"Would you like me to get a paper bag and wear that instead?"

"No. It's just I feel...awkward," she admits, coming over to the bed and flopping down. "This never happens," she mumbles.

"Sharing a bed?"

"Yes, no, maybe. But also..." she groans, dragging a hand down her face, before muttering, "Coming quickly."

Oh. *Oh.* Once again, I am king, and may I reign over the land of Maeve's pleasure. "Why is that a problem?" I ask, fighting off a smug smile.

Her lips are twisted with anxiety. "It's a problem because you're my friend. You're my brother's friend. I sat on you and then...*boom.* It's ridiculous and normally takes me, like, five supersize vibrators."

That's the highest praise in the universe. "You do know that's a compliment?"

"But I said we needed rules," she says, and her voice gets higher and higher as she berates herself. "I said we should set all these boundaries. I said only kissing, and then I sat on your lap, and one minute later, I was screaming in pleasure."

And I'd like to reign over multiple orgasm kingdoms. "Maeve, that's not true," I say, gently correcting her.

"What part is a lie?" She sounds worried.

"It was only thirty seconds," I say. And right now, giving in to the roulette wheel of red wasn't a bad idea. It was a brilliant one.

She pulls a pillow over her eyes, mumbling, "I can never show my face again."

"Why?"

"Because I will forever be Quick-Draw Maeve."

"Can we make a T-shirt that says that? That would be great."

She swats me with the pillow.

Somehow, that's the best friendship sign ever—the swat. It's a sign we *can* move past this...unexpected friendship benefit. Since we have to move on. Oh hell, do we have to. So I grab the pillow, set it down, and get out of bed, but before I reach the bathroom she calls out, "Um, do you want me to return the favor?"

With my hand on the doorknob, I snort-laugh. "Are you asking me to rut against you in my clothes and come in my pants?"

That earns me another pillow, this one thrown.

Deservedly so.

I toss it back to the bed and pad into the bathroom. But after I brush my teeth, wash my face, and return to bed, turning down the lights, I'm not thinking friendly thoughts at all. Not one bit.

I'm thinking how she felt when her body melted against me. I'm thinking about the way she moved like water when I ran my hands up her legs. I'm thinking about the soft, sweet shape of her mouth and the gasps she makes when I kiss her.

And I'm hearing her sounds in my head all over again.

I'm wide awake, lying next to her in bed, with enough space between us to fit a trunkful of complicated emotions and ten years of connections. I have no idea what to do with the fact that I'm a little wild for Maeve. That I'm a lot more into her than I'd realized. Sure, I've always known she was pretty. But for a long time, I was aware of that only on a logical level. Then at her brother's wedding, logic slammed into me on the dance floor and waved a big cardboard sign saying, *You're into your best friend and it's way more than logical, you idiot.* But when the dance ended, I ignored that sign. Ignored the feelings, too, maybe hoping they'd go away. News flash: Looks like they didn't leave. I'm not even sure they went dormant. I just let myself think they were gone. But now they're back, stronger than before.

Trouble is, it'd still be a bad idea to act on these feelings. Or, really, to act on them *again*. Once can be excused. But twice is flirting with danger. And I don't want to rock the boat. That is not my style. I hate problems that aren't on the ice. I can't stand trouble. I don't need to invite it in my life. Even though my gut twists over the next words, I say them anyway, knowing it's best to avoid danger: "I guess we should get annulled."

She pauses, maybe giving it some thought. After a few seconds, she nods. "Yeah," she says, a little wistful. But then she turns to me, chin resting on her hands. "But wouldn't it be funny if we played a joke on my brother?"

Ah, hell. I can't resist *that* temptation either. "Tell him we got married for real?"

Mischief dances in her hazel eyes. "Yes. Let's wind him up. Besides, we're getting annulled when we return to San Francisco since we don't have to do it here," she says on a yawn.

"It's a plan," I say, and it feels like a return to the way we were. That's fine. Really, it's fine. It's the smoothest path back to friendship, and that's what we both want *and* need, clearly.

As she settles under the sheets, Maeve adds, "There's something I have to tell you."

"My dick is so extraordinary you came in thirty seconds? Yes, I believe your actions already told me that."

"Your ego is so big."

"That's not the only thing."

"I know!"

"I'll take that as a compliment too."

"You would," she says.

"It was a compliment," I say, preening. Fucking preening.

She's quiet for a beat, sighs, then says, "It wasn't just your dick. It was your kissing, if you must know."

King Asher rules the world. I park my hands behind my head and don't bother fighting off a grin. "My lips and my dick are both extraordinary, you're saying?"

"Oh shut up."

"But you like my mouth," I tease.

"You're the worst."

"That's not what you said fifteen minutes ago."

"What did I say then?" she asks.

I meet her eyes. "It was sort of like...*oh, oh, oh.*"

"You're mocking me for having an orgasm? Real nice, Asher."

"You can climb on me and have another," I say.

"That won't be awkward at all."

I drop the teasing, then return to what she said earlier. "What were you going to tell me before? You said you had something to tell me." I pause, since I've got a feeling what it is, and maybe I want to beat her to it. The words taste like sand, but they need to be said. "Were you going to say that it can't happen again?"

She grimaces. "No, that wasn't what I was going to say. But that probably shouldn't happen again."

My chest aches, like I've been punched. She's right, and I can't stand that she's right, even though I was the one who suggested that the moment on the couch is best not repeated. "It shouldn't," I say.

"I don't want to screw things up with us. Our friendship. My brother. It would be too messy," she says, her tone sad.

"It would," I say evenly. "It definitely would."

"Sex and stuff complicate everything," she adds, like she needs to sell me on the one-time only aspect of tonight.

I don't want her to think I'm anything but on board. "Sex is the most complicated. Well, not if you're dry-humping me," I deadpan.

She swats me again, and I want—oh, how I fucking want—to grab that hand and press kisses all over it. To draw her close. To run my hands through those waves of blonde-brown hair. But I don't. There will be no encore. "Look, I know it'll be hard for you to resist me, but I have faith in you," I say.

She smiles softly, yawning again. "I'll do my best. Also,

what I was going to say is I'm Quick-Draw Maeve at a lot of things," she says, then ten seconds later, she's fast asleep.

And I'm wide awake. Like I am most nights for a while. I usually read myself to sleep, but tonight, my thoughts are keeping me company.

I'm thinking about how she felt in my arms. At the beginning and during the middle, and then, yeah, at the end. I turn and watch my wife as she slides deeper into slumber while the lights of Vegas flicker in the distance. Something tugs on my heart, and I wish I could stop time and just experience this moment with her again and again.

Which is a whole new problem entirely, and much more complicated than a box of condoms.

17

DOUBLE CONGRATULATIONS

Asher

Not only do Vegas hotels pump something into the air to hold you hostage in the casinos longer, but they must also lace the water in the rooms with sleeping potion. Because when I finally bust out of dreamland, I'm blinking, bleary-eyed, and—I check the time—totally fucking late.

We missed our eleven a.m. flight.

I fly up. Maeve has a party tonight, and this is all my fault. I should have set triple alarms even though I never sleep in like this. I never sleep this deeply. I turn to rouse Maeve, but she's not in the bed. Rushing out of it, I pad to the bathroom and raise a fist to knock but stop short when the door swings open.

She's dressed in jeans and one of her signature T-shirts with a slogan on it—*In My Defense, I Was Left Unsupervised*—which is so very Maeve. And so's the fact that it slopes down one shoulder, and just like that all the breath escapes my lungs. My flamingos are at full attention.

"Huh," I manage to grit out.

"Hi," she says with an *I know what you meant* smile as she pats my bare shoulder. It's the friendliest get-a-move-on gesture in the world. Hmm. Is she sending me a message? Like, *get over last night, buddy*? "We need to go. The airline canceled our earlier flight, so now we're on the one-thirty," she says, cheery, but also just shy of frantic. "I tried to wake you up ten times, and you kept telling me you wanted to sleep a few more minutes."

"Don't listen to me," I say, a little annoyed at myself. But maybe good sleep seduced me. No time to mull on it though. I turn slightly so I can try to angle my way past her without her noticing I'm too turned on by her.

"You're a lot bigger and a lot meaner when you're half-asleep."

"Meaner than you?"

"Shocking, but yes," she says, looking dewy and freshly made up, her loose waves of golden-brown hair piled in one of those artfully messy buns that look impossible to do. Seriously, I've watched her loop all those strands through a scrunchie, and it still makes as much sense to me as the alchemy women perform when they take their bras off through their sleeves. More girl sorcery for you. "Our car is coming in fifteen minutes," she says as she sails past me, clearly ready to leave this city behind.

But I'm stuck on last night. Maybe that pat on my chest *was* a message. Not simply to get a move on now, but to move past it.

Yeah. That's what I need to do—let it go. Which'd be easier if my best friend wasn't such a bombshell. I steal one more glance at her, my chest aching as she retreats into the bedroom with her makeup bag. As she sets it down in her suitcase, I catch sight of that gleaming gold ring on her finger. The reminder that she's not just my friend. She's my wife. For another day or so till we get this union annulled back in San Francisco. Something nags at me though, an unformed thought, as I call out, "I'm going to take a quick shower."

"We don't have much time."

"Don't worry. I shower like you come," I say.

She snaps her gaze back at me. "Who's the mean one now?"

Before I can think the better of it, I say dryly, "You are, since you left me hanging last night."

Her jaw drops as I shut the door. With this annoying erection—which is the story of my last twelve hours—I consider locking it, but then...would I really be bothered if she came in while I showered?

No, I wouldn't.

Even though it would be a very bad idea. Especially since we're in two very different places, it seems. But she doesn't ever need to know I'm feeling more for her than the one-night-only variety of lust.

She doesn't come into the bathroom while I'm showering though. And I don't jack off under the stream of water either, since how pathetic would it be if I were late for our rescheduled flight on account of flying solo beforehand?

I'd hate myself more then.

Ten minutes later, we're both dressed and hustling out of our room when I stop suddenly at the door, the unformed thought taking shape now. "We should take off our rings," I say, feeling like a douche for saying that. But it's necessary douchery.

Maeve doesn't even blink. "Good thinking."

We tug off our bands, tuck them away, then leave Las Vegas. No one will know what happened last night but Beckett.

And no one will know how much more I wanted to happen.

* * *

Later that afternoon, when the plane touches down in San Francisco, Maeve lets out a relieved sigh, her shoulders visibly relaxing. "I need to get to that party in two hours," she says, checking the time on her phone with a small frown of concern. She read some on the short flight—one of her mother's books called *If Found, Please Return.* One I've seen her read before. Many times. But she didn't make it through too many pages. I get it. She's probably stressed about the party.

"Do you need supplies or something?" I ask, as the stress flickers across her face.

"I do. I'll go home, grab them, then call a Lyft," she says, biting her lip, clearly calculating the logistics. But that sounds like a lot to deal with in a short amount of time.

"I'll help you," I say quickly. I feel terrible that she's cutting it close for such an important job. If I hadn't wanted to win big at the auction, she might not be in this time-crunch right now.

"Really?" Her eyes widen, a ray of hope softening her expression.

"Yeah, really," I say, trying to sound as casual as possible. But maybe I'm trying to prove to myself that I can jump right back into the friend zone too. "No big deal."

"Thank you. It's a lot to wrestle with," she admits.

We snag a ride back into the city, where she texts the party's event planner to let them know she'll be there at five, as planned. She tucks her phone aside, saying she'll deal with anything else later. "I just need to get in my painting mode," she says, by way of explanation.

"I get it. I'm like that before a hockey game."

"So the hockey zone and the painting zone are one and the same," she says with a laugh.

I glance at my phone. A few messages blink up at me from Soraya, responses from yesterday about the upcoming fundraisers, as well as a couple texts from Everly, and one from Miles, and *also* one from Max, but I ignore them for now, instead reassuring Maeve that we'll make it on time and focusing on being present with her, as her friend.

When we reach her place in Hayes Valley, the Lyft waits for us while we race upstairs. I drop off our bags in her living room while she disappears into her bedroom and reappears in two minutes, dressed in a simple black dress and short black boots. It's elegant and understated, and a part of me wishes I were dropping her off at the party knowing she'd return to me later in that dress and tell me stories of the event, then beg me to undress her. I'd grant her wish, naturally. Especially if she crawled to me. I'd reward her so good for coming to me on her knees.

I pull myself from the fantasy and focus on the reality of Maeve in a snug black dress. "Wow. You look...wow."

"I do?" she asks hopefully. "It's a fashion designer's party and the event planner told me to show up in all black."

"That dress is incredible," I say, even though it's her that's incredible, not the fabric hugging her body.

"Thank you. I want to look like a pro and totally blend in. We're not allowed to network, but you never know who you might meet," she says breezily as she grabs her easel and paints.

"You don't blend in, Maeve," I say before I can think the better of it.

She stops at the door, her brow knitting. "I don't?"

I close my eyes for a second, then open them. "You're too pretty to blend in." I shouldn't say it, but she is my wife for another day or two.

"There you go again. Making me feel good," she says.

I take the easel and paints and add hoarsely, "You should feel good."

We return to the car, heading toward the fashion mogul's home in Cow Hollow. In the backseat, she turns to me, her eyes brimming with gratitude. "Thanks again. For everything. I do feel better heading into this party after—" She stops, like she's weighing her words. "After last night. All of it. It really was an adventure, Asher." Her smile widens, her face lighting up at the word "adventure."

"Good. I'm glad it was..." But I don't know what to say about a night that turned ludicrously sexy, so I finish with, "What you needed."

We're not talking about the kissing anymore. Or the make-out session on the couch. We're not talking about it because it can't happen again. Because we need each other as friends.

I'd do well to remember that. Which reminds me...

"Before we forget, why don't we take a pic of us in our rings for Beckett," I say. "If Mrs. Matrimony sent those shots, you can send them later too. He'll lose his shit."

"He will. Let's do it," she says, then dips her hand into her purse, fishing around for her ring.

She slides it back on. I try not to watch, but I also can't look away, even as I take mine from my pocket and put it back in place. The weight of the ring feels different this time—heavier in a way. Filled with wishes that won't come true. But they also feel more surreal in the light of our hometown. Like last night was something out of a fevered dream. And I'm merely trying to hold on to it to tell the story.

"Selfie time," she declares, leaning close in the back of the car as it swings into Cow Hollow. We hold up our hands, showing off our bands. And I try to lean into the moment. To the joke. To the fun. To the cherry on the ice cream sundae of last night. Not to the way I feel a little more than I'd expected I would.

When she lowers the phone and checks the photo, she nods approvingly. "This is going to be better than when I put pink dye in Beckett's conditioner when he was fourteen."

"You are mean," I say with a low whistle as she clicks open a text to her brother.

"It wasn't permanent," she counters with a playful grin, and this is fine—this banter. Really, it is.

"But I bet it was funny."

Her smile turns sly, her eyes twinkling with satisfaction. "And it was worth the return prank of mayonnaise in my lotion bottle."

The thought of it turns my stomach. "So this really is payback."

As she sends the picture to Beckett, her phone rings. She gasps, freezing in place for a few seconds. She shows it to me—Angelina's name is flashing on the screen. But Maeve looks like she's trapped between hope and dread.

"Answer it," I urge. An agent calling on a Saturday can almost always only be good news, but I can see the worry in her eyes.

With a deep breath, like she's trying to steady herself, she picks up the call.

Angelina's brassy, confident voice carries over the silence as we turn onto an elegant block, where stately homes preside over meticulously manicured lawns. "First off, congratulations," her agent exclaims.

Maeve furrows her brow, then asks tentatively, "Thanks?" She glances at me as if I'd know what her agent is congratulating her about. But it could be a lot of things.

"And second, congratulations," Angelina repeats.

Maeve shakes her head, clearly baffled. "Um, sure. But for what?"

"They decided last night, they told me. You got the job."

Maeve's hand flies to her mouth as the car turns down the street toward the party. "I did?" The words come out like a squeak.

I pump a fist, mouthing, "*Told you so.*"

"You did," Angelina says, her voice full of warmth and pride. "I know you have that party right now, so have a blast. Paint your heart out, knowing you got this job. And I'll get you more details by tomorrow. But you'll be meeting with the owners soon. In a couple days. And they're hoping you can start pretty much straight after that. They're very excited."

Must be gallery owners she's meeting with, and that is excellent. A gallery commission would be a huge win.

"Thank you," Maeve says, in a voice choked with

emotion as the car pulls up to a mansion. "Thank you so much. I was so sure it was all over. Oh my god. This is a dream come true."

"You deserve it, sweetie." There's a pause, then her agent adds, "Or should I call you *Mrs. Callahan*?"

18

PAY IT FORWARD

Maeve

A weathered valet with thinning hair and a pale complexion swings open the car door before I can fully process the last words from my agent, let alone the fact that I got the gig with the Sea Dogs. For a huge commission. The biggest of my career. A mural that will be seen by thousands every time there's a game. A job I didn't think I'd land.

But right now, I need to focus on *this* job. The valet offers me a hand, looking me up and down. "You must be the painter. Come inside. Mr. Vincenzo is eager for your contributions."

He's the eccentric fashion designer hosting this party.

That's when it hits me—the man in front of me isn't a valet; he's a butler, and he's Serious with a capital S.

"Great, um. I have someone with me," I say, pointing to Asher, still in a daze. From the Sea Dogs job, but also...did

Angelina actually call me Mrs. Callahan? That's...well, I don't want to think too long on why she would.

The butler offers a thin-lipped smile. "That's perfectly fine to bring an assistant," he says.

"Oh, he's not my assistant," I say, nodding to Asher, who's stepping out on the other side, giving me a questioning look.

The butler jerks his gaze to Asher, quickly scanning him with robot eyes and efficiency. "Your partner then? Lovely."

My stomach drops. "Actually," I say, but the rest of the sentence dies on my tongue.

There's only one reason Angelina would call me Mrs. Callahan. Somehow, the news that we got married is already out there on the Internet.

But we weren't wearing our rings earlier when we left the hotel. Did Mrs. Matrimony leak the photos? That doesn't seem like her style, but who knows? It couldn't have been Jen and Hal—they took pictures of us before we got the brilliant idea to honor a marriage pact.

The driver scurries around to pop open the trunk, and I briefly contemplate sliding my ring off, but there's no real privacy. As I grab my gear, Asher comes up next to me, whispering out of the side of his mouth, "What can I do?"

"I don't know," I mutter through clenched teeth because...butlers. They're terrifying.

I bet part of a butler's job requirement is to have bionic hearing. I'm sure Mister Pale Butler watches everything like a hawk too. I can't very well take my band off in front of him now. He might think I was acting single to try and pick someone up. It'd be obvious if Asher slipped his off as well.

But maybe I can get away with claiming I don't wear it while I paint? If the butler asks? Then Asher can subtly slip his band off, and we can clear up this misunderstanding.

Yes! I am brilliant. Hear me roar!

But just as I turn to the older man, ready to say something like, *Oh, I'd better not paint in my wedding band,* I notice he's no longer alone. A woman with light brown skin, a newsboy cap, and a Nikon camera stands beside him.

"Just go about your business. Pretend I'm not even here," she says with the ease of someone used to giving direction.

Um, how? Also, what if I don't want photos taken?

I freeze for a second, but Asher steps up with a kind but firm, "We'd prefer no pictures, actually."

The woman looks up from her camera, offering a bland smile. "That's nice, but the invite said we'd be taking candids all night and posting on his feed, along with the live painting, so you've pre-consented. It's Mr. Vincenzo's thing."

"Documenting his life and times is important for Mr. Vincenzo. For posterity, of course," the butler adds, still humorless.

"When he publishes his memoirs someday," the photographer says, then adds proudly, "I'm his personal photographer."

Oh well, fuck me with a croissant. Not only is the host rich and eccentric, he's loaded with digital film.

His personal shutterbug keeps snapping away. She takes picture after picture of my husband and me, rings on and everything. What started as a prank on my brother —leaving on the rings—now feels like a very big problem.

* * *

Once we're inside the mansion, I barely register the sleek, minimalist design as the butler leads us down the spacious hallway. The polished concrete floors and stark white walls are a blur. All I can think about is finding a moment of privacy to snag my husband and figure out this newfangled mess.

"I just need to use the ladies' room for a second," I tell the butler, pasting on a false smile for Mister Robot.

He nods curtly, gesturing down the hall to the nearest amenities, and I quickly slip in that direction, motioning for Asher to follow me. The butler doesn't react—he's no doubt seen it all before.

I set my paints and easel down in the hallway and head inside the room, Asher right behind me. A frameless mirror stretches across the wall above a floating vanity, and the air smells faintly of eucalyptus. But I don't have time to admire the swank bathroom or these plush hand towels that no doubt cost more than my couch.

As soon as the door snicks shut, I push my hands into my hair, not even caring how messy it will get. "What do we do?" I ask Asher as I pace in the large bathroom. "Everyone thinks we're married, obviously. And now my fancy-ass fashion designer client is going to post pics from tonight as part of his memoirs, saying I painted here... with my brand-new husband. WHO'S A FAMOUS HOCKEY PLAYER!" I whisper-hiss.

"Semi-famous," Asher deadpans.

"You and your ass are plenty famous! What are we supposed to do?" I drop my voice even more. My palms are getting sweaty. I rub my hands together, trying to get rid of this clammy feeling. I need to unlock my phone to find out why everyone knows we're hitched, but I'm terrified of what I'll see.

"I just landed this huge commission, and I don't want my new client or any potential clients here to think I waltzed into this party pretending to be married. Or married by mistake. Or drunk married. I don't know who they are. I don't know their values. I don't know how they view any of that. They might not want to hire an artist who's, gee, even flightier than artists are known for being!"

My heart is racing. I'm breathing too hard. I'm on the cusp of a big break, and I don't want to lose it for being wild and drunk in Vegas, especially since we were only tipsy.

But...semantics.

I take a big, shaky breath, willing my pulse to settle.

Asher takes out his phone. "I'll check social in a second," he says, advancing toward me and setting his free hand on my arm with focused concern. "But are you having a panic attack?"

What? No. Of course not. "I don't have panic attacks. I'm just panicky right now." I press my palm to my chest, feeling even more flustered. "Anyone would be panicky right now. You should be panicking."

But he stays calm because he's always calm. "Take a breath," he says, letting go of my arm to reach for my hand.

Oh god. He really thinks I'm having a panic attack, and *of course,* he'd know what to do. "Asher, I'm fine. I swear. I'm just trying to figure this out," I say as calmly as I can. I don't take his hand. "The world thinks we got drunk-married!"

"But let's remember we didn't really get drunk-married." His voice is as level as ever. "Whatever is happening online, whatever people are saying about last night—remember, *we* don't have to say anything. We *could* just take the rings off. If anyone asks, we can say that it was a marriage pact. A dare. We did it just for fun. We *are* friends. It's plausible."

It's a reasonable point, but sometimes Asher fixates too much on other people and not enough on himself.

"But even if we could pull that off, what about beyond tonight, Ash? You're launching a charity *soon*. You're focused on helping kids with sports and mental health. You don't want to look like the kind of guy who knocked back some cocktails and got hitched by an Elvis impersonator after midnight *for funsies*." A muscle in his jaw ticks as the weight of our actions no doubt registers. "I mean, I bid a hundred grand on you so a beauty influencer wouldn't smear your reputation. And then I went out and smeared it myself." I groan. "I am such an idiot. Why didn't I think about this last night?"

"You're not an idiot and you didn't smear it," he says, his voice quiet but commanding. "I should have considered...*this*. The ramifications."

I shoot him a tough look right back. "If I hadn't been in a funk—"

He holds up a stop-sign hand. "Enough, Maeve. I have no regrets."

Do I? Not really, and yet I feel entirely selfish for saying this. "I don't either, but Asher," I say, like I'm begging, "I don't want to draw attention to myself here. I don't want to tell them *hey, it was just a big adventure*, and then have Mister Memoirs document that for posterity." And I really don't want to be the center of attention right after I've landed the biggest break of my career. Only, I haven't even told Asher about the mural opportunity yet. Guilt washes over me. "The commission I just got? It's with the Sea Dogs," I say, bracing myself for the fallout—will he be annoyed I kept it from him?

He tilts his head, confusion flickering across his handsome face. "You're painting for *my* team?"

I clutch my stomach as the anxiety knots tighter in me, mingling with excitement. Why do I always have to feel everything all at once? "They commissioned a huge mural project. It's all sorts of scenes from San Francisco. They're doing a huge mural inside the arena, and they wanted a local artist." Emotions swim up inside me. "And they hired me. Until they figure out I'm the kind of unreliable artist who attracts media attention by getting drunk married to one of their star players and it's clear my appointment was a mistake."

His smile is double-take worthy. Head-turning. Movie-star quality. "Maeve fucking Hartley," he says, beaming. "It's not a mistake. You got the commission because you're good." He squeezes my arm, then runs his hand down it. God, that feels good. I wish I could bask in his touch. It... settles the wildness in me. "I'm seriously proud of you."

I let go of my nerves and allow myself to enjoy this moment with Asher, touch and all. "I'm really excited," I say quietly. Speaking louder might shatter the reality of what's happening.

"I knew it. I totally knew it," he says.

And the thing is, he did know in a way. He's always believed in me. But that doesn't solve the problem of our spontaneous Vegas marriage or keep it from biting me in the butt. Or him. He doesn't need a drunk marriage—

since that's how it'll be seen—trailing him when he rolls out his charity. "Thank you. But I still don't know how to handle this."

It's a raw confession. Asher closes the distance between us, his gaze steady and reassuring. "Then let me."

Let me.

Two simple words that soothe my hammering pulse.

"I haven't checked social since last night," he says, taking out his phone. "It's distracting, and I just wanted to have a good time. Now, I want to know how this got out. Our marriage. I'm pretty sure that's why Everly and everyone were texting earlier."

As he scrolls, I let hope climb the stairs inside me. Maybe it's no big deal that everyone thinks we're hitched. Maybe everyone will have a laugh about our Big Adventure. Maybe the world will understand. We were just having fun.

Then, his jaw comes unhinged.

My pulse spikes. "What happened?"

"Hal and Jen," he says ominously.

"We weren't married then!" I exclaim, disbelieving the obvious. "And they were so nice. What happened?"

"They *are* nice, and they posted a great picture," he says heavily. He scrubs a hand across the back of his neck with a guilty grimace, and I know I'm not going to like what he has to say. "Shit, Maeve. I told them to tag us. I suggested they post it. And they did."

Right. He'd thought the team would want that pic, for the fans and all. Plus, Everly encouraged auction winners to post photos online. "How did that lead to someone figuring out we got married hours later?"

Asher spins his phone around and shows me the shot

of us in the lobby with the tired but grateful parents. The caption under it says, "Lucky us! Tonight in Vegas, we met this great couple. He's the face of CheekyBeast, and she's his good luck charm. And can you believe it? They gave us their extra room...just to be nice! I say we pay it forward! When in Vegas tonight, spread a little kindness and do a favor for a stranger!"

I...I can't...I can't believe it. "But the wedding didn't happen until much later," I say, even though something tugs at my brain, like a clue I'm starting to decipher.

Asher hesitates, flicking through the images on his phone. "CheekyBeast shared it to their socials. And it became a thing, people talking about how they then paid it forward and spread kindness." A hint of embarrassment colors his tone as he tells me, "We went viral in Vegas."

This is more surreal than marrying my best friend for fun. "We spread kindness and didn't know it?"

Scrolling some more, he says, "And since they posted that we were in The Extravagant, some people took pictures of us, calling us Mister CheekyBeast and The Good Luck Charm. Random shots. Like at the concert, when I held your hand as we walked to our seats." A shiver runs through me at the memory of his possessive touch. "Then a shot of us walking through the hotel." He quotes, "'Spotted Mister CheekyBeast in Vegas and then opened the door for a stranger. When in Vegas, pay it forward.' Or this—someone shared that pic and then said they gave up their bus seat for a senior. Someone else shared it and said they picked up litter."

"We went viral for doing something...nice?" This doesn't compute.

"Evidently," he says, as surprised as I am.

"That's..."

"Cool?"

My heart squeezes with warmth. "Yes. But did Mrs. Matrimony share the wedding pics, then? She's the only one who had actual proof of us being married. We took our rings off when we left this morning."

Asher sighs heavily, shaking his head. "It happened when we were playing roulette, Maeve."

Oh.

Oh shit. I didn't even think about the rings we wore in public. My focus was solely on betting on a kiss. But I remember Asher draped an arm around me and tugged me close, then stared daggers at a redheaded man next to me. I have no idea who took the shot, nor does it matter.

But when a memory swims to the surface, I decipher the clue. At the table, a woman in a fuchsia jumpsuit shouted, *When in Vegas!* and tipped her drink toward me. Was she toasting *us*? She must have seen the pic. *When in Vegas, pay it forward.*

It's all my fault that we went viral. I'm the one who suggested roulette.

"Can I see it? The roulette pic?"

He shows me a photo of us leaning against the roulette table, his arm wrapped around my shoulder, with a claiming vibe. The shutterbug has two more pics, zoomed in on our rings.

My stomach flips with nerves and some seriously lusty chills. I don't even know what is going on in my life right now, and my body decides to get a little turned on? What the fuck, hormones?

I try to ignore them and zero in on the problem.

This pay-it-forward movement is wonderful, but it's making my career situation even more complicated.

Or am I just being overly cautious?

"We could let it blow over, maybe," I suggest, desperate to fix this mess. I'm the girl who's too much, too clingy. But I can't lean on my best friend to fix *my* roulette mistake. Not right now. He has too much on his plate with hockey and his charity.

"Maybe we could," he says, and his brain is clearly spinning in search of solutions too.

"So what if everyone thinks we're married? Who do we have to prove this to? Beyond tonight? Beyond this party? No one, right?" I ask hastily, nearly convincing myself.

He nods. "Maybe it won't matter. No one has a long attention span these days anyway. The Sea Dogs might not find out. They might not care. It'll be fine."

For the first time in fifteen minutes, I almost believe this ridiculous situation will work. I always find trouble, but I always find my way out of it too. "We'll have a laugh later, I'm sure."

"Definitely."

Mister Butler clears his throat from the hallway—there's no time to linger. We exit the bathroom with the conversation unfinished but with hope we'll get out of this mess unscathed.

In the hall, the liveried man shoots me a look that says I'm an agent of chaos and I've met my match in him.

"Let me show you where you will be painting for the guests," the butler says, his tone tinged with irritation. I can't afford for anyone here tonight to be annoyed with me. The fashion designer has connections—he might recommend me. No one wants to hire a painter who becomes the center of attention at the party.

"Thank you for everything," I say, trying to smooth things over as I pick up my supplies. "I appreciate it." Asher grabs the easel, and I turn to him, improvising a bathroom scenario. "And thank you for helping me fix the zipper on this dress."

"Anytime," my temporary husband says.

"How utterly thoughtful," the butler deadpans as he leads us down the hallway, polished shoes clicking. "It's always helpful to have a partner who can assist."

As we tread the mansion's sleek halls, Asher drops a few feet back and whispers, "We'll lie low tonight." He nods to the front door. "I can leave if you want."

No. God no. My heart rate gallops. I need him here. "Can you stay?"

"Of course," he says. "I'll keep out of the way."

"And we can talk later?"

"Of course. And listen, if anyone *does* ask, we can say the marriage pact was part of this act of kindness, somehow. A viral stunt. Like we did it to get attention for this pay-it-forward thing."

That's not a bad idea at all.

"Yes! That's so brilliant I could kiss you," I say as we reach the giant sunken living room where I'll set up in the corner. But then I wince. My desire to kiss him is what got us here in the first place—the bet for a kiss and all. "We can sort it out when I get a break. Sorry, and thank you."

"Don't think twice about it. I'll fix it." He sounds happy to help solve problems—because he always is. That's what he does.

My throat tightens with emotion. He deserves so much better than someone like me. I'm a soda bottle shook up. A frothy drink spilling over. I reach for his arm and whisper in a choked voice, "You're the best."

For a second, he looks like he wants to kiss my forehead. And for a second, I linger on how much I'd like that —a soft, reassuring kiss that I could melt into.

That's new—this longing.

But maybe not so new, given last night? And the way I rode him like I was test-driving a new vibe that does zero-to-*O* in thirty seconds.

As Asher disappears into the arriving partygoers, I set up and get to work.

19

MY WIFE

Maeve

Soon, the living room fills with art world types. Women in avant-garde jumpsuits and short dresses that look like they've stepped straight out of a runway show. Men in colorful pants and tight shirts. I try to capture scene after scene with my brush.

I paint Mr. Vincenzo as he sails through the house, interacting with his guests with some sort of Dachshund-Chihuahua mix tucked into the crook of his arm. He's a short, stout man with thick glasses and a dapper polka-dot suit. I paint him, too, when he asks me if I'd be *so kind as to please make sure to get DaVinci—the dog—in some of the scenes.*

"I never skimp on dogs," I say, then he smiles and weaves back into the crowd, stroking the dog's long ears as he goes. I paint gallery owners who exude an air of refined taste. I paint artists who stand out with their eccentric styles. I paint models who move gracefully through the room.

I don't stop even when a tall, wiry man with high cheekbones and toned arms in a tight shirt strides right over to me. No idea who he is, but his *je ne sais quoi* makes me think he's a model.

"Mabel Hart?" he asks when he arrives by my side. He's British, posh, and very imperfectly interesting-looking in the way models are today.

"Maeve Hartley," I correct with a smile as I keep painting. It's hard to keep track of names, so I don't take it personally.

"My apologies. You do the geometric shapes art, if memory serves? They're so lovely." His tone is a little slurry like he's had one too many pints. "So insightful. So bright."

I don't do geometrics at all, but I say kindly, "Actually, I'm more of a stylized realist, but I like to play with light and shadow."

"Yes, that's exactly what I was thinking," he says, his voice smooth as he moves right next to me, maybe an inch away. "I met you at a fashion show one night, didn't I? I believe it was for Isla Beaumont's collection. You were doing these brilliant paintings then too."

Well, I *was* there, but I was hired to cater, thanks to Aunt Vivian, not to paint. "She's a wonderful designer. I'm sure you wore her clothes well."

He brings a hand to his heart. "Oh, thanks, love. I'm so flattered you remember me. I'm Nigel," he says, dropping his voice and glancing around as if making sure no one can hear him.

Thanks, love? My, my, aren't we friendly. "Nice to meet

you, Nigel," I say politely as I dip my brush into the palette and, well, carry on.

"And yeah, it was so great to wear Beaumont's designs. She has some very sexy clothes, don't you think?"

I don't actually know much about her style because I was too busy serving food, but that's neither here nor there. "Yes, she does," I say.

He leans closer, watching me work. It's not the first time someone has watched me closely when I've been party-painting. It is a sort of a party trick, after all. But it's the first time someone has gotten so up close and personal. Too personal—the fit of his pants makes me feel like I know him in the biblical sense. "Mmm, yes, that's so wonderful," he says, staring at my canvas.

Or perhaps...my chest.

I try to ignore how near he is. I try to ignore the liquor on his breath as I paint a stocky young man chatting amiably with a gray-haired, strong-nosed woman. I catch sight of Asher heading toward the conversationalist a few feet from me, the first time I've spotted him all night.

Maybe Asher will talk to the man and woman, and I can paint him too. I don't know if I've ever painted Asher. I think I want to. *A lot.* As I imagine the colors I'd use for his light brown hair, a rush of warmth slides down my spine.

Then, Nigel places a hand on my shoulder.

What the...?

It's clammy, and my skin turns cold from the unwelcome touch. Keeping my focus on the canvas, I try to subtly wriggle away from his spindly fingers.

"You have such a knack for this," he says as his hand curves over my shoulder. "It's like you were born to do it." His voice dips into something that he must think is sensual as he keeps his hand on me, his fingers now stroking my skin. My gut churns, but I try again to shake him off without breaking my focus on the party. I have a job to do, after all.

"You do have a real talent for playing with light and shadow. I'd love to see how you handle something...more intimate. Would you like me to pose for you after the party?"

I snap my gaze toward him. "No," I say. Firm, but not too loud.

A throat clears, and I look up to see Asher right next to us. Like a superhero arriving on the scene, he's towering over the far-too-handsy and way-too-tipsy model.

"My wife is so talented, isn't she?" he tells Nigel smoothly, but there's a hard edge to his voice now.

Before I can react, Asher cuts in front of him, knocking the model's hand off me. Asher grabs my chin and tilts my face up to his, pressing a kiss to my lips that's anything but subtle. It's possessive, demanding, and unmistakably territorial. When Asher finally pulls back, there's a challenge in his eyes as he stares down the man. "But *my wife* doesn't have any openings for nudes."

As if she appeared out of nowhere, the woman in the newsboy cap click-click-clicks, and she's captured the kiss on camera.

I can barely catch my breath. Beside her are the butler and the host, holding his dog. Mr. Vincenzo narrows his eyes at Nigel, and DaVinci seems to, as well.

"Oh, shoo, you little monkey bat," the host says, flicking his fingers at the creepy model. "You arrived at my last show hungover and projectile vomited on the runway. You're permanently banned from the house of Rafael and DaVinci Vincenzo! Do not come to my parties and hit on the talent! Do not even think about crashing my parties again! Now, go!"

I'm still reeling from the way the host said *talent* when Asher lifts a casual hand. "I'd be happy to see him out."

Still holding the judgy dog, Mr. Vincenzo claps with glee while the hockey star curls a hand tightly—probably too tightly—over Nigel's shoulder, cutting through the crowd that's watching with avid eyes as he sees the creep out, the butler by his side.

As they go, Asher's words repeat in my head—*My wife is so talented*. The way he said them, the way they felt like warning shots, the way they made my stomach flip...

But I stop lingering on them when Mr. Vincenzo turns to me, with utter concern in his eyes. "Do you need anything? Anything at all? A moment to rest? Some chocolate? A Xanax? An aperitif? Would you like to pet DaVinci?"

"I'm...good," I say, "but I will take you up on the last one."

He offers me the dog's sleek head, and I stroke it a few times. "He's very soft."

"We both use the same shampoo."

Of course they do.

Asher returns a minute later, dusting his hands. The tiny man reaches for Asher's arm and thrusts it in the air. "You saved my party! You're a hero, and you've earned a spot in my memoirs!"

So much for lying low.

20

SAFETY NET

Asher

I should feel bad for interfering in her work life, but I don't.

Sure, she didn't want to be singled out, but that jerk crossed the line. Even though Maeve's busy painting again, the sight of his hand on her still burns through me.

I duck away from the action to call Soraya. She's been texting me all evening about the upcoming fundraiser— something I should be paying attention to—but I'm still stuck on that bastard. And the way he touched my wife. My fists clench.

"So, does that work for you?" Soraya asks.

Shit. I wasn't listening. I stop pacing, drawing a deep breath. "I'm sure it will, but could you go over that again? I think I missed some of it," I say, playing it off like I wasn't distracted.

She chuckles softly. "Sure, and also...congratulations!

I'm sure you have a lot going on, being a newlywed and all," she says.

I close my eyes, not even surprised anymore. Is there anyone who doesn't know?

Not after that kiss in front of the photographer, genius.

"Yeah, life's been a little wild lately," I say.

"Understandable," she replies. "Anyway, I was saying it would be great if you could bring your wife to our first fundraiser. It's coming up soon." That's the picnic for the families. "I didn't want to bring it up before when you were single, but..." she says with a relieved sigh, "It's better optics if you have a plus-one now. The donors will enjoy meeting your wife. It looks better than showing up solo," she adds, a little apologetic.

I stop in my tracks, letting her words sink in. And... yeah, I'm smiling. A little wickedly. I like what she said more than I should. But oh hell, do I like it. It feels like a stay of execution for this marriage, and I'm a little elated for the reprieve.

No, *a lot.*

We finish the call, and I head back to the party. Once the painting session wraps up, Maeve grabs my arm and pulls me toward a secluded corner behind an abstract sculpture. The party's still humming in the background, but here, it's just us.

She turns to face me, her hazel eyes sharp. "What was that about? I didn't want to make a scene," she says, her voice steady, no hesitation.

I should feel guilty, but I don't. I'd do it again in a heartbeat. I meet her gaze, standing firm. "No one should make you feel uncomfortable like that. You were clearly trying to get away, and he kept touching you," I say, anger bubbling up again. I want to erase the feeling of his hand on her. "No one gets to treat you like that, Maeve. Not while I'm around."

She blinks, like she's surprised by the intensity in my voice. But she doesn't back down. "I could've handled it. I was handling it."

"I know," I reply, my tone softening just a little. Normally, I don't get this...protective. But she's different. She's my person. "You shouldn't have to. Not when I'm here."

"Asher, I appreciate the whole caveman thing, but I was supposed to blend in. That was the opposite," she says.

A fire burns in me. "That asshole touched you," I point out.

"I know, but..."

"And the host didn't want him here anyway."

"I know..." She pauses, shaking her head like she's taking it all in. Honestly, this reaction is new for me too, so I get it. Her expression softens. "It's just...we were supposed to fly under the radar," she says, her voice gentler. "Isn't that what you wanted? To try to, I don't know, keep things quiet?"

I did. But now? I'm not so sure I do.

"I did, but this was different. That guy's a prick. I'm sorry if it brought more attention to you," I say, crossing my arms. "But I'm not sorry for stepping in."

She sizes me up. "Well, that's clear. You're unapologetically possessive."

"I am," I say, not backing down.

She blows out a breath, then relents. "Fine, he was way out of line. I did need you. And this whole caveman thing? The *My wife is so talented*. That came out like a hiss?

It's kind of a hot trait in a..." She stops, lifts a brow in question, then says, "fake husband?"

I wasn't faking anything earlier with that Nigel prick, but I just nod. "Sure, fake husband works."

"Anyway, I wasn't expecting it. Or another photo either. Or becoming the center of attention again," she huffs out a laugh. "Are we magnets for trouble?"

"Looks like it," I say, scratching my jaw, but smiling now since she seems to have cooled off.

"I guess we're pretty bad at lying low."

I laugh too, because what else can you do? "We're terrible at it." I pause. "So you forgive your husband?"

She smiles. "It's hard to stay mad at you. Especially since Mr. Vincenzo invited me back. To paint another party."

I beam. "Told you my wife is talented."

Her smile from those words hits me right in the heart. "So yeah," she says, "it...weirdly worked out."

Which is an apt way to describe us right now. "About that," I say, moving on because there's another topic that's demanding my focus—one that I like far too much. When we arrived and she needed me to play along as her real husband, I was all too happy to do it. Hell, if she needed me to continue for a day, a week, a month, I'd say yes. But right now, I need her to help me out, and I'm not entirely sure why this thrills me so much. I shouldn't want this so badly, and yet...I do. "I talked to Soraya as the party was wrapping up."

Maeve raises an eyebrow. "And?"

"She congratulated us on the wedding, like Angelina did earlier," I say, then lay it all out about the upcoming picnic. "She also asked if you'd be joining me." I take a beat, then with some vulnerability ask, "Will you?"

I want her yes too much. Why am I dying for it? Why do I want it when she's made it clear she wants to be just friends?

Maeve parts her lips, then sputters out, "So, we're definitely not lying low? We're...what? Stepping out as husband and wife?"

I should feel bad for roping her into this marriage last night, and now again for the next few weeks. But I don't. "Will you go with me? It would look a lot better if I attended with my wife," I explain, since it would. A man showing up with a plus-one for a charity focused on kids looks better than a man showing up alone. Especially if that man married his brother's best friend on a whim in Vegas, then annulled the marriage. That wouldn't look so good at all.

Which is why I'm hoping we don't annul it quite yet. Then, I let myself be vulnerable as I add, "I need your help, Maeve." I hold up my hands in surrender. "I guess we do need to prove this to someone. Beyond tonight."

She blinks, shakes her head, like she can't believe what I'm asking. But then her answer is magic when she says, "Of course I'll do it. Remember, I'm the one who bid on you to save you from that woman, after all."

"I guess you're unapologetically possessive too," I say.

"Maybe I am," she says.

Then, since there are details to sort out but pillows calling our names, I add, "We can figure it out tomorrow. How long we're keeping up the act. I'm sure we don't need to do this for more than a few weeks. Maybe a month at the most."

She nods a couple times. "You're right. That's probably all it will take. A mural can't take too long. Maybe we can stay married till it's done? And then we'll be on our way."

A month. It feels long and far too short all at once. But I'm not about to say that.

Her phone buzzes. She snags it from the pocket of her dress and glances at the screen, her eyes widening. "It's Angelina again," she says, but she doesn't sound enthused. "The couple who owns the Sea Dogs? They invited me to brunch on Tuesday. And they want me to bring...*my* husband."

I fight off a grin. I should not be so thrilled about brunch with Eleanor and Spencer Greer. But I am.

Even when she looks up at me with a mix of fear and desperation and says, "I wanted to get this on my own merits—"

"You did."

"But what if I'm keeping it on *your* merits?"

I step closer, cupping her cheek gently. "Hey," I say softly, "according to your agent, they decided last night."

I'm not sure she's convinced, but she manages a smile. "Well, whatever the reason, it looks like we've got two performances to prepare for as Mr. and Mrs. Callahan."

The weight of her words settles over me, and I realize just how deep we're in. A spontaneous, tipsy decision has snowballed into something much bigger. But the funny thing is, as quickly as this marriage escalated, I'm not mad about it at all. And I think I know why.

I'm not so sure she wants to be just friends, and I can't leave that possibility alone.

Not after last night.

Whether it's a bad idea or not, I mostly want this marriage to last a little longer because these feelings for her aren't going away. They're getting more insistent, demanding I face them head-on.

A fake marriage could be a safety net as I work

through them. I'm no good at making relationships last anyway, but no one will get hurt with a built-in, predetermined expiration date. It's a relationship we control. It's like a game of hockey—you give it your all for three periods, then it ends, and you move on to something else.

Our buzzing phones interrupt us. I glance at mine, and a grin tugs at the corner of my mouth when I see who's messaging.

"Beckett," I say, holding up the screen to show Maeve his text. "'Why am I the last to know?'"

We laugh for a few seconds, but when I pocket my phone, something still nags at me. "Stay here," I say.

Heading to the nearest bathroom, I grab a washcloth and run it under warm water.

Maeve looks at me, puzzled when I return. "What are you doing?"

I step close, gently taking her arm. "Getting that guy off you," I say, my voice low but resolute. I scrub her shoulder where Nigel's hand had lingered, wiping away any trace of him.

When I'm done, I press a kiss onto her shoulder.

Marking my wife.

21

AND NOW I SHALL EXPLAIN MYSELF

Asher

I push up the chrome bar with a quiet grunt, the weights straining my arms, but it feels damn good. Not everything does, though—like the way Beckett's looking at me. We're in a quiet corner of his flagship gym on Fillmore Street, the early Sunday morning lull giving us the place to ourselves.

"So, let me get this straight," he says, brow furrowed as he spots me, almost like he doesn't want to. I grip the bar tighter just in case he's considering taking me out. "It's temporary? A mutual arrangement. For her project and the charity? Did I get that right?"

"Pretty much nailed it," I admit, drawing a deep breath before pushing the bar up for one last rep. My muscles burn, but I focus on the movement until I set the bar back in place and sit up, escaping his death stare. Sure, he sent that easygoing text last night to both of us, but it was followed by one to me alone, saying, *Be prepared to explain yourself tomorrow morning.*

Now I have, and I'm hoping he gets why his sister and I are staying hitched. But Beckett's shaking his head and muttering, "Dude."

That *dude* is never good. Not the way he says it. I wipe the sweat off my forehead and brace for impact.

"It's fine," I say, trying to reassure him. "I'd never hurt her. You know that, right?"

Maybe I was wrong to think he'd find our wedding funny. It's not just a wedding anymore. It's a marriage. So, yeah, him wanting to kill me feels reasonable-ish.

Beckett scratches his jaw, his eyes narrowing. "Yeah, I know you wouldn't hurt her. It's just..." He pauses, then sighs. "Think about the stakes, man."

I toss the towel aside, meeting his gaze with a serious one. "I am thinking about them, Beckett. All the time."

"Me too. Because you're my friend, but she's my little sister," he says, crossing his arms, reinforcing the point I already know. "She's trying to make her way in the world, dealing with an overbearing aunt. You're already a successful hockey player. If this goes south, you'll be fine. But she might not be."

He has no idea how much that only makes me want to protect her more. I square my shoulders. "I won't let anyone hurt her," I say solemnly.

Beckett studies me for a moment. "You really mean that?"

"One hundred percent. No—one thousand percent."

"You're gambling with a lot here," Beckett continues, his tone careful. "It might feel like fun and games, but you're throwing her into the public limelight. The art world—it's not like our world of sports and fitness. Art is all about perception, value, and reputation. It's all about who knows who. If this goes sideways, it could mess things up for her."

"I know," I say quietly, guilt slicing through me. I'd never want to hurt her. I only want to support her. I long to see her shine and share her light with the world. I hope I didn't make things harder for her. But that's all the more reason to look out for her with everything I have. "She's my friend too."

Fine, I wasn't so friendly with her the other night in the hotel room. But no need to mention that. Maeve and I agreed it wouldn't happen again, so there's no need to bring it up.

"Yeah." Beckett nods, relenting a little. "You guys are as good friends as you and me."

"We are." I'm glad he knows that. What I feel inside, though, is way more than friendship. "I care about her."

"I know you do." He takes a beat. "Sorry for giving you a hard time. It's just...when Mom and Dad died, I had to look out for her. I can't stop looking out for her. Maeve's like a Pokémon that keeps evolving but also keeps trying to run away."

I shoot him a *Did you really go there?* look. "Did you just compare your sister to a high-maintenance Pokémon?"

"Yeah, I did," he admits.

But I don't see her that way. I see her as the woman who remembers every birthday, every anniversary, every little moment. As the friend who goes to battle with you, who makes you laugh, and who shows up whenever you need someone. I see her as the human who finds inspiration in the sky, the stars, and everything in between. I see her as chaos and beauty melted into one gorgeous, joyful, complicated person who understands I'm not always as happy as I let the world see.

But that all feels private, like what happened in the hotel room. So, instead, I say in a firm voice, "You have my word. I'll look out for her. Always."

He claps me on the shoulder. "You'd better." His tone is lighter, but there's a real warning in it. "I worry about her."

I furrow my brow. "What do you mean worry?"

"She's my sister and all."

But why would he worry about her? Is something wrong? "But about what?" I try to sound casual when I don't feel casual.

"Just normal worry," he says with an offhand shrug. He turns to adjust the plates on the bar, taking off one and then another. "Someday, I'll bench more than you," he says.

He's moved on, so I try to put my worry aside. "Someday, I'll run a business as well as you."

He laughs. "Fair point, Callahan." But before lying down, he adds, "So, you two are going to be husband and wife at the picnic?"

"That's the plan."

"Weird, but I guess I can handle it."

"How big of you," I deadpan.

"I don't need to get you two a blender or anything, do I?"

"No, but maybe I should get you one," I say, offering an olive branch since, well, he could have been a supreme dick, but instead he was simply a protective big brother. If I had a sister, I'd probably behave the same.

He grins. "I've had my eye on that new Vitamix."

Later, when we finish working out, we head to The

Oasis up the block to meet Soraya for a quick planning session. She's jogging down the street toward us, wearing workout gear and a ball cap holding back her long hair.

"Hi, guys," she says when she comes to a stop. "Asher, anything exciting happen overnight? Did you buy an amusement park? Start a space camp? Invest in a yacht with your new wife to use as an animal sanctuary?"

"Nope. But the amusement park and animal sanctuary are excellent ideas," I say.

"Glad I could be helpful," she says.

Beckett lifts a hopeful finger. "Can you leave me the yacht in your will?"

"Only if you take the animal sanctuary that goes with it," I say, swinging open the door to the shop.

"Obviously," he replies.

"While we're laying claims, I'd like the amusement park," Soraya says.

"Sure. I'll have my lawyer get right on it," I say.

We go inside and order, then sit down and catch up on our plans for Total Teamwork over smoothies while Soraya makes notes on her phone.

When we're nearly done, she sets down her phone with a smooth finality. She's such a good leader. "And thanks to that one hundred-grand donation from *someone*," she says playfully, knowing full well that someone was me. Though, Beckett deserves the credit since he got the ball rolling with the donation to the auction charity that set the whole back and forth of the money in motion "We should be able to expand our services even more."

"Someone was looking out for us," I reply.

"Yeah, me," Beckett says, pointing to his chest.

I point to mine. "Dude, me."

He shrugs. "Though originally, I suppose it was Maeve since she technically started this all."

"Speaking of Maeve," Soraya says brightly, "we should have a great turnout at the picnic—donors, families, and community members. I'm excited your wife will be there."

A pang of guilt twinges in me. Yes, Maeve *is* my wife. But Soraya thinks we meant to get married. That we plan to stay married. That she's coming to the picnic *as* my real wife. "Me too," I say, and while that's true, I'm not being honest with Soraya, and that doesn't sit well with me.

But it has to be okay since my goal is to protect Maeve and make sure no one ever knows we'd once planned to get our marriage annulled this week.

Soraya scans her notes and laughs lightly. "I can't believe I almost missed this. We have a board dinner this Friday. Did you want to bring Maeve to that too? Reina is going, and so is Aram," she says, mentioning her partner.

Beckett shoots me a hard stare, which I translate as *Remember what I just said?*

Of course I remember. And I also don't mind spending more time with Maeve. "I'd love to. I'll ask her," I say.

Soraya smiles. "It'll be great to have her there. Board stuff—you know how it goes."

I don't know, but she's the non-profit pro, so I say yes.

When the meeting ends, I say goodbye to Soraya and Beckett and jog home, texting Maeve about Friday night as I go.

Asher: Want to be my date?

I stare at the message after hitting send, liking how it looks. The word *date.*

> Maeve: A board dinner? I take it this means I can't wear my new Sorry I'm Late, I Saw a Dog T-shirt.

> Asher: Maybe save that for the picnic.

> Maeve: Noted. Also, you are just filling up my calendar, Callahan.

I'd like to fill her up. But that can't happen.

> Asher: Yes. So I can have you all to myself.

Which is too true. As I reach home, I leave my texts and pop over to Google to order that Vitamix for Beckett. Then, I add one for Soraya too.

Well, who doesn't love a blender?

But once I'm back at my house, Beckett's words climb back up the stairs in my head. *I worry about Maeve.* Is there something to worry about? Is she, I dunno, depressed? Are her career worries turning into something more?

I flip open my laptop in the kitchen, not even bothering to sit down. On the Mayo Clinic site, I look up depression and study the symptoms. Maeve's not listless, she's not angry or irritable, and she doesn't seem to have lost interest in things she loves. If anything, she's painting and working her ass off, doing pole classes, and seeing her friends as much as she ever has. I breathe a sigh of relief, feeling somewhat settled.

Okay, so it's normal to worry. Beckett was right. And since I don't have a sibling, it's natural that I'd turn to Google.

I close the laptop and check the time. Need to get to the arena soon, but there's one more thing I have to do. Can't put this call off any longer. Time to call my dads. Thirty minutes until morning skate, and telling the two people who probably wanted to help me pick out a tux feels way harder than I'd expected.

Deep breath. I pace along my terrace, overlooking my backyard with a garden shed I had converted into a sunroom of sorts—a little space for coffee outdoors, not that I do that very often. The how-to-relax gene skipped me. I turn away and hit *call*, waiting for John to pick up. Normally, I'd start with Carlos for practical stuff, but this feels like a "John thing." He's the emotional one.

"Hey, Dad," I say when he answers.

"Hey, Ash," he replies, a little sterner than usual. "Something you want to tell us?"

He knows. Of course he knows. "I don't know. Is there?" I try to joke.

"Gee, I wonder. I'll get Carlos on the phone," he says, then calls out, "Hey, babe, it's our son—the one who got married without telling us."

Seconds later, I'm on speakerphone with both of them.

"Was our invitation lost in the mail?" Carlos asks, all innocence.

"It was kind of last-minute," I explain, feeling defensive. I don't want them to feel left out, but they were.

"No, really? You don't say?" John shoots back, his sarcasm sharp.

I feel like a kid again, explaining myself to one or the other, like when I drove John and me to hockey practice before I even had my license. Back then, when I was thirteen and fourteen, John was often too sick to drive, and the first time Carlos found out what I'd done, he wasn't happy with either one of us, but me more so. "You should have called me at the office," he'd said. "I would have figured out what to do." But there wasn't always time for a phone call to strategize, as I learned. Another time after practice, John was driving me home, and his heart was beating too fast and too unevenly, so he had to pull over. He told me he'd be fine and just needed to wait it out. But I didn't buy that. I switched places with him and drove straight to the nearest hospital. They checked him in immediately, telling me it was a good thing that I brought him there so they could treat him *in time*. They used those words—*in time*. Soon after, he was diagnosed with an unusual thyroid virus that left him weak, dizzy, and occasionally, unable to focus. They put him on meds to manage his thyroid, and he's still on them. They work wonders, but it's hard to forget what it was like knowing nothing, just worrying about worst-case scenarios.

Thankfully, Maeve and I dodged our own worst-case scenario by agreeing to stay married instead of looking like idiots in front of the world.

"We did it for fun," I admit, but the words sound hollow. "Listen, we need to stay married, and...well, I need you to play along with it."

"Okay," Carlos says, shifting from teasing to supportive. "Tell us what's going on."

And just like that, they're in my corner. Sometimes it is that easy. I leave the terrace, explaining everything as I head inside. I pace past the Lego plants on my living room table. Real plants don't survive in my care, but I can build the hell out of Lego ones. They don't get sick or die when I'm on the road.

"Well, consider us the happy father-in-laws then," Carlos says when I'm done.

"Um, babe. I think it's *fathers-in-law*," John corrects.

"You see what you have to put up with in marriage, kid?" Carlos quips.

I laugh, but inside, I'm thinking it's not so bad.

And this call wasn't either. Before I hang up, I remember John's elbow. "Hey, J-dad, how's your arm?"

"What do you mean?"

"He's still worried about your sore arm from pickleball," Carlos explains.

"Don't worry. I used it to destroy the other team last night. I'm all good," John says.

"And you're taking your thyroid meds?" I add.

There's a pause. "Every night before bedtime," he says, sounding kind but also like he wished I wouldn't ask. "Don't worry about me."

But I do. And I always will. "I won't," I lie, then tell them I have to go.

It's time to play, and I'm beyond relieved. Sometimes life is too damn complicated. But hockey? It's the perfect escape and always has been. I need it so damn much.

22

SECOND WIFE

Asher

I hop in my electric car, turn it on with the app, and drive myself to the rink for morning skate, skipping the usual ride with Max. I need some time alone to shake off the madness of the past day and the tough conversations this morning. Time to get my head back in the game.

On the drive, I flip on the satellite radio, tuning in to a comedy station. A few minutes of Tiffany Haddish does the trick, loosening me up as the city blurs by through the windows. By the time I pull into the Sea Dogs arena, I'm relaxed and ready to block out everything except practice this morning and the game tonight.

I park, grab my phone, and head inside, passing framed photos of past Sea Dogs stars in the familiar hall leading to the locker room. Inside, music is blasting, courtesy of Wesley and one of his pump-us-up playlists.

"What's up, boys?" I walk in like everything is good in the world. "You ready to make Chicago cry tonight?"

"Fuck yeah." Hugo grins, pulling on his pads at his stall. But then the bearded brute of a defender gives me a funny look, head tilted, eyes narrowing like he's about to drop some wisdom. "But...did you cry?"

That's...odd. "What do you mean?"

He shrugs amiably. "At your wedding. It's okay if you did, man. I was pretty emotional at mine. No shame in some waterworks. Fuck toxic masculinity."

Christian Winters, our captain, nods solemnly, sitting in front of his stall, taping his stick. "Same here. I teared up at mine. Weddings will do that to you."

I stop, raising a brow. I smell a prank. "Okay, but I didn't," I say slowly, wondering how we ended up talking about my marital status instead of, you know, the game tonight against Chicago right here in our barn.

Max shoots me a skeptical look as he adjusts his leg pads. "You didn't cry? Well, shit. I figured that's why you didn't invite us—because you didn't want us seeing you bawl your eyes out."

Ah, hell. "It was kind of last-minute," I say, keeping it casual as I explain my wedding.

My wedding.

It's still such a strange thought. I'm married. Just for a few more weeks, but still, I'm *married* to my best friend. Naturally, my teammates want to know what's up.

"Last-minute?" Miles echoes, pulling on his jersey and giving me a serious glare with those dark eyes. Our center's like the laidback professor who's scary smart—he can see right through you. "You sure about that? Because I'd be willing to bet my fine scotch collection you've been obsessed with her for the last couple of years." He clears his throat. "Do we need to remind you of the DickNose board observations of the top-five times you said something cute about Maeve?"

"Right, Professor Falcon," I say, hoping I sound as confident about my wedding as I do about hockey. Did we even talk about what to tell our friends? We were busy taking hits from surprise after surprise.

I head to my stall, shedding my hoodie. "It was...spur of the moment." I feel bad lying, but I don't know how Maeve wants to play this. I do know that letting the whole team in on the secret is a surefire way for it to leak, and neither of us needs to be branded a liar right now.

Plus, it *was* an impromptu wedding.

Miles scoffs. "The DickNose board disagrees."

"And the DickNose board doesn't lie," Wesley puts in.

But whether the board is an oracle of romance or not isn't the issue. I'm not about to spill my guts to my teammates about my feelings for Maeve when I've barely begun to figure them out. I grab my jersey, ignoring them. It's not like they need me this second since they're too busy talking *about* me.

"But don't worry," Max says dryly. "We're here for you. Even if you weren't here for us."

"First off, did you ever consider maybe there's a reason I got hitched in Vegas instead of, ahem, near all of you assholes?" I ask as I tug off my shirt. "Second, have you ever heard the phrase *when in Vegas*? So, there you go."

Here's hoping that throws them off the scent.

"Sure, Callahan," Max says, like he believes me, then tosses me a private look that says *something's up*. But he won't press now, and I appreciate the tact—if that's what it is.

Wesley pipes up from his stall, "And just to show there are no hard feelings about us all being snubbed from your special day, we made you a 'Top Five Things To Do Now That You're Married' list." Sheepishly, he adds, "Josie loves lists. She got me addicted."

I groan and drag a hand down my face. These fuckers. Why did I not see the DickNose board coming?

The team captain strides to the corner of the locker room and taps the whiteboard with his stick. I stand at my stall, arms crossed like I can brace myself for the hell of all hell they're about to give me. He clears his throat and brandishes his left hand, speaking in a voice full of authority. "Number one: Get a silicone ring for when you're on the ice because gold isn't going to cut it in the rink."

Oh.

I glance down at the simple gold band on my finger, then at his silicone one. That's actually a good point. "I hadn't even thought of that. Fair enough," I mutter.

Max joins Christian and points to the next item. "Number two: Get her a diamond. Pretty sure she didn't have one in the photos. And you can thank Everly for noticing that."

My pulse spikes. Why didn't I think of that either? But if I play this wedding off as an elopement, we're good. When you elope, engagement rings probably aren't top of mind, but...yeah. I'll still have to fix that. Fast.

"We eloped, but you're right. Good thinking," I add, grateful for these guys.

Wesley grins as he taps the board now. "Number three: Start doing cute couple shit. Farmers markets, carving her name into a tree, swinging at the park. You're in your domestic phase now, Callahan."

I groan, rolling my eyes. I might be known as the resident *good guy*, but no way am I going to embark on a saccharin tour of couple Pinterest. "I'll save that for you and Josie. Next."

"Watch your mouth. Josie and I are aces at cute couple shit," he says.

"They are," Christian grumbles.

Miles takes his turn, lifting a finger, dark eyes serious. "But don't wait too long for number four: Make it official on social media. You can't go under the radar too long." There's a heaviness to his voice, maybe even regret. He's definitely speaking from experience. Then he adds, like a warning, "Nothing counts until it's on social, right?"

Pretty sure they've guessed this whole thing is fake, but I keep my game face tight. Because their advice is solid, and I appreciate how, in their messed-up way, they're looking out for me. "Got it."

Hugo rises from his stall, heads over to the board, then nods to the final item, his tone dripping with innuendo. "Take it from me because my life's goal is keeping my wife happy—give her a hat trick before you score even one goal for yourself."

Christian, Max, and Wesley raise their sticks in agreement. So does Rowan Bishop, one of of our defenders. He's here too, watching with amusement on his usually grumpy face.

"Well, thank you. You're all the best marriage counselors a guy could ask for," I say.

The room erupts in laughter, and I flip them off as I grab my gear. I'll talk to Maeve about all this stuff tonight when she's done with her catering gig. It'll be fine. We've been in sync on everything. We'll be in sync on these housekeeping details too.

I sit on the bench and lace up, then Rowan smacks his forehead. "Wait. How the fuck did we miss this?"

I turn to him and arch a brow. "Miss what?"

He's shaking his head like he's disappointed in himself. "Let us know when you move in together. A friend of mine owns a moving company. Happy to hook you up."

My brain short circuits. "Move in together?"

"It's that thing people do when they get married," Wesley deadpans.

"Or when the captain asks you to do him a solid," Christian chimes in with a smirk and a shake of his head.

"And thank you for that," Wesley says to Christian. That's how he wound up with Josie, the love of his life. He volunteered a spare room when the captain asked if any of us had a place for his sister to stay at the start of last season.

Hugo turns to me with some concern on his face. "You *are* moving in together?"

I hadn't given it any thought, but since my teammates quite possibly think I'm really married, I play it off, rolling my eyes. "Obviously."

Before I head to the tunnel, I glance at the board one last time. It's like the to-do list I didn't know I needed.

But I put moving in together out of my mind. It's too tempting a thought being that close to her, and I don't need more temptation than I already have in my wife.

* * *

The first two periods against Chicago are fast, brutal, and exactly what I need right now. With ten minutes to go in the third, I sprint across the ice, chasing down the puck as a Chicago forward winds up and fires a slapshot toward our goalie. Lambert's a beast in the net, though, and he easily swats it away. Bergstrand is there to grab the rebound and flicks it to me. I'm off again, skating hard toward Chicago's net, dodging a couple of defensemen. For a moment, I think I've got a clear shot—until, out of nowhere, I'm slammed into the boards. The hit jolts me, pain slicing through my abs, my jaw rattling.

They want to play rough? Fine. I'll play rough.

I shove the guy off with a sharp elbow, flashing him a grin that, in hockey lingo, translates to a clear *fuck you*. I skate after the puck again, avoiding a penalty. Maybe it's the smile, maybe it's the good guy rep. Whatever it is, I'll take it.

The game barrels on like that. Elbows, hits, bruises, crashes. This is the best kind of hockey—rough and physical, demanding everything I've got. This is where I thrive. Forgetting the world and just...playing.

Life will be there for you later.

It's what my dad, Carlos, used to say when I was younger, whenever I was too worried about John, even after he went on meds for his condition. I took Carlos's words to heart, and I still do. I can hear the roar of the crowd, but I keep it in the background, not letting it distract me. Until—

I make a pass to Falcon after the next line change, and my attention is momentarily yanked toward the stands at center ice.

What the...

Did that just happen?

I snap my gaze back to the ice, but I'm a fraction too late and almost trip over my own skates. A woman in the second row just flashed her bra at me, and I'm pretty sure the sign she's lifting over her head says, *Call Me If It Doesn't Work Out.*

I blink, forcing the bizarre moment out of my mind. We're down by one with seven minutes left. I jump over the boards for the line change, grabbing my water bottle and taking a swig. I park myself next to Bryant on the bench. "We'll get it in the next one," I say.

"We fucking will," he replies, giving me a fist-bump.

As Winters flies down the ice, I focus on the game, but something about the crowd noise tickles the back of my brain. It's growing louder.

And it sounds like...*second wife*?

I glance at the Jumbotron. I'm not surprised often, but this? This throws me. I've seen my share of signs like *Meet Me at the Players' Entrance,* or *I'll Make Your Night Worthwhile.* Even the occasional phone number.

But this is a first—*Can I Be Your Second Wife?*

Bryant elbows me and shoots me a disbelieving look. "And ten thousand hockey fans are devastated you're taken," he says with a chuckle.

I shake my head, still not quite processing the news. But there's no time to dwell on it. Coach calls for a line change, and I'm back on the ice. The moment my skates hit the surface, everything else fades away.

This time, I'm nothing but focused. Determination powers me as I fly down the rink. Falcon races ahead, and he's open. I flick the puck to him, the pass perfect, and he lunges for it, sending it screaming past a Chicago defender and right into the net.

The horn blares—we're tied up.

Two minutes later, Winters sends the black disc my way, and I send it home. The arena erupts, and when the game ends, "Tick Tick Boom" blasts through the sound system, signaling our victory.

The guys are pumping fists and slapping shoulders as

we skate off the ice. But once again, something in the stands catches my eye. I can't help but steal a curious glance. There's a sea of signs waving my way.

You Might Be Wifed Up, But You're Still My Fantasy Hockey MVP!

Taken, But You Can Still Score With Me!

Call Me If You Need A Backup!

Falcon catches my eye, grinning. "You're getting hit on even more? Dude, can I have your luck, please?"

"I'm sure you do just fine," I say.

He scoffs but adds, "Who knew all of San Francisco would be heartbroken that your ugly ass is hitched?"

Honestly, I'm still a little stunned that everyone knows. I head through the tunnel in a daze, both from the last-minute victory and the fan reaction. After I change out of my gear and tug on a workout shirt at my stall, I head to the media room with Everly for the post-game press conference.

The usual suspects are there. Gus, a weathered reporter who has covered us for years, clears his throat and asks the first question. "Asher, you made the assist to Falcon in the third that tied the game. What was going through your mind on that play? It looked like you were lining up for a shot."

I nod, giving a measured answer. "We were down by one with five minutes left, so I knew I needed a more aggressive approach. But when I saw Falcon open, I went for it. The pass lined up just right, and he nailed it. I'm lucky it paid off, but this team never quits."

Gus scribbles a note, seemingly satisfied with my response.

Then Claudia, a podcaster, raises her hand, wasting no time. "So you're married now. When did things start with your wife? The night she won you at the auction? That was pretty fast."

Everly shoots her a friendly but pointed look, her tone polite but firm. "If we could keep the questions hockey-related, that'd be great."

It's not surprising that a reporter has asked a skeptical question. And I appreciate Everly's save, but if I dodge the question, that'll only fuel the speculation.

I think about this week. The brunch with the owners on Tuesday, and the dinner with the Total Teamwork board on Friday, where Soraya will be relieved I have a date. I remember Beckett's warning to protect Maeve as I think about all the pieces of our story that have slipped out of our control—photos of the kiss after the auction, the pic of us at the concert, shots of us around the roulette table.

Everyone else is telling our story. Random strangers are putting together the pieces of our romance like we're a jigsaw puzzle.

But I'm not moving the pieces, and that doesn't sit well with me. I hate it when things spin out of control. It makes me feel jittery and frustrated. Like a teenager again, help-less to do anything when my dad was sick. So, I don't take the out that Everly is offering. Instead, I do what I promised Beckett I would—protect Maeve.

"I can only speak for myself," I say to Claudia, with ease and confidence even, "but this has been going on for a long time."

Everly gives a professional grin to the media scrum. "Next question."

Another reporter asks one that's hockey-related, and I answer it, but my mind is already racing. I don't regret what I said, but we need to get our story straight if I'm going to keep my promise.

I'll text her as soon as I return to the locker room. I'm not going to fuck up this chance.

For her, of course.

I don't want to mess it up for her.

Especially since I was only speaking the truth to the press.

23

SUCH A LOVELY FLIRT

Maeve

From unexpected drama while live painting at parties to disappearing into the crowd while serving canapés. All in twenty-four hours. On Sunday evening, I swing past a group of art collectors at the Julien Aldridge Gallery in the Marina District, offering a final tray of champagne before the opening night ends. One woman—a blonde with a sleek bob haircut, dressed in a pantsuit with a plunging neckline—takes a flute without glancing at me.

"Thanks, love," she says, her voice dripping with casual indifference. She turns back to her group, her manicured hand gesturing as they discuss the thoughtful colors of the light installation on one wall. Neon blinks in and out, spelling provocative questions across the room in bold, electric letters.

What even is success?
Don't you have enough?
But will you ever be happy?

The words flash like a challenge. Honestly, they're kind of rude. Like, I don't need a light installation seeing into my soul. But then again, is it too early to hope? Too soon to think success might finally come my way once my name is out there on the Sea Dogs mural? It's a heady thought and, frankly, one I could get lost in if I'm not careful.

So I make my final lap with the champagne before slipping into the back—the prep area, where the real work happens. Stainless steel counters hold trays of food, half-filled platters, and the last of the champagne flutes as the catering staff tidies up for the night.

"It's almost a wrap," Vivian says with a satisfied smile, glancing up from her tablet, her brown eyes pleased behind her red plaid glasses. It's still jarring to look at her, even ten years after my mother died. Light brown hair, untamable waves, brown eyes—they looked so much alike they were often mistaken for twins, despite my mom being two years younger.

"You did such a wonderful job tonight, Maeve. I was impressed with how you handled the other servers."

She'd assigned me to be the so-called lead server for the evening, and I appreciate the promotion. I want to be good at this job because it pays the bills. And I know it'd matter to my mother—to show up for family.

"Thanks," I reply, trying to sound genuinely grateful. It is a compliment, after all, even if I don't feel like I did anything special tonight.

Vivian adjusts her glasses, inspecting the flutes. "Marriage won't get in the way of this, will it?" she asks suddenly, her tone light, but there's no mistaking the worry beneath it.

Ah, there it is. The topic she's been dying to bring up

since the moment she saw me arrive tonight when her gaze swept to my ring, and she said, "I'm so thrilled for you! Tell me everything!" But as she asked when it started, how I fell for him, and how long it's been going on, I detected a hint of nerves in her tone too.

That's understandable. In her mind, the idea of me married to a rich man probably scares her. I suspect I seemed a more reliable option to take over her business when I was merely a single flighty artist.

Good thing I barely had the time to answer her questions when I arrived. Still, I'm not really sure what to say to her now. Because I'm barely sure of a damn thing in this brand-new marriage. I hardly know what our forty-eight-hour-old marriage means. And I don't want to get too far ahead of myself with this bloom of hope that a mural job will vault me to name-brand artist level, like that's even a thing. I'd just like to make art regularly, art that matters, art that makes people feel a little joy as they move through their days. A bright painting of birds perched on a playful tree's branch on a restaurant wall that makes someone smile, a mural of ladybugs and honeybees outside a flower shop that makes people think about Mother Nature and caring for her, and of course, scenes of kisses, so many scenes of kisses, that make you feel like love is worth chasing. If I could be like Lichtenstein, like Klimt, like Hayez...

I almost, *almost* sigh, the happy, dreamy kind, before I steer out of the fantasies and focus on the moment, and the question—will my marriage change anything?

"Not really sure," I say, and isn't that the truth? I wipe off the champagne glasses and straighten a few plates on the counter to avoid looking directly at her. I don't want to let on that Asher and I are making things up as we go along. Like, oh, say, the whole damn thing. Freaking viral photo. "We haven't really talked about it."

But I can't tell her the whole truth of my marriage and how fake it is. She's too practical. Besides, she's my...*benefactor*. Aunt Vivian makes it possible for me to keep making art. She ensures I get these regular catering gigs. Though, maybe she thinks Asher is the one supporting me now. The thoughts make my head spin.

"Then let's all get together *and* talk about it," she says. "There's so much to discuss with him in the family now. How about dinner?"

"Dinner would be great," I say, but then pivot. "Or a hockey game."

That'll be easier. Less chat time and more shouting-at-the-ice time.

"Good," she replies, smiling crisply. She does everything crisply. "Because just look at that out there." She waves a hand subtly toward the open doorway that leads to the sleek gallery space, where the rich and beautiful continue to admire the blinking neon installations. "It's hard to make a living as an artist, Maeve. Even if you're married to an athlete. Besides, their careers are so unpredictable. They could end any day. And really," she adds, lowering her voice to a whisper, "what are you going to do for work—make light installations? It's like winning the lottery, hoping people will care about your art. But food?" She nods firmly. "Food is reliable. People always need to eat. And these days, everyone wants to be entertained with pretty food and events—especially with the way the world is going. Might as well give them what they want. Feed them as the world burns down."

Her practicality isn't new, but it still stings the way it always has—she doesn't believe in me. She doesn't believe in the dreams I have. Not like my mom did, or my dad, before his demons took over and he descended so deep into his grief that he was never coming back out of it. But, just maybe, I'll prove my aunt wrong.

I plaster on a smile. "Thanks, Aunt Vivian. I appreciate the job."

"I know you do, sweetie," she says with a hopeful smile.

I don't want to disappoint her more than I already have, so I grab a tray and head back to the gallery floor, shaking off the conversation and all its uncertainty.

As I pass through the main room, collecting half or mostly empty champagne flutes, I feel a little out of place but not entirely defeated. The crowd is elegant and polished— the kind of people who glide through life as easily as they glide through galleries like this. And then there's me, catering instead of attending. But for the first time in a long time, I feel like someday, my paintings *could* hang on these walls.

The possibility makes me a little giddy, as if I have a good secret powering me on. It's a secret I hold tight in my heart as I complete my final round. Hardly anyone pays me any mind, which is how it should be, of course. I'm not paid to stand out but to blend in.

It's funny, though, how a mere couple of nights ago in Vegas, people noticed us. With Asher, I'm Mrs. Callahan. With Asher, I'm...someone.

But perhaps someday, I'll be someone on my own too.

For now, I focus on finishing the job and then saying goodnight to Vivian.

On the bus home, I pull out my phone from my purse, sliding it past the copy of *If Found, Please Return* that lives in my bag. I want to ask Asher if he wants to get together before our brunch with the owners to hammer out some of the bajillion and one questions I have about what it means to be his someone. But when I tap my phone, I see he's already texted me.

> Asher: Hey, wife. We should probably get our story straight before brunch. Meet me Tuesday morning for coffee?

> Maeve: You took the words right out of my mouth.

> Asher: Such a lovely mouth too.

That giddy feeling spreads as the bus rumbles toward my tiny place in Hayes Valley. But this lightheadedness comes from the question echoing in my head.

Is my husband a flirt?

I think he is. And I think I kind of like it.

I lean into his compliment, typing a reply.

> Maeve: It has many uses.

Hmm. That's not flirty. It's downright dirty. I erase it and try something more playful.

> Maeve: Flattery will get you everywhere.

> Asher: I happen to like everywhere.

Oh. That's a little naughty from him, isn't it? I mean, I'm *everywhere*, right? I glance around the bus to make sure no one is peering over my shoulder. No one is, so I write back as night falls deeper over the city.

> Maeve: I'm feeling very "pet me and tell me I'm pretty" thanks to your texts.

I wince, though, as I re-read it. That's a little clingy. Once again, I delete the message. *Be flirty, but don't be needy.* I can do that. I send a reply.

> Maeve: Same here, husband.

As the bus swings into the heart of Hayes Valley, the bubbles dance on my phone. I clutch it, on the literal edge of my seat.

> Asher: You know what a good husband would do for his wife?

Fuck her into next year with that big dick? But I behave. I don't write that either.

> Maeve: Dying to know.

> Asher: Get you a ring, stat. I want you to wear a diamond. Something that broadcasts to the whole damn world that you're taken. Got it?

A pulse beats between my thighs. And this time, I don't debate the response. I write it and hit send so fast.

> Maeve: Yes, please!

24

GIVE THIS GIRL A BADGE

Maeve

"So, please say we get to go ring shopping with you. Like really soon?" Leighton's sea-blue eyes sparkle mischievously as she grabs her tea from the counter at Doctor Insomnia's on Tuesday morning.

Everly, Josie, and Fable are already sitting at a table in the back, waiting for us. As I snag my chai latte, I glance at the clock on the wall—I'm meeting Asher in thirty minutes, but I have to see my girls first.

"So we're all going ring shopping together?" I ask it while meeting Leighton's gaze since I know she prefers being able to see someone's face when they're talking to her.

"Yes. Because we need to make sure he gets you a proper, big, gaudy diamond. You're married to an athlete, after all. Even though it's a"—she stops to lower her voice —"*you know what* marriage, you can't be seen with small bling."

We reach the group and sit down, and Fable gives a long, emphatic nod. "She's right. You need the biggest."

I gesture toward the billionaire's girlfriend, rolling my eyes playfully. "Says the woman who will probably have a fifty-carat diamond when her man proposes."

"I should hope so," Josie chimes in, taking a sip of her coffee.

"If Wilder Blaine doesn't give you the biggest rock in the history of the world, I'll eat my Louboutins," Everly adds, then looks at me over the top of her mug. "But seriously, emerald cut? Princess cut? Solitaire? Or maybe a sapphire or ruby?" She tosses her head back. "Gah! I can see them now—sparkling before my eyes."

"And are you taking me with you?" Leighton asks again, far more into this ring-shopping idea than I'd expected. She always seemed a little more, I don't know, badass with her black clothes, multiple ear piercings – including a pair of flower studs she wears every day—as well as flower tattoos on her arms. "*You* actually want to go ring shopping?"

"Don't sound so surprised." Leighton waggles her fingers. Her nails are a bright shade of copper. Silver bracelets jangle on her wrists. "I like shiny things. I'm a boudoir photographer—of course I'm into all things romance, especially jewels. Oh, you two could even do a couples session. Married couples are doing those more. Dating couples. It keeps the spark alive, they say."

"But this isn't a real romance," I remind them.

Turns out they knew before I even did. Everly first heard news of our wedding on social like the rest of the world. But that makes sense since she'd be tracking team news. Before I went to my catering gig the other night, I told them everything over FaceTime—the marriage pact, the wedding, and why we're staying married.

"Not a real romance?" Fable stares at me, doubt in her eyes. "Keep telling yourself that."

"Now, now," Josie says, cutting in and giving our redheaded friend a knowing glance, "just because one person in our friend group wound up in a fake-romance-turned-real doesn't mean that'll happen again." Josie coughs for effect. It's a pointed reminder—Fable ended up falling for her fake romance with her boss over the holidays.

"It's not going to be like that with Asher. The ring is for show. Because we're friends. Just friends," I insist, but then why do I want to shop alone with him? Maybe because it is fake? Maybe because if they go along, it'd feel too real? I'm not sure. "This is just..."

I'm not even sure how to label the unexpected marriage of convenience to my best friend. In Vegas, saying *I do* was fun. Now we're stuck together for at least a few weeks as...what exactly? A cover-up? A solution to both our problems? A viral hitching? My thoughts whirl with all the ways our temporary arrangement feels like it doesn't belong to us but to the world.

"It's just...what?" Fable presses gently, seeming to sense my hesitation. "I mean, you did have that kiss after the auction."

And many more kisses in Vegas. The hottest kisses of my life that ended with a surprise *O*.

I part my lips, tempted to tell them everything that happened in the hotel room on the couch. But I stop myself. What's the point? It won't happen again. It can't happen again. But also, that detail—the way I felt falling apart with Asher—feels too private. Too personal.

"It's just a performance for a few weeks," I say, speaking only of our fake marriage now. "It's a rom com without the rom. A make-believe match."

"That's a good name for a book," Josie says, a gleam in her eye.

"I bet it already is a book," Leighton adds, setting down her mug. "Or a movie."

"Why don't you sell your life rights, Maeve?" Josie teases. "You always live your life in full color, and it ought to be on screen."

I pause for a moment, letting her observation sink in, like a coda to the words my mother shared in her final days. *Follow your dreams.* It was as if she was speaking to the deepest part of me that she alone understood—the part that has bold, wild, too big dreams. The truest part of me ever since I was little. I've never been the shy one. I've never been the wallflower. I'm the one who climbs the highest trees, who swings from branches, who jumps into rivers. I'm the one who tries the zip lines too, rides the upside-down roller coaster, dives headfirst into the crashing ocean waves. But that's not always the healthiest way to adult, is it? Maybe I need to turn down the volume on me from time to time. Like my exes have always told me.

"Look, you know I want to go shopping with all of you. But," I say, stopping to meet all of their gazes, these women I love deeply, "maybe it's best I don't make too big a deal of the ring shopping. I don't want to get caught up in things. You know me. I get invested. I get too interested. I can't let that happen with a fake relationship."

My heart sinks a little saying that, but my friends nod and murmur in understanding.

"I get that," Leighton says, practically, but then seems

to drift off into a memory for a beat, adding, "We can't always have what we want."

I give her a curious look. "Something going on?"

Leighton quickly shakes her head, but her fingers drift to one of those flower earrings. "No. Sorry. I didn't mean to steal focus. I'm just saying I understand and no worries on the ring shopping. Do it your way."

"Just send us pics after you get it, okay?" Josie asks.

"Obviously," I say, and I love that they accept my answer. I'm glad, too, that I finally understand why I want to go alone with Asher. So I don't get too caught up.

I glance at the time then shift gears, my stomach swooping as I think about the brunch looming closer. "We have to meet with the team owners soon. Any tips for that? That's where I could really use the help."

Before anyone can answer, footsteps grow louder, then I feel a presence behind me. I turn just as Asher reaches us, and my breath catches. My eyes roam up his tall, rugged frame. It's the first time I've seen him since Saturday night at the party. Have his shirts always hugged his muscles just so? Has his grin always been that lopsidedly sexy? Has his thick hair always looked so invitingly tousled? My fingers tingle with the desire to touch him.

"Hi," I say, too breathy. Too excited.

"Hey," Asher responds, scanning the table. Five women, one man. "Hey, Fable, Josie, Everly, Leighton. Everly, good to see you again. Leighton, how's everything going with your photography? Maeve said your business is growing a lot? The studio work and the sports photography?"

"I did. And I'm keeping busy. Thanks for asking," Leighton replies brightly, twirling her cup of tea. She's doing more than keeping busy—business is booming for her, especially in boudoir, but she's also shot a few promo events for the Sea Dogs.

He shifts his gaze to Fable. "Fable, fantasy baseball season coming up?"

"You know it, and I might even let you into my league," she shoots back with a grin.

"Hold a spot for me. I can't wait. And Josie," Asher adds, turning to my librarian friend. "Your love of lists is rubbing off on Bryant."

Josie pumps a fist. "It's all part of my master plan."

Holy shit. Asher just acknowledged each of them individually. That's not new—he's always been thoughtful and considerate. But now, it feels different. Like I'm seeing him in a new light. Most men admire women, want them, date them, but many don't always see them as people. And here's Asher, taking time to genuinely connect with my friends about their interests, and warmth spreads through my chest, like that honey-hazy feeling I get when I start a new painting, that glow of inspiration that lights me up.

Asher turns to me, his gaze softening. "Did you have a good time catering on Sunday?"

Catering? I can barely remember catering. My chest is tingly, and my head swims with new ideas and possibilities. With images of him and me, all over again. Him and me, not stopping. I'm at a loss for words, and Josie jumps in.

"We were just helping Maeve with some tips," she says playfully. "She asked us for some."

Asher arches a brow, intrigued. "What kind of tips?"

"Marriage tips." Josie pats the empty chair.

"I asked for tips on the brunch with the owners," I point out, finally managing to snap out of my thoughts, then gesture to my outfit. I'm normally all about cute skirts—either short denim or long and flowy, but today I went a little fancier, just in case. Slacks. Gasp. I paired them with an orange and white polka dot blouse, so at least I've got a little splash of color.

"And we just decided we'll give you marriage tips," Josie says.

I sigh.

Asher slides onto the chair, playing along. "Lay it on me."

Fable's grin turns wicked. "We have a lot to teach you, Asher."

Where are they going with this? No place good. "And I'm officially terrified."

Leighton leans forward, locking eyes with my fake husband. "First rule: Maeve gets super grumpy when she's hungry. So, you'll want to keep snacks handy at all times."

I scoff. "That's not true."

Fable gives me a deadpan look. "I've seen how you look at a bag of chips, Maeve. Don't lie."

"I feel attacked," I mutter.

Asher laughs. "I've noticed she does have a thing for... warm nuts."

"Oh, she's into the whole package," Leighton adds. I want to strangle her but she's too fast with her sass. "You're not denying it," she points out before glancing back at Asher. "Maeve loves surprises, so take her on dates —just don't tell her beforehand."

"That's not what this arrangement is about," I say, but my heart lurches as I glance at Asher, checking in. Did I hurt his feelings with that comment about dates? I hope not, but his expression is amused, so I quickly push the worry away. He hasn't given me any indication he wants to go on dates. He needs me as his wife for his new charity, and that's it. That's also fine with me.

Fable jumps in next. "Oh, and remember, Maeve loves her independence, so don't crowd her. But that doesn't mean you shouldn't cook for her."

"I never said I wanted anyone to cook for me," I protest.

But the thought lingers. *That sounds really nice. I do like food.* Except, wait—why would he be cooking for me?

Everly, who's been mostly quiet, adds, "And she might act like she's not up to speed on hockey, but she knows all your stats, Asher. Every single one. Do with that what you will."

Asher turns to me, his minty green eyes lighting up. "So you're a closet fan, Maeve?"

My cheeks burn. "It's not a secret!"

"Feel free to quiz her later," Everly whispers with a sly smile.

Before I can protest, Josie jumps in again. "And don't forget, Asher, you'll have to make some changes too."

He rubs his palms, *bring it on* style. "I'm up for it. What have you got in mind?"

"Marriage is all about compromise," Josie says with a teasing smile. "That means one reality show for every two football games." Then she pauses, tapping her chin thoughtfully. "But you should probably establish a chore list too. No one likes fighting over who's doing the dishes."

Asher turns to me, his eyes glinting with curiosity. "You watch reality shows?"

I lift my chin high. "They're my guilty pleasure."

Asher leans back, clearly delighted in a whole new way. "I had no idea."

Before I can respond, Leighton chimes in, "Oh, you'll learn all about her guilty pleasures soon enough."

He will?

Fable smirks. "So, you might want to swap out the lotion on your nightstand for coconut oil."

My face flames. "I'm going to kill you guys. We're not moving in together."

Asher's smile freezes, but his eyes flicker with...excitement as he takes in this detail. "But if we were, I should stock up on lube?"

Red. I am all the red in every crayon box in the universe. "You're all dead to me," I hiss at the traitors known as my former best friends.

Leighton stands, grabbing her bag and tossing a look over her shoulder. "It goes both ways. You should probably lock the bathroom door when you're enjoying yourself in the shower."

The devils. The absolute devils. "We're not living together. And you all need to go!" I groan.

"Unless you want Maeve to walk in on you," Fable adds with the sauciest of winks as she pops up, along with Everly and Josie.

Groaning, I drag a hand down my face. "Don't you all have somewhere to be right now?"

"Other than divulging the details of your vibrator collection?" Josie calls over her shoulder as she grabs her bag, and an elderly woman at a nearby table shoots me a look and then a wink.

I hold out my hands at my friends, like *how could you.* "You're all the worst."

"Did you mean we're all equal opportunity here?" Josie says, with an oh-so-innocent look behind her glasses. "Since we're concerned about his needs too."

"Yes, concern. Exactly. You're sooo concerned," I say dryly.

Leighton's jaw drops as she stares at my face. My cheeks to be exact. "Maeve. I didn't know you could get embarrassed."

"It happens once in a blue moon for our chief trouble-maker," Everly chimes in, setting a hand on my shoulder.

"Why are you all still here?" I ask with a groan.

"We can stay and give you more tips," Fable offers.

"By all means," Asher says, sweeping out a hand, and now he's in trouble too.

I flick my eyes to him and raise a finger. "Do not feed the animals at the zoo," I warn.

"That's good advice too. It kind of applies to you as well. Asher, if you leave out the coconut oil, Maeve might never go to work," Josie calls over her shoulder as she heads out, "since she likes a lot of private time."

I bury my face in my hands as the clicks of their shoes finally, mercifully, fade. And when I manage to peel my palms off my cheeks a millennia later, Asher slowly turns to me, a hint of a smile playing at his lips. "That was interesting."

How do I even begin to explain what just happened? I did not expect that ambush. "My friends are dicks. What can you do? I'm sorry."

I'm especially annoyed that they mentioned that he'd want to engage in some self-care since the images flashing through my head right now are obscene. Deliciously, delightfully obscene, and I'm probably going to need to block out a whole lot of time tonight with my battery-operated friends.

But the images aren't going away as I look at him mere inches from me. I stare a little shamelessly, cataloging my best friend, from that tousled hair to his smirk to the way he fills out that Henley. His chest muscles call out for my hands. His abs demand my attention. His arms need to be explored. "Why Henleys?" I blurt.

He furrows his brow. "What do you mean?"

"Why do they look so good?" I say, then instantly regret it. I need to shut up. Like I wanted my friends to do.

He plucks at the forest green material, then looks back at me, holding my gaze. "Oh, this? You like it?" It's asked as a challenge. In a rasp. Like the way I imagined he'd said, *you have a lovely mouth.*

"It's nice," I say, like I'm simply conceding when really, the way the shirt fits him is too hot for my own good.

"Nice? Did you mean it's having a flamingo effect on you?" he asks, and great. Now I'm thinking about what he's wearing under those clothes. Then he leans closer and says in a husky voice, "Or really, I should say peacocks today."

It takes my brain a few seconds to catch up, but when it does, I clamp my legs shut, then suck in a breath. I should leave this alone. Really, I should. But I've never been good at resisting a cookie. "Fitting."

"Is it?" he asks, with a curve of his lips. He loves toying with me.

And I think...I love being toyed with by him. That heady feeling spreads through my soul again, flooding me with warmth.

I flash back to the promise we made in Vegas—that nothing physical can happen again. There's too much at stake, especially now with this marriage for appearance's sake. "But none of that can happen," I add quickly, shifting the conversation back to safer territory.

Asher's voice lowers, teasing, "Self-care, Maeve? Is that what can't happen?"

I swallow. *Is he daring me to admit it?*

"Nothing physical between us," I blurt out, a little too loud.

Asher holds my gaze, unblinking. "I know. You told me that in Vegas."

Right. I did. No need to keep repeating it. There's a reason we're here, and it's not to get lost in the heat between us. "Our story," I say, trying to string words together, but it's hard because my mind is absolutely else-where—it's in bedrooms, in showers, on the couch in our hotel room, on the street with that first kiss, at the party the other night when he claimed me before a crowd. "People are asking about our story," I continue, forcing myself to concentrate. "My aunt did on Sunday night. Oh, she also wants to have dinner with us. But instead, I invited her to a hockey game. I figured we can grab some-thing after?"

"Brilliant."

"And my friends asked, too, though they know the truth about...this marriage." It still sounds weird to say—*this marriage*. It's still strange to be married to my best friend.

His brow furrows. "They do?"

"Well, yeah," I say. "I couldn't not tell them." I feel awkward and unsure around him for maybe the first time. Is it because we were intimate? Because we're flirting? Or because my friends basically looked inside my skull and bared my thoughts for Asher? "Is that a problem?"

He scratches his jaw, looking like his mind is spinning in a million different directions. "No, it's fine. It's just...the guys were giving me hell the other day, and I wasn't sure what to say. What you'd want me to say. I didn't want to tell the whole team, so I just went along with whatever they said."

"Oh." I hadn't thought about that—what he would have to juggle. "You can tell the guys if you want. That's what I did with my friends." I pause though, mulling this over. "You're not mad that I told them, are you?" I ask, worried.

He shakes his head, looking at me with a soft, thoughtful expression. "It's kind of hard for me to be mad at you."

I blink, a little taken aback. "Why?"

He shrugs, then gives a small smile. "The fact that you wanted to tell your friends? That's not really something to get mad about."

It feels like he's saying something else, or maybe *not* saying something. Maybe he's holding back in some way. Sometimes it seems like he is. Sometimes he's easy to read. Sometimes impossible to figure out.

But I want him to understand where I'm coming from. "I just told them how it all came together, how you wanted me to have a good night in Vegas, and how it sort of spiraled." I roll my lips together, debating how much more to say. "I didn't tell them what happened in the room if that's what you're asking."

A smile shifts the corner of his lips. "I wasn't. Asking."

Oh. Maybe he doesn't mind them knowing we were intimate? I feel a little silly now, but then again, this whole thing between us is so complicated when before it was the easiest thing in my life. I almost want to go back to the way we were, even though a part of me likes how we are now. "It just seemed personal. Quick-Draw Maeve and all," I explain because I keep putting my foot in my mouth. Maybe it can go farther down my throat. Hard to say since it's past my esophagus right now.

"And, as you said, Quick-Draw Maeve isn't going to happen again. And hey, we're not living together either. Or so I hear," he adds with a smirk. He's clearly amused with me, or maybe at me. Honestly, I probably deserve it. I feel a little all over the place today. It's hard to get my bearings with him being so damn handsome.

"Well, it's just that there's no reason to do it. We don't need to live together to pull this off," I say. Do I sound like I'm making excuses? Am I making excuses?

"Exactly. We don't. And I promise we can pull this off," he says, a little bossy, and I like the command in his tone.

Time to focus then on why we're here this morning. To get our story straight. "On Sunday night, my aunt asked me how we got together, and I mostly avoided it. But she'll ask again when we see her," I tell him, matter-of-factly. "And I feel like the owners are definitely going to ask, and I want to be better prepared. The board members probably will too. We should plan what to say. So we're on the same page."

"You're right. We should." His gaze turns serious as he leans back in the chair, his hand scrubbing across the back of his neck, his Henley stretching deliciously across his strong chest. "Especially since the media asked me that question Sunday night after the game."

"They did?" My voice pitches up. My head spins with this new information, but of course, it makes sense they would ask him. Still, I'm dying to know how he handled it. "What did you tell them?"

His eyes are thoughtful as his gaze stays on me. "I went with what seemed like the easiest solution." He pauses, but not like he's hesitating—more like he's giving this the weight it deserves. "I said it's been going on for a while."

Oh.

Oh wow.

My heart feels a little fluttery. I press a hand to my chest, unsure of what to do with that piece of information. Or perhaps unsure of what to do with this hummingbird beating in my heart.

"For me, at least, it seemed like the easiest way to explain everything," he continues and there's an intensity in his voice that feels new. "So why don't we say that we always planned to get married eventually? That we started dating before the auction. That we planned to go away to Vegas for fun, but once we were there, we just knew it was what we wanted—getting married. And we couldn't wait."

Flames spread inside me from the way he's guiding me through this speed bump. From the way he's telling our story and making it feel...so incredibly real. Like that could actually be how it happened. How *we* happened.

"Does that work for you, Maeve?" he asks.

It works too well, especially the way he says my name, like it tastes delicious in his mouth. "It does," I say, trying not to sound too...aroused. Too breathy.

"Good," he says, then leans closer. "And listen, the guys reminded me of something else. We need to announce this on social, and we need to do it soon. Or people will suspect it's not real."

My mind is in overdrive. There's so much to do. So much to get right. "Right. Sure. Of course. But where do we start?"

He must sense how jittery I am, since he covers my hand with his, soothing my nervous energy. "Don't worry.

I've got this. We'll get you a big ring, and then we'll get a picture for social. After brunch."

I exhale, long, a little calmer as he takes charge so completely, like he's wrapping an arm around me and guiding me safely across a rocky shore. "Good plan," I say, but then my brow furrows as I snag on one little thing. Something that didn't even occur to me when my friends mentioned rings. "Buuuut." This is awkward. We haven't talked about money, but it's sort of obvious I don't make athlete bank. "I can't afford a big ring. We'll get costume jewelry, right? Or cubic zirconia. Oooh! Here's an idea— why don't we go to a consignment shop and find a vintage ring? I'm an artist. I can totally pull off the look." I do the bling show-off move. "Oh, this art deco ring? We hunted all over Paris for it."

He laughs. "Maeve, when did we go to Paris?"

"Let me have my fantasy."

"Fine, but someone is going to spot the lie in that. We weren't in Paris."

"Okay, okay." I sit up taller, reboot my routine. "We hunted up and down San Francisco for this ring. It's from the 1920s. Rumor has it, it was once worn by Zelda Fitzgerald during a lavish gilded age party. Isn't it divine?"

Asher dips his face, smiling. Then he raises it, and his smile disappears. His eyes hold mine. "Maeve, I'm buying you a big, beautiful, gorgeous ring. And that's that."

Oh. Well. Bossy Asher is in the house. "Asher, you can't—"

He sets his finger on my lips. "I can. But more so, I want to."

I swallow and try to protest, but I can't find it in me when he's so...determined to get what he wants. *For me.* "If you insist."

"I do." Asher checks his watch. "Actually, that story part didn't take long at all. We've got an hour. Let's get you a ring now. There's a jewelry shop up the street."

My pulse speeds once again. Everything is happening so fast, but when he rises and reaches for my hand, I don't hesitate to take his in mine. I like the way he sets the pace. I like that he's bossy. Most of all, I really like that it's only us going ring shopping, and that he never lets go of my hand the whole time as we walk to the shop.

* * *

Twenty minutes later, I'm inside a glittery store, picking out an absolutely blinding ruby. It's set low in a thick platinum band, the rich red stone gleaming with a deep, fiery intensity. The ruby is perfectly oval, framed by a halo of tiny, sparkling diamonds that catch the light with every movement. It's both elegant and bold—timeless but with just the right amount of flair. *It's bold, just like everything in my life seems to be right now.*

When I'm with Asher, that is.

"You like this one?" he asks, as I gaze at the beauty in my palm a little longer.

"I do," I say, low and reverent. I'm so tempted to tell him I've checked it out before. That I've walked past this shop and stupidly gazed at it. Of course I have. I'm the dreamer. But what are the chances it'll fit? Slim to nil.

"Let me see it," he says. A demand.

I hand it over to him.

And in no time at all, he's down on one knee.

My chest seizes up.

"Will you be my wife?"

"Yes," I say, without thinking because I don't need to think at all. It's the *only* answer.

Remember, you're faking this marriage.

But that voice quiets down when he slides the ring on my finger easily. A surprised breath escapes my lips. "It fits," I whisper.

"Meant to be," he murmurs, his thumb brushing over my skin in a way that sends a shiver up my arm. Maybe those words do too. Our eyes meet, and for a second, something shifts between us once more. For a long beat, I can't look away. I can only feel—this new thing between us, charged and unspoken as I look at my best friend, then at the stunning ring on my finger. It's only for show. And yet my heart is beating too fast. My skin is warming too much. The words *meant to be* echo. They're so romantic, but I don't want to get caught up in dreams of romance when really and truly, our friendship is what's meant to be. Our friendship feels written in the stars.

But his eyes are heated, vulnerable too. Like how I feel. "Is that your proposal play?" I ask finally.

"Yes," he replies, his voice full of certainty, then he presses a soft, tender kiss to the top of my hand.

My knees wobble.

How is that so sexy?

Why am I shivery everywhere from a kiss on my hand?

But I am—my cells are vibrating with longing. A pulse beats between my thighs. And I ache.

He rises, standing to his full height, several inches taller than I am. I look up. I swear the walls in the store feel smaller. I lean in closer, like I want to kiss him. No, it's not *like* I want to. I *do* want to kiss him. This man made me swoon with his kisses. And for several not-so-fleeting seconds I want all the swoons again.

But we agreed to stay chaste. It's too risky to kiss him. There are lines we shouldn't cross again or we could lose this precious friendship.

As he pays for the ring, I shove the thoughts aside, and whisper playfully. "You didn't have to propose, you know. I'm already your wife."

Asher's expression says he needs zero reminders of our status. "I wanted to propose to my wife," he declares. There's something outrageously pleased in his voice, and the glint in his eyes, as if he's in on a secret only the two of us share.

And I know at last why I wanted to be alone with him. Because I like being alone with Asher. The warmth in my chest swells again, but I resist the pull to close the distance between us.

Actually, I deserve a badge for resistance. Maybe I should make one for myself for each milestone I reach during this fake real marriage.

Resisted Kiss Badge.

No Hands on Abs Award.

Didn't Indulge in Self-Care Yet Medal.

Yet being the operative word.

Before we leave, I reach into my purse and take out something I've been carrying all morning, waiting for the right moment. I hand the gift to him—a black silicone ring. "And now yours," I say.

He blinks. Several times. "You got me a ring?" He makes it sound like it's a Ferrari.

"I did."

"How?"

"There's this thing called Amazon. You can order from it any time of the day."

He drags a hand through his hair in disbelief. "The guys were saying I needed one. And you got one for me."

It's like no one has gotten him a gift before but that's not true. I've gotten him gifts. A hot sauce set. A Lego plant when I learned he wanted to try making one, since he used to love building Lego sets as a kid. A hand-painted hockey puck with the words Puck Off on it. And our photo albums, though we share custody of those.

"I thought you'd need it for when you play. It's better for athletes," I explain.

"Put it on me," he demands in a gravelly, commanding voice.

He tugs off the gold one and tucks it into his pocket then offers me his hand. I slide the black band on, wiggling it over his knuckle. And it happens again. The sparks, the shivers, and the chills erupting down my spine.

I meet his eyes. They're glimmering with flames. I bet mine are too. I feel like I'm shimmering. I swallow roughly, then look at his big hand, adorned now with *my* ring. "It looks good," I say, and I feel a little possessive, a little territorial. A little like him.

"No. It looks perfect, Maeve," he says, his voice raw, piercing even. My throat aches from the sound of it.

Then he takes my hand, and together, we leave, telling the story now with our new rings.

25

SHOWTIME

Asher

"You're utterly ah-maze-zing," Eleanor Greer says to Maeve as we sit down for brunch at their home. "The very second I saw your portfolio, I just knew—you were the one to bring my vision to life on the walls of the arena."

I knew she had real talent. I've known it for years. I'm tempted to chime in and say, *Yeah, she's fucking awesome*, but I also know my role here is to support her.

Maeve's cheeks turn a little pink as she offers a grateful, "Thank you so much, Mrs. Greer. I'm excited to start on the mural."

"And we'll be moving fast. This week. Did your agent tell you it's this week? I hope so. I've already been telling my friends about you," Eleanor says, sounding like she's had too many espressos from the gleaming Rocket espresso machine on her kitchen counter.

"I can start this afternoon," Maeve replies gamely.

Eleanor's eyebrows rise. "Let's go to the arena after

brunch. We can do the site assessment today. Initial measurements. Photos. Clementine will be there too," she says, mentioning the team's general manager, and yup. Eleanor's got the energy of a Border Collie.

We're in their grand mansion in the Presidio, where the massive dining room is adorned with portraits of their Maltipoo mix, Holmes. He wears a suit in one painting and in another, a Sherlock Holmes deerstalker hat. Holmes had greeted us at the door earlier, offering a paw for shaking before trotting off to his tartan dog bed with a pipe stuffy that looked custom-made for the cute little dude. "Bye, Holmes," Maeve had called out, which must have scored her major points with Eleanor.

"I'm there," Maeve says, matching Eleanor's energy with equal enthusiasm.

"Wonderful. As I was saying," Eleanor continues, her sleek blonde bob looking custom-ordered from the rich white ladies' bougie catalog. "Even after I saw your work, I opened the search to other artists. I felt like I had to. Just to be thorough, just to make sure I wasn't falling in love at first sight. But I kept coming back to you." She sets down her water glass and offers a confession to all of us. "I have this dream of owning a museum. I don't know if that will happen, but for now, I can put art on the walls at our team's arena. It was meant to be." She glances at her husband, Spencer, next to her on their side of the table. "Don't you think?"

"Just like you and me," Spencer says, adding for our benefit, "she's got a great eye for talent."

He seems comfortable to take the back seat, which makes sense because, well, they both own the team, but Eleanor calls the shots. Years ago, she started a venture fund with him that made billions, and they bought the team together. "Once Eleanor has her mind made up, there's no turning back," he says, proving my point.

He leans in to give her a quick kiss on the cheek, and she flashes him a smile that's just shy of flirtatious, paired with a knowing look. Then, returning her focus to Maeve, she enthuses, "And finding out you're newly married to one of our star players? Well, that made it seem like kismet. And," Eleanor adds, "we love to work with the players' partners when feasible. Like Cookie Melissa, Hugo's wife."

"What does she put in them?" Maeve asks brightly. "Because I'm addicted to them."

"Me too, and I'm dying to get her recipe." With a tap on the table, Eleanor seamlessly shifts topics. "You must try the quinoa salad. It's one of our favorite recipes." She nudges the platter toward us. Her gaze brims with curiosity as she looks between us. "And tell me all about you two. I want to know everything."

It's showtime, and we've put in the practice. "Well, we've been friends forever," I say, glancing toward Maeve as I serve some quinoa onto our plates.

"Friends to lovers," Eleanor says, then looks to Spencer with a playful smile. "Like us."

"Yes, love," he says fondly.

Eleanor returns her attention to us. "How did you first meet?"

Ah, hell. I steal a glance at Maeve. We didn't discuss how open we should be about the past particulars. Should I admit we met at a grief support group? She's intensely private, never wanting people's sympathy as the *orphan.*

I don't want to add a lie when we're already in deception territory. But, like on the ice, I'm quick to spot an alternative play when I'm blocked, and I take that opening now.

"We met at a community center," I say. It's true—our group met there. "And right away, I noticed how big her heart was."

Also true.

Eleanor gasps, her eyes shining a little. Spencer smiles at his wife, clearly touched by her reaction.

Luckily, I can share the real story without giving away the private details. "She was caring and thoughtful, and she helped a lot of people with her openness," I say, looking at her.

Maeve smiles at me, her eyes soft. "So did you."

Eleanor reaches for her husband's hand. "That's love-ly." She pauses, then asks me, "Did you know then that you simply had to marry her?"

Did I? When she walked into that meeting ten years ago, I saw something special in her hazel eyes. They were sad, deeply so. But also hopeful. She knew she needed people. She knew she needed to talk and found what she needed. And I suppose I did too. We bonded over late nights snacking and watching comedies. Anything to escape the ache—me for Nora, who'd died before we could even try to be just friends, and Maeve for a life without her parents. We started visiting dive bars and diners, conducting hot sauce tests on burgers—veggie burgers for her—and we parlayed that into a decade of big adventures.

"I was impressed with her ability to handle hot sauce," I say dryly.

Maeve gives me a look, shaking her head. "No, you were jealous that I can take it hotter than you can."

"You're so mean, Mrs. Callahan," I tease the woman next to me.

She bobs a defiant shoulder. "It's just the truth."

Looking at the Greers, I point my thumb to Maeve. "She never lets me live it down. Fair, I suppose, since her heat tolerance is ghost pepper-level."

Maeve stage-whispers, "He's still in the green pepper stage."

Spencer tosses his head back, chuckling, then dead-pans, "No shame in that, Asher. At least you're decent on the ice."

"I won't quit the day job, then," I say, laughing.

"You'd better not," he says sternly.

Eleanor presses for more romance. "So you bonded over hot sauce, and then you knew it was meant to be?"

Spencer tuts, squeezing his wife's hand. "Darling, I'm sure it took them time to figure it out."

Time. So much time. Was it wasted, though? Did I squander all those years when I could have been...what? Romancing my best friend? I dismiss the thought as pointless. Something in me is broken and has been for just over a decade. I wasn't even in love with Nora when she died, so it's not like I'm hung up on my first love. But losing her—someone I had loved, someone I wanted to keep as a friend...It's the kind of moment that changes a person. You realize all the ways that real love, in all its shapes and forms, can go wrong. But Maeve and I aren't doing this romance for real. So I give Eleanor the rom-com vibe she's after. "Well, the funny thing is," I confess, "we made a marriage pact two years ago." It's another bit of edited truth, and it fits with *our* public story. "I suppose that's when I knew it was meant to be."

"Ah, I love it. A pact," Eleanor coos.

I picture Maeve and me at Beckett's wedding the night we made the pact. The night I first noticed Maeve's glossy raspberry-colored lips and discovered how perfectly she fit in my arms. The moment I came face-to-face with how hungry I was to kiss her.

"Yeah, I knew it then," I confirm, my words thick with the memory, heat rushing through me.

Maeve's smile fades as she stares at me, lips parted, eyes wide like she's never seen me before. Or, rather, this side of me. "You did? Back then?" she asks, like it's just the two of us here.

In for a penny, in for a pound. I shrug, owning it. "I did."

She's quiet for a beat, her brow furrowing at the unexpected revelation. Well, it was certainly unexpected to me. But Maeve recovers with an easy smile, picking up the story and sending it toward the goal. "I thought he was joking about the pact," she tells the Greers with a chuckle.

"But why?" Eleanor's eyes sharpen, her nose twitching like a Bloodhound as she gestures to Maeve's hand. "He gave you that ring. Clearly, he wasn't joking."

Oh, dammit. No wonder Eleanor's dog is named after the famous English sleuth. Why didn't I think about the inconsistency in the ring timeline with a marriage pact? Is Eleanor trying to deduce why, if Maeve and I were engaged before Vegas, is she wearing that big, shiny gem for the first time today? Because pics will prove this ring is new. I'm convinced the words Sham Marriage flash in ruby-red neon over our heads.

But Maeve serenely raises her hand, admiring the ruby, seeming even a little transfixed by it. "The ring is only new. But I suppose it was meant to be too. I was looking at this ring months ago in my favorite jewelry shop. It's my color—red. And when we returned from Vegas, Asher surprised me with it. It still hardly feels real."

My shoulders relax. What a perfect response and a brilliant save.

"Nothing says real like a big ring," Spencer tells me in a man-to-man tone.

"Don't I know it," I say, leaning into his vibe for the moment.

Then Maeve locks eyes with the romantic across the table from her. "Actually, Eleanor, the whole thing kind of feels like a dream. Or like a dream becoming reality. And I suppose when we made the pact, it was sweet and playful, and I wasn't ready to believe it could be real."

Another perfect detail painted into the story. It prompts me to carry the tale forward.

"It was real," I say. "It was also..." I trail off, unsure how far to go, how much truth to infuse into the tale.

"A promise?" Eleanor offers eagerly.

"I suppose it was." I settle back into my chair, feeling pretty damn good about the play we're presenting. "Now, I can see it was a promise I needed to keep. Once she bid on me at the players' auction, and we went away, well, it all clicked."

"And you went viral. I just loved all the photos—you and the couple you gave the room to, the concert, the roulette game. Even the auction kiss."

"Ah, it's so lovely." She turns to her husband. "Maybe we should pay it forward too. With a kiss."

She doesn't need to tell him twice. Spencer leans in and presses a quick, affectionate kiss to Eleanor's lips. Except...nope, it's not quick. It lingers. It lasts longer than I'd expected.

When he finally pulls back, he shrugs, but his smile is cocksure. "My wife is irresistible."

"It's good that you feel that way." I think back to earlier at the coffee shop when Maeve and I re-established our rules—nothing physical. Maeve seemed to need that line in the sand, so I'll respect it. I keep my hands to myself for the rest of brunch as, at last, the conversation shifts to the mural and away from us.

"By estimates I've been given, it should take several weeks—anywhere from eight to ten," Eleanor says.

Maeve's eyes widen. "Oh. Really?"

Shit. Does that bother her? Eleanor picks up on Maeve's surprise and asks, "That won't be a problem, will it?"

Maeve quickly recovers. "Of course not."

When brunch ends, we offer to clean up, but they decline. Eleanor says she needs to gather her notes for the mural and then arranges to meet Maeve at the arena later.

"I'll bring Holmes," she tells Maeve. "He likes to keep me company. Does that work for you?"

Maeve snorts. "I believe the question is—does that sound like the best way to work?"

Eleanor smiles. "Like I said, kismet."

"It is," she agrees and waves at the dog when we pass him on the way to the door. In the foyer, Eleanor tilts her head, assessing us like puzzle pieces, roaming her eyes over Maeve and me.

"I remember the honeymoon phase," she muses. "We couldn't keep our hands off each other. But maybe young people today are different."

Wait. What the hell?

I feel like I've just been checked into the boards. My

head is rattling. She thinks I'm not into my wife because I didn't touch her ten million times like they did?

"That's not the case," I say quickly, defensively. I reach for Maeve's hand, but she's holding her bag, and I miss it.

Great. Just great. Now I look like an awkward teen flailing around on his first date.

Spencer offers me a sympathetic smile and a clap on the shoulder. "There, there. You'll figure it out."

I stare at them, dumbfounded. A perfect routine, which I fucked up by not touching her like the Greers touch each other. We didn't stick the landing, and that's what the judges will remember.

We leave, and once inside my car, I grip the wheel hard, dropping my head on it. "So much for that show."

When I look up a few seconds later, Maeve gives an apologetic wince. "I guess we need to be as handsy as they are next time. Who knew? I'm so sorry."

"Don't be," I murmur, frustrated I missed that detail. I don't like to fuck up. I don't like to make mistakes. I don't like asking my next question, but I have to know.

"When she said the mural could take eight to ten weeks—did that bother you? I know it's longer than we'd planned to stay married."

"No," she says quickly, cutting off that notion. "It's fine. I'm good. I was just worried about you. Are you okay staying married that long?"

So good with it. "Definitely. With the charity launch and everything, it makes sense." I try to keep my response casual, though I'm pumping a fist virtually.

"I promise I'll get better at acting." She nibbles on the corner of her lips. "I'm just not that good at faking it, I guess."

And I could take that a million ways, but I take it the

right one. I know she liked holding my hand earlier outside the shop. I know she loved it in Vegas when I kissed her like I couldn't get enough of her. And I would bet my entire hockey career on how very much she'd like to ride my cock again.

That's not what she has a hard time faking.

What's tough for Maeve is *not* being her true, authentic self. She means she wanted to touch me. So she wasn't that good at *not* touching me.

I fight off the biggest, cockiest grin ever. My wife wants me. The Greers want authentic? I'll give it to them.

"I have an idea," I say.

"Count me in," she replies without asking what it is.

We drive to the Marina, and along the way, she turns to me, her expression shifting. "Do you think it's true? That I was her first choice all along?"

"Of course," I say as we cruise toward the bay, glittering in the afternoon sun. "Why wouldn't that be true?"

"She said they like to work with players' partners. What if they waited until we were married to hire me?"

She sounds so vulnerable, and it tugs hard on my heart. "Maeve, they hired *you, not me.* It's your name going on the mural, not mine."

"Right, but what if they did it to make you happy?"

Oh hell. How can I ever reassure her? "Look, I'm not even in a contract year. They're not sucking up to me. You got this job on your merits," I say, trying, desperately trying.

She flashes a smile that quickly turns to a frown. "I don't want to be handed things because I'm...Mrs. Callahan."

"You're not," I say emphatically, wishing she could see what I see in her talent. "You got this on your own terms.

She said you were her top choice. Hell, she opened up the field just because she was blown away by you and wanted to make sure she was being fair. And she came back to you."

She shudders out a sigh, then nods like she's trying to absorb that truth. "Thanks, Asher. I seriously appreciate that."

"Get used to it, wife. There's more where that came from," I say. I'll do whatever it takes for her to know I believe in her.

"And I think you deserve a badge for being a great temporary husband," she says.

But to earn it, I need to do everything I can to make everyone believe in this marriage.

I park near the water and take her hand as we walk across Crissy Field. When we stop, I hold out my phone, the Golden Gate Bridge rising high behind us.

"Smile for social," I say.

She does, bright and beautiful—a clear smile that burrows deep into my heart. But it's not enough.

I don't want a smile for the camera. I want to show the whole damn world that I can't keep my hands off my wife. But I don't want to presume she wants a kiss too, so I start to ask. "What about—?"

"A kiss for social?"

It's the best finished thought ever.

"Yes." I tug her against me, her back to my chest. I wrap an arm around her waist, and then, with my free hand, I cup her jaw and turn her toward me. I kiss her, long, slow, deep—the kind of kiss that's a prelude to how I want to fuck her.

I mentally record her reaction—her sighs, her hungry murmurs, and most of all, the way she surrenders to the kiss. She tilts her chin, she parts her lips, and she invites me to kiss her thoroughly with everything I've got.

That's who she is. Someone who gives fully, who loves deeply, who wants with her whole soul. I kiss her by the bridge and in front of the ocean so we can tell our story.

When we break the kiss, she sighs—a deep, satisfied sound. "You kiss me a lot."

She's not wrong. "Want me to stop?" I ask like it'd be no big deal. Only, it'd be a terrible deal.

"No," she says, then smiles up at me. "Who knew my best friend was such a good kisser?"

I drop a kiss onto her nose. "I guess you know now."

"I do know," she says in a feathery whisper.

I drive Maeve to the arena so she doesn't miss her appointment with Eleanor, telling her goodbye as she goes inside.

But I don't take off yet. I do what the guys said I should do—make this official on social.

I post the bridge photo with a caption, keeping it cheeky.

Can't spell kindness without kiss. And I can't kiss without my brilliant wife, Maeve Hartley. What have you done to be kind today?

I tag the Sea Dogs and Maeve, hoping the Greers see it.

If anyone doubted I want my wife, they'd better not doubt it now. But for all Eleanor talked about loving our photos, she doesn't even like this one.

Well, you can't get lucky every time.

26

THE FOLD PROBLEM

Maeve

If the brunch with the Greers was an out-of-town tryout, this dinner three nights later with the Total Teamwork board is opening night for the Broadway show. *Presenting Mr. and Mrs. Callahan.*

And I plan to earn a standing ovation.

It's been a busy week, working on the sketches for the mural both at the arena and at home. But on Friday night, at Everly's place, I put murals, paint, acrylics, and ladders out of my mind as I zip up my navy blue sheath, one of my painting-party dresses.

My friend smiles approvingly. "You look amazing," she says. I can't believe you snagged this at Goodwill."

"I can't believe someone bought this and never wore it. The tags were still on when I found it," I say.

"Thank god for fancy ladies who buy too much."

"Indeed," I say. I look in the mirror, admiring the shoes Everly let me borrow—basic nude heels. "Tasteful dress. Styled hair. Understated pumps. Will my husband even recognize me without an outrageous outfit on?"

"Oh, I'm pretty sure he'll *always* recognize you," she says, knowing. "The man doesn't take his eyes off you when you're around."

Scoffing, I shoot her a look. "Please."

"Don't *please* me. You know it's true."

My stomach has the audacity to swoop. I like her suggestion too much. Which means it's best not to focus on it at all. I don't want to cling to my temporary husband. "Anyway, give me your best tips for a fancy-pants dinner."

"Don't use the word labia," she says.

I jerk my gaze to her, jaw falling open. "Why would I use the word labia?"

"I don't know but I wanted to pass on the tip," she says earnestly.

"Did you say labia at work today? Tell the truth."

"God no," she says, frowning. "But I was in a bookstore the other day and overheard some of the employees talking about words they don't love in romance novels. One of those words was 'folds,' which then turned into a conversation about different sizes of folds, which then turned into a conversation about labia, which then turned into a discussion on how nobody should discuss labia so I thought I should pass it on."

"I am shooketh," I say.

She nods in solidarity. "I am also shooketh."

"And yet you still said labia."

"That is how much of a good friend I am to you. I don't want you to run into the fold problem. So I'm passing on the tip."

I let my gaze turn skyward. "How on earth am I going to make it through dinner now without saying folds or labia?" I narrow my eyes and look at my friend. "Thanks, Everly. Thanks a lot."

She smiles. Serenely. "You are welcome."

"You are not helpful," I say, wagging a finger as a text from Asher pops up on my phone, letting me know he's here.

"Oh, but I think you'll find I really am," she says. "I guarantee you won't say labia."

"Stop. Just stop speaking," I say, then I give my friend a hug and head downstairs to meet my husband.

Husband.

Such a strange thought. But I glance at my ruby ring, and something feels a little fizzy in my chest. I head outside and find Asher waiting on the steps, looking mouth-wateringly hot in tailored charcoal slacks and a purple dress shirt that shows off his firm chest and strong biceps.

I stop in my tracks for a second. His eyes widen. "Wow," he says, right as I say, "You clean up well."

We both laugh, a little awkwardly. Is this how newly-weds behave? I don't know. They're probably used to compliments. I back up and try again.

"You look great," I say.

"And you're stunning," he says, then holds my gaze for a long, weighty beat that makes my pulse skitter. "Should we go?"

"Right. Yes. We should."

He walks me to his car at the curb, his hand on the small of my back the whole way.

And the whole way to dinner, I'm thinking of his hands on me, and his lips, and how he kissed me the other day by the Golden Gate Bridge.

Well, that's a better thing to think about than folds.

* * *

Asher and I step into the restaurant's private dining room, greeted by a long, elegantly set table filled with flickering candlelight and soft conversation. The board members of Total Teamwork are already seated, with Soraya at the head of the table, her usual poised and warm smile in place.

"Mr. and Mrs. Callahan, right on time," she says, standing to greet us. "Glad you could make it."

I flash a smile, hoping it hides my nerves. How do actors do this acting thing? "Wouldn't miss it," I say, hoping that sounds like *wife-speak*.

Soraya introduces us to the rest of the board members, who nod in greeting. There's Terrence, the retired football coach with a booming laugh; Lydia, sharp and no-nonsense, known for her commitment to charity; and Marcus, a laid-back sports psychologist. My brother, Beckett, and his wife, Reina, are also here along with Soraya's partner, Aram.

We take our seats, and the conversation flows easily—sports, the upcoming family picnic in the park, anecdotes about the others' work with kids. Soraya pipes up, saying they need to push the picnic out by a few more weeks due to a scheduling conflict with the park. "No problem," Asher says. "I don't have a game that day, so the new date works just fine." He turns to me. "And you?"

I'm flattered to even be asked, but yes, of course it works for me. He's staying married to me for the mural job, which will go for at least a couple more weeks after that so that's all good.

The conversation shifts to tales of past glory and present. Asher's in his element, flashing that easy charm of his. But it's more than charm—there's real passion behind it, and watching and listening to their conversation eases my mind.

After we order, my pulse settles more.

I've got this. I know the marriage script we wrote the other day. We've been friends for years, made a marriage pact for fun at my brother's wedding, and once we were in Vegas, we just knew it was what we wanted—getting hitched.

I'm ready for their relationship questions if they ask them, and just as appetizers arrive, Terrence leans forward with a grin as if on cue. "So, newlyweds, huh? Have you planned your honeymoon yet? Or are you two still in work mode?"

My stomach drops. Honeymoon? We didn't script that part. I glance at Asher, hoping he'll take the lead.

"We've been pretty busy," Asher says smoothly, "but we've talked about a few places."

"Bali," I blurt out, nodding as if it's the most natural thing in the world. "Or maybe the Maldives. Something tropical."

"Oh, tropical," Lydia says, raising an approving eyebrow. "Nice choice."

"I'd love to go to Bali someday," Aram chimes in.

"I think we all would," Lydia says. "Will you head over when the season ends?"

Thank you, Lydia, for giving us an easy out. "Yes, April should be nice," I say.

Asher clears his throat, shooting me a skeptical look. "April?"

Shit. What's wrong with April?

Beckett laughs. "Maeve, did you forget The Cup is in June?"

My cheeks flush. "I'm a terrible hockey wife. Of course, it won't be until June."

Asher turns to me with a smile. "And besides, I think we should go to Paris. I have a feeling that's where you really want to go."

My stomach flips. He remembered what I said about ring shopping in Paris. My fantasy. "I suppose I would."

"Good thing we asked," Terrence says with a chuckle. "Gotta help you get to know your wife, Asher."

Asher doesn't miss a beat. "I know my wife. She picked the Maldives for me. I like the tropics, being from Canada and all. But she likes Paris, and what my wife wants...she gets."

A shiver slides down my chest. I'm a little turned on from Asher's words. But that seems to be my new norm these days.

"Words to live by," Marcus says, lifting his glass of wine. We all do the same. Then Marcus glances at Beckett. "And now you've got a brother."

That's when the wine goes right out my nose. I grab my napkin, dabbing at the mess, mortified. I almost wish I'd said "labia" instead.

"Right," I sputter. "Beckett has a brother now."

Open mouth—insert nude heel because that's not a weird thing to say at all.

Reina cuts in, saving me. "And that's really what Total Teamwork is about, right? Everyone supporting each other."

Relief washes over me, but it's short-lived because right as I set down the glass, Lydia leans in, her eyes sparkling with mischief. "And how's domestic life? Figured out who does what around the house yet? That's the real challenge of marriage."

I freeze. We don't even live together. How do I answer this? Asher tenses beside me, but I jump in, keeping my tone light and teasing. "We're still negotiating that. Asher's convinced his method of folding towels is superior, but I'm not so sure."

Asher raises an eyebrow, clearly playing along. "Because you fold them into origami swans."

Oh, great. He just had to say that. "What can I say? I like birds."

Then Marcus, of all people, grins and picks up his napkin. "I love napkin origami. Can you show us?"

Wait. What? My heart stutters. Show them? Here? I throw Asher a wide-eyed look that very clearly says, *I'm going to kill you.*

My brother chuckles under his breath, and Reina looks away, hiding a smile. Meanwhile, Asher's just sitting there with that charming smile, seeming oblivious to the situation he's put me in. "They look like swans to me," he says, not helping at all.

I clench my jaw but manage a smile. "Give me a second. I need to powder my nose."

I hustle to the restroom, where I pull out my phone and quickly look up napkin origami on YouTube. Of course, the swan is ridiculously complicated. I opt for a fan, then a frog, then a bird—fuck it. I'm an artist. Where there's a will—or YouTube—there's a way.

I return to the table, grab my napkin, and fold the hell out of it, setting it down with panache. "Asher calls them swans, but really, he's just blinded by his love for me. They're fans," I say, patting his shoulder. "Next stop—swans."

Asher stares at the napkin in awe, lips parted. "You

have many talents," he says, his voice low. "You can fold the towels anytime."

I study the napkin a beat longer. It's not a bad fan at all. I can't believe I pulled that off.

Marcus raises his glass. "Impressive," he says with an approving nod. "You're full of surprises, Maeve."

"Thank you," I say, relaxing into the compliment, proud of my improv skills.

Asher leans in and drops a kiss on my cheek, his lips lingering for just a second longer than necessary. Under the table, his hand finds mine, giving it a light squeeze. It's subtle, but the warmth of the gesture feels like reassurance—maybe even something more.

And I can't wait to tell Everly that Asher said "folds" and it wasn't filthy.

When dinner is over, I'm relieved Asher and I pulled that off. We head outside with the rest of the board, and I turn to Asher, smile politely at the group, and say, "Well, I should head out. The next bus comes in a few minutes."

The words have barely left my mouth when I catch the strange looks from Lydia, Terrence, and Marcus. Lydia's brow furrows slightly, and Terrence's booming laugh is replaced with a confused blink. Marcus tilts his head, his curiosity almost palpable.

"Catch the bus?" Lydia asks, as if the idea is completely foreign.

I freeze. *Oh no. They think we live together.* As married couples do. My stomach flips in panic.

Before I can sputter out an awkward explanation, Asher smoothly steps in. "Honey," he says with a grin, sliding his arm around my waist. "You're still getting used to living with me. It's adorable."

He loops an arm around my waist, says goodbye, then steers me toward his car, opening the passenger door like a perfect gentleman. "I was going to drive you home anyway."

"I'm sorry," I say.

He turns to me. "Don't be. You were amazing. You saved me with that swan fan."

"And you saved me with the ride," I say.

"We saved each other," he says, then backs up and cruises toward my home in Hayes Valley, and the whole time I'm wondering what it would be like if we were really going to his place.

27

A BIG COMPLICATION

Asher

It's weird pulling up to her apartment now. Weird because I want to walk her upstairs. Weird because I want to take her home. Weird, too, because we're lying.

I'm supposed to be driving her to *our* home. Not her little apartment.

Since there are no parking spots out front, I pull down a tiny side street, past a park that's closed at night, then cut the engine.

But I don't make a move to go. I should. "I think we pulled it off," I say.

"Thanks to me! For a while there I thought you were tanking us with your swan comment," she says.

I'm still impressed. "How did you pull that off?"

"YouTube, *honey*," she says, using a term of endearment. I don't mind it at all.

"Very impressive, *honey*. Too bad Eleanor didn't see us.

She didn't even see that photo I posted the other day with the bridge behind us," I point out.

"If a hockey player posts a kissing photo online and no one sees it, did the kiss even exist?" she asks, going all faux philosophical.

"Good question," I say.

"How do you know?"

Well, that's an opening if I ever spotted one. I lift a hand and run it down her hair. She trembles as I touch her, and that drives me on. That, and the feel of her soft strands—god, I fucking love her hair. I drop a kiss to her forehead, lingering there.

It's innocent as far as kisses go. But I don't feel innocent when I touch her. I feel...powerless to resist her. "No one can see us now," I murmur, pulling back and gesturing to the tinted windows in my car.

Her breath hitches. "No one saw us in the hotel room either," she points out, like she's taking stock of the kisses that weren't for show. That weren't for the public or for performance.

The kisses just for us. I tuck a strand of hair behind her ear. I really shouldn't do this. We have a no-touching rule and I'm definitely breaking it right now. But I think of those napkin fans that looked like swans to me. The way she pulled that off. Her dress. *Her.* Just her. "Good thing no one saw us in the hotel room when you had that screaming orgasm."

"And you still haven't dry-humped me in return. Shame," she says, adding an eye roll, like she's making light of it.

My dick isn't thinking light of it though. My dick likes that idea too much. But is she hinting at something? Or is that only wishful thinking on my part? I glance around.

We're in my car, parked on a street, at night. But then again, no one can see inside.

I'm this close to saying *Tell me what you want, and I'll give it to you.*

But the thing is—I don't think she entirely knows what she wants from me. So I cup her cheek and draw her close, but somehow find the will to stop before our lips touch again. "You said this was complicated," I murmur.

"I did. It is," she says, but her lips move closer to mine.

She's millimeters from me now, and the scent of her skin and the softness of her mouth is going to my head. "It's very complicated," I say.

Then, before I risk another kiss, she slides a hand up my thigh. I groan. Her fingers walk closer. "A very big complication," she whispers, then her palm covers my hard-on.

She cups my dick through my clothes, and this should not feel so fucking good. It should not feel like a fucking revelation. My chest should not be burning, my stomach should not be tightening, and my brain should not be short-circuiting.

She's just stroking my hard-on, for fuck's sake. Yet it feels too damn good. I hiss a breath through my teeth, knowing, *knowing*, I should stop this. We're friends. We're fake married. We've got more than a month of this show.

But Maeve's hand on my dick is the best kind of complication I've felt in ages. So I crush my lips to hers and kiss her deeply while she strokes my hard-on through my pants. My brain pops and my chest heats. Everything in me is amped up, the volume turned high. My head goes hazy, and I'm going to come so fucking hard when I get home tonight. It'll be a wonder if I make it through the door without unzipping my pants.

Because...this is too good.

She kisses me back more deeply, her tongue stroking mine while her talented hand that made a napkin into a swan-fan, or a fan-swan cups my dick. Then she squeezes it—hard, firm, purposefully.

I grunt out a carnal yes, maybe a swear word, I don't even know. My mind is on fire. Maeve squeezes my cock again, then breaks the kiss, murmuring, "Or maybe it's not so complicated?"

She lifts a questioning brow, her eyes gleaming in the soft glow of the streetlamps.

"Maybe not," I rasp out because I can't really think straight right now. Not with her hand rubbing up and down. I'm in the driver's seat, my cock heavy in my pants and my best friend watching me with avid, curious eyes.

Watching and stroking. Turning me inside out with a lust that takes me hostage. My whole body is crackling. My cock is throbbing, and I'm so damn aroused I can feel a bead of pre-come forming at the tip. I grit my teeth and breathe out hard like I can hold back this desire banging at the gate.

She tilts her head, her eyes entranced, her lips curving up. The awareness of how into this she is sends my temperature shooting higher, making me somehow even harder. Then she licks her lips and whispers, "Can I?"

I don't have the willpower to turn her down. I don't even know what she's asking, and I don't care. My dick is jumping up and down for joy, saying *yes, fuck yes* before my mouth does. But I say it. Oh hell, I say it with my whole entire chest. "Yes."

Helping her along, I unzip my pants, and two seconds later, my wife dips an eager hand inside, covering the fabric of my boxer briefs. I shudder an embarrassing amount. That feels so good.

But it's the look on her face that sends me into overdrive. My mind short-circuits as her lips part in filthy glee. "*Asher*," she whispers reverently as she palms my cock through the cotton.

One word. My name. But it's the sultry way it slides past those pretty lips.

My dick shouts *it's go time*. My whole body jumps. Pleasure grips me. Everywhere. I lean my head back, gritting my teeth, trying to fight off the punishing wave of lust that slams into me. But it's no use.

I'm helpless.

My vision blurs. My brain goes offline.

That's all it takes. Two seconds later, I'm grunting, grabbing her hand, spilling into my CheekyBeasts, cursing up a storm. "Fuck, fuck, fuck."

The aftershocks don't stop. They pop in every damn cell. I feel drunk in the best of ways. Hazy, happy, wild, thrilled.

When I open my eyes, reality hits. I can't believe I came in my pants. But I can't believe the wicked smile on my wife's face either. She's too damn pleased. "Happy one-week anniversary, hubby. I guess we're even now."

It takes me a beat, and then I say, "Tomorrow's our anniversary. We were married after midnight," I point out.

"Details," she says, then smirks again at my lap. "I'd let you walk me to the door but looks like you have some other *details* to deal with."

I wave her off. "Don't be so cocky."

"Oh, I'm going to be cocky. I'm going to be so very cocky." She tilts her head to the side, that grin never leaving. "Also, thanks to your flamingos or whatever they are today, we still didn't break our no-touching rule."

"Shame. Such a shame."

With a playful glint in her eyes that near about kills me, she opens the car door, then tosses a sexy-as-fuck look my way. "Goodnight...Quick-Draw Asher."

"You're mean," I growl.

"And you like it."

And...she's right.

But I'm right about something too. I knew it was our one-week anniversary. "Maeve, there's a gift in the back seat for you. Take it and wear it to my game on Monday night."

28

THE WET BLANKET KIND

Maeve

Asher flies down the ice, hellbent on chasing the puck on Monday night, flipping it back and forth with Wesley and my heart slams against my rib cage.

"C'mon, c'mon, c'mon," I shout, urging him to score. "Get it, Asher!"

I rise to my feet.

When Asher winds up the stick and slams the puck past the goalie, I go wild, arms in the air. "That's how you do it!"

Asher and Wesley skate past the bench for fist bumps —or glove bumps, really—then glide past me. I'm behind the glass a few rows back, wearing my one-week anniversary gift—a Number Twenty-Nine jersey. He locks eyes with me and blows me a kiss.

In front of the entire rink. I catch it. It's part of our game—the public kissing game. But still, I feel giddy, even when he hops over the boards for the line change, and I sit down next to my aunt.

She's a hockey fan, but not the way I am. She's pragmatic to the core. "The game's not over yet," she warns me.

Yup. Like I said. She's the worst kind of fan. The wet blanket kind.

"I'm still happy they scored." I won't let her, or any other fans, get me down—like the women holding up signs offering to be Asher's second wife even though I'm right here.

But I'm the only one who made him come in his pants, so really, I think I'm winning the wife wars.

When the team goes on to win the game a little later, "Tick Tick Boom" blasting through the arena, I grin at Vivian. "See? My optimism paid off."

She shakes her head. "I can never cheer till it's over."

And that makes me a little sad for her.

* * *

Asher, Vivian, and I grab a post-game bite at a bar next to the arena. Asher keeps a close watch on the time. He needs to catch the bus with the team in half an hour, heading out to the Sea Dogs jet for a long road trip.

He orders a chicken sandwich, Vivian picks a burger, and I opt for a tofu scramble.

"You need more protein," Aunt Vivian says, tutting after I order.

"Tofu literally is protein."

She hums doubtfully. "Still, it's a good idea to have more," she says, her gaze drifting down my torso.

That's odd.

She shifts quickly, flashing a smile at both of us. "So,

dinner is on me. A celebration. Now that you're building a family."

Asher wheezes. "Excuse me?"

I blanch, then raise my hand in protest. "Nobody said anything about building a family."

Vivian shoots me a look that says, *Don't be ungrateful.* Then her eyes soften as she glances briefly at her own belly. "Well, you should try...before it's too late."

Children? That's not even remotely on my radar right now—or ever, honestly. There are too many things I still want to do.

"Don't you think, Asher?" she asks, turning to my husband.

His face is ashen. He parts his lips. But nothing comes out. I don't blame him.

"Vivian, we're not trying to have kids," I say.

"But you probably will. Someday." Determined, she turns to Asher and peppers him with questions about his career, his health, his injury status, his contract status, his standing with the team, and a million other things.

It's exhausting, and after thirty minutes, I feel like we've lived a thousand years.

He checks his watch and gives an apologetic smile. "I have to go. But thank you so much for dinner, Vivian."

"Of course. It was a pleasure," she says.

"I'll be right back," I tell her and walk him to the door of the bar. I step closer to him, so only he can hear. "Sorry about that."

He shakes his head. "Don't be. She just wants to know someone can take care of you."

"I can take care of myself," I say.

"I know, but maybe she doesn't know you like I do," he says, then drops a quick, firm kiss on my lips.

A kiss that I feel in my toes.

When he breaks it, my heart aches a little bit, then a little more when he says, "I guess we made it through our *three performances.*"

"I guess we did," I say, a little wistful. I enjoyed them, stumbles, fumbles, and all. Perhaps there's even a part of me that hopes for more.

But isn't that like me? Always wanting more. Enough is never enough. I hold on to everything too tightly, so before I do that to Asher, I smile brightly and wave goodbye.

"Bye, wife," he says softly, and I feel that in my knees. They're a little weak.

He heads down the block, then turns the corner, out of sight and on his way to a plane that'll take him across the country.

I sigh, feeling the pang of missing him already.

I run my finger along my bottom lip, remembering that kiss. Then, as I return to the table, I remember the kiss from earlier last week.

The one he'd hoped Eleanor would see. Well, I can make sure she does.

* * *

The next day, while working with Eleanor in her office at the arena, I show her some sketches on my phone—which happens to be open to that kissing photo from last week. Her eyes widen. "Great picture," she says.

"Isn't it?" I say with a happy, newlywed sigh. "Sometimes, he can't keep his hands off me."

"Well, that's clear," she says with a conspiratorial smile.

She waters the seed I planted, reposting the photo that afternoon with the caption: ***For every repost, I'll donate one dollar to any one of these three charities our team supports.***

Then she lists a food bank, an animal rescue, and the Friends of the Library Association. When I tell Asher about it that evening, he says, "I've always said you were a good luck charm."

Or maybe I just wanted to give him what he wanted.

THERE'S ALWAYS A CATCH

Asher

The third period is winding down, and New York clings to a one-goal lead. We have ten minutes to shave that. I race down the ice, passing the puck to Falcon as we hunt for an opening.

But New York's relentless, and their defenseman Karlsson won't lay off me. The second I spot an opening and try to sneak it past the goalie, he cuts across, swiping it from me, then flashes a dickhead smile. "You're a little distracted, Callahan. Must be all that kissing."

I know better than to rise to the bait. Assholes like Karlsson thrive on getting a reaction, and he's the league's leading asshole. If you don't give in, they've got nothing. But I can't ignore him completely—that fucker is talking about my wife. "Yeah, but I wouldn't expect you to know what that's like."

"Don't expect you to know what good hockey is like," he says, then races ahead of me.

I dig my blades into the ice, muscles burning as I chase him down. My breath comes in sharp bursts as I fight for control of the puck along the boards with Karlsson and a couple of New York guys. I grit my teeth, jabbing my stick into the scrum and snagging the puck, but Karlsson's still tight on me, his breath hot against my ear.

"You thinking about kissing her now, Callahan?" Karlsson's smirk is almost audible in his voice.

The puck bounces loose, and I rush to recover it. But fuck me—I swing too high, too fast. My stick clips Karlsson across the chest.

Before I can react, he drops theatrically to the ice.

"Are you fucking kidding me?" I mutter as the whistle blows, sharp and shrill. The referee's arm shoots up. High-sticking. It wasn't intentional, but that doesn't matter. The damage is done. Jaw ticking, I skate to the penalty box as New York fans chant, "Power play."

And New York scores ten seconds later.

I slam my stick against the boards in frustration. When the clock winds down, I'm back out there, determined to make up for it. I chase down the puck, race toward the goal, and fling it at the empty spot in the net—but the New York goalie deflects it.

Karlsson skates past me. "Bet your wife can kiss you and make it better."

She can, but that's not for him to know. I spin around, gloves halfway off, my voice razor-sharp. "Leave my wife out of this."

I've never been a fighter. I'm the one who stops fights. But right now, I'm ready to throw gloves. Before I do something I'll regret, Falcon grabs my right arm. Bryant grabs the left, holding me back.

"He's not worth it," Bryant mutters. He should know—
he used to play with that jerk.

I blow out a harsh breath and skate away.

Hopping over the boards for the shift change, I yank
off my helmet and drop my head in frustration. Coach
McBride strides by, cool and focused, like he always is. He
levels me with an intense stare. "Keep your head in the
game, Callahan."

"I will, sir," I reply with a tight nod.

Hockey is my happy place. My escape. It's where
everything makes sense. I need to get that mentality
back.

Pep talk done, I shove off the frustration and jump
back out there for the next line change, scrambling for the
puck. But New York's faster, and they keep it away from us
till the horn blares with their win.

When the game ends, Karlsson sails past me. "Maybe
next time your wife wants a quickie marriage, she'll
choose someone who plays to win."

He's not getting the last word in. No fucking way. The
game's over. The refs are skating off the oval. So I catch up
to him before he reaches the gate, flashing a fuck-off
smile. "Say one more word about my wife, and you'll be
picking up your teeth off the ice. Got it?"

His eyes widen, flickering with fear. Good. I like that.
He gulps—even better. But just in case there's any misunderstanding, I add with my best good-guy charm, "Sounds
like we're clear on that."

He mumbles something unintelligible.

Fine by me. I skate off to our tunnel, chest heaving—
not from exhaustion, but from frustration. This game got
messy fast, and I should have kept my cool.

I didn't, and that's not like me. When I hit the ice, I

treat it like a game. Like it's fun. And I have a good time. I'll have to get back to that.

Once I'm showered and changed into my suit, I do my best to put hockey out of my mind for the night. There's only one person I want to talk to, but I'll have to wait till I get a minute alone.

On the short flight to Boston, where we'll play tomorrow evening, I close my eyes, but I don't nap. I listen to a comedian, and when I'm finally in the quiet of my hotel room that night, I pull out my phone and call Maeve. The phone rings twice before she picks up, her voice soft but teasing. "Tough game?"

She watched it, and that...well, it thrills me. She's seen plenty of my games over the years, but Monday night was the first time she watched as my wife. What would it be like if she were in the stands regularly at home? I let my imagination run wild, seeing her in my jersey for every home game, cheering me on. That's a real nice thought, and it definitely perks me up.

"You could say that." I sink into the bed, rubbing the back of my neck. "Karlsson was chirping the whole game. But screw him."

She pauses for a moment. "What was he saying?"

I hesitate. She doesn't need to know the details. Part of protecting her—part of this fake marriage—is keeping her out of the mess that comes with my world. She's got enough on her plate already. "Nothing worth repeating. Just hockey stuff."

There's a beat of silence before I steer the conversation away. "How's the mural coming along?"

"Good but exhausting. It's easily the biggest project I've ever done. Normally, we'd start with the concept, but that was done as part of the submission. So we jumped right in and finished the sketches and the color palettes. Looked at them in the space itself."

"And was Holmes there?"

"He was. Don't tell Eleanor, but he's a little in love with me. Though, I think she figured it out when he tried to hump my leg."

"That might be a dead giveaway," I say.

"True, true. And I've been working through the sketches on my tablet back at my place. And my butt has never hurt more from the spring in my couch," she says.

"So it's a pain in the ass?"

"Bah-bump," she says. "And I'll probably work through the weekend. I have a lot to get done."

"Just be sure you get enough sleep," I tell her. I could rattle off a hundred benefits of a good night of rest. I know them all. By heart. But I stick to the big ones, so it's not obvious that I've researched this topic. "It's important for good health and brain function and creativity, which you need."

"Yes, Doctor Google. You always know what I need. It's like that time I thought I sprained my ankle when I was working on a mural for that new café."

I remember that perfectly—she twisted her ankle coming down from a ladder a couple years ago. "You just needed some ice and to rest it," I say, relieved again that she didn't need crutches. The sprain was minor.

"And you made sure I did just that. So, don't worry. I'll get plenty of rest this weekend too," she adds.

"Good."

The tension in my chest loosens a little. She has that effect—lightening my load without even realizing it.

We talk for a few more minutes, and by the time I

hang up, I feel more grounded. But the frustration from the game still lingers. I can't let it go.

So I pull up my phone again and start searching for articles about exhaustion, specifically, how it affects creativity. I want to make sure she'll be okay. That she's not going to work herself too hard. I scroll through pages from the Mayo Clinic, Cleveland Clinic, and more to make sure she's not hitting critical levels for exhaustion. Good news—she's not, by my diagnosis, but I'll be keeping an eye out for that as she works on this project.

Just as I'm about to put the phone down, Karlsson's comment from the game comes back to me. Maybe Maeve should know what he'd said to upset me, after all. I don't want to keep important things from her, and we're in this together.

Before I can talk myself out of it, I shoot her a quick text.

> Asher: Karlsson made some stupid comment about our viral post, something about all the kissing.

Her reply comes almost instantly.

> Maeve: Fuck him. I'll kiss you a thousand more times.

I can't help but smile. It's the kind of response only Maeve would give, and in that moment, Karlsson's chirps don't bother me anymore.

Friday night, we beat Boston in their barn, and after the game, Wesley appears at my door, riding a post-game high, insisting we go out to celebrate the victory. We don't travel again till tomorrow, so there's time.

"There's this place called Gin Joint that Josie told me about. Her librarian friends go there. And librarians know how to party," he says.

"I'm gonna trust you on that." I grab a jacket and follow him out.

Something nags at me as the door closes—the annoying feeling that I forgot to do something important.

We gather Miles and Max, who's joining us tonight since Everly's out with the Boston team's PR woman. Hugo's turning in early. We walk to the nearby lounge, and usually, I'd be all in for the casual strategy session, trading tips, and shop talk. But the nagging feeling is like there's a mosquito buzzing around my head that I can't swat away.

"What do you think? Is Boston tougher this year since they acquired Jorgen?" Max asks. "You're our stats guy."

I blink, realizing I've been zoning out as we walk in the cold February air. "Sorry, what were we talking about?"

Wesley laughs. "The time you stopped paying attention."

Miles gives me a curious look. "You all right, man?"

"Yeah, yeah, I'm good," I say, scratching my head. "But...what's today?"

"The day after yesterday and the day before tomorrow," Miles says, adopting a deeply philosophical tone.

"No, seriously. The date."

"Is your phone broken?" Miles retorts.

"I mean, is it like a holiday?"

"Yes, it's National Calendar Celebration Day," Max says. "Want to go calendar shopping?"

I wave them off, check my phone, and...it hits me. "I'm a dumbass."

Miles grins and spreads his arms wide as we reach Gin Joint. "Yes, he finally gets it!"

Wesley smirks. "Honestly, we all kind of knew you were just the pretty one. But why are you just realizing it now?"

I flip him the bird, grinning. "Pretty *and* smart, thanks. It's my two-week anniversary with Maeve tomorrow, and I need to get her something—something good."

Cue the jeers. Dear god, the jeers. They're worse than expected, and they don't stop as we head inside and order. But I don't care. Maeve will love a two-week gift for our fake marriage, especially after the one-week one. It'll show her what a good temporary husband I am. Besides, she deserves gifts. But what to get her?

After the server leaves, Wesley points to me. "This is going on the DickNose board."

"We don't need a top-five list," Max chimes in, stabbing the table with a finger. "This, tonight? You remembering a two-week anniversary? It's all we need on the whiteboard of Asher's Obsession with Maeve."

I stare him down. "Says the guy obsessed with Everly."

Max nods proudly. "As it should be." Then, he levels a no-bullshit stare at me. "What's the story, Callahan? You've had it bad for her for a while. You just went out and got married?"

His tone says he's not buying the story I was selling the other week at morning skate. He's waited almost two weeks for me to 'fess up on my own. I can't say I didn't see this line of questioning coming.

"The whole spur-of-the-moment thing did make me wonder if it was so spur of the moment," Miles puts in, tone curious, maybe a little skeptical too.

I scratch my jaw. "Yeah, the thing is..." But where to start? I don't want to get into the marriage pact. I definitely don't want to get into how Maeve was in a funk in Vegas and I wanted to cheer her up. But saying we got drunk-married does a disservice to the situation too. I try again. "It's complicated."

Miles's eyebrows shoot up. "As in the nine-month variety of complication?"

"Fuck no," I say, faster than I can shoot on an empty net.

"So what's up then?" Max asks again, never one to mince words.

These guys deserve the truth. "Look, the wedding just sort of happened. We were hanging out, having fun, and it seemed like a good idea at the time."

Wesley tilts his head, pauses, then cuts through the vagueness. "But you *stayed* married. And don't give us that whole kisses-equals-kindness bit." He rolls his eyes. "You seem way too into the two-fucking-week anniversary for this to be anything but something that maybe you want to keep happening."

Way to see right through me. I drag a hand over the back of my neck, weighing the situation again. These three guys are my closest friends on the team, and they've already sniffed out enough of the truth.

"Look," I begin, then fuck it. "She's...great. Okay? You happy now?"

Wesley offers his palm to Miles and Max. "Pay up, fuckers."

My jaw comes unhinged. "You bet on this? Assholes."

Max shakes his head, annoyed, but pulls out some bills from his wallet while Miles taps on his phone, presumably Venmoing some money to Wesley. "What the hell was the bet? You all were giving me shit about this forever."

Miles sighs heavily. "We bet on who'd get it out of you first tonight." He nods toward Wesley. "Bryant won."

I spread my arms out wide. "Seriously?"

"Like this surprises you?" Max asks.

He has me there. "Honestly, no."

"Also," Wesley says with a shit-eating grin, "I am very happy now. And two hundred bucks richer." Then he leans forward. "So what's next?"

I shrug. "No idea."

"But you're staying married?" he asks.

"For a couple of months, give or take." The words taste sour on my tongue.

"Good luck with your obsession, man," Max says. There's no sarcasm in his tone, just genuine concern.

I'm not sure how to answer him. Fact is, I am obsessed with my wife, and I don't know what to do about it. Maybe this is where I really do need some luck in my life.

When the server swings by with drinks, I'm grateful for the distraction.

Miles lifts his scotch, then says, "I guess that makes me officially the last man standing," he says, though he furrows his brow. "Sometimes, I wish that weren't the case."

"Is there someone?" Max asks.

Miles shrugs. "Maybe, but it's complicated."

"As in, the nine-month var—"

"No! God no." Miles tosses a napkin at me.

"In what way then?" Max presses.

As they talk more, I give in to the obsession, flashing back to the night Maeve and I got hitched, wondering what would make for a good present for her, then to last week, too, and the gift I got her. In no time, I have an answer. Now, if I can just find a place that works as fast as Maeve.

A few searches later, I'm placing an order for something special, asking the store to deliver it tonight. Then, I relax and knock back my beer, picturing Maeve's reaction when she opens the present.

When I return to the hotel with Max an hour later, I run into Everly in the lobby. She's just said goodnight to a friend, and once her friend leaves, she turns to me with a smile. "Just the man I wanted to see," she says.

"I thought I was that man," Max cuts in, growling.

She rolls her eyes at him. "I see plenty of you."

"Because I'm your type," he says, planting a kiss on her cheek before walking away to give her space. He's respectful like that when it comes to her job.

"What's up?" I ask, curious.

Everly waggles her phone my way. "Eleanor is going to be donating *a lot* of money with that repost," she says, then gives me the figure, and damn.

"That's nice," I say.

"Stop making my job so easy," she teases.

"That was all Maeve," I say, since my wife deserves the credit. Actually, she deserves so much more than credit. As I head into the elevator, a new realization hits me— Maeve isn't a good luck charm. She's a good luck catalyst. That wasn't fate or fortune looking out for us. That was

Maeve seeing what I wanted—for the Greers to know how I feel—and then *making* it happen.

My heart thumps harder at the awareness, and I grab my phone and send her a text, telling her the good news.

> **Asher:** You did this. You. Not luck. Just you.

> **Maeve:** I'm an instigator.

> **Asher:** The most diabolically clever instigator I've ever met.

> **Maeve:** The best compliment I've ever gotten. Also, here's a gift for you.

Attached is a digital badge, something she probably made in Photoshop. It's a blue ribbon and it says *Best Two-Week Temporary Husband.*

I laugh lightly, but the laughter fades when I spot the next image under it and the words *for you.*

A black-and-white pop-art sketch of a couple almost kissing. It's small, but it does funny things to my chest as I sink back into bed, running my finger over the silhouettes. I can't stop touching it. I can't stop thinking of her. And I can't help wishing for many more badges.

Most of all, I can't stop loving the words *for you.*

* * *

In the morning, another text lands. It's a photo of Maeve in the T-shirt I had made for her last night and rush-delivered to her place. She's giving the camera a look like she can't believe I did this, but there's a hint of a smile on her lips—even as she's flipping me double birds.

But I'm grinning too. In the pic, she's not wearing any pants, so really, I won. I've got a photo of my wife in her two-week anniversary shirt that says *Quick-Draw Maeve.*

She looks so spectacular, so…Maeve. Playful, sexy, all the things that make her, well, her, that I take matters into my own hand.

Happy anniversary to me indeed.

* * *

Later that morning, while I'm riding the exercise bike in the hotel gym before we take off for the next city, Everly marches in with a too-pleased smile on her face.

I pull out my earbuds, and she says proudly, "I've got some press requests about you," she says, all business now. "And they involve Maeve."

Didn't have that on my bingo card today. "Everything okay?" I ask, ready to do battle for Maeve if I have to.

She holds up her hands like she's telling me to stand down. "It's mostly feel-good stuff. You want the details?"

"I do," I say, still pedaling, my heart and legs pumping fast.

She rattles off a few lifestyle news sites that I've never heard of that want to do features. Stuff she can mostly handle on our behalf. Then, she adds, "Webflix has an entertainment news show that's pretty popular. *The Good Stuff.*"

"Yeah, I've heard of it." It's a soft show, focusing more on lifestyle than gossip.

"They love you and Maeve and the whole viral kindness thing. And they want to do a piece on the two of you."

Well, that sounds like something the Sea Dogs would eat up, and it'd raise Maeve's profile on her own merits, not just mine. "I'm interested. What's the catch?"

Because there's always a catch.

Everly glances around the workout room to check if the coast is clear. Then, lowering her voice, she says importantly, her meaning crystal clear: "They want to shoot it in *your* home. Where they think you and your wife live together."

I stop pedaling, my feet freezing mid-motion. "They think—" I start, but the rest of the words stall. *We live together.*

Then, they speed up on a loop in my head—*we live together.*

My pulse kicks into overdrive. This feels like Christmas, my birthday, and our anniversary all rolled into one, wrapped in a bow of dangerous temptation.

30

INSTANT WIFE, JUST ADD PLANTS

Maeve

"Put the ponytail palm next to the plastic orchid," I say, setting my real plants beside Asher's Lego creations in the spacious living room.

Beckett looks at me, frazzled. "Which one is the ponytail palm?"

Reina rolls her eyes dramatically at her husband. "The one that looks like a ponytail," she says, as if it's the most obvious thing in the world.

"It's the cute one," I explain, pointing to the small succulent with long, wild green leaves shooting from the top like an untamed hairstyle. "It looks like it has crazy hair."

"Like when I wake up," Reina jokes, tucking a strand of hair behind her ear.

Beckett raises both hands in surrender. "I'm staying out of trouble on this one, since your hair always looks beautiful," he says, backing away from the chaos that's taken over Asher's home. Me—I'm the chaos.

The door code Asher sent felt like an open invitation, and now here we are—setting up house. It's weird, no doubt about it. But also...kind of fun. "I'll handle it. It's highly recommended for any aspiring plant ladies," I say, grabbing the ponytail palm from the foyer table where Beckett had set it when he lugged in my plants from his car a few minutes ago. It's next to a stack of mail and a couple boxes that arrived for Asher this week. Things he asked me to bring in when he gave me the code. Like a wife would do and vice versa. Yep, we're playing house.

I carry the plant to the corner table in the living room, placing it beside the fiddle leaf fig I positioned earlier, adding another layer of green. My fingers brush against the smooth plastic of a Lego rose, and I pause, touched. I knew Asher had built the Lego orchid I gifted him years ago, but I didn't realize he'd made so many more. There are easily a half-dozen Lego plants now—roses and sunflowers and tiny shrubbery too. The table is a mix of real greenery and his creations. It's an odd contrast, but it works.

"This'll look good for the TV crew, right? Sort of a his-and-hers vibe," I say.

"Yeah, his-and-hers weird plants," Beckett teases.

Reina swats him lightly. "They're not weird."

"They're a little weird."

"You strip in your sleep. That's weird," she shoots back.

I cover my ears. "Okay, okay. I don't need to know about my brother's weird sleeping—or stripping—habits," I say, then drop my hands with a grin.

I adjust the fake and real plants a bit more. The

evening light filters through the windows, bathing the room in a soft glow. It's Thursday. I spent the day working on color palettes for the mural scenes Eleanor approved.

But I put work and the thousand-mile-a-minute speed of the project out of my head for a moment, pausing to take in Asher's home. After a long day, we're staging the house with some of my things, making it look like I actually live here for the camera crew that'll come this weekend. It's surreal, but in a few short hours, the house has started to feel more like mine. Will this feel as surreal to Asher as it does to me?

I walk around the first floor. Asher's not a minimalist. His game room houses a pool table and framed baseball memorabilia, newspaper clippings from World Series victories. Past the game room, there's a home gym, then a terrace overlooking a small backyard. They're so rare in the city, but of course so are homes this spacious and appointed. A small outdoor structure, like a sunroom, sits in the far corner of the yard, on a floating deck with evergreen shrubs and wildflowers surrounding it. I could see myself drinking a chai latte or a glass of wine there, but I'm not sure I can picture Asher relaxing there in the afternoons. He's not really a cat, like me. I turn around and head back. In the living room and kitchen, more art hangs on the walls and my heart squeezes because many of the pieces are ones I helped him choose: wildflower illustrations, fruit sketches, and San Francisco caricatures. Some of my own work is here too—prints from my "animal phase," which I am still in, like the dog painting with the saying *Every Bite You Take, I'll Be Watching You*, and a jungle-themed print of a monkey instructing the viewer to *Get Up to Monkey Business*. In the kitchen, a hook designed for dog leashes holds skate laces from each season he's played for The Sea Dogs.

Beckett and Reina move around beside it, setting up a few mugs they snagged from my apartment. "Everyone knows a woman needs her own mug," Reina says, organizing them.

"Or twenty," Beckett mutters.

"You wish I had twenty," she says.

"More like twenty thousand," I joke.

"Like I said, women need their special mugs. For their moods," she adds.

I leave them to their mug moods as I tend to my candle moods, moving through the home to place candles on every available surface. Lemon cake scent in the kitchen, vanilla in the living room, banana bread in the hallway. The scents mingle, making the place feel lived in. But I haven't ventured into the main bedroom yet.

"Are they going to film in the main bedroom?" I ask when I return to the kitchen, unsure how far we're supposed to take this TV shoot.

Reina gives me an uncertain look. "I don't know...That feels kind of personal?"

"I agree. But you never know. Should I put a photo in there or something?"

"Probably a good idea. And maybe a few of your things just in case," she suggests.

I nod, thinking of the items I stashed in the guest room on the first floor to avoid overstepping. My clothes, my lotions and potions—which, it turns out, have multiplied like Reina's mugs. I had no idea I owned two sweet plum body sprays, a sunset blossom one, a desert willow one, and a white lilies spray until I scooped everything off my bathroom shelf and tossed it into a canvas bag. But here we are. Evidently, I'm a girl who likes pretty smells—and pretty lotions, judging by the tons of bottles I somehow managed to bring.

"You could put them in the bathroom you're sharing," Reina says gently.

"Just make sure there are five of your things for every one of his. No one will ever doubt your marriage then," Beckett adds with a playful grin.

That earns him another swat from Reina, then a quick peck. "You're not wrong," she says, before she checks her phone and sighs. "We should head out—it's getting late."

It's past nine. I nod. "Go ahead. I can handle the rest."

They've already helped haul over suitcases, plants, and some of my artwork. Reina was careful to make everything look like I truly live here.

But once they leave, a strange quiet falls over the house. I walk slowly through the living room. It feels intimate, yet strange, to be here alone in my fake husband's home, like some kind of interloper in his life. This isn't a quick visit to my friend's house anymore, an evening hang, a game night, a dinner. This is his space, his life, and now...I'm here for several days, leaving pieces of myself in each room, like this belongs to me as much as it does to him.

No, like it belongs to *us*.

His presence lingers here, woven into every room, every scent, every small trace of him. I run a hand over the back of the couch, my fingers brushing the fabric as I imagine him sinking down on the cushions, filling this space with his easy confidence, with his warm, woodsy scent, with his cocky smile.

I imagine him everywhere. I close my eyes, and I can feel him here, in a way.

In a way I long for.

In a way that's getting harder to ignore.

But I have to ignore it. We set down rules in Vegas, then reestablished them the other week before our brunch with the Greers—nothing physical. Then broke them again after the board dinner. Because sex complicates everything. So do *feelings*. Those fuckers really complicate things. Our fake marriage is already one huge complication; that's why we have rules. Rules I'll need to work hard to stick to when he returns tomorrow.

I need to focus on *that*.

I open my eyes and shove those thoughts away as I head to the foyer and grab my small pink duffel bag—the one I didn't go through in front of Beckett or Reina. I rummage through it and pull out a small box of special things I brought to make this all seem even more real— framed photos and one piece of art. Something I hope he likes. I go room to room, adding the framed pics one by one. For the camera crew of course. For the shoot.

After I finish placing the last frame in the living room, I go to the foyer and grab one more thing. A piece of art I made for him—a little mirror with a sketch on it. A new design I'm playing with. But where should I hang it? I check out the walls. It's not really my place to hammer nails and hang items. So I bring it to the plant table and rest it against his Lego orchid.

I step back, staring at the room. What will Asher think when he sees all this? Will he be surprised? Uncomfortable? Amused? No idea.

When I finish, I take pictures of the rooms, then stand in the kitchen and text my friends, attaching the photos.

> Maeve: Look—instant wife. Just add pillows, perfume, and plants. But here's the question—where should I sleep tonight?

> Everly: That couch looks like it's made of pillows.

> Fable: The guest room looks like a five-star hotel.

> Josie: The carpet looks like you could fuck on it and not get rug burn.

> Leighton: Girl, sleep in his bed.

I glance toward the stairs leading up to his bedroom, my heart racing dangerously fast. Do I really sleep in his bed? It feels too intimate without him here. But where will I sleep tomorrow? My stomach flips. No idea. We didn't discuss that when he asked me to move in for the weekend. Maybe I should just head home.

I text Asher to let him know everything's set up and that I might go home for the evening. I don't want to presume I'm welcome tonight too. His reply comes instantly.

> Asher: Stay the night, wife.

It's like he can read my mind.

Maeve: Without you? Are you sure you want me taking over everything? Because I probably will. It's the inevitability of me.

Asher: My house is your house.

Yeah, except his house is about twenty times larger than mine.

Maeve: You've been warned.

Asher: It'll be more believable. It'll smell like you then.

Maeve: You like the smell of paint and struggling artist?

Asher: Yes, but mostly you smell like plums, sunsets, or wildflowers.

My breath hitches as I stand in the now-quiet kitchen. He's so casual about it, but something about the way he's cataloged my body sprays makes me shiver. I bite my lip, then reply.

Maeve: All three? At once?

Asher: No. It depends on the day. Keeps me on my toes. And yes, you can and should sleep in my bed. It's fucking otherworldly comfortable.

.   .   .

Talk about intimate. Talk about an invitation. I'm not sure I can resist RSVPing.

I grab my canvas bag and head upstairs, down the hallway to the main bedroom where I push open the door. The room is vast, with a huge king-size bed. Like it's enchanting me, I walk over to it, then drop my bag on the floor. I run a hand along the soft dove-gray duvet, then picture Asher in it. Taking up all the space with his big, strong frame, rippling muscles, tousled hair, and bossy, commanding charm. What does he look like when he goes to bed? When he wakes up? In the middle of the night when he dreams? I reach into my bag and set down a couple paperbacks on the nightstand. A new book I checked out from Josie's library since I needed a tear-jerker. And then my familiar copy of *If Found, Please Return*. With my phone still in hand, the thoughts of Asher weave around me as I wander to the palatial bathroom with a shower that's begging for me to try it. My phone buzzes.

Asher: And use the rainfall shower. You'll love it.

I'm convinced now he can read my mind. Or maybe he's spying.

Maeve: Are you watching me? Do you
have cameras? That's where I am.
Checking out this bathroom I could live in.

Asher: Shame, but no. I don't.

I shiver again from the innuendo. But does he really want
to watch me? I think of Vegas, his hands on me, his mouth
latched onto mine, his words in my ear.

Maybe he does.

I swallow roughly, past the wild uncertainty of this
situation. I turn around and glance at the framed picture
of us I'd placed on his nightstand earlier, then drop the
phone on the counter.

As I strip off my clothes, I leave a trail on the bathroom floor, my skin already buzzing from the thought of
him. The air feels heavier than usual as I step into the
rainfall shower, letting the heat and steam wrap around
me. I reach for his body wash, twist the cap open, and the
scent of him hits me instantly—clean and fresh with that
hint of oak. It floods my senses, and suddenly, it's like he's
here, standing just behind me. His hands skimming my
warm, wet skin. His mouth caressing my neck. His arms
roping around me, nice and tight. Most of all, his mouth
telling me to sink down to my knees.

My pulse rockets, and I ache everywhere.

I let out a shaky breath, trying to shake away the
thought of me on my knees, my hands on his hips, my lips
parted, but it clings to me like the steam. It's getting
harder to deny this attraction, especially here in the heat
of the shower where I want to give in.

Even though it's a very bad idea. Because giving in

could ruin this beautiful friendship that we both desperately need.

When I'm out, I wrap myself in a big, fluffy towel and twist another over my hair. I text him, though that's probably a bad idea too.

> Maeve: I showered. Because you told me to.

> Asher: Good. I like it when you do what I say.

I pause, staring at the heady words. It was one thing to pretend we were married while living apart. It'll be entirely another thing while we live together, even for a few days.

31

A HOUSEWARMING GIFT

Asher

I've lived with a few women over the years. The last one was Lila, a bakery owner I dated for—no surprise—six months, my usual expiration date. I didn't plan to live together so soon, if at all. But when her lease ran out, she moved in with me for a month. In that short time, I realized we were incompatible. It wasn't that she was a slob, though she was, or that our schedules clashed, though they did.

It was that she wanted more. I didn't.

Story of my life. She was outgoing and generous, and still, I couldn't fall for her. Because I'm broken.

So, living with someone? It's not exactly new to me. But what *is* new is this wild anticipation as I head home. It's been following me since Everly told me about the TV piece. It chased me on the flight home; it nipped at my heels as the team jet landed. And it's swirling around me as I drive home from the players' lot. It's Friday night, and I'm pulling up to my house—full of jitters.

Or maybe excitement? I'm not sure which one is winning the battle inside me, or maybe both are.

I can't stand how much I want to see her. It's surreal.

I park in the garage and close it, ready to race up the steps into my home when my phone rings. Her name flashes on the screen.

"Hey, what's up?" I ask, half-expecting her to tell me to close my eyes as I go inside. I bet she has some surprise waiting for me. That'd be so very her.

"I'm stuck here," she says, frustration creeping into her voice.

"Where?"

"At the arena. Eleanor wanted to go over a million options—timeline, materials, everything. The crew finished priming the walls earlier this week. I drew the grid for the outline. And she wants to finalize some details since she's trying to fast-track this so I can start painting it next week. Which means...I'm stuck here late. But guess what?"

"What?"

"I made you something."

I stop in my tracks at the door that leads from the garage into the house. "Food?"

"My famous mac and cheese."

My stomach growls. "With the cheddar, Monterey Jack, and cream cheese?"

"Yes, the one and only. There's some waiting for you in a vintage casserole dish I got at Goodwill. I went full 1950s housewife with it. I'm playing the part."

Playing the part.

Those words should remind me that this is just for

show. But when a vision of her in a tight retro dress and apron, and holding a martini pops into my head, I like it too much to be bothered by the performance of it all. "So, did I miss the martini too?"

She laughs, her smile coming through the phone. "Maybe I'll make that when the camera crew comes tomorrow. Good idea?"

"They'll buy it," I say.

"I'll be home later," she promises.

"Okay," I reply, trying to sound upbeat, but the disappointment sneaks in. I do love her mac and cheese, but I wanted to see her. It's been a week and a half on the road —New York, Boston, Toronto, then Vegas on the way back. I miss her.

"And we will do our best impression of the Greers," she adds.

I brighten. "We will."

"No repeats of that brunch."

I adopt the older man's voice, raspy and with a wink in it as I imagine him. "*I remember the honeymoon phase—we couldn't keep our hands off each other.*"

"Hey! I want a honeymoon. You'd better not stiff me on Paris."

I laugh. She has no idea how much I want to take her anywhere. "When the season ends *after* The Cup, I'll take you there," I say, meaning it, but knowing it won't really happen.

"I'll start planning," she says.

Briefly, I feel a twinge in my chest. It's late-February; I'm sure this will be over well before the season ends. We'll get through this piece tomorrow, and then surely, we'll fade quietly from interest.

Shame.

But what can I do?

I hang up and head inside. The second I turn the corner of the steps onto the main level, the air rushes out of my lungs. The place looks...different.

Maeve doesn't mess around. She's never done anything halfway, and this proves it. I look around, taking it all in—the plants, the tarot deck she nicknamed Tatiana on the coffee table, along with the books too. Art books from her favorites: Lichtenstein, Klimt, Cindy Sherman, Barbara Kruger. Even a book on graffiti art.

I pick it up, intrigued, but then my gaze shifts to something else—a photo on the table behind the couch in a simple silver frame. My chest tightens as I step closer.

It's...our wedding photo.

Holy shit.

I walk over and pick it up. In the picture, I'm holding her hand as Hitch reads the exchange of vows. I'm wearing that ruffled suit, she's in that Marilyn dress, and I'm looking at her like I can't look away.

I still can't. It takes me a long time to put it down.

When I do, I spin around and check out the plant table. She arranged her living ones with my Lego ones. But what's that? Something shiny rests against the orchid. I head over to a small oval mirror with a sketch on it that looks vaguely familiar. When I reach it, my heart sprints. That's...holy shit. I pick it up. It's the sketch of the couple almost kissing she sent me last week. But she's painted them into the corner of the mirror. Next to them are the words: *Keep snacks handy at all times.*

The first piece of advice her friends gave me weeks ago. I had no idea the sketch she sent me would find its way into a piece of her art. But of course, it would. It feels like a secret message to me, which is such a ridiculous thing to think. And yet, here I am, thinking it. Like I did last week with the image and the words *for you,* I run my finger along the advice. A key to Maeve.

But I know another key to Maeve—making her realize her work matters. And it matters greatly to me. I trot down to the garage, grab a hammer and a nail, and return to the living room, grabbing the little mirror.

Then I go to the foyer and hang it up—right by the front door.

Where it belongs.

Once I return the hammer, I wander into the kitchen, where I spot a dish rack full of her mugs. I smile stupidly. Yeah, this is all for show. I'd do well to remember that. But damn, did she ever understand the assignment. She left her imprint everywhere. My favorite is the white mug in the sink with the words *I'm a Fucking Ray of Sunshine* on the side and her lipstick marks on the rim. Raspberry. She's already drunk from this mug.

I might stare at the shape of her lips for a good long time. It's only when I realize I'm jealous of a mug that I tear myself away, letting it clatter in the stainless steel sink before I do something like, I don't know, drink from it just to touch the spot where her lips have been. I wouldn't put that past me at this point.

I go upstairs, and once I turn into the bedroom, I'm caught in a tractor beam, drawn to another photo, the one on my nightstand. It's one more shot of us at our wedding. And I'm kissing her.

I walk over to it, in a goddamn trance.

I sink down on the bed like I'm in another world, picking it up, studying it, and getting a little lost in time.

Maeve's eyes are closed, and she looks like every one

of her kissing paintings. Like she needs to be kissed by me. Badly.

I swallow past the dryness in my throat then scrub a hand along my jaw, taking this in. What she did with the mugs and the plants and the books—and most of all, the pictures. She made it a home.

But she's not the only one who can play house.

I go downstairs, rifle through the packages I asked Maeve to bring in for me from the lock box, and find the one I'm looking for. I rip it open and grin, pleased.

Yep, this is perfect.

Maeve had the right idea with the wedding pictures. But I made a promise to her brother the other week, and mostly to myself, to look out for her. To protect her. To show the world that she's fucking mine.

I ordered prints of some pictures of her, and had them framed. Photos from over the years, including the most recent one—a shot of her flipping me the double bird.

My personal favorite. I add them all around the house, setting down Quick-Draw Maeve in the T-shirt on my nightstand when my phone buzzes.

> Maeve: Another hour or so. Save some mac and cheese for me!

I type absently, my mind elsewhere.

> Asher: I will.

. . .

I'm not thinking of food because when I look at the photo of her once more, something clicks. Something she said when she gave herself that nickname back in Vegas. Something...demonstrative.

I know the perfect housewarming gift for my wife. I check the time. It's nine. Not too late. We live in a big city that caters to all sorts of appetites around the clock. I google the hours of a nearby shop, then grin like a cocky fucker when I see it's open till midnight.

I'm out of there in no time.

* * *

But traffic is a nightmare on Friday nights. It's slow-going, and by the time I make it to the shop, Maeve's texted me.

> Maeve: Well, I checked everywhere and can't find you. I can only conclude you've been kidnapped by aliens. 👽

Shit. She beat me home. But as I'm grabbing the last item, I fire off a quick reply.

> Asher: Back soon. Just needed to grab... something.

It's vague, but I can't spoil the surprise.

> Maeve: Happy grabbing. Your wife is
> exhausted.

A jolt of tension hits me. I really hope she's not overworking herself.

> Asher: Get some rest, okay?

But there's no response. And that's good. Really, that's good. I want her to get plenty of sleep. Once I finish the purchase, I hop back in the car, gift bag in hand. By the time I pull into the garage, it's almost ten-thirty. No further replies from her. I bet she's already hit the sack.

That settles some of my worries. I head inside, set the bag on the kitchen table, and make my way upstairs.

The lights are still on, and there she is—face-first on my bed, her bra next to her. But otherwise she's still wearing her clothes—leggings and a sweatshirt. Her hair's in a messy bun that's coming undone.

Two thoughts slam into me at once.

First, she looks too damn good in my bed. Second, I'm stupidly thrilled she chose *my* bed, not the guest room, to sleep in. A third thought crashes down next. I hope she sleeps better than she ever has here at my house.

I turn around, head down the hall, and grab a blanket from the closet. When I return, I gently cover her. She sighs softly, murmurs something incoherent, and rolls over, her lips curving into a faint smile. Her eyes flutter open for a moment, heavy with sleep. I'm a little jealous, but also wholly happy for her. She needs it.

"Hi," she says, but her lids don't stay open for more than a second or two.

I'm not even sure she's awake, but I sit down next to her. "Hey," I murmur back, gently setting a hand on her shoulder.

"You look...nice," she says with a dopey grin.

"So do you," I reply, my voice low and rough.

"I was...thinking about...this," she says, her words slow and slurred.

"About what?" I ask, dying to know what's on her mind.

"Seeing you," she says, almost in a dreamlike state.

"Yeah?" The tension inside me is near unbearable.

"Yeah. I dreamed..."

But she turns quiet. I wish she'd wake the fuck up and tell me what she dreamed about me. "Dreamed about what?" I ask, leaning in, ready to hang onto her every word.

But she doesn't finish. Instead, her breath comes out in a soft, deep exhale. Her chest rises as her hand flutters to her chest, then glides down her body. Over her breasts. Down her belly. And just like that, the flames eat me alive.

Her hand slips between her thighs as she falls back into deep sleep.

There's only so much I can take.

I grit my teeth, suppress a groan, and head straight to

the bathroom. I'm naked in seconds, stepping under the shower, letting the hot water wash over me, imagining her here *last night*.

Out there *tonight*.

And all the things I want to do to her.

32

THINGS WE CAN'T UNSEE

Maeve

Mmm. The day swims before my eyes, syrupy and warm. But it's warm here, too, in this big, comfy bed. Fumbling around under the covers, I kick off a corner of the blanket...when my eyes float open.

Rude.

I'd rather be sleeping.

I glance down at my legs. Oh. I fell asleep in my clothes. My eyes are sticky and my makeup clings to me. I groan. I should change. I should brush my teeth. I should wash off my makeup.

I drag myself out of bed, half-awake. Or half-asleep. Maybe both. Definitely both. I trudge to the bathroom in the dark, a huge yawn taking over me and blocking out the world as I turn the knob.

Oh. There's a faint light on. Just one of several in the bathroom, keeping it dimly lit.

Wait.

Did Asher come home?

When the yawn ends a century later, I turn my head and I'm hit by steam, the rhythmic sound of the shower, and the sight of...Asher under the water, eyes closed, with a very ambitious erection in his big hand.

Fully awake, I squeeze my thighs together.

I don't move a single, solitary muscle. I roll my lips together, sealing in all my sounds, every breath.

Don't make a noise.

I bargain with my wild heart to beat quietly. With one hand grabbing the edge of the sink, I stare shamelessly at the man behind the glass, six feet away and diagonally across the room. His back's to me, but I can see the side view.

His powerful thighs, his muscular ass, his firm abs, and one incredibly impressive bicep, flexed nice and tight as he strokes.

It's a deliciously lazy stroke.

Like he's testing out the weight of his cock in his hand, and the interest of his dick in a quick ride. But the assessment doesn't last long. In a few seconds, his dick must answer with a *hell yes* since Asher's hand glides along his thick shaft with lustful purpose.

His grip tightens as he reaches the tip. My eyes pop, and I rein in a feral gasp as he squeezes it, then lets out a shuddery breath.

This is so wrong.

This is such a violation.

I should go.

I really need to leave.

Right. Now.

I'll just turn around and go back the way I came.

And I try, I swear I try, to will my leaden feet to spin

around so I can quietly slip out and pretend I never witnessed his self-care. Even though I can never unsee the hottest sight ever—Asher's hand curling tighter around his thick shaft, traveling to the base, then to the tip again. A harsh groan shudders past his lips. Those lush, firm lips that have kissed my neck, my shoulders, my face.

I grow infinitely wetter.

My cheeks are on fire. My entire body is engulfed in flames, but I have to tear myself away. I purse my lips, pivot quietly, and valiantly, I don't even know how, find the will to head for the door. Hand outstretched, I reach for the knob.

"Don't you dare leave now."

Chills erupt down my spine at the sound of his voice. The rough, carnal command in it.

"Don't go?" I ask, in a shuddery breath, not quite turning around in case I heard him wrong over the patter of water. There's no way he said *that*.

"Watch me," Asher says in a taunt. "You know you want to."

How does he know? Did he see me staring savagely at him? A flush crawls up my chest. I swallow, then turn around, guilty as charged. I gasp, no longer looking at his silhouette. He's turned, and he's wiping off the steam on the glass door with one hand. He's shifted his stance, giving me a three-quarter view of his impressive body.

And at last, I can see all of his cock.

My thighs clench.

Sure, I felt him through his slacks, then his boxer briefs two weeks ago. I had a rough idea of the goods. But now I'm seeing it. This man is blessed. I can't stop staring at his dick—it's the prettiest one I've ever seen. It's big, and beautiful, and my favorite color—pink.

But that's not the real reason I'm staring. Dicks are whatever. They hang, they dangle, they sway. Mostly they get in the way.

The reason I can't stop staring is he lowers his hand to it again and looks my way as he gives a tug, while never looking away from me. His green eyes flare with heat, a primal kind of lust. Now that he's cleaned off the steam, he's created a viewing area for me.

"What's the verdict, Hartley?" he prompts, sliding that big hand down his hard-on, casting a spell on me with his cock.

I nod slowly, like he's the puppeteer working the strings on my head. "I'll stay for the show."

With my yes in hand, he flashes a cocky grin that burns off in seconds. His hand slides up and down, up and down. In a slow, tantalizing rhythm. It's impossible for me to look elsewhere. I draw a deep breath, stutter it out and keep staring, my lips parted, my eyes hungry.

"Your eyes are big, Maeve," he says, his voice a teasing drawl now.

You'd think walking in on someone in the midst of his self-care would give you the upper hand. You'd be wrong. This man holds all the cards. There's not a shred of embarrassment on his face. Not a single sense of embarrassment that he was caught in the act.

I only see challenge in his irises. Heat. White-hot desire.

"Are they?" I finally reply to his question about my eyes.

On a tight, firm upstroke he rasps out, "Fucking huge."

His fist curls tighter around his cock. Strokes faster. He's unabashedly naked. He's shamelessly aroused. He's mercilessly jerking off.

And I am one frayed, sparking nerve as I watch him in the dimly lit bathroom, the rainfall shower cascading over his huge frame, his hand taking a tour of his erection, over and over.

I burn from head to toe. I tingle in every cell. My bones melt. My pulse pounds. My thighs shake. I've never been more aroused in my life than right now as I stare at my best friend jerking off to me. *At me.*

I'm so soaked I could shove a hand inside my panties and fly off in one, two, three strokes. Absently, I bite my lip.

He smiles, a lazy, lopsided smile, then tips his chin. "You like the show, wife?"

A tremble takes my body hostage. "I do," I manage to say.

"You were watching me for a while, weren't you?" He challenges as his fist flies faster.

"A minute. Maybe more," I say, breathlessly.

"Long enough to know what you like."

"I like this." But that's a lie. This is more than like. I'm absolutely enchanted by the way his hand shuttles along his erection, by the punch of his hips, by the rippling of his muscles.

"Good," he mutters as his dark green eyes tour my body like I'm the only one he's ever gotten off to. "So fucking good."

His big shoulders shake. His hand grips tighter. I'm so jealous of that hand. I want that hand to be mine. To be my mouth. To be my body.

I'm obscenely wet. My panties are a waterpark as Asher slaps his other palm on the glass shower door. "You like to watch."

It's a statement not a question, but still, I nod. "I do."

"You want me to finish?"

"Yes, please," I say, and it's like I'm begging.

Because I am.

With hard eyes and choppy breath, he fucks his fist. And when I say fuck, I mean fuck. His hips jerk, sharp and fast. And powerful too.

He fucks into his hand, his jaw tightening, his chest heaving, his filthy gaze locked on me.

The object of his desire.

Another pump.

His eyes squeeze shut.

One more.

Then, his whole body jerks as he tips his head back and groans a long, guttural, "Maeve."

Did I just come in my panties?

Almost. Fucking almost.

Because that's the hottest thing I've ever seen, ever heard, ever experienced—Asher spilling his release all over his hand as he grunts my name. It takes every ounce of self-restraint not to shove my hand inside my panties and rub my aching clit till I come too.

But this is a show. This is a game. This is some kind of negotiation. And the man is in charge.

I don't know who's supposed to make the next move in this friendship-with-benefits game we're playing, so I wait till his breathing slows, his chest stops heaving, and he opens his eyes. He tips his chin to the door. "Go wait in bed, Maeve."

And I fly out of there, the memory of his pleasure seared forever on my brain. Along with the question—did he want me to walk in on him? He was warned by my friends to lock the door after all.

33

COUNT FOR ME

Asher

After I drag a towel through my hair and halfway dry off my body, I cinch it around my waist, not caring that droplets of water slide down my chest.

Only one thing is on my mind—the gift I bought her.

I leave the steamy bathroom and return to the bedroom where the sight of Maeve steals my breath. She's so fucking obedient. Maeve's lying on the bed, propped up on a mountain of pillows. Waiting eagerly for instructions.

Her expressive hazel eyes flicker with obvious excitement. No, there's downright dirty glee in them. I stride over to the foot of the bed, press my palms on the mattress, and meet her gaze. "Nothing physical, right? Those are the rules?"

Her brow knits. She's clearly confused as she asks, "Um, yes?"

"And did you break them tonight?"

She nibbles on her lip, then asks, "No?"

I stare sternly at her. "Did *you* touch me?"

The hint of a smile appears. "No."

"Did *I* touch you?"

"No." She sounds both desperate and emphatic.

I let my gaze roam down her body, settling on her leggings. They're purple. Nylon probably, and I'd be willing to bet, the material is damp between her thighs. "Open your legs."

A gust of breath crosses her lips. She parts her legs slightly, revealing a wet spot and making me grin like a goddamn rock star.

"Like this?" she asks, playing along.

"Just like that, wife," I say, then nod to the bedroom door. "Want to see your housewarming present now?"

"I do," she says.

I tear myself away from the bed and pad downstairs, powered by determination and lust, and grab the bag from Risqué Business. I take the steps two at a time, returning to the bedroom in less than a minute.

When she sees the pink bag I'm holding, her eyes widen. "Asher," she says, my name like a filthy prayer.

I cross the dark blue carpet and sit on the edge of the bed, my dick hardening again. I set the bag down and lean closer to her. "I believe you once said it takes you five supersize vibrators."

A shudder runs down her body. Then she nods. "I said what I said."

"And I listened. I wanted you to have everything you need to be happy. Happy wife, as they say."

"Can I see them?" She sounds like it's Dirty Christmas and she's just discovered the battery-operated gifts of her dreams under the tree.

"I'll show you," I say, but first I take the bag to the bathroom, wash off each one, dry them, then return.

"Finally," she says with a pout.

"It's better this way." I dip a hand into the bag, taking out the so-called Thruster. It's long and thick. "Fourteen speeds," I say, and then grab another. The Flutter. It's a circle, but with an open end. "Goes inside *and* outside." I take one more from the bag. It's a modern take on the traditional rabbit with a shaft and vibrating ears, but with some kind of newfangled flutter technology. "This one I'm told is like an instant orgasm."

"Oh god," she gasps.

I show her the others. A Soft Touch, and a Finger Puppet. "Gotta love the name." I furrow my brow, holding up the pink finger toy. "Shoot. This is no good," I say, like I've just discovered a huge problem.

"Why?" she asks. No, she *whines*.

"Well, you said supersize. It's a bullet-size. My bad," I say, then drop it back in the bag. "It's not used so maybe we can return it?" I ask innocently, but she flies up, grabs my wrist, and shakes her head. "I want it."

Her voice is raw, husky.

"Well, it is your gift, I suppose," I say, then flash her a grin. "Should I leave you here with them?"

Like hell am I leaving her alone with five toys. But I need her to want this game. To agree to these rules. I need her to want it as much as she wanted to watch me get off.

She shakes her head so fast. "No."

I adopt a confused look. "No?"

"Asher," she says, like a plea.

"Yes?"

She closes her eyes, then like it pains her, she takes a deep breath and opens them. "You pick."

Music to my fucking ears.

I lean closer, sinking deeper onto the bed. "Right. Because sex complicates everything, right. Including a marriage?" I ask, smoothly, confidently, using her words on her.

"It does."

"But orgasms don't?"

"Orgasms are fine."

"Fine? Just fine?" I ask, playing with my food a little longer.

She bangs a fist against the mattress. "More than fine. God, please. Use one. Fuck me with it. Just fuck me with it now. I can't stand how turned on I am," she says, then shoves her hands into her hair, a desperate act of a woman undone.

And I'm a man breaking. But also holding tight to a shred of control—a control I need. I rise from the bed, leave her with the bag, then lift a finger. "But no touching, right?"

"Yes. Dammit. Fine. Whatever," she says, so frustrated, so wound up...

"Just a little horny, honey?" I ask, tilting my head.

She narrows her eyes at me. "If you'd watched *me* get off, you'd be horny too."

I bend down and dip my face to hers, dusting the tip of our noses together. "You're right," I say, then brush my lips dangerously near to hers. Everything inside me screams *kiss her*. My body burns with the need to touch her, but I don't. I'm having too much fun with her desire. "I *would* be horny, so let me help you."

I step away. Head to the closet. Grab some ties. When I return, I say, "Just to make sure you're not tempted to touch me."

She draws in a sharp breath. "You're going to tie me up and fuck me with a toy?"

"Just following the rules."

She smiles wickedly and moves quickly so before I can tie up her wrists, she hooks her thumbs into the waistband of her leggings and skims them down, pushing down her panties too, like she's afraid I'd leave them on.

And just like that, she's in control. Because she's half-naked and her perfect, pink pussy is on display for me. Wet, pretty, and glistening. I groan as I stare wantonly at her. It is going to be so fucking hard not to touch her.

But rules are rules.

And even if they weren't, I can hear the echo of her words loud and clear—*sex complicates everything.*

And sex can lead to regret.

I hate regret. And I hate the thought of Maeve regretting me. I won't fuck her till I'm sure she won't regret it. If, and it's a big if, we ever sleep together, I don't want her to tell me it was a mistake, to say we shouldn't have done it, to backpedal in the morning.

I want to fuck her, and taste her, and please her, and make her come on my face and cock and fingers with no regrets.

This, though? This game? This I'll allow.

I straddle her, my hard cock nearly touching her soft stomach from under the towel I'm wearing. I wrap a tie around her right wrist, binding her to the bed. Then her left, doing the same with that wrist. When I tug on the material, there's a little bit of give, but not too much.

"Safe word?" I ask.

Her lips twitch. She takes her time, then she says, "Warm nuts."

Fuck, I think I love her. I really do. But now is not the

time to get lost in those thoughts. Or feelings that are far too fizzy for my own good. I dip my head so she can't see the size of my smile. When I raise it, my smile burns off. I slide down her body, adjusting the towel I'm wearing. Half wondering why I'm even wearing a fucking thing at all. But maybe because she's still in that shirt.

Settling between her thighs, I reach for a vibrator. "You said you need five, Maeve?"

"Yes," she says, defiantly.

I start with the small one, sliding it onto my finger, then show her the vibrating pad. "Start counting," I say.

She gasps, as I slide my finger between her spread thighs, running the pad against her swollen clit. Her gasp turns into a long whimper. Love the sound of it, but rules are rules.

"Count for me, Maeve," I demand.

She swallows, shakes her head, murmurs, "One."

"Good wife," I say.

Then, she arches her back and moans so loudly, so recklessly that my dick pops out of the towel. I was hard already. Now I'm granite level since she's lifting her hips and rocking into my finger. I fight to keep my voice even as I muse, "Is it like a tongue? I wonder?"

She cries out a breathy, "Yes."

"Bet you'd like to be eaten, wouldn't you?"

"So much," she mutters.

How I fucking want to eat her. Bury my face between her thighs and feast. Instead, I turn off the Finger Puppet, then grab the Thruster. "Count again," I tell her, holding up the long, thick toy.

She's a mess already, hair wild, cheeks red, eyes shimmering. "Two," she pants out.

"We have a way to go, Quick-Draw Maeve," I say, then

turn on the new device, rubbing the tip of it against that needy clit of hers.

Her wrists strain against the ties as she mutters a long, "Ohhhhhh."

My dick thumps. My chest swells.

She arches up, stares fiercely at me. "Fuck me with it. Now."

Tempting, but no. "So greedy," I muse, then turn it up, sliding it through her slickness. "Like this?" It's asked innocently.

It's answered wantonly with a loud, "Inside me, you tease."

"If you insist," I say, then slide it inside her pussy, and my cells turn molten. She's so wet, so hot that she takes it all easily.

Then, I turn it all the way up. And seconds later, she's fucking it. Grinding down, riding it, seeking it out. And driving me wild.

"I'm close," she pants.

I had a feeling she might be, and I *could* let her come. But I could also drag this out. I'm feeling like I want to edge her, so I turn it off.

She whimpers. "What did you do?"

"You said you need five," I say, feigning innocence.

"Asher," she warns me.

And since I really don't want her to say warm nuts, I'm speedy as I switch to the circle vibe, sliding it into her sweet cunt, watching her take one curved end in while the other fits over her clit.

She arches her hips. Soon, she's chanting. Begging. She's close again. And I'm an asshole since I ease it out.

"You dick," she mutters, thrashing around on the bed like she wants to throttle me.

"Oh, did you say dick?" I grab the rabbit-style one, brandish it.

She lifts her hips, spreads her legs wide open. My god, she's going to be a dream to fuck. But then, she's pretty much my dream girl. My heart hammers ruthlessly.

Settle the fuck down, man.

I try to clear the emotions cluttering my brain, focusing only on the physical. "Keep count," I tell her, dangling the toy in front of her.

"Four," she says, breathlessly.

"Such a good wife," I praise, then I slide it inside her soaked pussy.

She keens. It's gorgeous and animalistic all at once, and it goes to my dick and my heart. But I fight off the feelings, focusing only on the task. Edging her like she's never been edged before.

I thrust it all the way in, flick on the ears, and let it ride her lovely, hungry clit. In no time, she's writhing against the shaft, her lips parted, her cries telling me she's so damn close. She tosses her head back. "Asher," she groans, groans, nearly there, nearly coasting over that precipice.

And I *should* let her come. Really, I should. I could get her over the cliff in a couple more deep thrusts. But I turn it off.

"Screw you," she shouts.

"We can't, Maeve. Remember?"

"Asher," she seethes.

"Need to use your safe word?" I ask, hoping, fucking praying she says no.

She glares at me with narrowed eyes. "Five. Give. Me. Five."

I smile. And I can't resist a second longer. As I grab the

last vibrator—the Soft Touch, the one that simulates a tongue and lips—I lean over her, and this time I don't steal a kiss. I *take* a hot, deep one as I turn on the new toy, slide it between her thighs, and rub it against her.

She moans and I swallow the sound with my lips.

She cries out and I kiss her while I rub faster.

She pants and I stroke.

Then I let go of her mouth and she screams.

"Yes, yes, yes!" she calls out as she comes utterly, fantastically undone in my bed, for me.

And, I'm pretty sure, with no regrets.

Fifty thousand years later, she smiles woozily at me. "You're so mean."

"I'm the worst. But you're right, Maeve," I say, then cage her in with my arms. "It does take you five supersize vibrators."

"Actually, it was four supersize vibrators and one little one with superpowers."

"Is that a challenge? You want to try again with five big ones?"

She laughs but then shakes her head. "Actually..." Her gaze drifts down my body. Come to think of it, I'm feeling a breeze. My towel must have fallen off at some point. My hard shaft bobs against her shirt.

She glances down at it then up to my face. "Come again, husband," she whispers sensually, pausing, looking down at her chest. "On me."

In case it wasn't clear.

She's a siren. She's a dreamer. She's an artist. She's my best friend's sister. She's my best friend too—my rock. But right now, she's simply the woman I can't resist.

"If you insist," I say, then push up her shirt, so the tank sits tight under her arms, groaning when I set my eyes on those gorgeous tits for the first time, with perky, dusky rose nipples and plenty to hold onto. There's so much I want to do to them. Lick and bite and kiss and fuck. For now though, I straddle her chest, a knee on each side of her. I give my aching cock a stroke. Yeah, this won't take long. "There's only one little problem."

She shoots me a coquettish smile. "I wouldn't say it's little, Asher."

Glad she appreciates the goods, but it's best not to gloat. Instead, I meet her curious irises. "But the thing is," I say, giving my cock another tug.

Her eyes go glossy as she breathes out hard. "Yeah?"

"It would help," I continue, taking my time with every filthy word as I slide my hand down it again, "if it were a little wet."

She licks her lips and stares at my dick like it's candy before nodding vigorously. "I can help."

I bet she could, but I'm not thinking of the kind of help she'd give me with that lovely mouth wrapped around my cock. "I know you can," I say as I stare down at her, gripping my shaft again and sliding my palm down to the tip. "But right now, I need one thing from you."

"What is it?" she asks breathily.

I take my time, letting the charged air crackle some more. Making her wait for it. I grip my dick tighter, bring the tip closer to her mouth. "Spit on it," I tell her.

Her eyes widen. Her mouth falls open. Her breath escapes in a rush.

I will remember this look forever—it's how she looks when we've gone to an amusement park and she's convinced me to ride the upside-down roller coaster, or when she drags me into the crashing waves of the ocean, or when she spots a door to an ice-skating rink that says closed but she decides to sneak in anyway, bringing me with her.

It's a look of pure thrill, but tonight it's both thrilling *and* dirty.

Saying yes with her body, she brings her face closer to my dick. Swallows visibly. Works up some saliva. With our eyes locked together, she parts those raspberry lips and lets it dribble onto my dick. Drop by fucking drop.

It's the hottest show I've ever seen. I groan in appreciation.

When she's done, she pops her lips and asks innocently, "Like that?"

I look at my dick. A drop of pre-come forms at the tip, my dick showing its appreciation too. "That'll do," I deadpan.

Then I slide my hand down my cock, lubing it up with her and me. When I'm done, I settle between her tits, pressing my hands against the outsides of them. Like that, I hold on tight as I fuck the valley between them, gripping them like they're her hips. A few thrusts, a couple pumps, and pleasure is roaring down my spine, frying my brain and destroying any last bit of reason.

I paint her tits with my release as she cries out *yes*, almost like she's as turned on as I am. Not sure that's possible. Not sure anyone has ever felt like this. My whole body is shaking.

My vision blurs. My brain goes offline. I can't catch my breath. My entire world is reduced to pants, moans, and aftershocks. When the last one jolts through me, I finally register the perfect mess I've made of Maeve's tits. She's covered in my come. It's such a good fucking look. I want to rub it all over her chest, mark her with me. But I should check in with her first. She's tied up after all. I raise my face and take in the flush on her cheeks, her wild hair, her excited eyes. And her arms stretched above her head, straining against the knots of my ties. "Let me undo them," I say, recovering my senses. "And then I'll clean you up."

"Don't."

"Don't undo them?"

"Don't clean me up."

She is the lottery. And if all I get is one night like this where we bend the rules, I will take it and savor it. I will hold onto it forever. I quickly undo the ties, kiss her right wrist, then do the same to the left.

When I lift my face, Maeve's hands are already busy, spreading my climax all over her breasts. "I'm painting myself with your come," she says.

That's it.

She needs another orgasm. "Rules are rules. You need three-to-one orgasms."

"I can't handle five more orgasms," she laughs.

"Have it your way. But we need to be even."

"Says who?"

"I say." My tone brooks no argument.

"I had one in Vegas, and you had none there. We're even."

I grab the Rabbit. "Not for long. Can I fuck you with this?"

"Well, when you put it like that..."

A minute later, she's coming again, and it's a sound I'm already addicted to. I head to the bathroom and grab a washcloth to clean her up.

Sometime later, she's in her cami and a pair of sleep shorts, and I'm in giraffe boxer briefs. We get back in bed, and there's a moment, maybe several, where everything's awkward under the covers.

Where I fear she'll want to lay down rules.

Or say that can't happen again.

Hell, she'll probably say it tomorrow.

But for tonight, all I want is to sleep next to my wife. I preempt her, striking first as I tug her into my arms. "Let's just go to sleep, okay, honey?"

The implication is clear—*I can't talk about this right now. Don't hurt me right now.*

Don't tell me that was a mistake right now.

"Okay," she says softly.

And like she promised the first night we spent together three weeks ago, she's out in seconds. I'm not. I never am. When the world goes still, my mind whirs too fast, replaying the day, or shooting ahead to the next one, reviewing problems I need to solve, things I have to deal with. This time is a little different though. I'm wide awake in the dark, but I feel more peaceful than I usually do. I'm smelling Maeve's sweet plum perfume, touching her soft skin, dreaming of more nights like this.

But knowing they may not come.

I'm tempted, so damn tempted to grab my phone and google—what to do when you've fallen in love with your best friend.

I'm not sure Doctor Google will have an answer I like.

Because there's no way this can end well for us. Relationships never end well for me—they always end.

But even if I weren't broken, even if romance weren't radioactive, there are never any guarantees. Something will always go wrong. Something will always break. And I hate when things spiral out of my control. I hate it more than anything. I don't even know what to do when shit starts falling apart.

Hockey's different. It's unpredictable, yes. But when I play hockey there are *always* solutions. Find a new opening, skate faster, fight for the puck harder, chase it farther. *Achieve*.

But life isn't a game played in three periods on an oval two hundred feet long and eighty-five feet wide. The outcomes are too varied, too unpredictable, too permanent.

I close my eyes and try to sleep.

I breathe in, breathe out.

But my thoughts race away annoyingly. Soon, I start turning over brand-new scenarios. Imagining what-ifs I've barely let myself entertain before.

Like...

What if I stopped holding up all the walls and let myself explore whatever this is with Maeve? What if I let myself feel all these things for her? What if I romanced my wife?

Here's the biggest problem with those what-ifs—what if it all goes wrong?

I shudder at the thought.

Fucking shudder. A visceral sensation that runs jaggedly through me. I wince, then turn to look at her, sound asleep, happy.

Maybe this will be enough.

34

YOU'RE GETTING TO BE A HABIT
WITH ME

Maeve

I'm kneeling on the grass, wearing cut-off shorts and a black T-shirt that says, "Make Art, Not Hard-Boiled Eggs," while sniffing a lavender bush. It's a candid shot of me at the lavender farm in Darling Springs, taken a few years ago on our Big Adventure there. In the corner of a photo, a black-and-white hound of some sort is looking at me. I'm petting his head as I sniff the flowers.

"When did you take this?" I ask, my brow furrowed. I don't remember him taking the picture. I remember the farm dog though. His name is Hudson, and the owner of the farm—Ripley Addison—and I talked about his rescue for a while. She even recommended the organization if I was looking for a pet. I wish I could have a dog. My apartment's a bit small though.

I shake off the dog dreams and turn to Asher, adding, "This photo." So he knows what I'm talking about.

"When we were there," he says easily.

"No, I mean...I don't remember you taking it," I say, glancing at him, confused.

He shrugs, turning away to make coffee. "Must have sneaked it in," but now he sounds a little evasive.

I hold up the frame again, inspecting the one he must have set on the kitchen counter last night. Usually, I'm the one taking selfies or dragging him into them.

"So, like, a drive-by shot?" I joke, but I feel unsettled.

He fiddles with some lever on the fancy coffee machine. Maybe it's an espresso machine, now that I think of it, with all these knobs and levers.

"Yeah, exactly."

"And you had it framed? Like the one on the night-stand?" I ask. I noticed that picture of me in my Quick-Draw Maeve shirt when I woke up. But why am I so focused on *this* photo here? Oh, maybe because it's easier than talking about what happened last night. In *his* home. Now *our* temporary pretend marital home. When we indulged in all the things.

I can still hear him saying *spit on it.*

I can still feel how aroused I was from that filthy command.

He turns around, brow furrowed. "For the news crew. I wanted it to be believable."

Right. Of course. I don't know why I thought it might be for another reason. How stupid of me. I did the same thing with our wedding shots.

"It's great," I say cheerily, despite the knot forming in my chest. I don't want him to think I don't like it. "It's really thoughtful."

"So were yours." The words feel so...false. Like two people tiptoeing around each other. Like we had a fight, and now we're being overly polite to avoid breaking something fragile.

When I woke a little while ago, the bed was empty. He'd probably been up for hours. I threw on a sweatshirt and wandered downstairs to find him making egg-white omelets and saving some for me. Now, he's brewing coffee. I don't even like coffee that much. I thought he knew that. But I'm not about to complain. I'm a guest, after all.

That's it. That's why I feel so weird. It's always awkward to be a guest in someone's home, even when that someone is your best friend—or more? It feels like when I visit Aunt Vivian or when Josie invited me to her mom's house one time after college. Everyone was lovely, but I felt so out of place. Maybe because I don't even have a family home to go to.

And now I'm standing here, feeling like I don't know how to behave with Asher after last night. Our tryst in Vegas was one thing—it was practically chaste by comparison. Last night was entirely different. We were drenched in orgasms. We were naked. We were shameless. We crossed all sorts of lines and yet held back at the same time with that technical no-touching rule—intimacy veiled by a boundary. But I need boundaries or I'll fall into old patterns—clinging, needing, holding on too tight. The way Gideon said I was with him. And I can't do that with Asher. I have to let go of people...like I was forced to do with my parents.

My chest squeezes uncomfortably at the reminder, then aches with memories of them. Back when they were happy. When she was well, when he was the man madly in love with his wife. When no one was sick, or dying, or heartbroken. But if I cling too hard to those memories, I'll get lost in them, and we have a show to put on today.

Focus on the present.

I wander out of the kitchen, feeling Asher's gaze on me. It's subtle, like he's watching me from the corner of his eye as I move through the house. Maybe he wants to say something, but he doesn't. I pretend not to notice, walking toward the living room where I stop in front of another frame he must have placed here last night. It's me, tossing my graduation cap in the air, celebrating my studio arts degree. This one makes sense. I remember him taking it.

But as I keep wandering, I find other shots—me huddled in mountains of jackets while in our room at the ice hotel and a shot of me in the tree tent, reading a book in the sleeping bag. I'm not saying I should remember every photo taken of me, but these? I don't remember them at all. Does Asher make a habit of snapping candids of me?

It's like finding out a friend speaks another language and you never knew. Has photography always been his secret language and I never noticed?

I'd better find out, especially since the TV crew will be here later today. I definitely should know these things about my husband.

I march back into the kitchen, setting my hands on the counter. "Photography's a hobby of yours?" I ask, but before he can respond, the smell of cinnamon and nutmeg hits me. Does he put those spices in his coffee? Because I hate to break it to him, but even yummy spices won't make mud taste better.

He looks over his shoulder, one eyebrow raised. "Why are you asking?"

"I figured it's something I should know before the crew arrives. Like...it's a hobby of yours, right? Like the Lego plants?" I gesture vaguely. "I mean, you have all these pictures, so..."

His shoulders bunch up as he fiddles with a lever on the machine. He looks...tight. Like he could use a massage. My fingers itch to touch him, to rub the tension out. I'm good with my hands. They're strong. I could help. I *want* to help. I take a few steps toward him, already imagining my hands on his shoulders—but then I stop myself. Would that be too much? Too emotional? Too interested? Too clingy?

Fuck you, Gideon.

I drop my hands.

"It's not a hobby," he says, and I shake my head, feeling even more confused. What's happening here? Why do I feel like I'm missing something? I shouldn't press—he might think I'm trying too hard. Or that I'm not respecting our marriage-of-convenience boundaries.

"Well, you're good at it," I say, cheery, since that's nice. I can be nice without being too much. "Did you see the wedding pictures I put up?"

"I did. Last night," he says, cool and in control. "That was smart of you."

Smart. Because this is a sham marriage. The unspoken question lingers longer in the air: Was last night a mistake, then?

Asher turns away from the gleaming espresso machine and hands me a mug. It's my favorite one. The one that says, "I'm a Fucking Ray of Sunshine."

I blink down at the chai latte he's offering me, my eyes widening. "You...you made me a chai latte?" I ask, amazed. I had no idea he had barista skills.

He shrugs again, this time with a hint of a smile. "Well,

my wife really likes them. Isn't that something a husband ought to do?"

The warmth of the mug seeps into my hands and under my skin. Asher learned how to make a chai latte for me. If I'd done that for him, Gideon would have said it was too much. But I love the too-much-ness of this.

Something shifts inside me. There's so much I want to say—that I love the way he's noticed these things about me, that I love how he touches me, that I love the way he thought to take photos of me when I wasn't looking, like I'm someone worth capturing.

But I can't. I won't ruin this temporary thing with too many feelings. Instead, I take a sip and sigh happily. "It's the best I've ever had."

"Yeah, right," he says dryly.

"It is," I insist.

"Thanks."

For a moment, the tension loosens, and for the first time today, it feels like we're both being wholly honest— even if it's just about a drink.

I hold the mug a little tighter. "Asher, the photos are great," I say, meaning it. But there's so much more left unsaid as I drink the rest of it while he downs his coffee.

"I should get ready. They'll be here soon," I say, looking toward the door when my gaze catches on a new reflection. Curious, I make my way over.

My heart climbs into my throat. He hung my new mirror. The one I set on the plant table the other night since I didn't want to be presumptuous. And he hung it exactly where I had imagined it would go. "Asher," I say quietly, more emotion in my words than I'd expected, but I am so damn touched. I try to clear it away, raising my voice as I turn toward the kitchen. "You hung the mirror."

He leans against the doorframe, tilting his head my way. "Because my wife's art should have a place of honor."

Oh, right. Sure. For the camera crew. Of course it's for the crew. I fasten on a smile. "Yes. Thank you." I take another sip to cover up the funny feelings in my chest—something warm mixed with a familiar worry. But it's one I ought to ignore. "Anyway, I'd better shower and all that. And then later I need to meet my agent for a drink. She texted earlier. Some new opportunities."

He nods to the staircase. "I'll leave you to it."

The implication is clear. He won't come upstairs and find me in the shower like I did to him last night. And my heart feels a little heavier for it.

35

REAL CHARADES

Asher

So far, this interview is like a breakaway shot. A clean, open path to the net. We show Rachel Mehta, the reporter from *The Good Stuff*, around *our* home. Her camerawoman shoots video as we go and it sure as shit looks like we happily live together in this space, what with all the pictures I took over the years set out, and the wedding ones Maeve framed. My *habit* of taking pics of my friend came in handy. I even point out the mirror by the door, a proud husband showing off his wife's work, like I told Maeve I'd do. Rachel smiles and says *keep snacks handy* are definitely words to live by.

With Maeve's ruby ring and my silicone band, and our hands held—learned my lesson from the Greers, thank you very much—we look unequivocally married. While we wander through the living room, passing the wedding photos and plant table, Rachel shoots us a professional smile.

"So, it's true you call your wife your good luck charm?"

"I do call her that," I say, casually looping an arm around Maeve's waist. I'm grateful for the easy interview and glad I took the notes to heart after our first *performance* when I didn't touch her enough. That won't be a problem today. If the world wants to see a man who can't keep his hands off his wife, they'll get it.

Hell, maybe last night was good for us when it comes to this facade we need to present for the world. Maybe it connected us even more. Made us look more married. Maybe if we just keep up this touching, this closeness, it'll feel like we've already talked about what went down. Like last night doesn't need explaining because it's obvious, right? I don't want her to say, *'It can't happen again,'* because maybe that would make those words real.

Best if we live in this limbo lust land for a little longer. Where nothing can go wrong.

"Any reason for that? Her being your good luck charm?" Rachel asks, a tablet tucked under her arm.

I squeeze Maeve's waist a little tighter. "She's been my biggest fan. She's cheered me on from behind the boards, and at the auction every year for the last two seasons. And I haven't missed a game since. So there you go."

"It's all me," Maeve says, laughing brightly, almost too brightly as she leans into me, her shoulder bumping mine.

"Can't mess with a streak," I add, dropping a kiss on her nose.

Maeve giggles. *Actually giggles.* That's not like her at all. She's not a giggler. But then again, I've never been this touchy in public with girlfriends. *She's your wife now*, I remind myself.

Be that as it may, I'm not a big PDA guy. But with

Maeve, I'm being extra, because that's what the situation calls for. But also, because I want to, even though this morning was awkward, even though we haven't talked about last night, even though I may never want to talk about it. I just want to keep doing it. So much that I feel this uncomfortable ache in my chest, this deep and terrible longing. I don't think it's just a bottomless desire to touch her. It's from the way I want to keep her close. Closer than I should.

I take a beat to center myself, then focus again on Rachel and the questions. "And I was extra thrilled when she bid on me at the auction."

Rachel arches an eyebrow. "Did you plan to get married in Vegas? Was that part of the whole 'good luck charm' thing?"

Ah, I hadn't thought of it that way before. But luck and Vegas? That makes sense. I roll the dice and say, "Yes."

Maeve runs her hand affectionately down my arm. "Definitely. We feel very lucky."

Rachel's brow furrows in confusion. "I'm sorry," she says, holding up a hand to the camerawoman. "Can we stop for a moment?" The woman cuts, and Rachel glances between us. "Could I trouble you to maybe...not touch so much?"

"Sure." I straighten immediately, feeling Maeve tense beside me.

"Oh, okay," Maeve says, her tone light but clearly thrown off.

Rachel gives an apologetic smile. "It just looks a bit distracting on camera. Like you're acting."

Maeve snorts, loudly. "How ridiculous."

"I know, right?" I jump in. "Who would do that?"

"Exactly," Rachel agrees, glancing at the camera-woman as she resets.

Maeve shifts next to me, her smile stiff. "Sorry. Didn't mean to be distracting."

"Honestly, this sounds cheesy, but just be yourselves," Rachel offers, as if she's trying to ease the awkwardness.

But what if being myself means I want to touch my wife a lot? Maybe I especially do since she hasn't pulled the 'that can't happen again' card. And maybe by making sure I protect her, that I look out for her, that we're damn good at this charade, she won't want to pull that card.

I hear Beckett's voice echoing in my head: *She's trying to make her way in the world, dealing with an overbearing aunt, while you're already a successful hockey player. If this goes south, you'll be fine. But if this blows up, she might not be.*

What if the idea to channel the Greers was wrong? Maybe I should just be myself.

Somewhere in the back of my mind, I know this is more than a game for the cameras. More than for charity. More than a pretend marriage sparked by a viral kindness campaign we didn't expect. If I could just be myself, I'd let on how I felt. I'd admit that at Beckett's wedding, that wasn't simply a momentary lapse of reason. That it was the start of something. Something that's been slowly, steadily, persistently building up strength inside me. Like a storm that was barely a few winds in the ocean and has now been upgraded to a category five, fueled by all these fucking feelings for my best friend.

But I can't go there. Not now—not with Maeve's wish to keep things simple. Then another voice asks—but aren't they already complicated?

I try to shove that voice aside. I'm not ready for all the complications. And she sure as shit isn't.

Rachel nods toward the couch, and we sit. "Let's focus more on the viral kindness campaign," she says. That's why she's here, after all. That's what interested *The Good Stuff*.

"Sure," I say, settling into the cushions.

"It's so rare we see a true feel-good story like this. Something about doing good. We're just so tickled at the way that's taken off. Did you expect that kind of response?" Rachel asks.

I turn to Maeve, speaking from the heart about our night in Vegas. "No, not at all. I honestly just wanted to help out a couple we met and then to have a great time that night."

"And we were just as surprised as anyone when it blew up the next day," Maeve adds, her voice more natural now.

Rachel scrolls through her notes on her tablet, stopping at one. "Your team says the owner has raised..." She pauses, checking her tablet, and then looks up with an eyebrow raised and shares an eye-popping number. "And that's since the post of you two kissing she shared."

"That's amazing," Maeve says, seeming genuinely impressed.

"We're touched," I add.

Rachel's gaze shifts to me. "Has charity always been important to you? You're starting one, right?"

Maeve jumps in before I can respond. "He is, and I'm seriously proud of my husband. He's always cared about more than just sports. He thinks about the whole athlete —their mental and physical health. And he wants kids to have all those tools too. Anxiety is a real thing, affecting so many people, including athletes, and it's not often talked about. It's important to talk about mental health. To destigmatize it for kids. Seeing him create this organization is so...incredible." She looks at me, her expression fond, and I feel something new stir in my chest.

We've talked about Total Teamwork before, but hearing her say it all makes my heart soften more for her. Like that was possible. But evidently it is.

Rachel smiles, as if she's noticing the shift. "And now you'll be by his side as he moves into this new venture?"

Maeve leans against me, her hand resting on my arm, and this time Rachel doesn't object, maybe because this time feels wholly real. "Absolutely. I'm really proud of him."

My heart slams against my chest. This wasn't supposed to happen. We weren't supposed to go from being too touchy, to suddenly feeling warm and...honest.

I try to focus on the rest of the interview, but the way Maeve admires this side of me isn't helping. It's making me feel too much. It's opening the valve on emotions I've been keeping at bay for some time now.

But her words are also like a wide-open window. The sun's shining through it. And it's illuminating the truth as I glance around my home.

It's so much better with her here.

And I can't let her leave.

36

I'M NOT A TACO

Maeve

"It's the woman of the hour."

Those are Angelina's words when I stride over to a corner table at The Spotted Zebra, her favorite watering hole in Hayes Valley.

She opens her arms and gives me a warm hug. She's from Guatemala and has a big sister vibe about her, where she's always looking out for me. It's everything I could want in an agent, and I take the hug, though I'm not letting myself believe her words mean something special.

"You're the woman of the hour," I say, deflecting as we let go.

She flubs her lips—actually flubs them—and waves me off. "Please." She pats the zebra-print stool next to her. "You are, darling." She says "darling" in an exaggerated, snooty tone.

I laugh and sit down. "Darling? Are we doing that now?"

"Seems fitting." She gives me a playful smirk.

"All right. Darling," I say, leaning into her vibe.

As I settle on the stool, Angelina looks me up and down, as if she's assessing my light blue T-shirt with orange piping that says, *I Can't Make Everyone Happy—I'm Not a Taco,* and my flowing black-and-white polka-dot skirt.

"Is this what you wore on camera? It's so cute. Screams *artist*."

I pluck at the shirt. "Does it?"

"Who else could rock mismatched styles and still look this good? You've got creative energy, and it shows."

I lean in, whispering, "I wore it just for you."

Well, she deserves to feel special too.

"Oh, baby, you sure know how to make an agent feel good." She laughs, lifting her martini glass. "Now, let's get you a drink so we can toast to all the good things."

All the good things sure sound good to me, but I don't want to get ahead of myself, so I simply ask for a white wine when the bartender swings by. A fancy cocktail feels too presumptuous, and besides, Asher wouldn't want me to tempt luck. That thought hits me—*did I just adopt one of my husband's luck mantras without realizing it?*

Maybe I did. He'd get a kick out of hearing that. I should tell him. I picture the mirror he hung last night, and my stomach does a little flip. That was such a nice touch.

Then I catch myself when I realize what I'm doing— acting like all these moments are real. *Don't get ahead of yourself, girl. This is a pretend marriage only. Sure, your temporary husband wants to sleep with you, but that is all. At least, I'm pretty sure he does. If buying you five toys doesn't say "I want to bang you into next Tuesday," then what even does?*

I lift my wineglass and clink it against Angelina's chocolate martini. Her rule to live by—*don't skimp on chocolate or art*—is one I can get behind.

"To all the good things," I say, but I'm measured, careful in my tone.

"And there are many coming your way. I'm thrilled about the opportunities I see happening," Angelina says, her bracelets jingling on her arms as she talks animatedly with her hands.

"More live-painting parties?" I ask, guessing that's what she means.

She snorts—and, oh my god, did her martini just come out of her nose? I don't even bother to stifle a laugh, nor does she.

"Excuse me," she says, dabbing at her face with a napkin. "If anyone asked me the most ridiculous thing a client ever said, it'd be when Maeve Hartley asked if her next opportunity was *painting parties*."

Excitement sparks through me, but I hold it down. I don't want to hope too much. "I actually like the painting parties," I say with a happy shrug. "They keep me on my toes."

She waves a hand dismissively. "That's good, and we'll still have plenty of those. But I also had a call with *California Style*. You know them?"

Of course I do—it's an online style magazine. But why would they want to talk to *me*? "Sure," I say, tentatively.

"They want to include *you* in a photo spread," Angelina says, then lifts her hand and counts off on her fingers. "You working on the mural. We'll need team approval on that, but I'm sure it'll be no problem. Then you in your studio, then a shot of your home with some of your art, and even one of your live-painting events. I already spoke to Mr. Vincenzo about using a photo from his party three weeks ago, so we're covered there. And getting one at the arena should be easy. But they'd love some shots of your new home too. They like to showcase homes of artists, designers, architects," she adds.

"Wait, what?" I stammer. "You mean athletes, right? They do features on athletes?"

Angelina shakes her head, laughing. "Oh, sweet summer child. I meant *artists*. You do know the Sea Dogs commission is a big deal, right? They're excited about it, Maeve. You're making waves. This is a spread on rising star artists."

My heart stops because that is too good to be true.

I don't know what to say. The world feels like it's spinning. "But...we're not really..." I start, before quickly clamping my mouth shut. Angelina doesn't know that this is a marriage of convenience. She probably believes the story we spun for the Greers—that Asher and I started dating before the auction and eloped in Vegas because we knew it was right. I guess in a way, she's always seen me as someone who'd make bold moves like that. She's been telling me to trust my instincts for as long as I've known her.

I clear my throat. "We're not really moved in yet."

Angelina gives my hand a reassuring squeeze. "Of course. It's all happening fast. But don't worry—you'll be settled soon. And there are so many exciting opportunities ahead this season."

This season.

The weight of it lands all at once, heavy and unavoidable. This isn't just a fake marriage for a day or two, like we first thought. Then for a few weeks, like we figured after that. We have the picnic and the mural, and now the media features are rolling out. *California Style* wants a photo spread, and the world wants to know more about *us* as a picture of us kissing, somehow, incomprehensibly, has led to thousands of dollars in charitable donations.

Angelina talks excitedly about my rising profile, but I'm barely hearing her. It's all surreal. Maeve the caterer, Maeve the broke artist, Maeve the wild one who struggled to get commissions is now suddenly getting attention because she's Mrs. Callahan. My new profile thanks to a man doesn't sit entirely well with me, but I'm not stupid enough to turn away from the opportunities.

The problem is, I can't invite lifestyle editors to my tiny apartment with a couch best known for its broken spring, pigeons fornicating on the windowsill, and a bathroom where the toilet faces the wall.

It's not that my place is small or humble—that wouldn't matter. I'm an artist. Almost all of us start like that. But I can't do it because the world believes I live with my *husband*. And I don't. Not really.

And then, a terrifying thought takes hold. If I ask Asher if I can stay a little longer—to keep this going—I'll be the clingy one. My stomach twists into knots. I hate the idea of asking that.

Since I'm always the one asking for more.

37

DOUBLE OR NOTHING

Asher

I should focus on beating Miles at pool. I'm only a few shots from bragging rights. The trouble is, as I line up the cue, I can't swat away a persistent thought—*how the hell do I convince Maeve to stay?* My chest tightens, and my brain keeps replaying the question on a loop as I move around the pool table with my teammate, post-workout.

It won't leave me alone. I wish it were a simple question I could ask Google. I line up the shot, but the thought nags at me again, and the ball goes screaming past the pocket, just missing.

Miles shakes his head, giving me a sympathetic look from behind the black glasses he often wears off the ice. "I am so, so sorry you suck," he says, then pushes up the sleeves of his Henley, revealing ink of an arrow on one arm. For focus, he's said. And focus the fucker does. It's almost like he's saying *sit down and watch how it's done* as he moves around the pool table, cleaning up the rest of the balls with practiced ease.

When he's done, he wiggles his fingers. "Now, pay up."

"In my own home?"

"Even more so. That's embarrassing, man—for you," he says with a grin.

"With friends like you..." I say, but I'm not ready to end the game. The last thing I want is to be left alone with my spinning thoughts. "Double or nothing?"

"You are a glutton for punishment, and I can't resist," he says, already resetting the balls for another round.

But once he starts racking them up, the question plays in my head again. Shit. I need to deal with this. "Dude," I start.

He stops, looks up, no doubt hearing the urgency in my tone. "What's up?"

"I want Maeve to stay."

His brow knits, then he nods. "This isn't fake for you."

That's all he has to say. He knows the score. They all have, honestly. For longer than I have maybe. But in Boston, I barely admitted I had feelings for her, only saying *she was great*. I'm getting a little tired of that refrain.

"It's not," I admit, sighing heavily. "Not one bit. Not at all."

He pauses, the cue in hand. "Okay, so ask her to stay. Make it work. Give it a shot." Miles studies me. "Right?"

"In theory, yes. But it could never work for real."

He scoffs. "Why?"

I don't want to get into my faulty heart right now and the way it sputters out, so I just say, "We're friends and all."

"That's your reason, man?"

"That's a damn good reason," I argue. "I mean, we have a lot of history and...stuff. I don't want to risk that."

"Sure, I get that. But all that *it's complicated* stuff is just bullshit at the end of the day, Callahan. If you want her to stay, ask her. Sounds like the perfect opportunity to work your shit out. Maybe, if you're lucky, you can win her over. Stranger things have happened. And maybe it's finally time—you've been in love with her for years."

I drag a hand through my hair, letting that one word sink in—*years*.

No.

That can't be possible.

It can't have been years. I've barely come to terms with my feelings for her since we said *I do*, with the depth of them, the weight of them, the danger of them. There's no way it's been going on for years. That's just not possible. But it's definitely been for longer than I'd realized. Problem is whether or not I'm in love with her doesn't entirely matter, given my track record, given my past. "Just because you're in love doesn't mean you stay in love," I point out.

"True, but so what?"

I furrow my brow. "So what?" I repeat.

He levels me with a stare as he lines up his next shot. "You think love comes with a guarantee? It's not a Hydro Flask. Does hockey come with a guarantee? Every time you get on the ice could be your last time. Every time you leave your house could be the last time," he says.

Like I need the reminder of everything that could go wrong. "I know that."

"But you play anyway. You play a dangerous game for a living. You get in a car. You get on a plane. You fucking breathe. Of course you might not stay in love. But why are you letting that stop you?"

Because we're friends. Great friends. I'm closer to Maeve than I am her brother. She's my best friend more than he is, and I do not want to lose her. Not after nearly losing my dad. And not after all the losses she's endured. After the hurt she's been through. After all the people who are gone. "It might not work out," I say. Even though I'm thinking *it probably won't.*

Miles stares blankly at me. "And?"

I shove a hand through my hair roughly, breathing out hard, my shoulders tensing. "I don't want to risk that."

He nods a few times, then shrugs. "I get it. You're a pessimist," he says. "But this thing between you two—it's doable. It's not like she's the coach's daughter."

I blink, taken aback. "Wait, do you have a thing for Leighton?"

He wags his finger. "We were talking about you."

"And yet, you brought up Leighton." Come to think of it, didn't he give her a ride home after a community outreach event we all did last fall for The Garden Society? "You know...you *do* seem to gravitate to her at events."

He scoffs. "We hardly have any events."

"And that's not a denial."

He stares menacingly at me. Fine, fine, the dude does give good glower, I'll grant him that.

"Photo ops," I correct, thinking he'll admit it that way.

"We're talking about *you* now." Miles tips his chin my way, making it clear that's all he's saying. His dark eyes brook no argument. "It's my turn to give you a hard time, Mister Pessimist."

"I'm a realist," I counter.

"Then be realistic for yourself, man. Yes, it's risky.

Yeah, it might not work out. But do it anyway—ask her to stay for longer. You're clearly not getting divorced any time soon. Look around. You hung up a million pictures of her."

It's the bare truth, and I can't even pretend it was just for the camera crew earlier today. Fact is—I took those pictures. I like those pictures. And asking her to stay isn't the same as risking pouring out the truth of my heart to her. I can do the first without doing the second.

"Okay," I say, letting out a decisive breath. "I'll do it."

"Sooner rather than later," he says, pointing his cue my way.

We start the next round. With each shot, I feel looser, freer. I'll find an opportunity and I'll seize it. We make a game plan for our upcoming game against the Los Angeles Supernovas in two more weeks, especially how to score on his brother Tyler, who plays for them while raising two kids on his own. Younger than Miles by a few years, Tyler's carved out his own solid career for our rivals.

We finish our round, with Miles taking all my money and making a show of pocketing it. "Always a pleasure cleaning you out."

"I bet."

I walk him to the door, opening it just as Maeve's coming up the steps, looking like she's got something on her mind.

"Hey, Maeve," Miles says with a grin. "Be nice to Asher if he asks you something."

"Asshole," I mutter to him.

He flashes me a grin, holding his arms out wide. "Like you'd expect anything less?"

"Did he say I was the mean one? Because he is, I swear," Maeve asks, playfully.

Miles just waves goodbye, then trots down the steps.

Maeve comes inside, but the easy zing-zing-zing I felt with Miles is erased the second the door shuts. Her expression is serious, her brow furrowed. Something must have come up with Angelina, and the weight of whatever she's thinking seems to hang between us. Maybe this isn't the moment to ask.

"What's going on?" I ask.

"A lot," she says, her voice shaky. No idea if that's good or bad.

"Talk to me," I say, nodding to the couch in the living room.

Once we sit, she breathes out like she's girding herself to say something hard. I tense, preparing myself for bad news, when she says, "Angelina has a bunch of opportunities for me. For a few months."

I don't even think twice. I take the chance. "Stay here with me. Through the end of the season. Just stay." Then, so she doesn't think it's for show, for the Greers, for appearances, or for any other reason than pure want, I add, "I want you to."

Her smile is radiant, so damn beautiful. "Really?"

"I mean it. Stay." It's both a command and a plea, and I hope she doesn't hear the desperation in my voice.

"Asher," she whispers, her eyes wide, like she's afraid speaking any louder would break the moment. "Confession: I was going to ask if I could stay."

Damn, this feels like some kind of luck. And I can't help myself. I rap my knuckles subtly against the back of the couch. It's not wood, but it'll do for knocking. "So, we're married through the end of the season," I say, though it's more of a statement than a question. I lift a hand, tucking a stray curl behind her ear as I set the time-frame for the rest of this union. At Mr. Vincenzo's party three weeks ago, we said we'd do this for a month or so, till Total Teamwork officially launched and the mural was done. But now? Now I have even more time with her. I've got a few months, and I want to make the most of them.

"We are," she says, and she sounds...relaxed. Excited too. I like both of those sounds—a lot. "And I still have my sub-lease on my place. So don't worry. I won't crowd you too much. I'll be able to return to it when this is over."

When this is over...The thought curls my stomach. I don't even want to acknowledge the statement. So I side-step. "You could sub-lease your place for a while. Pocket the rent."

"Oh. Do you want me to pay rent here?"

I scoff. "No."

"Asher," she presses.

"No. Just no. You are not paying rent, even if you lease your space. In fact, you'll never pay rent here, and you'll always be welcome," I say, meaning it. Hell, this home feels like it was meant for her.

"If you say so."

"I do." I exhale, relieved, settled even. "Now that that's settled, be a good wife and tell me what's going on. What are these opportunities?"

She laughs, then begins. "There's *California Style*."

As she shares more of her conversation with her agent, I smile confidently. Knew it. Called it. "I told you big things would happen for you."

Her mouth is soft, grateful as she says, "I don't say it enough, but I really appreciate how much you've believed in me."

Please. That's easy. I hook my thumb toward the hall-way. "That mirror of yours? I hung it for you. Not for the crew. Not for show. But because I legit love it. Because I'm proud of you. And because it's great."

She dips her face, smiling. "Stop making me feel so good."

"That won't happen," I say, and this is the perfect chance to deal with something else. Something I didn't deal with last night. Or before I left for my road trip. Something, frankly, I didn't deal with well in Vegas the night it happened. The night *we* happened, when I said it shouldn't happen again.

Fuck that.

I meet her eyes and ask the tough question without agenda, without preempting her, with only the hope for her *yes*. "What do you want to do about what happened last night?"

And I don't have to wait long.

Her hazel eyes glimmer with that look she gets when I kiss her, when I touch her, when I edge her. "I can't stop thinking about it," she admits. "But I don't want to lose our friendship."

"I don't either," I say, my voice thick with desire and something more. But something I won't let on now. Not yet. Not this soon. I can't risk scaring her away with the depths of my feelings. But the depths of my desire? That's a whole other story, and I am ready to tell it.

She pauses, clearly thinking. "Maybe we need to get it out of our systems."

Oh hell, do we ever. "We should enjoy the marital benefits then. It is our three-week anniversary after all."

Her smile is the sexiest *yes* I've ever seen. "And I know what I want—friends with benefits. Husband and wife with benefits. Same idea?" she asks, like she's testing out new terms.

Do I want more? Yes. But will I take what I can get for now? I absolutely will. I am *not* going to press my luck by saying anything further.

"Yes." I let out a slow breath and wrap a hand tightly around her head. "And now I'd really like to fuck my wife the way I've been wanting to for a long, long time. With no regrets."

38

WHEN YOU KISS ME LIKE THIS

Maeve

It doesn't surprise me that Asher has a plan. He always has a plan. He always knows how to handle any situation.

Including, evidently, *me*.

Except I'm not entirely sure what to expect next, especially when he cups my jaw with a firm grip, levels me with a dark stare, and then says, in a voice that's not at all friendly, "Don't move."

Like I'd do anything else but obey him. A shiver rushes down my back, and I nod. He runs his hand along the side of my hair, over my shoulder, along the top of my arm. Then he rises from the couch, watches me for a beat as he moves around the piece of furniture, and stands behind me.

Anticipation thrums through my body, like bubbles in a champagne glass, and I look up and back at him, wondering once more what his plan for me is but thrilled that he clearly has one.

He places both hands on my head, then runs them down gently over my hair. Stroking it. Once, twice, then a third time, before he gathers all my strands between his hands, sliding his fingers through them, fashioning them into a ponytail. His touch is soothing and sexy all at once. I'm warm everywhere, like honey.

His thumbs stroke my hairline tenderly. Then he lets go, bends down, and brings his face near mine, his breath coasting across my cheek. "Do you have any idea how sexy your neck is?"

I tremble, shaking my head. I'm not even sure I was aware that he was into my neck.

"Sometimes I stare at your neck. When I think you're not looking. And I imagine kissing you there," he says, his voice a husky rasp.

"You do?" I'm kind of amazed at the specificity of this... want.

"Let me show you," he says. Then he sweeps my hair up to the left side and dusts a soft, sensual kiss to the back of my neck. My shoulders bunch up in pleasure. He takes his time, his lips traveling over my skin, then down the side of my neck toward my collarbone, pushing the T-shirt over an inch or so. He presses open-mouthed caresses there while he cups the side of my face in his left hand.

He's holding me in place, in a firm grip that has me at his delicious mercy. He tugs my head to the left, stretching my neck and sweeping more dizzying kisses along my flesh. I murmur, shuddering with each druggy kiss he bestows.

It's safe to say when he told me he wanted to fuck me, I didn't think he'd start like this. With this slow, languid, exploration that has me feeling all loose and warm.

"Fucking gorgeous, Maeve," he whispers. "I've wanted to do that for so long."

He said that before—that he's wanted me for so long. Since the auction, he must mean. Since I kissed him that night.

"What have you wanted?" I ask, needing to know what he's pictured since then. If it's been some of the same things I've imagined.

"I want to watch you melt. I want to hear you moan. Want to see you beg, crawl, fall apart."

I gasp at the promise of all those things. "I'll beg. I'll crawl. I'll come very hard," I say, an easy promise since he's made everything easy so far. His hands and mouth seem made for me.

I reach for him, lifting my hands to tug him a little closer. But he grabs my wrists, spreads my arms out wide, and curls his hands over mine, pinning them in place as he devastates my neck with the most luxurious, intoxicating kisses known to womankind.

I'm panting and gasping, caught up in a kiss trance. Both turned on and intrigued, I ask breathily, "What are you doing to me?"

Because I truly don't know what his plan is.

He smiles down at me, a little wicked. "Why don't you tell me? Or better yet," he says, nipping at my jawline before he tips his forehead down to my lap, "show me."

It takes me a few seconds to catch up to his meaning. When I do, my pulse beats wildly between my thighs.

Show me.

Like when he said *spit on it.*

I reach down, gather the soft cotton of the hem of my skirt, and pull it up above my knees, stopping at my thighs, then teasing him with, "Like this?"

It's asked ever so innocently.

His breath hisses out, harsh and ragged. His mouth comes down on my shoulder, biting it. I jump, but it's not a harsh bite. It's a passionate one, like he's putting all his lust into it, leaving teeth marks on my skin.

"Yes, like that. Like a good wife would do," he says.

A burst of heat flares inside me, chased by a warm, safe sensation. That's how I feel when he calls me *wife*— like he'd take care of me.

Like he's both my safe harbor and the man who wants me, all in one.

Sitting on the couch with him behind me, directing the scene, I tug the skirt up, up, *up* my thighs, then to my waist, revealing my panties to him.

"Fuck." The vibration from the growl lands in my ear. I can tell he's staring down at my white cotton panties.

"But you can't see exactly what you've done yet."

A soft laugh falls from his lips. He cups my jaw, turns my face to him. "What a good point. Be a good wife then and let me taste you for the first time."

I shiver, expecting him to come around and drop down between my knees. But instead he nods, urging me on. "Come on, your husband is hungry. Slide your finger inside."

I shudder but obey, gathering up my own arousal, then lifting my hand to him. With his face next to mine, he sucks on my finger, and I swear I go up in flames from the sounds he makes. It's like he's eating the most extravagant meal. Then he grabs my face and crashes his mouth down on mine. His tongue strokes inside. His teeth nip on my lips. He's voracious. When he breaks the kiss, I feel dazed, drunk on him already.

In a flash, he's around the couch, down on his knees,

peeling off my panties. He looks up at me. "Now, I can kiss you in a whole new way."

39

KING SIZE

Asher

I could drown in her.

She tastes incredible. Like I knew she would. But somehow even better. I guess that's what it's like when you finally have your dream girl. She's better than your dreams. Because she's real and sweet and addictive on my tongue. I kiss her pussy like I can't get enough of her because I can't.

My hands find their way up the soft flesh of her thighs as I spread her nice and wide. She murmurs and cries out as I lick up her pussy, sucking on her. She arches and shudders, and that drives me on. I trace a circle around her clit with my tongue and suck her into my mouth, making her cry out. I listen for her cues, and I follow them, shifting from soft, fluttery licks to hungry kisses, lavishing the attention her sweet pussy deserves from my mouth. Nothing has ever felt so right. No one has ever felt so much like mine, even though I know that's not true. But it's a heady thought and a thrilling one all the same as I lick and kiss and stroke.

"God, Asher," she whispers, then curls her hands around my head. A bolt of pleasure rushes down my body, making me even harder.

"Yeah," I mutter against her, urging her on. "Grab my head."

She laughs softly, then murmurs, "So controlling even when you eat me."

I pull back, look up at her, not even smiling. Just arching a brow. "Yes, I am. Is that a problem?"

Excitement flashes across her features as she shakes her head quickly. "I like it."

"I thought so. Now grab my head and use my fucking face like I told you to, wife."

She huffs out a breath like she's annoyed when her wet pussy says the opposite. So do her hands as she wraps them tighter around me, gripping harder, letting me know she likes this too. Every second of our back and forth. She arches her hips and soon she's following my orders, thrusting her hips at my face.

I push on her thighs, opening her wider, lifting her knees up so her feet are at the edge of the couch. I keep her open for me, holding her in place like that as I lick her and eat her. I glide my hands under her ass, squeezing it hard, and fighting off a torrent of pleasure that slams into me. Her ass in my hands is fucking spectacular. She whines and I love that too.

It's so very Maeve. I catalog this detail—Maeve is a whiner because of course she's a whiner. She's the girl who doesn't hold back. She does everything with her whole heart and body. So it's not really a surprise, but it is a fucking delight that she puts her whole heart and body into getting eaten out.

She's thrashing and writhing, rocking into my face and using me exactly how I want her to. Her nails dig into my skull, and I pray she leaves marks. I flatten my tongue, giving her wet pussy a long, lusty stroke.

She jerks, and I try not to come in my pants *again* while she goes wild on my mouth. My chin. No, my whole goddamn face. It's like my mouth is a toy and she is fucking it the way she wants. I will not be Quick-Draw Asher again. Not this time.

And the thing is...I've never been happier, I've never been more turned on, I've never been more aroused than when she snaps her thighs to my head. Clamping them down like a vise, she surrenders and screams at the same time. She's so loud, so into this, so very her.

"Oh god, oh god," she chants. Wild and unleashed. And it's everything.

My head swims with an overdose of desire as I lick and kiss her through her orgasm.

When she gently pushes back on me, I let go and wipe the back of my hand across my wet mouth as I look up at her. I don't take a picture. *Of course* I don't take a picture. But I snap this shot in my mind.

It's perfect. Wild, disheveled, hypnotically beautiful Maeve.

Yeah, I was right. Disheveled Maeve is a very good look, and I can't get enough of it. It's mine. This look is all mine. I want to remember it forever because I'm pretty sure I've wanted this—her giving herself to me—for so much longer than I even realized.

I rise, slide a hand over my very needy hard-on in my jeans. With a contented sigh, she blinks, then her eyes travel down my body, stopping at my erection before she locks eyes with me again. "Well, are you finally going to let me feel that big dick of yours?"

I take a beat, tilting my head, giving her a lopsided grin. "I will on one condition."

"What's that?"

"If you come all over it, nice and bare, like a good wife. Exactly the way I want you."

"Bare," she repeats it like I've invited her to Tahiti. Like going bare is a fancy tropical destination.

Well, yeah.

"I've been tested for everything. Negative. Are you on protection?" I ask the last question because it's the right thing to do, though I already know the answer. I saw her pills on the bathroom counter this morning. But it's important to ask. It's important to talk about it.

"I'm on the pill and I'm negative too."

A grin works its way across my face as I imagine filling her with my come. "God, I need to fuck you right now, honey."

"Honey," she repeats, as if she's savoring the word on her tongue.

"You like when I call you that?"

She offers me her hand, meets my gaze with bold, hungry eyes. "Asher, I like everything." She presses her chest flush to mine. "So, so very much."

I want to record those words. Play them on repeat in my head. Drink them down, eat them up, subsist on them. *I like everything. So, so very much.*

Instead, I scoop her up, then toss her over my shoulder, easily. "Asher, I'm five-eight," she squeals. "How can you pick me up?"

"I'm six-three and weigh more than two hundred

pounds. I'm supposed to be strong. If I can't carry you upstairs, I should be banished from the game."

"All right. Do it then," she says in a playful challenge.

One I fully accept as I head upstairs, carrying her the whole way, my hand on her sweet, bare ass. She hums happily as I stroke the curve of her cheek where it dips and meets the back of her thigh, the delicious crease.

But once we're in the bedroom I'm not so playful anymore. I am horny as fuck for my wife.

I set her on the end of the bed and slide my hands up her thighs, pushing her skirt up. "You need to ride my cock right now," I say in a tone that says I'm not fucking around when it comes to fucking. "I want to stretch you as far as I can."

She slides her teeth along her lower lip and says, "Bet you want to watch my tits bounce too."

I shudder out a harsh breath, then slide my thumb roughly along her bottom lip. "The sass in you. I want to fuck it right out of that pretty mouth."

She purses her lips then blows me a seductive kiss. "Then I really should get on my knees."

The image of her plump, pretty lips wrapped around my cock is branded on my brain, but no way can I have her the way I want if she's sucking me off. I will come in seconds. "Next time. Right now I want you to take my clothes off and see what you've done to me," I tell her.

She grabs at my shirt, then tugs it over my head in one swift motion. When she drags her nails over my pecs, I shudder from the feel of her fingers, from the reminder that even if I tell her what to do, she is still in charge. Hell, she holds me in the palm of her hand even if I'm setting the pace.

This woman simply owns me.

I can't look away as she runs those long cherry red nails through my chest hair, playing with it before roaming down my abs, then to the button on my jeans, and undoing them. In no time she drops to her knees, and she pushes my jeans down. Then shrugs. "Oops, I couldn't wait."

"Maeve," I say in a warning.

She pouts. And yep, I knew she'd be good at that too—pouting. She does everything to the fullest. "But I like your dick so much. Are you sure I can't suck your big dick?"

I close my eyes for a second, then open them to run a finger over her lips. "I think you really like saying that."

"I can't help it. I like king-size in everything."

I tip my head back and laugh. Then smile smugly, but grateful, too, that I've got the goods she wants. But I don't have it in me to deny my wife. "Then take it out and I'll let you have one good, long lick before I fuck you the way you need to be fucked."

She pushes my jeans down and I step out of them. When she sets eyes on my boxer briefs, she wiggles her brows. "Monkeys swinging on vines?"

It's not really a question. It's like an insider secret as she hearkens back to Vegas and to the night she became mine—when we walked past the monkey business ad from CheekyBeast.

Soon after that, she became mine for a night, but then unexpectedly mine for a little longer. And this time, she's deliberately mine for now. She pushes down on my boxer briefs with the monkey prints till my cock springs free, hard, throbbing, leaking at the tip.

She rubs it against her cheek. I think I might die of lust. Pleasure's burning a path through my body as she drags my hard shaft over her soft face, along her cheek, over her lips. It's the hottest thing I have ever seen in my life, like she's a cat, marking her person. Only Maeve is marking my dick. Or maybe I'm marking her. I don't even know anymore.

She parts her lips, looking ravenous. "It's seriously so pretty I want to paint it."

I laugh again. "I thought you didn't do nudes."

She shakes her head. "I don't. I think I'm a little obsessed with your dick. Is that okay?"

I stroke her hair. "I'm obsessed with your hair." I run the backs of my fingers against her cheek. "Your face." I brush a thumb over her lips. "Your mouth."

Then silently...*you.*

She drops her face and draws the tip between those pretty lips. My bones crackle. She looks spectacular, then even better when she opens wider and swallows me inch by inch, her eyes sparking with lust and excitement as she takes me deeper. My blood heats like the sun.

My wife, on her knees, craving my cock is officially the sexiest thing that has ever happened to me. But when she sneakily shoves a hand between her thighs and strokes her wet pussy, I revise that statement. Because *this*, right here, is even hotter. So hot I yank my dick from her mouth.

"What?" she asks innocently. Too innocently.

"I will come on your face if you play with yourself."

Her eyes widen, flickering with filthy excitement. She wraps a hand around my dick. "I want that soon."

I know what she means. Of course, I fucking know what she means. But I have to ask the question. "You want me to come on your face?"

"I do." Like she said when I married her.

She is killing me, and I need her. I strip off the briefs then lie down on the bed, parking my hands behind my head on the pillow. "Get naked and sit on my dick now." She slips off her skirt, pulls off her T-shirt, and unhooks her bra. She stands naked before me and my mouth goes dry.

My efforts to control everything fly out the window.

My heart stutters. Thumps harder. My best friend is naked and gorgeous. This is so unreal, and yet here she is climbing up on the bed, straddling me and saying, "So this is how you want me."

I can barely breathe. I want her so much. I want her in every way. I nod since I'm unable to speak. I would probably only grunt anyway. I grip the base, offer her my dick. And finally manage to use my words again, gritting out, "Take it, honey. Take it all."

It's a barren rasp, full of raw emotion.

She has to hear the truth in my voice. To know this is so much more than sex.

But maybe she's lost in the moment too, since she bats my hand away so she can wrap her fist around my dick. She rubs the head of my cock against her pussy. I close my eyes because it's almost too much. The hot, slick, silky feel of her.

I shake. I breathe out hard, biting off a string of curse words so I don't shoot right now. Everything feels too good. Every single thing.

Like Maeve, guiding my cock along her pussy, getting ready to take me deep. Like Maeve positioning the tip. Like Maeve drawing a deep, steadying breath and sinking down on my dick.

In one smooth motion she takes me into her body, and I toss my head back, letting out a feral groan. "Fuuuuck."

She's tight and hot, and she has my last name.

Nothing has ever been better than this. I grab her hips and fuck Mrs. Callahan, using all my strength and every ounce of control to thrust up, to fill her and take her and have her and mark her.

And to wrestle back what I need most—control. "Lift your hands into your hair," I tell her, in a clear order.

She complies, raising them, lacing her fingers through those lush waves as she leans her head back and gives me the most perfect view in the entire universe.

It is glorious to witness. The sight, the sound, her scent, her pleasure as she rides my cock. Her tits bounce, her skin glistens, and her pussy stretches as I fill her deep. Every nerve in me is raw, exposed as I slam her down on me then grind up into her, setting the pace under her until she's gasping and groaning.

I let go of her right hip to slide my thumb between her thighs, rubbing her needy clit. With a few quick circles, she's shaking, shuddering, coming, and I really need to follow her there.

But not like this, when she's got me by my balls, so to speak.

When she lets out a final gasping, satisfied breath, I lift her off me. "On your back. Knees up high. Hold them open."

I set her down on her back and she complies, sliding her knees up to her tits. "You want to watch your dick slam into me?"

She knows me too well. That's the problem. But that's also the joy. "I fucking do," I tell her.

"Is that your kink?"

I take a beat, letting the moment breathe as I shake my head, stroke her cheek, and speak from the bottom of my damaged, greedy heart as I say softly, "You are my kink."

She gasps, but I don't give her time to linger. Her sounds turn into long, greedy moans as I sink into her all the way. I stare down at the place where we meet, watching her glistening pussy stretch around my cock. She reaches for the headboard, gripping it with both hands. "Like that?" she asks as if she knows what I'm thinking. As if she knows what I need.

For her to let me fuck her hard. For me to take her.

"Yeah, just like that," I say. Sparks rattle down my body, shooting straight to my cock. I'm not far off. Not at all. I pick up the pace. Faster, deeper, racing to the edge.

Trouble is, this isn't enough.

I need more of her pleasure. I make a game-day decision, stretch out an arm, and grab the aptly named Finger Puppet that we used last night. It's in a drawer. I shove it toward her. "Let go of the headboard. Fuck yourself while I fuck you," I tell her.

Maeve needs no instructions. She holds onto the slats with one hand, puts the toy on her index finger, and shoves it between her legs, stroking and moaning.

That's all it takes. I fucking explode in pleasure. It takes me hostage. It steals my brain. It robs me of anything else but the sheer and utter bliss of coming hard and deep inside Maeve as she shouts my name.

It's hot and electric. It's raw and passionate, and it is not nearly enough. I want so much more. I want it all. I want everything.

When I ease out, my come drips down her thigh, a slow slide that I can't look away from.

Lying next to her, I slip my hand between her legs and rub my finger through my release, push it back into her pussy with two fingers, and hold them there till I'm satisfied I've filled her.

She blinks, her breath hitching. Then she parts her lips, meeting my eyes, whispering, "Asher."

"Yeah?"

But she says nothing. She's not really asking anything either. It's just said as an observation like she can't quite believe I did that. Honestly, I can't either. I ease out my fingers, shaking my head, a little shocked. "I've never done that before."

She's quiet for a moment. "Me neither." Another pause. A crinkle of her brow. "Was that how you wanted to fuck me?"

"It's one of the ways," I say honestly.

"Will you show me the others? We have time, you know." It's asked with raw hope. Like she thinks there's a chance I'd say anything but yes.

"I will. I promise." Little does she know I'd probably promise her everything. Damn the complications. Damn the risks. Damn the challenges.

I run my other hand over her freshly fucked hair. She sighs, long and contented as I stroke her strands with no plans to stop. But we probably should clean up. "Do you want to shower?"

I should add *with me*. So she doesn't take the question the wrong way. But before I can say another word, she says, "Your shower *is* better than a sex toy. I'll get up in a minute. But right now I'm kind of into the bed."

A laugh bursts from me. I barely know where to start with that statement. "Would you like some sex toys *in* the shower too, Maeve? You can have a collection of five supersize vibrators there as well."

"I require six," she says, then settles into the bed with a

contented hum. "It's hard to get out of your bed. It's so nice." There's a pause, then she adds, "I slept so soundly here."

My stupid heart speeds up from that statement. Maybe the bed will make her want to stay longer. But I also picture Vegas and how she conked out right away. "Maeve, when do you not sleep soundly?"

She snuggles up against me, her chin resting on my shoulder. "I'm just saying...I did."

"I think it's in your nature to sleep soundly," I say, since I'd be a fool to get ahead of myself and think it's me. But I did sleep well with her too.

"I'm a sleep champion. What can I say? Maybe someday you can have a nap date with me. Wait, do you even nap?"

"I nap before games," I point out.

She scoffs. "That's like exercise. Like eating broccoli because it's good for you."

"It's still a nap."

"I meant like a nap where you don't have anything to do, anywhere to go. Where you lie in the sun and let afternoon dreams take you away."

"No."

"You hate relaxation."

"Not true," I say.

"A little true."

"Fine," I grumble. "It's a little true."

"I know you well," she says, pleased, and I *mostly* am too from those four words. She does know me. She knows I'm more wound up than I let on. She knows I like to be in charge, to fix things, to play hard and have fun on the ice, to show up for my friends, to hang out with my dads, to go to new places with her, and now, I suppose she knows *this*—how I like to fuck.

But would she want to know me better? See more of me? Discover the parts she doesn't know? To know what keeps me up at night? What stresses me out? More so, will she ever catch up to where I am? And while we're at it, what do *I* want? Besides for her to really like my big bed.

Those questions ping through my brain, repetitively. I try to ignore them, but they're making me antsy. And, well, so is the fact that there's a wet spot on the bed. I turn to her and swat her ass. "Shower. Now."

"Are you saying I'm dirty?"

"You're filthy," I tease.

"Pot. Kettle."

I point to the bathroom. "Go," I tell her.

"So filthy. *And* so bossy."

"You say that like you don't love my kind of bossy."

"So cocky too," she adds, hopping out of bed with a playful grin, and heading straight to the bathroom.

But I can't move. The sight of her naked, walking so casually, so comfortably into the bathroom is stealing the air from my lungs.

Yes, she's sexy as fuck with that gorgeous heart-shaped ass. But it's the *way* she looks in my home.

Like she fucking belongs.

It's killing me.

And exciting me.

And fucking me up.

Dragging a hand through my hair, like it'll sort out my wild thoughts, I get out of bed and follow her to the bathroom. She's already looping her hair into a messy bun on top of her head, then stepping into the shower.

She turns it on, and yep—she owns this place.

And, really, me.

I dim the lights, step inside, and shower with my best friend for the first time. I grab some of her body wash, and rub it onto her stomach, her breasts, her ass, then I get down on my knees and clean her thighs, looking up at her.

"Thanks for making a mess of me. And thanks for cleaning me up," she says, in a tone I haven't heard from her before.

It's soft, maybe just shy of romantic. I want to hear that tone again. Mostly, I want to earn it. I stand and drop a kiss to her forehead. "Anytime," I say, and that barely covers the scope of things.

But for now, it'll have to do.

40

AFTER ALL THIS TIME

Asher

This won't be our first night together in bed. It'll be our third as husband and wife. But we've shared beds before this too. Like the one in the ice hotel. We shared a room on that trip—that was the point. To freeze together.

Then, there were our sleeping bags, lined up next to each other in the tree tent.

Another time when we went on a tour of amusement parks up and down the California Coast, we shared a room in the All Aboard Inn, a hotel with suites built from old train cars. We pretended we were rich Europeans solving a murder mystery.

But this time is different *for me*. Since it's the first time I'll get in bed thinking too hard about the future rather than the present.

It's all I can think about even after we forage the fridge for leftovers, even after we return to the bedroom, even after we slip under the fresh sheets and covers.

I meet her gaze once more, taking in her still bee-stung lips, the flush on her cheeks, her playful eyes. Then, those two books on the nightstand. They're just books, but they're also the signs of Maeve. They're positioned a little haphazardly, like she does live here. Not like she was trying to make them neat as a guest. But like she's comfortable in my home.

Is this even real? I run a hand down her arm like I need confirmation. Yep, real. She's here, and she's not leaving, and she's not laying down rules, and she's got my ring on her finger.

She's my wife for the rest of the season.

It's a wild, addictive thought, and my mind won't stop thinking it, over and over. It's barely ten. I'm not at all tired. I'm not even sure she is, so I say, "Do you want to watch something?"

"As long as it's not a drama."

"Do I look like I'd play a drama?"

"Nope," she says with a pop of her lips, then runs a hand up my chest, playing with the hair on my pecs. It's a familiar gesture, one I hope she turns into a habit. But her brow furrows. "Asher?"

That tone. The question in her voice. I tense. "Yeah?"

"I was afraid we wouldn't be able to be friends. If we had sex," she says, vulnerable, looking up at me. "But this is nice. I think we can. And I'm so glad."

Has there ever been a more double-edged sword in my existence? Her words should be good. But they're a reminder of how far apart we are. And what we stand to lose if this goes sideways. Still, I say from the heart, "Me too."

Because I don't want to lose her. *Ever.*

When I reach for the remote on the nightstand, Maeve

slides closer, snuggling tighter against me. Fuck, that's nice. My heart thuds hard. So loud she has to be able to hear it. I will it to quiet down.

I run my hand over her hair again. I can't seem to stop touching her as I aimlessly search the streaming options, barely paying attention to the screen.

But then she freezes for a few seconds before she inches away from me.

"What's wrong?" I ask.

She backs away more. "I don't want to crowd you in bed."

That won't do, her slipping away. "You're not crowding me," I say, meeting her gaze in the soft glow of the room, shaded blue and then green as the TV screen reflects on her face.

Worry lines her eyes. "It's cool. Not everyone likes to cuddle."

"I'm not everyone."

"I know."

"Is this your way of saying you don't want to cuddle?" I counter, slightly guarded. I hope that's not what she's saying.

"No. It's that...I want to be respectful of your space," she says, full of tact.

I scoff. "Fuck respect," I say, then raise my arm, inviting her back into the crook of my shoulder. "Get over here. And fuck those everyones who made you think guys don't like to cuddle."

She smiles. "Well, well, well. I guess I've learned you're officially a cuddler."

"Shut up and cuddle," I say, then haul her against me.

"There you go again—giving me orders."

"And you love them," I tease. She does, and it's easier

to just *be* in this moment rather than think too hard about what happens tomorrow, next week, and next month.

She primly pulls the covers up. "I'm an independent woman. I don't want a man to tell me what to do." She pauses and shoots me a mischievous look. "Unless we're in bed and he wants to hold my throat."

That's a hell of a roadmap. She's in her sleep cami, so I slide a palm over her chest, up her throat, then around it, gently holding her in place. "Such a good wife," I say, low and smoky.

She shivers, then whispers, "Next time."

Two perfect words. A simple promise of more. I'll take what I can get for now. Rather than push my luck, I find a comedy and turn it on.

* * *

Sometime into the second episode, she goes quiet. Then, her breathing evens out. She cuddles even closer in her sleep. I pet her hair. It's perfect. Totally perfect with her here post-sex. With her comfortable with me. With us slipping back into the way we were.

With no regrets.

But even so, I don't fall asleep. There's too much happening in my head. Too many questions. Too many thoughts. Quietly, resting her head on the pillow, I slide away, tucking the blanket over her shoulder. I get out of bed in my boxer briefs, pull on a hoodie, and pad downstairs. My laptop's on the kitchen counter, and I wish it were baseball season. I could fuck around in some baseball forums, talk trash anonymously about the city's two teams even though I promised Everly I wouldn't do that again. I need something, anything, to keep me busy because my mind's a cluttered freeway right now.

I stop at the silver machine, flick it open, and toggle on a browser window. But I don't have anything to ask Google.

Instead, I close it, head to the hall closet, and open it quietly, taking out a small box from the top shelf. It's a Lego plant—a prickly pear.

Maeve got it for me for Christmas as part of a whole succulent collection. I go into the living room, flipping on a lamp. I pop open the box and quietly sort the pieces on the coffee table. It's like a jigsaw puzzle, and I need something to focus on now besides my own tangled thoughts.

But as I'm building the terracotta pot, my attention snags on a frame on the other side of the room.

I set down the plastic arm of the cactus, and head over to the frame to inspect the picture more closely even though I've seen it before. It's the photo of Maeve reading in the tree tent on one of our Big Adventures, curled up on her side in the sleeping bag, a book light illuminating the well-worn pages. I can't tell what she's reading, but I bet it's one of her mother's books. She loves those, says she reads them till the pages fall out. Pretty sure that's what she was reading that night.

As it grew darker over the Sierras, I snapped some pictures of the starlit sky from the tree, then turned around and saw her like that in her orange sleeping bag. I remember thinking she'd want to look back on that someday. I took the photo for her so she could remember it.

That was six years ago.

I stare at the photo till my vision goes blurry with memories.

I set it down, but I don't return to the couch. Something is tugging at me. There's a pull in my chest. A quiet chorus in the back of my mind that's growing a little bit louder. Telling me to keep going. Keep asking. Keep looking.

I circle back to the kitchen, pick up the photo of her in the lavender field with the dog in the corner. That was three years ago. She'd wanted to visit Lavender Bliss Farms so fervently that she'd planned it for months. There was one weekend for the peak bloom, she'd said. So we drove to Darling Springs and wandered through the lavender maze, then scoured the fields, the farm's dog trotting at her side, like he wanted to adopt her. No surprise—Maeve has that way about her. She'd scratched the dog's head, tossed him some tennis balls, then sniffed every lavender bush, it seemed. She told me scent was most directly linked to memory. "And the more I sniff the lavender, the better I'll recall this feeling someday. This sweet summer joy I feel right now," she'd said. "Someday I'll paint this and call it *That Summer Memory*."

I didn't want her to miss that feeling, so I took a picture.

Or so I told myself.

But now I wonder...

I turn and take a tour of all the photos of her I've framed. The graduation shot, taken more than seven years ago. The ice hotel from five years ago. One from four years ago after she rode a double-loop upside-down roller coaster, and her cheeks were flushed and her hair a mess when she stepped off it. "My heart has never beat so fast," she'd said.

So I took a picture.

Telling myself it was for her.

It was for her to remember.

It was for her someday.

I walk over to the small mirror by the front door. The one I hung up last night. Her art. Her almost kiss. Her friends' advice—*keep snacks handy.*

And in the reflection, I'm looking at the truth of my actions. I didn't hang her art for the camera crew.

I didn't hang it for Maeve.

I hung it for me. Because I love it, and I love making her happy. So she'd feel at home here.

All these other pictures? I didn't take them so she'd have a record of all our days together. I didn't take them so she wouldn't lose a memory.

I took them...for me.

So I'd have them.

So I could look at them.

So I could return to them.

As I return to each one, I finally see what I was doing seven, five, four, three, two years ago from behind the lens of my phone.

I was slowly, over time, day by day, falling in love with my best friend.

Miles was right. He was so damn right.

I circle back to the lavender photo in the kitchen. *That Summer Memory.* My heart thunders mercilessly in my chest. It hammers so hard it nearly hurts.

Because here, after midnight, with Maeve sound asleep upstairs, and me being chased by relentless thoughts all day, I have an answer I didn't know I was searching for.

My heart isn't broken.

I don't come with an expiration date.

I'm not radioactive with romance. Nothing lasted after

I met Maeve because I was falling in love with her all that time.

And I didn't even know it was happening. Last night, I realized how I felt. But now, I can see this feeling started years before we made a pact at her brother's wedding. I run my finger absently along my silicone ring as I stare at the photo in the dim light of the kitchen, wondering how I missed this all along.

I can't miss it now, and I feel freer, lighter, joyful even at the realization. I'm more than capable of love—for all this time, for all these years, it was always her.

I'm not cursed at all. True, my other relationships didn't last for more than six months. But the real six-month curse is that half a year was as long as I could be distracted from the actual love I've felt all along for Maeve.

I breathe out a long, relaxed breath, feeling like one big, huge question has been answered.

But in its place is a whole new one. How do I get my wife to fall hopelessly in love with me too? Ideally, before she moves out at the end of the season.

41

THE GREAT BANGING

Maeve

I don't wait long to tell my friends. I can't keep news like this from them. On Sunday morning when I'm alone and Asher is working out, I head to the terrace, savoring the view of the backyard. There, I fire off a text as I drink the chai latte he made me before he left.

> Maeve: *taps mic* I have news.

> Josie: *Sits up* *bats lashes*

> Leighton: Don't make us wait any longer.

> Fable: I've already been waiting too long. Spill.

> Everly: It really better be good.

> Maeve: Oh it is. As in…we banged. We banged again. And again.

> Leighton: I'm so shocked.

Everly: And they say text doesn't have a tone, but I heard all the deadpan in that, Leighton.

Leighton: As you should.

Maeve: Hello! Did you forget about me? Does no one want to know how it was? ASK ME HOW IT WAS!

Josie: I'm sure I speak for all of us when I say TELL US NOW.

Maeve: Let's just say I used to think vibrators were the gold standard. Safe to say my husband is.

Fable: Well, marriage-of-convenience has clearly been good to you. And I believe this calls for drinks and dish this week. I want to know everything.

Josie: Yes, like...WHAT DOES THIS MEAN?

Maeve: I'm going to be living with him for the next few months, and my "palace" is now vacant.

Josie: I meant, what does it mean in an existential sense, not necessarily a practical one, but good to know you're becoming a landlord.

Leighton: *raises hand* I need a place to stay. My roommates just started hooking up and they're LOUD.

Josie: Oh god. I have secondhand embarrassment. Or is that firsthand since I hooked up with my roommate?

Leighton: You started a trend. And now I'm suffering from it!

Maeve: Consider it done. My place is yours.

As I finish the latte, Leighton and I message separately about my sub-lease, where I tell her she'll become a sub of a sub of a sub, or something like that.

Leighton: Sounds fun. And like the perfect place for a photographer trying to eke out a living.

Maeve: You can take pictures of pigeons fornicating on the windowsill. That'll really add to your boudoir portfolio. But they might be as loud as your roomies.

Leighton: Former roomies, you mean?

Maeve: Why yes I do.

Leighton: Also, that sounds more like sports photography :) Which works for me too.

And I feel good that I'm helping another artist. I've been lucky that I've had friends—like Asher—who've helped me. It's nice to return the favor. But as I set the mug in the sink, I return to Josie's question. What does this mean? I wish I knew. I don't, though, so I get ready to paint. At least with my brushes, my sketches, and my imagination, I always have answers.

* * *

I don't play nice with the dawn, so when it has the audacity to wake me up at an obscenely early hour on Monday morning with light—fucking morning light— filtering through the windows, I flip, grab a pillow, and cover my eyes, murmuring, "Must get blackout shades soon."

Sighing, I settle back into the world's comfiest bed, which I never want to leave, especially since I worked late last night on the mural. Then it hits me—it's eerily quiet. I peer at Asher's side of the bed.

It's empty and neat. The duvet's already covered up his side.

Hmm.

I swing my gaze to the clock. It's barely six. Asher's not a farmer. Or a banker. Why is he up now? He's been up before me every morning we've spent together, except the one in Vegas, but we'd been out and engaging in bedroom activities till three then, so that hardly counts. Maybe he normally exercises at this inhuman hour? Still, worry tugs at my chest. I flip off the covers and pad quietly down the steps, along the hallway, and toward the dim light of the kitchen.

Just one set of lights is on, and it doesn't sound like he's cooking. I turn into the doorway.

Oh. He's standing at the counter. His back's to me. He's on his laptop, a mug of coffee next to him, the strong aroma drifting past my nose.

"Hey," I say quietly, my voice froggy with sleep, but my chest a little heavy with worry. Why is he on his computer at this early hour? It's...odd.

He looks up, turns to me, his gaze soft. "Hey, you."

"Are you already up?" I don't really know his private habits yet.

"Yeah. I remembered something in the middle of the night about the thyroid meds my dad is on, and I wanted to check," he says.

Right. He's mentioned in the past that John has hypothyroidism. Wrapping an arm around my waist, he shows me the site he's on. It's a health news site and he's reading an article about the long-term effects of a medication. I'm secretly relieved Asher's not doing something else online, though I am concerned for his dad on his behalf.

"He's been on that for a while, right?"

"I just remembered if you're on it for a while though," he explains, "it can *potentially* lead to osteoporosis, so I'll send over some info on what to do about that. Things to do for good bone health and all."

"Oh, that's thoughtful," I say.

"I'm not sure they read them though. The articles I send. The studies and stuff. So it's probably easier if I go pick up some new vitamins. Calcium and vitamin D." He pauses, clearly thinking. "Nope. I'll order online for delivery today."

I furrow my brow. It sounds a little like he's parenting his parents. But I don't know what it's like to have parents as an adult, so I say nothing on that front. Besides, isn't this just what he does? He likes to look out for the people he cares about. He's always one step ahead, with the right info and details, whether it's a sprained ankle or that time I got the flu, and he paid attention to the symptoms so it wouldn't turn into pneumonia. "All right. But don't spend too much time on Amazon or you'll wind up with a lava lamp and a red-light therapy mirror," I add.

"I'll be sure to avoid that rabbit hole," he says with a smile.

On a yawn, I nod to the stairs. "Your comfy bed is calling my name, so I'm going to listen to it."

"It's *your* comfy bed too," he says.

My chest flips a little from that word—*your*—then I glance at the clock in the kitchen. "You have a game tonight. You need to rest as well."

He lifts his mug. "Coffee and me are tight."

I shudder. "Coffee is gross." I wave and turn around, heading back upstairs.

A minute later, as I'm settling into bed, the mattress sinks, and Asher's right next to me, wrapping an arm around me, dropping a soft kiss to the back of my neck.

"Did you send them the articles?"

"Yeah, but I think I forgot to check on another side effect," he says, his voice tight. "So I'll have to do that."

"You can do it later," I say softly, hoping he lets go of this worry.

He sighs, then settles into bed.

I drift off, but I have a feeling he doesn't. When I wake up for good a little later, he's gone once again. My jaw tightens. I wish he'd sleep more. But maybe my husband is a vampire.

On Wednesday after I complete my work on the mural for the day, I slip off to the tiny studio to finish some lamps I need to bring to the next night market. The other artist I share space with isn't here tonight, so it's all mine. I make good progress, so I'm done sooner than expected. Asher said he'd pick me up after his evening workout (thank you, goddesses, for his commitment to his abs and glutes), which means I've got a free hour. I shift my focus to mirrors, playing around with one I've been working on for a while, picking up a fine paintbrush to add some red to the tiny outline of a woman's dress in the corner when a few strands of my hair fall out of my messy bun. I brush them away from my eyes and continue working.

As I gently, but precisely blend the red to the perfect shade, I lose track of time until sneakers slap on the concrete floor, then I catch the scent of soap. The temperature in me ticks up as I raise my face, meeting Asher's gaze. One of the other artists must have let him in. The studio space is divided into multiple small rooms. He's right next to me, and his green eyes glimmer with that mischievous look he gets sometimes. His lips curve up in the slightest grin.

"Hi," I say, my own smile forming to match his. "Why are you smiling?"

He leans forward and brushes a finger across my cheek, swiping a daub of...red. He holds it up. "You have paint on your cheek."

"Shocking," I say.

His gaze drifts down. "Also..."

I follow his eyes. "Oh."

That smile of his deepens when I lift a hand to swipe the red off my chest, right above the V-neck of my shirt, visible even though I'm wearing a smock. But he's faster, catching my wrist before I can touch my skin. "I've got it," he says, then slowly strokes his finger through the smudge like it's the highlight of his day.

Well, right now it feels like the highlight of mine. So does watching him walk to the nearby industrial sink, wet the corner of a clean rag, then return to me, finishing up what he began with lingering, sensual caresses. "All gone now."

"But you liked the way it looked," I say, teasingly.

"So much," he says.

When we return home, he shows me exactly how much he liked it when he hikes me up on the kitchen counter and gives me the real highlight of my day. After we're both panting and satisfied, I say, "Things I learned today—my best friend thinks I look good in paint."

* * *

I climb down from the ladder on Thursday afternoon, wipe my hands on my paint-stained T-shirt, and take a few steps back to survey my work. I've only just begun the mural, but the corner looks good with the start of a stylized trolley car. I take it in, then let my gaze wander down the length of it. This thing is no joke. I finished sketching the chalk outlines onto the grid earlier this week. Now I'm finally painting it, which should take a month at least. Still faster than most other murals of this size, but that's Eleanor for you. She operates at top speed all the time, and I suppose that's good since Angelina has been working with *California Style* on sending a photographer in a couple weeks for the spread.

Such a strange thought. A cool one too. I wipe my hands on a dust rag, then gather up my supplies to set them aside for the night when a peppy voice echoes across the cavernous hallway, accompanied by the lope of paws.

"It looks so good!"

I turn to find Holmes and Eleanor striding my way, the woman's Converse sneakers smacking against the floor. She cuts an interesting image in slacks, a blazer, and Chucks. But if the fashion world has taught us anything recently, it's that heels can go fuck off. Holmes reaches me first, parking his fluffy little butt down and wagging his tail.

I bend to scratch his chin, and his tail thumps harder. "Hey, cutie," I say.

"Thank you for not embarrassing me again in front of the talent," Eleanor says to the dog, who's not humping my leg but is looking at it like he dreams of doggy-style.

As for me, I love being called *the talent*. "He's a very good boy," I say.

"And that is a very good start to the mural," she says, admiring the trolley I've been drawing. She parks her hands on her hips, checking out the grid that extends for more than forty feet. There's a proud smile on her face. "Look at us—living the dream. Making art and talking trades," she says.

That catches my attention. "Asher?" The word flies out before I can think twice about it.

She shakes her head. "No. Not him. I've no plans to trade him away," she says, and immediately I wonder if he has a no-trade clause. I think so, but I should ask him. "But I have my eyes on some talent. We'll see how things go. I asked my GM to make some calls today."

Am I her new best friend or something? Why is she telling me about her wheeling and dealing? "That's... cool."

But then she waves her hand, her huge diamond ring sparkling as she sets it on Holmes's little head. "But that's all in a day's work."

Oh, okay. It's no big deal she's saying that. I breathe a sigh of relief. I'm lucky Asher's played here his whole career. Maybe that means he won't ever be traded.

As I put my chalks away, footsteps click across the concrete.

"Hey, honey."

His voice slides up my spine like warm fingertips gently tracing the lines of me. I turn to see my husband heading in our direction. With eyes only for me. With an intensity in his gaze. A purpose in his step.

When he reaches me, he loops an arm around my waist, then drops one of his signature possessive kisses to my lips. My head goes hazy even from the quick kiss.

But when he lets go, and I catch Eleanor watching us, looking thrilled, I want to whisper, *Good job* to Asher. Every day this week, he's driven me here to the arena, he's made sure to meet me at the end of work—except when I went to the studio—and he's kissed me in public. He hasn't forgotten the brunch lesson from that day at their house.

Maybe he hasn't forgotten that Holmes has a crush on me, too, since he turns to the dog and says, "Sorry, bud. She's all mine."

Eleanor cracks up. "I guess you heard."

"I did. But I get it. She's pretty irresistible," he says, tugging me closer.

Eleanor smiles at us approvingly, like all is right in the world.

And really, in this moment, it is. Even though I know this affection, though real, is also all for show. It's for her benefit. But who am I to complain? I'm enjoying the benefits, too, of Asher's performance.

After I pack up, Asher walks me to his car in the players' lot. "Pole class now? With the troublemakers?"

I pat my pink duffel bag I'm carrying. It has my clothes but also a gift for Asher. Something I've been holding onto for a few days. I've been looking for the right moment to give it to him. "I'm ready for it."

He looks me over with hungry eyes as we reach the car. "You should show me sometime."

"My pole moves?" I ask.

"Yes."

My mind is racing ahead to what he might like. I think I know, so I smile as I slide into the car. "Consider it done."

On the way to class, he cruises through early evening traffic, slowing at a light. His expression is a little serious and a little hopeful when he says, "Would you want to come to the game next Sunday with my dads?"

My heart warms, heating my whole chest it seems. I've always loved watching him play. "Of course."

As we wait at the red light, he gives a small smile. "Good. I want you there again. Been thinking about it since the other week when you and Vivian came. I like you there as my wife," he says with confidence but a trace of vulnerability too.

That warmth spreads, heating me up from the possession in his tone. "Then I'll be there as your wife. I mean, that'll look good, right?"

The light changes and he hits the gas. "Yes, but that's not why I want you there. It's not for show."

"It's because I'm your good luck charm," I add lightly.

He shakes his head. "I thought we cleared that up. You're an instigator, you're an agent, you're a force to be reckoned with."

"Clearly that's all true. But I also like the idea that I can bring you luck."

A small laugh seems to escape his lips, but he says nothing, just shakes his head slightly, like he can't quite win on this count. I'm not sure what to make of the moment, but there's no time to dissect meanings since he pulls up to Upside Down a minute later. "I bet you'll be hungry when you're done. I'll handle dinner for us," he says.

"Damn. I love it when you order food," I say with a low whistle, touching his chest because I can. "I like these marital benefits too."

"Good. I want you to." He grabs my hand, making my stomach flip. He drops a quick, hot kiss to my lips and nods to the studio door. "Go do your thing, Maeve... Callahan."

A tingle slides down my spine from the way he says his last name. But before I exit the car, I stop, my fingers curled around the door handle. "Do you have a no-trade clause?"

He smiles. "I do." He pauses, his lips curving up, almost like he's amused. "I've told you that before though."

Hmm. He probably has. I'm sure it came up at some point—when bowling, while exploring the weird new offerings at the local farmers market, while playing party games at Josie and Wesley's some night. Yet this time feels different. Because I'm asking for me.

42

LONG LIVE MESSES

Maeve

It's open studio night at Upside Down, so we're all working on our own moves, some basic, some advanced, getting one-on-one instruction as we go. I've been flirting with inverts, but I'm not there yet. Mostly since, well, I don't want to break my hands. Or my neck. I like both body parts.

The studio is lit with soft, ambient light that highlights the sleek poles, mirrors lining one side of the room.

As the class winds down, I glance at Everly in the mirror. She's so determined, and now she's working on her Ayesha—a move I'm not sure I'll ever be able to master. The level of strength required is beyond me. I look over to Kyla, the main instructor and manager, who's a few feet away. I grip my pole, trying to prep for my basic climb, something I love to work on all the time since it's good for my hands and my hands are my life.

"Good job today," Kyla says. "You'll be working on your Ayesha in no time."

I laugh, nodding to my friend. "The thing about me is I think I can do stuff like that, and then I can't even invert well."

"Yes, you can, Maeve," she replies as she steps closer. "I've seen you do it."

"You know what I mean—without looking like a limp, wet pool noodle."

"You look like one of my badass students working on her skills, just like Everly. And you're fearless."

I glance around the studio again. The air feels different now, quieter, with only a few of us left working. "Speaking of fearless," I say, lowering my voice, "can you help me with some floorwork?"

Kyla raises a brow. "What are you thinking?"

"Pin-up girl, leg sweep, maybe a backslide."

She grins. "Someone's planning a fun evening."

I smile, a little secretive. Like a cat about to catch the canary—or, in my case, the hockey player. And honestly, I can't wait.

* * *

After class, we head to Sticks and Stones, a lively bar with pool, games, and excellent cocktails. The five of us squeeze into a booth where the music isn't playing too loud. When Gage, the tattooed owner, swings by to take our orders, things seem normal with my friends. But the second he's gone, all eyes turn to me.

Josie huffs.

Fable taps her fingers on the table.

Everly's gaze sharpens.

And Leighton points to an imaginary watch. "If I'm not mistaken, it's been almost four weeks since you *married* your husband, and you only told us a few days ago about the great banging. We're going to need every detail, plus the biggest apology for keeping this from us."

Her voice carries that mix of playful annoyance and genuine fury that only friends can muster.

Josie crosses her arms. "Exactly. What the hell? I can't believe you've been keeping this from us."

"I *told* you the other morning!" I protest. "Hello! I texted about the great banging."

They all roll their eyes, perfectly synchronized like they've been rehearsing for some eye-rolling contest.

"You gave me hell about my boss having a crush on me for over a year," Fable chimes in, leaning closer, her hazel eyes searing. "You didn't let up. And now, you went off and did *this* in secret. I think you're going to need to serve some time in friendship jail for this."

"I don't need to go to friendship jail," I say, half laughing. "That sounds terrible."

"Then explain yourself," Everly presses. "How could you not tell us about Asher?"

My instinct is to defend myself. "How do you even know it's been going on since we got married?"

Everly rolls her eyes again. "I wasn't born yesterday, Maeve."

"Maybe it's the way you blushed when we gave him marriage tips a few weeks ago," Leighton adds.

And he didn't follow them. He left the door unlocked when he showered, and I've never been happier. Still, denial is fun. "That proves nothing."

Josie shakes her head, mock disbelief written all over her face. "I know you, Maeve. That proves everything."

"And the fact that you were getting special tips for a certain dance in pole class tonight?" Everly teases, her eyes sparkling. "Kind of hard to deny it's been going on for a while when you're asking for moves like the backslide. You weren't exactly subtle. And I don't think you'd dance for a guy you've only boned for one night."

Damn. Sherlock has nothing on my friend.

"I'm triggered," I joke, but they're right. I didn't tell them the details. I kept everything close. But where to start? Do I take them back to Vegas? Do I tell them about that night when we said *I do*—about how I was so hot for him I could barely control myself? It all feels too personal, too private. It's *ours*, and I'm not sure I want to share it.

But then again, they're my best friends. Each of them owns a little piece of my heart. As much as I like to tease, it's been hard keeping this from them.

"Fine," I admit with a smile, "it started in Vegas. We kept trying not to give in, kept saying it couldn't happen again, that it would be a one-time thing, and then..."

Everly and Josie exchange knowing looks, like they've been there before, done that.

"And then you couldn't resist," Josie says gently, her voice soft with understanding. That's kind of what happened with her and Wesley.

Fable squeezes my arm. "Friend, I really get it. So...is that what it's like for you? You kind of can't get enough of him?"

That's exactly what it's like. But if I admit that, am I just like them? Not that that'd be a bad thing—Everly, Josie, and Fable are all in happy, stable, committed relationships. But I'm in a fake one with an expiration date. As much as I adore Asher, I can't pretend I'm where they are. It's different. Messier.

Plus, I don't want to fall back into my old patterns, clinging to things that aren't meant to last. Lord knows I hold on too hard, like I do to that book of my mom's I brought to Asher's home. The idea makes me feel exposed, vulnerable, more than I want to be, more than I'm naturally prone to be.

"It's just an arrangement," I say, trying to mask the uncertainty creeping into my voice. "Friends with benefits, but we're married...technically."

Josie snorts. "You're living with him, sleeping with him, hanging out with him...How are you not going to fall in real love with your fake husband?"

I open my mouth to protest, but nothing comes out. I don't have an answer to that because it's terrifyingly possible. But it can't happen. It can't because my fake husband is my real best friend. And if I hold on too tight as his wife, I might lose him as my friend. That's not a risk I'm willing to take.

"Because I'm too much of a mess!" I blurt out, half joking but half serious. "I have so much going on—there's no room for new emotions. Besides, I don't even know how to act with him, much less feel with him."

Everly gives me a sympathetic look. "You're not a mess."

I side-eye her. "But I am. I promise you, I am."

Josie shakes her head. "We all think we're a mess. We're just working through things, trying to be the best versions of ourselves. That's what you're doing too. Maybe there is room for new emotions."

Leighton leans in, her gaze soft but intent. "But it sounds like that's what you're already feeling with him, isn't it?"

I pause, her words sinking in. Sure, maybe there are

new emotions slipping in, but they can't be love. Not yet. How could I handle that on top of everything else? My life is already chaotic—between the Sea Dogs mural commission, and the new projects my agent mentioned (including a plant-based café that begged me to come in this week and draw a painting of a tree with humming-birds on the wall and I could not resist, because...hello, dream job!), and me trying to finally, after years of trying, carve out a meaningful career, and now Asher...it's too much.

Especially when I think of my mother and her final wishes for me. *Follow your dreams*. The last piece of advice she ever gave me. What if I get distracted from my dreams? What if I end up like Dad, losing sight of every-thing else because I got too caught up in a romance?

I can't let that happen. Not now, not when everything is finally falling into place.

"Feelings," I say, sidestepping the topic. "I'm feeling too many of those damn things. That's sometimes the problem."

The bartender arrives with our drinks.

I lift my mojito, trying to quell the rising panic in my chest with a toast to, well, to this thing I deeply need—friendship. "To The Padlockers. And your uncanny ability to get anything out of me."

Josie clinks first, peering at me through those glasses. "I'm surprised, Maeve. You're usually an open book. It took you long enough."

Everly lifts her glass. "For the record, I confessed early about Max."

"And I told you all practically the morning after things happened with Wesley," Josie adds, and out of the corner of my eye I catch Leighton fiddling with her napkin, then her earrings. The flower ones specifically. Hmm. That's some nervous energy right there.

I clear my throat. "Does anyone else have anything she needs to get off her, ahem, *bosom*?"

The table's quiet for a long beat, and slowly, we all turn to Leighton. "What?" she asks, with wide blue eyes.

"Spill," I demand, stabbing the table.

She lets out a long, anguished sigh. "Fine, I had a thing with Miles Falcon late last summer before I knew who he was and that he works for my dad, and it won't happen again, and it can't happen again. And you really can't say a word."

"Last summer?" Everly's voice shoots up. "Before the start of the season."

Leighton nods guiltily. "It was pre-season. One night. Well, one day too. One amazing day together," she says wistfully.

"Like a perfect date one day?" Josie asks, voice both sad and hopeful.

"Pretty much," she says.

"Wow. That was before I saw you again in your dad's office in the fall. Before you took pictures of the community center gardening event," Everly says. That was one of the promo shoots Everly arranged when she was rehabbing Max's image a few months ago.

"Yep," Leighton says, a heavy admission. "It hasn't been easy running into him those times. He drove me home too after that gardening event."

"Where is my popcorn?" I pull my chair closer. "The coach's daughter and one of the star players. This is going to be good."

And it is very, *very* good when she tells us about her one perfect day and night with him. About the earrings too. When she's done, I lift my glass once more. "To wonderful, fantastic, knee-weakening messes."

"And finding our way through them," Leighton finishes.

We all clink glasses once again, and in that small gesture, I make a silent promise to my parents that I'll try to find the way through mine.

43

THAT GUY

Maeve

When I walk through the door a little later, something smells good. Wait—scratch that—everything smells good. Like a dog, I lift my nose and sniff the air as I kick off my shoes and pad into the kitchen.

Where...

Oh god.

It's the hottest thing I've ever seen.

My husband is cooking, and he's cleaning up as he goes. Is this a dream? I walk slowly into the kitchen, practically in a trance. Or maybe I'm under the spell he's casting.

I flash back to the coffee shop with my friends, when they gave Asher their "care and feeding instructions" for me. *Keep snacks handy at all times. Maeve loves her independence, so don't crowd her—but that doesn't mean you shouldn't cook for her.*

I'd protested, saying I didn't need anyone cooking for me. But actually? I think I like it.

A lot.

It's strange, though, letting someone in like this. I'm not used to having someone take care of me, not since my parents. And Asher—he's not just cooking. He's paying attention, knowing exactly what I need without me asking.

My heart swells. New emotions, indeed.

"Hi." It's not the most artful opening, but it'll have to do. He turns around, and he's wearing an apron that says *Suck This*.

I crack up. "Where did you get that apron?"

He stirs something on the stove—basmati rice, maybe? Butternut squash? Possibly curry?

"I got you a shirt that says *Quick-Draw Maeve*. You think I can't find an apron to amuse you?"

I stop in my tracks. He got it to amuse me. I'm not used to men doing things like this for me—really, anyone doing things like this. I'd have to go way back to when my parents were still alive, when my mom used to send me silly photos of the dog I grew up with, posed as if she were reading my mom's books. Mom would caption them with sayings like *This is good in Woof*.

And now, Asher cooking for me not only makes my stomach growl, it makes my heart feel warm and squishy. Only, I don't know what to do with this feeling, so I ask an obvious question. "Are you cooking us dinner?"

He holds up a wooden spoon, adopting an inquisitive look. "Let's see. There's food on the stove, dishes on the table, and wine. I'd call that dinner. It's a butternut squash and chickpea curry. But," he adds, his smile widening, "I also made an appetizer."

"Stop. I love appetizers," I say, maybe a little too excitedly. At least I don't squeal. I give myself points for that.

He gives me a look like, *Tell me something I don't know.* "Snacks, appetizers, dessert—yeah, I've got your number, Maeve Hartley."

Hartley. I've always loved my last name. It's the one my mother used on her books. It makes me feel close to her. But...when he calls me Mrs. Callahan, I feel something else. Something warm. I like it too—maybe more than I should. But I'm not going to point that out. Not now. That might be too much.

"Where's this fabulous appetizer?"

"Here. It's your favorite," he says as he reaches for a white ceramic dish next to him, covered by a cloth napkin. He turns the heat down on the saucepan, strides over to me, and dramatically whips off the napkin.

"We can get to the bottom of the warm nut conspiracy."

The hair on my arms stand on end. "You made warm nuts," I say, like it's the nicest thing anyone's ever done for me.

Honestly, I think it is.

He runs his thumb over my wrist, and the heat of his touch travels all the way to my core. "What my wife wants, she gets."

What I want...is him.

* * *

"What did you put in this?" I ask, taking another bite, savoring the rich flavors.

"Tofu, cilantro, butternut squash, and chickpeas," he says.

It's making my taste buds dance. "How did you know I'd like it?"

"You like chai lattes. You like hot sauce. You enjoy interesting dishes, variety, the unpredictable. But you also like cilantro, and Carlos grows it, so I picked some up from him earlier today," he says with a knowing grin, gesturing to the herb I'm a little obsessed with.

In short—he's paid attention. *To me.* He made the effort. *For me.* This is all so new. So foreign. "No one's ever cooked for me before," I say, a lump rising in my throat. "I mean...in a relationship—" Crap. We're not in a *real* relationship. I shouldn't use that word. "I mean in a—"

But he's cooked dinner for me as a friend. We've had meals together with Beckett and Reina, with his teammates, and with Josie and Wesley. "I mean...well, you have. Obviously. There was the time you made enchiladas using Carlos's family recipe, and the mushroom risotto..."

He gives me a soft smile. "I like cooking...for you."

For you.

He's not talking about cooking for the group. He's talking about me. And he's opening up to me. I should do the same. I take another bite of the delicious dish, then try again. "I guess I was saying no one has done this for me..."

"Romantically?" he suggests, his voice gentle, like he knew I needed him to finish the thought.

"Yeah, that," I say, my chest warm from putting that word between us. It feels like it has a life of its own, a pulse, a heartbeat...*romantic.* "Gah. Why are words so hard?"

He laughs, the sound free and easy. "Maybe because my dinner is seducing you and stealing all your senses?"

"Clearly. And the warm nuts were more perfect than they were at five miles high. I guess we've solved the conspiracy," I say, but there's something else on my mind. The same thought from earlier with my friends still lingers. I don't know how to act around him sometimes. But maybe there's a way to fix it—by telling the truth. "Sometimes I feel out of place here. In your home," I admit.

His brow furrows with concern. "What do you mean, Maeve?"

He knows my spotty romance history. He knows how Gideon left me flat on my ass. But I've never told him *why*. I didn't want to plant that doubt in his mind, didn't want him to see me that way.

No one likes a clingy woman. It's the kiss of death in romance. Men want someone a little hard to get. No one would ever accuse me of being that.

I set my fork down, the weight of what I'm about to say pressing on my chest. "Gideon told me I was too clingy. He couldn't handle all of my needs. He said he didn't think any man ever could. And sometimes, I wonder..." I stop, my throat tightening as I force myself to take a breath. "I wonder if you'll get tired of me. Of having me around. Even here, over the next few months."

The words hang in the air, thin, reedy, full of raw emotion. I hate how vulnerable they make me feel.

Asher sets down his fork too, his eyes never leaving mine. They're intense. Steady. "Maeve, I'm not that guy. And you're not that woman. You're not too much. You're perfect just the way you are."

I swallow hard. "You're only saying that because it's easier."

He leans in, his gaze steady, serious. "No, I'm not. Listen to me. Hear me when I say this—I've known you for ten years. I'm not kicking you out, and you won't scare me away."

His words make my heart swell, but there's still a part of me that needs help believing it. And maybe...this is the place to ask for it. "Just...tell me—will you let me know if I'm asking for too much? Or if you need space? Will you tell me how much is too much?"

Asher's lips are a ruler. His eyes lock with mine. He nods solemnly. "I promise," he says, taking my request as seriously as I mean it.

"Thank you," I say, and it's a relief to be understood. To be accepted.

"But you won't be too much."

"You can't know that," I say.

"I can," he says, then reaches for my hand. "But I also hear *you*. So if you want to figure this out for yourself, if you want to know what's too much, or too little, or just right, I'll tell you."

"Good. I want to know what you like." I pause, hesitating on the words, or really making sure I have the right ones. The one that was hard to say moments ago. It's not so much now. "In a relationship."

"I can do that," he says easily.

"Thank you." I draw a deep breath, feeling more settled, assured. It's the Asher effect. I'm so lucky to have someone in my life like him—someone who takes me as I am. My girlfriends do that, of course. But so does this man, and that matters to me. Which means now's as good a time as any for the gift I made him. "I have something for you," I say.

"You want to get naked right now?"

"Oh, I got the message loud and clear from your apron what you want. But first, this," I say, then hustle over to my duffel bag, where I grab a little something I made for him the other night. It's another mirror—this one with a small rectangular gilded frame with dragon scales painted on it. In the corner is a tiny painting of one of my pop art couples, kissing of course. I pause though, the frame in hand, as a pit forms in my stomach briefly, coated in the worry that he won't want what I have to give. But I push past that uncomfortable feeling and bring the gift back to the table.

"I snuck into the tiny studio for a couple hours this week to make this. I get a little...batty if I don't make my decorative art too. And I had this idea," I explain, then hand the mirror to him.

His eyes gleam as he takes the gift, tracing a finger over the words I painted on. *It's the little surprises, like dragon underwear, that keep the spark alive.* I watch as his fingertip follows the lines, then he looks up, locking his gaze with mine. There's something new in his expression —something that perhaps says I'm a mystery he's eager to solve.

"Advice from Jen and Hal. That night in Vegas," he says, and a small gasp escapes my lips. I wanted him to remember, and I'm glad he did.

"Good memory," I murmur.

"I remember a lot of things. Seems like you do too. And I'm sensing a theme behind these mirrors."

"What's the theme?"

He taps the frame, giving it some thought. "Advice on the proper care and handling of an artist. That's what this is, right?"

"Maybe it's a roadmap to me, but I think the general lessons apply too. People keep wanting to give us tips, so I thought I'd put it down."

"Is this your way of telling me I should wear dragon underwear next time?" he teases.

I nibble on the corner of my lip, a little nervous. "Maybe it is. So, tell me—was this too presumptuous? The gift?"

He laughs, shaking his head. "Not at all. In fact, I'm going to hang it up tonight."

That's a relief, but still, I'm compelled to add, "You don't have to. I'm not trying to, I don't know, redecorate your home."

His gaze is unflinching as he says, "You could though. If you wanted to."

I furrow my brow. What do I make of that comment? But then it hits me, like a ten-pound bag of obvious. This is fake. Like I told my friends earlier. Just because I might feel some new emotions doesn't change the score. And I shouldn't try to read anything more into his comments. "Right. For the photo spread." Of course that'll help. If this place looks even more like I live here, it'll be good for this marriage of convenience—for my work and for his charity rollout.

Briefly, frustration seems to flicker on his face.

"No. Just for you. You're living here now. And you don't have to go to the studio you rent to make your mirrors. You can do it in the guest room. You already have your easel and paints in there. Do you want to paint in there? Make your decorative art in there?"

It's a generous offer, but the guest room is a guest room. "I think sometimes I just need a little distance from where I sleep to create."

"I get that," he says, though he sounds a little wistful. I think he wants me to like the guest room.

But also if I did that I'd be taking over, encroaching on

all his space. "Thanks for the offer though. And the feedback on how I'm doing."

"Anytime," he says with a slow, teasing smile. "But I can give you feedback in other ways too."

My pulse quickens. "Oh, you can?"

His gaze roams up and down my body, his voice dropping to a low murmur. "Yeah. I'll tell you exactly what I like. But first, I can't get something out of my head."

"What's that?"

"What you promised me before I dropped you off at class. Because all I thought about while I was cooking dinner was what those pole moves might be."

Funny, me too. "But we don't have a pole," I say playfully.

He points to the door. "I'll get you one right now."

Oh. I sit up straighter. He's serious—he'd really install a pole for me. But that won't be necessary. "The thing about pole dancing is...there are plenty of moves you can do on a chair." His eyes glint with excitement, then darken when I say, "Or...on the floor."

He hauls in a breath. "Good, then I'd like to see you get down on your hands and knees, wife."

And just like that, dinner's over, and it's time for the show.

44

JUST RIGHT

Asher

I'm parked in a chair in the living room, sultry music pulsing from my phone, my wife on her back on the carpet, with one knee up. She rises, her back arching in the sexiest way possible.

My throat goes dry.

She's not even looking my way, and that's the point.

She's lost to the dance as she puts on a show for me. She teases me, clad in heels, tight shorts, and a cheetah print bra which hugs her perfect breasts. She's pushing her hips off the floor and sweeping one leg to the side.

I groan.

As the bass thumps low, she turns around and locks eyes with me before licking her lips. "Let me know if it becomes too much for you," she says. A taunt. A challenge.

"It can never be enough," I reply.

She waggles her ass.

"Are you sure, handsome? I don't want to overwork my favorite customer," she says, getting into character.

My dick strains against my jeans. "You're definitely working me hard," I tease as she arches her back and then dips it down, meeting my gaze once again. "Tell me what you want next."

I want you. I want to give you everything.

But I can't say that. Not yet. If I tell her how I feel now, I might lose her. *I* might be too much. So I'm showing her through cooking her dinner and giving her orders—since she loves both food and when I take the reins. "Need you to crawl to me, wife."

She lifts an eyebrow provocatively. No surprise. Maeve does everything provocatively. As the music changes, she starts moving toward me—gracefully and sensually.

It's fucking breathtaking. It's been a fantasy of mine for so long. And now it's happening right in front of me. As a man who craves control, there's nothing better than having the woman of my dreams obeying my every command.

She slides one palm along the plush carpet, then the other, then a knee. When she reaches me, I curl a hand through her hair, twist it in my fist. Give it a nice tug. She lets out a soft whimper and looks up at me with a submissive expression. "Yes, sir?"

I am molten. Fire licks my veins. "You want to know if it's too much?"

"I do."

"You think I can't handle it? Turn around and tease me," I bite out.

Maeve grins mischievously, then stands up and says, "Let's find out." She spins around, giving me a seductive look over her shoulder before grinding down hard on my erection.

I inhale sharply. "Fuuuuck."

"I'm sorry, sir. Is that too much?" she asks innocently.

"No, but I need to make sure it's not too much for you," I say, as I dip my hand around her waist and under her panties. She moans as I slide my fingers through her warm, wet pussy. She's heaven and so, so soft.

"You can take more," I say, then ease out. "Now, get down on your knees, and show me you can handle every inch of me in your throat."

"On one condition," she says.

"What's that?"

"I decide where you come."

It's like electricity fries my whole body. She's everything. Not because she wants to suck me off, though that does help. It's because she gives so completely.

And I want everything she has to offer.

"Fair enough. Now take out my dick and take care of your husband," I demand. "I made you dinner, after all. Show me how much you enjoyed it."

She drops to her knees, tap dances her fingers up my thighs, then unzips and pulls down my jeans. I assist her eagerly, pushing down my briefs. She stops, eyes popping when she sees the design and, well, the positioning of the animal right over my hard-on. "Roosters? I had no idea CheekyBeasts' repertoire included roosters," she says.

I run the back of my knuckles against her cheek. "It's a prototype for a new design. They asked me for ideas the other week. I suggested a rooster. Since you like cocks so much."

Her eyes gleam. "So they're sort of for me."

"It's for you, Maeve." The meaning isn't lost on me—

everything's for her. She might not know it yet. I might not be showing her all my cards since I don't want to scare her away. But still, I know that everything is for her.

Even the new underwear.

"Good," she says, then frees my cock. When she sees it, her eyes widen and her tongue darts out. I don't know if she's aware that she does that every time she sees my dick, but I won't tell her. It's like a game of poker, and that's her tell—it gives away how much she wants me.

She wraps those pretty lips around my shaft and my thighs clench. She murmurs as she takes me in, inch by inch. Heat builds low in my stomach.

I urge her on, grazing my thumb over her top lip. "You've got this, honey. Take it all," I murmur.

She nods against my length, looking like sin and all of my dreams. My Maeve, my best friend, my temporary wife who doesn't feel temporary at all is worshiping my cock with that lush mouth.

I slide my thumb down her jawline then wrap my hand gently around her throat, stroking it as if I can help her open wider. She swallows against my hand, relaxing. "That's right, baby. It's not too much for you, is it?"

She shakes her head, then flashes me a mischievous smile. A look that says, *You might be able to choke me with that cock, but I've got you by the balls.*

Then, for a few minutes, she sucks fervently, sparks crackling across my skin. It's filthy and perfect and everything I could want. My hands scrape through her hair. She runs her palm up my thighs. I ease out, letting the tip graze her lovely lips. The view makes my whole body tremble. I push my thumb inside and warn her. "You'd better decide soon."

"I'm a last second kind of girl," she says, then drops

her mouth all the way down on me again, devouring my cock. I start pumping my hips in the chair, filling her throat. My breathing turns frantic.

Briefly she coughs, but she shakes her head and holds up a hand. *Don't stop,* she's telling me. And I don't. I pump faster as she sucks brutally hard, giving me a raw, passionate blow job until my thoughts are this close to blanking out. My pulse pounds everywhere. But still, I grunt out one question. A harsh, urgent: "Where?"

She drops me from her mouth and grabs my cock, pointing it at her face. "On me."

"Yes. Let me make a mess of your pretty face, wife."

I hold the base while she guides the crown to her lips. I tremble, my mind blurring as I paint her lips, and her chin, and, yes, even her throat.

Finally, when the pleasure ebbs, I breathe out hard, open my eyes, and manage to say, "You look so fucking good with my come on your face."

She runs her tongue along her lips, licking it all off. "Just right."

The other thing that's just right? When I get on the floor and tell her to sit on my face. To be as loud and as wild as she possibly can.

She complies. She rides me hard and relentlessly, using my face for her pleasure, giving everything.

She doesn't hold back.

That is another thing that I love about her. The list keeps getting longer.

Yes, I tried to win her over with dinner.

But the fact that I give her screaming orgasms can't hurt my chances in this game of love.

* * *

Things I've learned about Maeve in the two weeks we've lived together:

Watching her nightly skin-care routine is like witnessing a science experiment. Use this serum. Add this lotion. Mix in this toner. And every night, she offers me something—a dollop of moisturizer, a dab of night cream. She loves to share.

Her showers are hotter than even girl-hot. I legit looked up how hot is too hot for a shower, but I guess she hasn't hit that limit yet. And I've learned I can handle Hades-level temps since I hate to let her shower alone.

I've learned she talks to her plants when she waters them. "You were hungry, Rover," she'll say, since she gave her plants traditional dog names.

I try not to smile stupidly every time she calls them by their names.

I didn't learn she tends to run late, since there's no way I could have missed that Maeve-ism over the last ten years of friendship. But I've discovered she moves faster when I drive her to work since she doesn't want to make me late for morning skate.

Which is how I've learned she mixes up her body spray at whim, so every day when I get in the car with her, I lean over and inhale her scent. She's started offering me her neck for sniffing when we're at a red light, and she plays along too. "What am I wearing today?" she'll ask. Then I give my best guess.

Things I learn about myself? I fucking love knowing all these details about my best friend.

The best thing I've learned? Her favorite way to end the day is with sex and an episode of a reality dating show that she only makes it halfway through since she'll inevitably fall asleep when the date starts to go south.

On Saturday night, after she drives me wild by fucking herself in front of me with the rabbit vibrator, and I drive her wild when she's on all fours, we get ready for bed together. As she brushes her teeth in the sink next to mine, my heart jumps up and down. I want to shout, "See? This could be us."

Because this—right here with her—brushing our teeth together is more perfect than it has a right to be.

Instead, I just flash her a grin and keep my thoughts to myself, focusing instead on showing rather than telling.

Like doing the things she enjoys.

When we're done, we get in bed, and I grab the remote. "We have to see if Tia wants to give Jonah another chance."

"I can't wait to find out," she says, and we turn on a new episode of *First Dates.* But a few minutes in, she winces, then lifts her hand behind her head and gently— or maybe not so gently—tugs it to one side.

Her neck pops, and I cringe at the loud cracking sound. "Are you okay?"

"Yeah. I think I pulled something in my neck earlier."

I turn to my side, on alert. "From sex?"

She laughs, shaking her head. "No, and if it were a sex injury it'd probably be lower body, Asher. And as big as your dick is, you didn't pull a muscle in my vagina."

She turns back to the TV, cracking the other side of her neck.

"But you injured your neck today?" I press.

"No. I just pulled something at the café," she says, since she worked pretty much a double-shift of sorts today. She was at the arena during the week, and the café all day today, squeezing in the quick turnaround on the tree painting.

"Do you need to see someone?" I ask, because that noise sounded bad.

She looks back to me again with question marks in her eyes. "It's okay. It happens. I work on a ladder a lot and I'm looking up or down, so sometimes I feel neck strain and I like to crack it. It's just an occupational hazard."

But what can we do about it? There has to be a fix. "Right, but do you want me to give you a neck rub? Do you need to do some neck stretches? I could get you a physical therapist if you want."

She takes the remote and hits pause. "Thank you, but I'm fine. It happens and I rub it or do extra stretches." She takes a beat, studying my face, then in a reassuring tone says, "I work with my body too. Just like you. So sometimes it's going to hurt. Same as you."

But it's hardly the same as me. I don't worry about me. But her? I have to figure this out and help her. What if it gets worse and she's not aware? What if this leads to a problem she doesn't catch in time? "Let me at least rub your neck for you," I insist.

She smiles. "Well, that I won't turn down." She snuggles closer, points the remote at the TV again and says, "*First Dates* and a neck rub. This is the full temporary husband treatment."

Not temporary if I can help it.

I rub her neck as she watches the show. But by the time the next couple breaks up at a cheese tasting because he ate the Gouda she wanted, I'm rubbing with one hand, grabbing my phone with the other and typing one-handed. How to relieve neck pain. Causes of neck pain. Exercises for neck pain.

"What do you think?"

Oh, shit. I both stopped rubbing and stopped paying attention to the show. I got so focused on Google.

"Second date," I say, taking my best guess as she turns to me with curious eyes.

"You stopped watching," she says—not an accusation, but more a curiosity.

I wave my phone, showing her the screen. "Sorry. I was just googling about cures for neck pain."

She laughs, then says, "Orgasms, Asher. More orgasms."

Well then.

Setting down the phone, I reach for one of her favorite toys in the nightstand drawer, taking control back from her. "Ditch the panties and spread your legs nice and wide for me, wife."

She complies, and I slide a thumb in her mouth. She sucks eagerly. I add another finger, and she swirls her tongue around it. "Good girl," I say, then I ease out, and gently caress her pussy while kissing her neck, slow and soft till she's wet and murmuring.

When she starts arching into my fingers, I switch it up and turn on the Soft Touch, using that on her till she's breaking apart beautifully on my bed.

And falling asleep just like that.

I'm not though. I stay up for a while, researching neck strain again since it's really best to address small problems before they become big problems.

But if she's proactive and does some stretches and exercises, she should be okay. So I email her some new videos for neck stretches and exercises too. And set a reminder on her phone to do them.

Sometime later, I get back in bed.

* * *

In the morning, while she's sleeping, I set a gift for her on the kitchen counter. It's wrapped in white paper with a pink bow. I leave a card under the bow with the words on it: *Wear this to the game tonight.*

I'm not saying this little gift will make her fall in love with me. But she loves gifts, and I love giving them. As I head to the terrace to finish my coffee, I come up with one more idea.

On the way to morning skate, I make some calls, then at the arena I turn off the world and focus on hockey since our rivals are in town tonight and I plan to beat them.

Well, I want to impress my wife.

45

THE STRETCH

Maeve

It's the number one rule of being a good hockey fan—thou shalt not miss the warm-ups.

But I've never been so warm from them before. I blame my husband. Asher's on the ice with the Sea Dogs for their pre-game warm-ups, and he's currently doing *the stretch.*

I sigh happily from my seat in the rows behind the players' bench. "I'm so glad his dads aren't here yet," I tell Leighton. Her dad got her tickets, and she's meeting up with some friends from college to watch the game, but she's joined me here first.

"I'm pretty sure they've seen him stretch before," she says.

I elbow her—because I'm mature like that. "You mean...*humping the ice.*" Bless them, that's what most of the guys are doing now. They're in their full uniforms, on their hands and knees on the ice, lifting their hips up and down.

"Stretch those hip flexors, handsome," I shout to the hotshot winger, though I doubt he can hear me.

Leighton shoves my shoulder. "You're going to get us in trouble."

"With whom? Your dad?"

"Um, other fans?" she points out, glancing around. The arena is less than a quarter full, crowds straggling in slowly. But the ones here early are hardcore, decked out in Sea Dogs jerseys and beanies.

"Pretty sure Asher wants everyone to know I'm here for him," I say, gesturing to the back of the jersey I'm wearing, the one he left for me on the kitchen counter this morning. The one he had custom-made. Then I lower my voice to not entirely a whisper and hold her gaze as I ask, "Or do you think the Feral Falcon will swing by and hear *you*?"

Groaning, she rolls her eyes. "First of all, let's make sure that doesn't stick as a nickname."

"The Filthy Falcon? The Fucking Falcon? The Flirty Falcon! Yes!" I thrust my arms high at that last one. "And we have a winner!"

"He's hardly flirty." She drops her voice. "Well, not in public. Also, did I say we fucked?" She gives me a saucy look.

"No, because you're a mean friend," I say with a pout. I turn back to the ice action, waving a hand in front of me like it's too hot in here. "Goddamn," I murmur to myself. My husband looks so sexy, moving his body like that. Then, screw it. If other people can hoist signs asking him to bed them on the side, I can let him know I think he's a fine drink of man. I stand, cup my mouth, and shout, "Looking good, Twenty-Nine."

He heard me because he pops up with his hockey stick and flies across the rink, sending a spray of ice toward the boards when he stops right by the empty bench. "You're coming home with me tonight, Mrs. Callahan."

And yes, I already knew that, but he's declaring it— loud and cocksure for the other fans to hear.

A woman a few seats over whines. A guy nearby cheers me on. But Asher only has eyes for me. He takes off his gloves and beckons me closer. "Get over here, wife. I need a good-luck kiss."

My stomach flips. Leighton nudges me, saying, "Go."

She doesn't need to tell me twice. I hustle down a few rows. When I reach the bench, the only spot where there's no glass, he leans over and drops a quick, possessive kiss onto my lips.

Immediately, he lets go, skates backward, and points at me, shouting, "You're mine."

Is my heart supposed to flutter so much in a tempo-rary marriage? Is my chest supposed to tingle like this? Should my cheeks feel this flushed? I press a hand to my face. I'm hot all over even though I'm surrounded by ice.

With a dopey smile that won't disappear, I rejoin Leighton right as Miles glides by, giving the quickest of chin nods in her direction. She steals a glance at the coaches on the ice, then flashes a barely-there smile to Miles before he skates behind the net and away from her.

I turn to her and sigh sympathetically, squeezing her arm. "Pining Falcon," I say quietly but clearly enough so she can hear. "Maybe that's more apropos."

"I don't know about that," she says wistfully. Then she quickly changes the subject, waggling her phone at me.

"Guess who snapped a picture of your husband kissing you before the game?"

This makes me unreasonably happy. "Let me see."

She shows me the shot—I'm stretching for a kiss, and that feels fitting too. It feels true. It feels like us. My heart balloons as I stare. "You're good," I say, then meet her eyes. "Can I post it?"

"That's why I took it. I had a feeling you'd want it."

"Thanks, babe," I say.

As she sends it to me, we chat briefly about the sub of a sub of a sub, and she tells me how the place is working out. "Thank you again," she says. "I needed this. I have a lead on a place I can move into in the summer, but this has been perfect for now."

The summer. When this arrangement between Asher and me ends. When we return to our regularly scheduled lives.

That thought weighs on me as I post the photo on my social, but then I furrow my brow at my profile. "Um, do I have a bunch of new followers?"

Leighton stares at the number on my phone. "Do you?"

"I do," I say, and it's weird and wonderful at the same time. "It's not entirely earned, is it? They're not really here for me. They're here because I'm...Mrs. Callahan."

Leighton nods a few times, her expression thoughtful. "The world isn't fair, Maeve. People don't always get what they deserve. But, don't you forget—Maeve Hartley got the Sea Dogs mural gig before she became Mrs. Callahan."

"Love you," I say, then I smile thoughtfully. "And I've only known you for a few months. How did that happen?"

"I'm easy to love," she says.

"You are. You're like a dog."

"High praise." She throws her arms around me and then takes off to join her friends.

Feeling contemplative, I look at my phone again and the picture I just posted. I don't deserve all this attention, but I'm getting it anyway. Including from Eleanor, who's already liked the new snap.

Well, at least the kiss is real.

The other real thing? The way my heart scampers a few minutes later after Leighton meets her friends and two familiar men come down the aisle toward me. The tall, strapping one with the roguish good looks and burly charm is John, and the lankier, wiry one is Carlos.

When they reach me, I'm up on my feet since it's so good to see them. "It's been too long," I say, meaning it.

"I know, girl. I know," Carlos says then wraps me in a hug.

"Especially now that you're family," John says, giving me a hug too.

Yes, they're in on the deal. But there's no "wink and a nod" in *family* at all. They say it like they mean it, and my throat hitches. That's an inconvenient reaction—this surplus of feelings.

Letting go of John, I try to tamp down the emotion, giving them both a smile as the three of us sit. "And family goes to hockey together," I say. Wow, that did not help me feel any less.

"Of course they do. Our first date was a hockey game," Carlos says, looking at his husband with affection.

"Shut up," I say, my jaw dropping.

John nods, big and proud. "What can I say? I was confident. I wanted to impress him, so I shelled out for tickets."

"It was a minor league game," Carlos points out, laughing.

"But you were still impressed," John insists, his gaze drifting down to his husband's gold band.

"Fine, fine. You got me there." Carlos gestures to the ice, where Asher's lobbing easy shots on goal as the warm-up winds down. His tone shifts from teasing to genuine as he adds, "And hockey was somehow meant to be for us when we decided to have a family."

"The universe had a plan when the adoption agency found us a son," John says, heartfelt too, and...*dammit.*

My throat constricts. All this talk of *meant to be* is making my eyes a little watery too. No, not a little. *A lot.*

I swallow, trying to stave off this waterfall. The last time I felt this way was when their son slid a ruby ring on my finger, and said it was *meant to be.*

The way I've felt about our friendship for so many years.

The way I always want to feel about it.

But the dreams of romance are getting harder to ignore when Asher's always a step ahead of me, cooking for me, caring for me, looking out for me. Most of all, lifting me up, supporting me, and knowing what I need maybe before I know it myself.

"Your son's amazing," I blurt out to the two men who raised him.

They smile warmly and say in unison, "We know."

Carlos squeezes my shoulder, shifting gears. "How was dinner the other week? I trust the cilantro made the meal?"

"Of course it did," I say, impressed but not surprised with Carlos's finesse with herbs—he works in finance, with a focus on restaurants and the food-service industry.

"Oh!" John says excitedly to Carlos. "You should give him a recipe with rosemary next time. Your rosemary is to die for."

Carlos's deep brown eyes light up. "I detect no lies in that statement. I'll drop some off tomorrow."

"With some vitamins," John adds with a laugh.

Carlos laughs again, a warm, loving sound that tells me they aren't making fun of Asher. "Yes, since we already have plenty." Carlos turns to me, explaining, "He sent us some vitamins the other week, even though we told him we're all set."

And Asher sent me neck exercises late last night and set an alarm on my phone to make sure I did them. But I don't add that, though the neck stretches were, admittedly, helpful. Still, I don't know what to make of Asher's concerns. Especially since John looks great, and I have no idea why Asher's worried about osteoporosis, except well, he's kind of a worrier, and I suppose you can't tell anyway if someone has it just by looking.

But I file away the fact that they already have the vitamins Asher was so determined to get them. I don't say anything though, since it's not my place to ask. Except, it already seems I have the answer to one question—*does Asher worry a lot about your health?*

He does.

"So tell us all about the mural job," Carlos says. "We're so excited for you and it sounds like it's leading to all sorts of things."

"Asher said you're getting new gigs from it," John adds. "He was really excited when he got the cilantro. Such a huge break for you."

It's happening again. My throat is tightening, and it's not only from the fact that Asher told them about my life and career. But from the fact that they not only remember, they also care enough to ask me.

I tell them about the café where I'm finishing the tree painting tomorrow, then a request from a new night market to carry some of my decorative mirror designs, and even some requests from galleries to look at my pop art kiss portfolio, and it's so nice to share with his parents. They dote on me and treat me like their real daughter-in-law and it's almost embarrassing how much I love it.

But I love even more the reaction my jersey gets when Asher races onto the ice at the start of the game against the Los Angeles Supernovas. I rise and cheer him on with everyone behind me seeing the custom-made jersey— custom made for one woman only.

Me.

It has his number and his name, like all the other Asher Callahan jerseys.

But this is the only one that says *Mrs.* in front of his last name.

Carlos hoots when he sees it. "Damn, he likes claiming you," he says.

"He really does," I say, and once again, I feel like a part of their family, and I love it far too much for my own good. I can't let myself get too caught up in the moment.

"Besides, it's a damn good name," John says, and Carlos laughs, like they have an inside joke.

"That's why we picked it, babe," Carlos says to his husband.

That raises an interesting point. Do both his dads have the same last name? I don't actually know, because do you really need to know your friends' parents' names? "Did you pick that last name for Asher? Rather than use a hyphenated name?"

Carlos grins. "Actually, neither one of us wanted a hyphenated name, so we picked a new last name and moved our given names to middle names, and that way the three of us could have the same last name."

My heart swells. It's just a name, but the gesture and the reasoning fills my heart. "That's lovely," I say.

They both smile my way. They invite me to their thirty-fifth wedding anniversary dinner in a few weeks' time, and they don't stop including me for the rest of the game. They involve me in everything. From their discussions about their favorite shows—they're hooked on *First Dates* too—to trade rumors surrounding Miles's younger brother, Tyler, who plays for the Supernovas, as well as their predictions for when that trade might be. "Trade deadline just passed. Bet they get him in the off-season though," John says confidently.

Oh! Maybe that's the trade Eleanor was dropping hints about. Possibly she was discussing it, but it didn't come to pass before the deadline? Then I laugh quietly. I don't know the ins and outs of trade machinations, but maybe she does like me if she's dropping breadcrumbs about trades.

That makes me feel like maybe I do deserve some of the attention I've been getting. Asher definitely does when he scores the first goal of the game near the end of the first period. After he fist-bumps with the guys on the bench, he turns to me, locks eyes, and blows me a huge kiss.

I catch it, then turn around, looking over my shoulder, showing off the back of my jersey just for him. He mouths *Mrs. Callahan.*

And he looks even more pleased than he did when he scored that goal.

46

KEEP IT TOGETHER

Asher

"I'd say I'm sorry for your loss, man, but I'm really not," Miles says, grinning at his brother in the corridor after the game.

Tyler scratches his thick beard with his middle finger. "I'm not sorry for telling the press you slept with a stuffed bunny till you were twelve," he shoots back as we head toward the media room.

Miles's face turns pale. "I did not."

I chuckle, enjoying this. "Wait—dude, you slept with a stuffed bunny?"

Tyler nods, smug. "Sure did. He was scared of thunderstorms."

"No shame, man," I say to Miles, trying to keep a straight face. "I'm scared of stuff too. Like anacondas. And climate change. But thunder? That's loud, so I get it."

Miles huffs, clearly not amused. He turns to his brother with a scowl. "I mean it, Ty."

Tyler gives him a playful pat on the cheek. "Maybe don't gloat, then."

"You'd do the same," Miles grumbles.

Tyler shrugs. "Yeah, you're right. Gloating's fun. Go ahead, but just know I'll gloat ten times harder when we beat you for The Cup."

With that, we stride toward the press room. Normally, Everly only corrals the Sea Dogs players for post-game comments, but tonight, with the brother-versus-brother angle, she's wrangled Tyler for a statement too. The press can't resist the photo ops of the two Falcons in the NHL.

Me? I'm on my way out. "Catch you guys later," I say, stepping aside when they reach the media room.

"You're not staying to rub it in?" Tyler asks with a raised eyebrow.

"Nope," I say, nodding down the hall. "I've got somewhere to be."

Miles smirks. "His wife and his dads are here. Pretty sure it's his wife he's rushing to see."

With that word—*wife*—Tyler's smile fades as something dark flickers in his eyes. It's subtle but unmistakable —a shadow of someone who's been through the wringer when it comes to love. His jaw tightens for just a moment before he nods. "See you later."

If it were another night, another time, I'd ask how he's doing. But we both have places to be, so I give a crisp nod to my rival, then look to my teammate. "Thanks for the tips on how to score on your brother, Miles," I call out over my shoulder.

"Don't forget—I know your secrets, Callahan," Miles fires back with a grin.

Shit. He does. I backtrack. "No shame, Falcon. I slept with a stuffed rabbit myself."

"Good man," Miles says, and with that, he and Tyler disappear into the media room.

In my post-game suit, I walk down the hallway, the noise of the arena fading behind me, my thoughts drifting ahead to Maeve. For a moment, I let the scene play out in my mind. Days like today. Nights like this one. A life with her.

It hits me hard, nearly stopping me in my tracks. This deep, heady desire—this overwhelming need for her to be here, to be with me. To be part of my life in every way that counts.

I drag a hand through my hair, trying to catch my breath. The intensity of it all—the desire to make it happen—surges through me.

I want this. I *need* this.

Before I reach Maeve and my dads, I check my phone. There's a response to the calls I made earlier—some texts letting me know that yes, what I want is possible.

Good. That's really good. Because one thing I learned after googling "how to make your wife fall in love with you" is to be the man she needs, to give her what she wants, to *be* there for her.

I can do that. I *will* do that.

When I finally reach Mrs. Callahan at the end of the corridor, I tug playfully on her jersey then plant a kiss on her cheek. She startles with a soft "oh," then touches the spot where my lips just were. "Hey, you."

"Hey," I reply, as the scent of her sweet plum body spray works its magic. I'm unable to resist her. I drop another kiss to her lips, quick but lingering, savoring the feel of her. Maeve at my game, sitting with my dads—it's perfect. Absolutely perfect.

I turn to my dads. "Glad you guys could make it. Especially since I was pretty fucking good tonight."

"Language," John chides.

"J-dad, where do you think I learned it?"

Carlos gasps in mock surprise. "Babe," he says to John.

He just shrugs but smiles as he says, "Can we take you two out for a bite to eat?"

It's said like that's all the two of them could want—time with Maeve and me. I glance at Maeve, and her eyes are already shining with a yes.

"Sounds great," I say.

As the four of us slide into a booth at Sticks and Stones a little later and order a late dinner, I can't shake the feeling that this is the happiest I've ever seen her, laughing and teasing, talking and eating. I'd do just about anything to bottle this moment, to recreate it for her—to give her the moon.

* * *

The door clicks shut behind us as we step into the quiet of the house, heading up from the garage, leaving the cool night air behind. After we toe off our shoes, we head to the kitchen, like we both feel an inevitable pull to keep the evening going—or really, the talking. I toss my suit jacket on the back of a stool. She sheds her jacket, the jersey still on. Flicking on the light, she leans against the cool, marble countertop, the soft hum of the fridge filling the silence for a moment. There's a warmth in the air that wasn't there outside, and her small, thoughtful smile tells me she's still replaying the evening in her mind.

"Did you have a nice time?" I ask, moving closer, my fingers brushing the hem of her shirt.

"I did," she says with a nod. "Your dads are...really wonderful. They made me feel so welcome." She hesitates, her expression shifting, more pensive now. "It kind of made me miss my parents."

There's a twinge in my chest, one I've felt before when we've talked about them. I can't imagine what she went through. It's my worst fear—losing the people I love. I've asked her this before—of course I have—but I ask again anyway. "Do you miss them a lot?"

"I do," she admits quietly. "Especially in moments like this, when everything feels so...cozy, you know? I'm really glad I had tonight, but yeah—sometimes I just wish they were here to do these normal things too. See a game. Have dinner." There's a pause, then she swallows roughly, almost choking out the next words. "See my mirrors. Check out the mural." She draws a steadying breath. "Isn't that selfish?"

I reach for her shoulders, cupping them, rubbing them. "Are you kidding me? No. I love when my dads see me play. Of course you wish your parents could see your work. You put so much into your art, and they'd be so proud of you." I never met them, but I know this deep in my bones. They'd be so amazed by the woman she became.

"You think so?"

"I know so," I say with utter confidence. "Your mom wanted you to follow your dreams. You did follow them. You still do. You keep doing it. Every single day."

"She wanted that for me, you know?" she says softly, then her brow knits again. "That book of hers?"

"*If Found, Please Return*?" I ask, thinking of the one on the nightstand.

"Sometimes I read passages again, looking for a

message from her." She sighs, closing her eyes, maybe ashamed. "That is why sometimes I think I hold on too tight." She opens her eyes, and those hazel irises are etched with such vulnerability that my heart slams harder against my chest. "Isn't that silly?"

I ache for her. "No. I think it's normal to want to find that connection. Even now. Even when they're gone. You want to feel like they're still talking to you."

"I really do," she says. She pauses, biting her lip, as if weighing her next words. Then, with a nervous laugh, she asks, "Was that too much to tell you? About missing them? About the book?"

Scoffing, I shake my head immediately. "No. Not at all. I want to know. I want to know everything you want to share." My voice is firmer now, certain. "And I'd feel the same way."

"You would?"

"I would. I'd look for signs too, Maeve," I say then take a moment to collect my thoughts. I want to say the right thing. "I'd want...I don't know, a sense that they aren't forgotten. I kind of do that now, maybe preemptively. Maybe that's why I hunt out luck—good luck charms, stepping right foot first onto a plane. Maybe I do that because I want signs somehow that I'll keep this luck. I've done that ever since Nora died."

"Do you feel lucky? Like it could have been you? That you weren't riding with her?"

I've never been a bike rider, so no, I didn't join her for that training ride. But I'm acutely aware that things can change in a split second. Someone can be here today and gone the next second. "No. But losing a friend—someone I wanted to stay friends with—made me want to hold onto...what I have." But perhaps, it's deeper than that. Maybe it goes further back. This sense of holding onto what I have. Because I don't actively miss Nora. But I do feel that too-familiar heaviness of loss at times. I venture on, stepping into territory I rarely visit. "When I was fourteen, I thought John was going to die." The words come out quietly, almost cautiously, and I realize I've never told her this before.

"Asher," she says softly, reaching for me, her hands on my arms. "What happened?"

"He had this health scare. Well, he'd been having a lot of them. But this time was worse. One day after hockey practice, he wasn't just dizzy or faint. He was having heart palpitations. Like, this really uneven and way-too-fast heartbeat. His breath was short; he complained of chest pain. It happened while he was driving so he swerved, but managed to pull over and I could have called 911. But I didn't even think there was time to wait. I had to drive him to the hospital. It was just the two of us..."

I was never afraid of getting hurt playing hockey. But I was devastated when I thought I was the difference between my father's life and death. That drive is indelibly etched in my mind. The way my heart seized up too, but I had to ignore my fear and somehow get him to the emergency room. There was no time to waste.

"You didn't even have a license," she says softly.

"I knew how to drive, though," I admit.

"You did?"

"I had to. There were times beforehand when he was dizzy. Sick. Faint. Before he was diagnosed. For maybe a year on and off. So I learned early. I had no choice."

She reaches for my hand, squeezing it. "I didn't know

that," she whispers. "I knew he was sick back then, but I didn't know...you almost lost him. Or that you had to... step up like that as a kid. I didn't know what you went through. You must have been so scared."

"I don't like telling the story. I don't like talking about it," I admit, my voice thick with something I can't quite shake off. "Because every time I do, I feel that fear. No, it was more than fear. It was absolute terror."

My throat tightens as the memory presses in, vivid and raw. My hands on the wheel. The press of traffic. The curves in the road. The panic that threatened to rise in me. The words I repeated in my head—*keep it together, keep it together, keep it together.*

And I somehow did. Maybe it was luck. Maybe I took the right turns, hit the green lights, remembered how to drive through sheer luck. "I was so scared," I say quietly, taking measured breaths with each word, sharing something I don't like to share, something I don't like to feel, something I've kept inside me. But now, with her here, I want her to know. To understand.

Maeve squeezes my hand tighter, her thumb brushing gently across my knuckles.

"You saved his life. That's a gift, but it's a lot to carry with you too," she says, somehow understanding me completely.

I lean into her, feeling something new. Something rare. I feel the depths of her understanding in my soul. Like she knows so much more of me, and I hope—*I fucking hope*—I don't scare her away.

We stand in the dim light of the kitchen, the hum of the fridge the only sound around us. She steps even closer, her arms slipping around my waist. I pull her in, resting my chin on the top of her head, the feel of her body, the scent of her skin, the beat of her heart grounding me. "Was that too much?" I ask, more vulnerable than I ever want to be.

"No. Not at all," she says, then holds me tighter. And I hold her. And we hold each other.

47

JUST RIGHT

Maeve

The *California Style* photographer, Gillian Rivera, swings by the arena on Thursday while I'm painting a section of the Golden Gate Bridge. The magazine wanted the most iconic representation of the city, and the bridge felt like the perfect choice. Eleanor joins us, praising me as usual. It still feels surreal how much she looks out for me, almost like she's adopted me as one of her own.

When the shoot wraps up, I climb down from the ladder, stretching my neck and wrists while Eleanor chats with Gillian. Their conversation drifts toward tomorrow's shoot at the house—without Asher since he's on a road trip. It feels strange to do the shoot solo.

"Don't you want my—my husband there?" I ask, hesitating over the word "husband," only because it's still so new to me.

"No, we want you," Gillian says, her tone firm, no nonsense. "We don't need him."

The comment feels foreign to me, but I do my best to roll with it. We set a time, and after Gillian leaves, Eleanor turns to me with a triumphant smile. "Told you so."

I laugh, shaking my head. "Well, thank you."

Eleanor is insistent, making sure I hear her as she says, "No, really. I recognized your talent right away. I knew I wanted to work with you. And look at you now, getting all this attention. Just remember, darling, you're the one he wants to come home to."

My pulse skips. Lately, that feels more and more true, but I don't dare say that out loud. Besides, who am I even comparing Asher to? Gideon? All the men before him who called me high-maintenance? Screw those exes.

"Do you have any other marital advice?" I ask, because she always seems so keen to offer it.

Eleanor taps her chin with one finger. "A little spritz of perfume never hurt anyone."

I grin. "I'll keep that in mind."

"Sometimes, we have to make them feel special. Men fall deeply, and when they do, they become so focused on us. They'll treat us like queens if we let them."

I think about that. It's something I've never really considered before, but it's how my dad treated my mom. "And a queen has to look out for him now and then, right?"

Eleanor nods knowingly. "Exactly. Hence, the perfume. Something to make him feel special, because the right man will lay gifts, love, and adoration at your feet."

That's the complete opposite of the men I've dated before, and it's new to me too. I mentally add her words to my growing notebook of advice. It's getting longer every day.

The next day, Gillian arrives at Asher's house as planned. I let her in, feeling like I'm the lady of the manor. Sure, I've been staying here for nearly a month, but today feels different. I'm giving someone a tour of his house as if it's my own—when it's not. Not really. I'm still just playing pretend.

It feels bizarre to walk around this place without him. What's even more bizarre is that sometimes I feel like I belong. Maybe it's from all the photos he's hung up. Maybe it's from the way my plant collection mingled with his Lego plant collection. Maybe it's from the way we've been sharing the bathroom, the kitchen, and the bed—of course, the bed.

I lead Gillian through the house, showing her some of the art on the walls. She pauses at a series of wildflowers and peaches. "These are beautiful," she says, her eyes scanning the pieces. "Are they yours?"

I blink, surprised. "No, they're not. But I helped him choose them before we were married."

"Oh, really? Is that part of how you fell in love?"

The question stops me in my tracks. Am I in love with him? The thought is sudden, overwhelming. I know I'm falling for him—harder than I want to admit. Back when we picked those pieces, I thought we were just best friends, gallivanting around town, going to art festivals, choosing things for his walls. But now? Now, it feels like it's becoming more. But can it? We promised to stay friends. We promised these benefits wouldn't hurt the friendship. But the way we are together, in and out of bed, feels like a lot more than just beneficial.

"You know, maybe it is," I say, the words feeling heavier than I'd expected. How do I even trust this storm of emotions inside me? The desire I feel for him, the way I count the hours when he's away, the excitement when his texts pop up on my phone, the way my heart flutters when he comes home.

Gillian walks to the foyer, turning her attention to one of the mirrors I've been working on. "Tell me about these," she says, her face lighting up.

I smile and laugh as I show her one with an inscription about dragons and underwear. "We've been getting a lot of advice since we got married—maybe it's a newlywed thing. So I started a series inspired by it. I just finished a new one. Want to see it?"

I grab the latest mirror I worked on in the studio when I got a free hour, and the woman I shared the space with wasn't using it. I painted it in seashell blue. "We all need a hot friend in our bed, don't we?" I say, quoting one of the inscriptions.

"Words to live by," Gillian laughs.

"The woman who married us said that," I explain.

"Is that what started the 'love lessons' theme?"

"Actually, it was a lesson about dragon underwear. And I'm going to add Eleanor's latest—'a little spritz of perfume.'" I smirk, thinking of her words from yesterday. "It's the little things we do to make our partners happy—if they're worthy of us."

Gillian smiles warmly. "You're right about that—we need to make sure our partners are worthy. And I guess I just gave you some advice too."

I laugh. "You did."

"Are you planning to sell these at the night market?" she asks.

I pause, considering. Then I smile. "Yes, I'm doing a series. And you know what? I think I'll turn this into a full line."

Impulsive as always, but this feels right. I've always thought there should be a line of pieces inspired by all this love advice. People keep giving it to us—why not use it?

That evening, Asher calls me from his hotel room. "How'd the shoot go?" he asks.

"It was great," I say, reflecting on the day. "I'm going to turn the mirrors into a line."

"I love that. You should," he says. "They're fun and clever and romantic."

"I think so too. And for the first time, I feel like people are hiring me for me, not because of you. Is that weird?"

"No," he says. "It's amazing."

And it does feel amazing. When I go to bed, I feel this quiet strength burrowing inside me. This knowledge that I have real talent—a belief that I'm not simply getting jobs because I'm Mrs. Callahan. Sure, I'm having a blast playing that role. But people are hiring Maeve Hartley, the woman who can paint. The woman who has great ideas. The woman who's following her dreams. I pick up my mother's book, flipping through it, looking for a message. But maybe the message is in the thing itself—the dream she followed.

And I'll keep chasing mine because it feels so good to know...that I am worthy.

Me. Just me.

A few days later, Gillian comes back to the studio space I rent with other artists for the final shot of the *California Style* photo spread. I never fully moved my art supplies, my canvases and paints and brushes, into the guest room at Asher's home. That felt like taking over. But more so, I suppose I also simply prefer working in a studio rather than a bedroom, even a cramped one like this, even one I need to share.

In the studio, I work on painting a tiny image of a couple on a mirror while Gillian captures photos of me painting a pop art kiss. "You inspired me," I tell her. "But really, I suppose my husband did since I started making them for him."

"I bet he loves them," she says, framing another shot.

With complete certainty I answer her. "Yes. He does." I pause, thinking once more on the art, but also the meaning behind these mirrors. "I guess my lesson is that when you find someone worthy, you give a little piece of yourself each time—and hope they do the same."

The words hang in the air along with a wish—that I'll know that when I feel it. Someone loving me the way I love them.

* * *

I keep wondering if I will recognize it that weekend when he returns to town. I wonder if that's what I feel on Friday night when I spritz on some perfume and rush downstairs after his text that he'll be home in five minutes. After Max drops him off, I fling open the door to find him striding up the steps two at a time.

Like he's rushing to me too.

His smile is crooked and his eyes are bright. My heart goes a little wild and this feels like more than friendship.

Still, I don't trust my own compass. I don't want to assume the way I feel is normal when it's always been extra. When I've been extra. I want my own love lessons; I need them too. I want to know what all this means, and how it feels to be accepted for who I am. I don't want to assume, even as he scoops me up into his arms and says, "I've fucking missed my wife."

"Missed you too."

After he kicks the door closed, we waste no time as he carries me to the living room and sets me on the couch. There, we grab each other, hands and fingers rushing to tear off clothes. He strips off my T-shirt and I hastily unbutton his shirt. "I hope the NHL never changes its travel suit rule but right now I wish it didn't have one," I say.

"Me too," he mutters as I slide off my skirt.

Quickly, I unzip his slacks and free his cock. It's hard and ready and hot. A quick slide of my palm down his shaft and he's shuddering. He grabs my hand, squeezing me, squeezing him. "Do you have any idea how much I missed you?"

I shake my head. "No. How much?"

"So fucking much."

I stroke; he breathes hard.

"Do you have any idea how beautiful you are?"

I shake my head again because I like this game too much. "How beautiful?"

He opens his eyes, his gaze searing. "So fucking hot. So fucking beautiful."

I grip him harder, sliding my fingers over the head, spreading a drop of the liquid arousal.

He hisses through his teeth.

"Maeve, do you have any idea..." He just bites off the end of that sentence; maybe he was going to talk about sex? His cock throbs against me and he grits out a command, "Put me inside you fucking now."

His demand makes me wild with desire, so I comply,

then rise up and down on him while we both grunt in unison as he fills me up. We fuck, fast and frenzied.

My first orgasm hits me like a tsunami, but after it crashes over me, he adjusts us, putting me on my back, sliding between my thighs, and then he eases out slowly before thrusting back into me. He slows the pace, a long, lingering fuck that dangerously feels like making love. When I look into his eyes, I swear I feel like he's falling for me.

I close my eyes as that thought hurdles into me. That's the stuff I can't let myself think about. That's too much.

But when I open them again, it's hard to believe anything else. Still, when we're done, I have to ask because I have to know, "Was I too much?"

"Too much for what?" he asks incredulously.

"In the way I wanted you?"

He breathes out hard, his gaze more intense now. "That's just not possible."

* * *

I snort. Not attractive—not one bit—but I can't help it as I swipe on blush and ask Asher to repeat himself. "Did you actually just say 'better optics'?"

He nods, tugging on a Henley. Ever since I jokingly asked him at that coffee shop why Henleys, he's never stopped wearing them when he's not working out or dressed in a suit. He has other clothes—polos, pullovers—but every day it's a Henley. Like it's just for me.

Like the warm nuts he roasts at night. Like the dinners he cooks. The endless orgasms he gives me. Or really, the words of affirmation he showers on me, which I'm starting to realize might actually be my deepest love language. The one I need the most. The one he excels at.

"Yeah," he says with a wry smile. "Soraya mentioned it's better optics to have a plus-one. Bringing my wife to the fundraiser looks better than showing up solo. Which translates to 'single men give off creepy vibes.'"

I crack up, pointing at him. "Your words, not mine."

"Question for you," he says, leaning against his vanity, watching me put on makeup. "Do I creep you out, wife?"

I turn to him, looking so ruggedly handsome in jeans and with a fine dusting of stubble. "I like that. Your stubble."

"I look like a cowboy, right?"

"Yes, let's put a cowboy hat on you," I tease.

"You'd like that."

"I would. Which translates to—you don't creep me out at all."

"Good."

I go back to swiping on blush when Asher moves behind me, wrapping his arms around my waist. He brushes my hair to the side and drops a kiss on my neck.

My breath catches, and I go a little existential. "What is it about neck kisses?"

"Maybe you should do a series of mirrors with neck kisses," he murmurs, caressing me more with those lush lips.

A tremble runs through my whole body.

I glance back at him. "Are you that greedy? You already have my pop art kiss mirrors. Now you want a series of neck kiss art."

"When it comes to you, Maeve, you know I can never have enough," he says, his eyes meeting mine in the reflection, intense like the night he came home and took me on the couch. That look right now—more passion than I can try to paint—makes my heart stutter.

I'm getting slightly scared of how far my emotions are running past the expiration date on our arrangement.

I focus on my makeup, but something about this moment feels so right—the two of us, getting ready, doing life together. And today, we're stepping into one of our last official acts as fake husband and wife. That thought makes me a little sad. After I'm dressed in jeans, Converse, and a cute hoodie, we head for the door. I pause, touching his hand. "This is our last performance," I say quietly.

His eyes soften, a bit sad. "Do you want to come up with another one?"

There's a touch of desperation in his voice—like he's eager to keep this going. Maybe I am too.

"I would. I can...I can come up with something. I can do anything you want," he says.

But the truth is, we don't have another performance lined up. No more shows to act out as husband and wife. I'll be done with the mural in a few weeks. Everything is winding down, just like the hockey season. Just like our arrangement. Just like these "benefits" that don't feel like only benefits anymore.

Two words tumble through my brain, over and over. Fake. Real. Real. Fake.

The lines have blurred so much I can hardly tell what I'm feeling, except a little melancholy. Whether we want another "show" or not, this is really our last scheduled performance.

We head downstairs, ready to go. Along the way, I curl my fingers into fists, so I can stretch my wrists back and forth. I swear I can feel Asher tense behind me. As I walk,

I turn back to look at him. "You stretch before games. I stretch after painting," I say.

His brow knits, but he gives a tight nod. Like he's accepting that I'm okay. That he doesn't need to carry this burden. At least, I hope that's what he's thinking. But when we reach the door, he stops. "Hold on. I forgot something."

He lets go of my hand and trots down the hall, up the stairs, and back to the bedroom. Is he...looking something up again?

But he returns a minute later with his watch, glancing down the hall at the terrace as he snaps it on his wrist. "You like the way I look in watches," he says by way of explanation.

"You noticed."

"I notice everything about you."

I'll miss that too—the way he sees me. But I shove these wistful feelings inside as, hand in hand, we head for the park.

* * *

"Go deep!" I shout to a group of grade-schoolers who had the audacity to challenge me to a round of frisbee on Crissy Field on this beautiful Sunday afternoon.

A sixth grader named Prahna, who plays soccer, sprints across the field, arms outstretched. "I've got it!" she yells, reaching for the orange disc I send soaring through the air. She leaps and snatches it mid-flight.

"You're better than a Border Collie," I call out.

"Goals," she responds with a grin.

We toss the frisbee back and forth a little longer

before she slows down, breathless. "I'm hungry. Do they have any gluten-free sandwiches? I can't eat wheat."

"Dude, I don't eat meat," I say, smacking palms with her. "Different food options for the win."

We head toward the sandwich boxes in recycled cardboard, joining her parents and the other kids and families. Some kids are here with their families, and some aren't—that's the whole point of this charity. It's for underprivileged kids, and not all of them have parents who can always be there for them.

I glance around at the kids digging into sandwiches, a warm feeling settling in. It's moments like this that remind me why this charity matters—why Asher and my brother are launching it. For sports, but also for support. But then a small tug on my sleeve pulls me from my thoughts.

Another girl, about ten, stands by my side. "Do you know where the restrooms are?"

"Sure, I'll show you, Lia," I say, reading her name tag, then walking her toward the facilities. She's unusually quiet on the way, her eyes downcast.

On the way back, she suddenly blurts out, "I miss my dad. He died last year."

My breath catches. I crouch down beside her, unsure of what to say at first, but the look in her eyes tells me she just needs someone to understand. "I'm so sorry," I say softly. "I lost someone important too—my mom and my dad. And you know what? Sometimes I still miss them."

"You do?" she asks, her voice small.

"Ten years later, I really do."

"Does it ever stop hurting?"

I pause, thinking about how to answer her. "Yes. But sometimes that hurt comes back out of the blue. When you aren't expecting it. And it wallops you. But you know what?"

"What?" she asks, eager for an answer.

"The love stays. That part never goes away."

Lia looks at me, blinking back tears, but straightens her shoulders like she's trying to be strong. "I feel it sometimes—the love."

I nod, smiling softly, my throat tightening as I feel that swelling in my heart—that love I believe my mom left for me. When she passed on to the next life, I believe she gave me all that was left in her heart. "Good. Hold onto that. It's what makes us who we are. It's a gift, really, to have that much love inside you."

She nods. "Thanks."

Maybe that's why I feel like I'm too much sometimes—because I have all this love in me with nowhere to go. But maybe it's not such a bad thing if I can help others unexpectedly, especially in moments like this. I squeeze her hand gently. "And thanks for sharing. It's good to talk things through."

She gives me a tiny nod. "I try to stay tough," she whispers.

"You are tough," I tell her. "But you don't always have to be. If you ever want to talk to someone, that's okay too."

"Maybe," she says thoughtfully. "Sometimes I just like to play soccer though."

"I get that," I say with a smile. "We all work things out differently. I do it through painting."

We walk back, the moment settling into my bones. I've been where she is—trying to be tough, trying to hold onto something that feels like it's slipping away. Sometimes, maybe all the time, holding too hard. But maybe holding too hard isn't a bad thing if you can help others with it.

When we return to the picnic tables, Lia heads off to talk to a counselor, and Asher finds me and introduces me to a few families. We chat with some board members from the dinner—Marcus, the sports psychologist is here, as well as Terrence, the retired football coach, and Lydia, one of the big donors.

"Are you still folding swan napkins?" Marcus asks.

"I'm working on a whole series now," I say, appreciating that he called them swans, even though they were fans.

"Maybe we can add that to the sports camps. Competitive napkin-folding," Lydia says.

"I'll teach it," I offer.

Asher smiles fondly. "You'd be great at that."

And optics or not, I can tell one thing—he likes having me here. And that's reason enough. "I would be good," I say, feeling his confidence in me, but also this newfound confidence in myself.

My brother swings by and pats me on the back, teasing, "Going great, huh? It's the optics, right?"

"That's me. I'm magic when it comes to optics," I say.

He smiles, but then his smile fades and he tips his forehead toward the water, a sign for us to step away from the crowd. I walk with him toward the edge of the picnic grounds. "What's going on?" I ask.

"Just want to see how everything's going with the whole...*thing*," he says in a low voice.

"It's great," I say, meaning it completely.

"Yeah?" It's asked like he doesn't believe me.

"Beckett, I swear it is," I add.

He blows out a breath, then nods a few times. "Okay. I can't help looking out for you."

"It's the big brother gene," I say, but there's affection in my tone.

"Guilty as charged." He sighs and looks toward Asher, who's chatting one on one with Marcus now. My brother returns his focus to me. "Anyway, so it's working out. You're getting lots of new gigs, right?"

"I am, but it's not because of the marriage," I say, believing it for one of the first times. Maybe there's more interest in me now, but these days it feels like the interest is in Maeve Hartley, the artist who's working on the Sea Dogs mural, rather than in Mrs. Callahan. I square my shoulders, something like pride filling my chest. "I started a new line of mirrors. And Angelina already heard from a couple local shops that might want to carry them," I say, sharing the latest news with him. I sent her some pics of the Love Lessons mirrors last week, and she made some calls, and quickly found some stores that like to carry local artists' work.

"Good, good," he says, rubbing his palms. "I don't want you getting hurt during this whole...*charade*."

"The opposite is happening," I say, because my dreams are finally coming true. "Maybe the whole *pay it forward* thing worked out in its own way."

He scratches his jaw, seeming to consider that as he nods a few times, his gaze drifting to Asher. "And the two of you? You're friends and all still?"

I snicker. I can't help it. It just bursts from me.

"What's that for?" he asks.

I roll my eyes. "We're all good," I say, but I'm not telling him anything more. My sex life is none of his business. Come to think of it, neither is my love life. I don't need anyone's permission to date.

"Okay," he says, not looking quite satisfied with my

answer but accepting it, nonetheless. He exhales, then nods toward the group again. But before we go, he turns to me one last time. "Do me a favor then."

"What is it?" I ask, a little skeptical.

He squeezes my shoulder. "Don't break his heart."

On that mic drop, he walks off to rejoin the others. I stand in place for a long beat, the words echoing. *Don't break his heart.*

Does my brother know something? Does he sense something? I catch up to him, grabbing his shirtsleeve. "Did he say something to you? Is that why you said that?" I whisper.

Beckett shakes his head. "No. He didn't. But I have eyes. Now let's go."

His advice—another love lesson—rings in my head as we return to the donors, the kids, the families, the board, and my husband, who's still chatting intensely with Marcus.

It plays on a loop as Beckett clears his throat, gathering everyone's attention. Behind him, the bay gently laps the shore, its waves soft like background music.

"I want to thank you all for coming today and supporting Total Teamwork," Beckett says. "None of this would be possible without Asher's idea to get it started, so I'll let him take it from here."

And the words ring in my head once more as Asher steps to the front of the picnic tables, his usual easy confidence shining. "Thanks, Beckett," he begins, glancing around at the gathered crowd. "This cause is so important, and I'm grateful to everyone who's helped make Total Teamwork possible. But today's not just about me—it's about the people who've supported me along the way. I've been lucky to have Maeve by my side, helping in more ways than I can count. I couldn't do any of this without her. So thank you—to my wife. My best friend."

His words hit deeper than I'd expected. Everything right now feels so real, from my brother's unexpected advice to Lia's watery eyes to my own dreams finally feeling within reach. But this, most of all—the goal Asher and Beckett had years ago to create this charity. They made it happen, and it's coming true at last.

Asher talks more about the charity, the picnic, the fun run, the upcoming summer camps, and the range of services available. When he's done, the crowd applauds, and I'm left standing there, feeling the warmth of his words, the heat of his gaze, the love that surrounds us.

Don't break his heart.

I don't want to. I'd never want to. But is that even on the table? His heart? As that thought grows roots, so does another one. Is my heart on the table too?

It beats louder, thumps harder.

My thoughts start to race. It's only been six or seven weeks—how could I possibly be falling in love? My emotions are so tangled, so blurred, I can't even tell what's real anymore. Is this part of the act, or am I starting to feel something deeper?

There's no time to figure it out, since I need to mingle more, so I push down the confusion that swirls inside me. Play the part. Smile. Focus on him, on being the wife. Optics, right?

* * *

Asher is amped up when the event ends. I've seen him like this after hockey wins. There's this charged energy around him, like he can't sit still even as he drives.

"Are you happy with how it went?" I ask on the short ride back to Pacific Heights.

"Hell, yes. This launch is better than I'd imagined. Had a good chat with Marcus for a while too. Smart guy. He knows a ton about working with athletes' mental health. Well, obviously," he says. "So we can definitely incorporate more of his skills. But that's not why I'm so fucking excited right now."

"Why, then?"

He grins at me, full of secrets, as we pull into the garage. "Let me show you."

"What is it?" I ask, his energy infectious.

"Patience, my wife," he says, then he leads me through the house, out onto the terrace, and into the backyard. Fairy lights twinkle along the fence—brand new and lighting up the yard with a soft glow. My eyes drift toward the little shed, the former sunroom.

It doesn't look like a sunroom anymore.

I gasp, barely able to breathe. "Asher?"

"Yes?"

"Did you make a—?" I stop, unable to finish. This is so much. This is unreal.

"A studio for you?" he asks, holding my gaze with the most satisfied, hopeful look ever. "I did. Well, I had it made while we were gone."

This is so much more than words of affirmation. This is everything.

48

YOUR FAVORITE COLOR

Maeve

"How?"

I can't even begin to process how he's pulled this off. It's stunning. I stand in the backyard, staring—no, gawking—at the sunroom, now completely transformed. Even at night, under the soft glow of string lights, I can see the changes. The large windows reveal it's no longer just a spot for a casual coffee break—which he never takes. There's an easel inside, the one I had tucked away in the guest room, and shelves lined with paints, as well as a workbench like the one I use to make mirrors.

"What did you do?"

Asher's smile radiates with pride, deservedly so. "*I* didn't really do anything."

"I mean, how did you pull this off?"

"I hired a couple of guys. They built the workbench in their workshop and brought it over. Then, while we were out today, they wired up the lights and added some blinds to control the sunlight. They moved out everything I never use and brought in your things." He hesitates, then adds, "I wanted to make sure you had a space of your own."

I'm afraid to say the obvious—that I'm leaving soon, I'm not staying here much longer—but I feel like I'd be pointing out the wrong thing at the wrong time. Instead, I say, "Are you sure? This feels like so much."

He arches a defiant brow. "Are you telling me it's too much?"

It's a bit of a challenge, in a tone that makes it clear he doesn't have the same fears I do. He's unafraid to show how deep and wide his feelings go.

I suppose we're all afraid of different things, and he's done so much to allay my fears.

But also to lift me up. "It's perfect, and I'm overjoyed," I say, my voice cracking as I let my emotions show. I let him see all the real things I feel, including the tears of gratitude that slip down my cheeks. "Thank you."

He seems to fight off a smile. "Even if you only use it for a couple more months, I wanted you to have it. You said you needed separation from where you sleep to make your art. So if inspiration hits at midnight or six in the morning..."

I laugh softly, brushing away the tears and swallowing some of these too-big emotions. "I'm not up at six in the morning."

He smirks. "Work with me, Maeve. What if you're inspired at nine o'clock at night or at midnight? What if something calls to you? What if you want to finish one of your mirrors or paint a concept for a mural? If you want to do it, you can do it here. If something calls to you, you have everything you need."

My stomach twists from all the what-ifs.

But especially the what-if of us. The future is racing toward us. The future where this temporary marriage ends when the season does. It's March, and the pages on the calendar are flipping too quickly.

"Are you sure? This is so big. So wonderful."

Asher steps forward. "We'll always be friends," he says, his voice thick with emotions. Then in a raw, stripped bare tone he adds, "You can always use it. It's yours."

Oh god. That's the biggest gift of all. He's giving this to me as my friend. He's giving it without strings or conditions. He's giving it *solely* because he wants me to have it. The way he gives so completely fills my heart like a cup overflowing with the sweetest wine, like sunlight flooding a room, like love finding its way through the darkest of places.

"Asher, I love it," I say quietly, and even though the words stop there, the truth lingers—*I think I'm falling for you, and I don't know what to do with all these feelings gathering strength inside me, marching relentlessly toward my bruised heart.*

"Good," he says with the confident smile of a man who knows he's pulled this off. He places a hand on my back. "Let's go see your new studio."

I'm giddy as he guides me along the stone path through the beautifully landscaped yard. The soft glow from the string lights makes everything feel peaceful, but festive too, like they're an invitation to create at all hours. We step onto the floating deck, built around a tree with a hanging chair swaying gently in the breeze. It's scary how perfect it is—how easily I can picture myself there.

He slides open the door, motioning for me to enter. "For Maeve Hartley, one of the top artists in California.

Too bad I didn't get it done before the photographer came out."

I laugh, feeling lighter than I have in weeks. "Are you kidding? I love it. I love it just for me."

"Good, because I didn't do it for *California Style*. I did it for you."

My heart stutters, then slams against my chest, pounding in a rhythm that feels too good. I feel like my veins are glowing.

Inside the studio, the lighting is soft, casting a warm glow over the carefully arranged space. It's a space for me to create, one I don't have to share with others, one I don't have to squeeze myself into.

But it's not just the space I love—it's the way the entire backyard leads here with the string lights, the landscaping, the peace and calm, the way I can shut the door and get lost in my art.

I'm overjoyed. "I want to try it out right now," I say, feeling like a kid at Christmas. Like he's just given me roller blades and I must race down the street now, feel the wind in my hair, the muscles pumping in my legs.

Asher walks over to the shelves, tapping his chin. "Let's see then. I ordered some of the paints you like. The ones made with non-toxic chemicals. They're all cruelty-free."

That's it. My heart is going to burst.

Tears prick at the back of my eyes. "How did you know...?"

He turns to face me, and his gaze softens. "You mentioned it once, how important that was—for you to find materials that didn't cause harm. I thought, if you're going to paint here, I want you to have everything you need."

I swallow hard, overwhelmed by how much attention he's given to every small detail. "This...means so much."

Then, with a playful gleam in his eyes, he lifts a tube of paint and adds, "And if memory serves, red is your favorite color?"

His gaze drifts down to my chest, and I'm sure we're both suddenly remembering that day in the studio, when he ran his finger across the red paint on my skin, when his touch lit me up, made me sizzle.

"Did you have something in mind to break in the studio, *husband*?"

His smile is sinful. "I sure do."

49

PAINT MY BODY RED

Maeve

I set a drop cloth on the floor and pick out a few paintbrushes—slim ones, soft ones, but also a few bigger ones. I've never done this before, so I'm not sure what will feel right.

"More is more," I say to Asher, offering them in a mason jar.

"With you, it is," he replies, his voice rich with amusement as he takes the jar, then carefully studies the options before picking a slim one to go with the paint he's selected —a tube I've never seen before. It isn't one I bought.

This man. He's ravenous, and also prepared. Which is very *him*. I don't even need to ask if he researched body-safe paints—because of course he did.

He sets the brush next to the tube.

I hand him a palette as I nod to the tube. "Let me guess—you went to Risqué Business again?"

With a glint in his eyes, he nods. "You know me so well."

He's right. I do. And I like that knowing. It's comforting, but it also stirs something else inside me. "And you didn't even have to ask them for the best paint for *kinky* painting night. You went straight to the shelves and found it."

"I did all my homework in advance." He steps closer, his smile fading into something deeper, darker—his green eyes glinting like gemstones, full of flickering want. He runs the back of his fingers along my cheek and murmurs, "It's your studio, but you're my canvas tonight."

Chills erupt down my spine.

I hadn't really thought about the mechanics of this—who's painting whom—but of course, this makes sense. He'll paint my body.

I sit down in the chair, the one I'd normally paint in, and fumble with the button of my blouse. "When the painter becomes the painted," I say softly.

He stalks over, cups my chin, and raises my face. "Take off your shirt, wife. I want to paint your tits red."

I shudder out a breath, my mind flashing back to a moment in time—back to when my friends and I were at the diner for lunch, and I was musing about the ideal man for me—someone who'd want to paint my body.

And now that someone is...my best friend.

My brother's best friend.

My husband.

My breath quickens as I undo the buttons, slip the shirt off my shoulders, and let it fall.

"Now the bra," he says, his voice low and steady.

I unhook it, my pulse racing. He looms over me, holding the brand-new paintbrush. As he steps closer, he curls a hand around the back of my chair, leaning in, his breath warm against my skin. "I'm not an artist. I just know what I like. And I like..." He pauses, as if choosing his words carefully. He licks his lips, maybe gathering his thoughts before he says, "I like *this*."

It's said like he's holding something back, like he's adjusting what he really meant to say. But I think I know what he's saying—he likes me. And I think *like* wasn't the verb he originally wanted to use either.

Or maybe I'm just hoping another four-letter word was forming on his tongue. Maybe I'm feeling far too much. Maybe all these emotions bubbling up inside me are making me want something I probably can't have.

He lifts the brush but doesn't touch me with it. Instead, he runs it across the back of his hand, as if he's testing its softness. Then, in a low, smoky voice, he says, "Lift your chin."

I do, and he drags the brush from the bottom of my chin, along my throat to the hollow at its base, then continues down, down, down my chest, between my breasts, all the way to my belly button. I'm trembling everywhere. The hair on my arms stands on end. I feel electric in my own skin—just from that one stroke.

He travels back up with the brush, stopping at my right breast, tracing the bristles around my nipple and I'm gasping, hoping, wanting—until the peak tightens into a little diamond.

"There," he says, his voice low and satisfied. "I think my wife is going to enjoy being my canvas."

"I think I am too," I say softly, breathless.

He turns away, so he can spread some of the paint onto the palette. Then he dips the brush, and adds with a teasing smile, "If you have any tips on how to paint this canvas, I trust you'll let me know."

My breath hitches again. "I will," I whisper. But I already know I probably won't say a word—because this man knows exactly what to do to me.

He dips the brush in the red paint and then slowly, dizzyingly, glides it around my right breast. The moment the brush touches my skin, it's like a spark ignites in my veins. The paint is cool and smooth, but the friction of the bristles sends heat rushing through me.

He's measured and deliberate as he paints circles around my breast, turning it the color of a summer cherry as my skin wakes up with each stroke.

When he reaches the nipple, I'm shivering as he paints that red too. Then he steps back, looking cocky, and also incredibly aroused.

He doesn't say a word, but he returns to me, only this time instead of dipping the paintbrush, he slides his finger into the paint and then drags the color onto me.

With each touch, I grow hotter, wetter, more aroused from the slow, sensual way this man who uses his body to play a rough, brutal sport is using me as art.

He looks at me like an artist who worships his subject. With adoration. With reverence. And with a desire that I recognize completely—not only the kind I feel when I'm creating, but the kind I feel for *him*. It's something rich and potent, something that comes from deep inside. Something that fills me up, when I felt empty before.

He squeezes more paint onto the palette, dips his fingers into it, and takes his time, painting my other breast with slow, deliberate strokes. When he finishes, he steps back, glances at his stained hand, and says, "I guess my hands are all red now."

It's said as an invitation.

"Then mark me," I whisper. I stand, sliding off my jeans and panties, leaving myself bare before him. "Mark me with your hands."

Without hesitation, he dips both hands into the cool paint, pressing them against my stomach. I shiver from the cold of the paint and the heat of his hands. He pulls back. We both look down. His ruby-red handprints are stamped on my body, vivid and bold. He moves lower, leaving prints on my thighs and calves before coming back up, his hands tracing my arms, wrapping gently around my throat. His voice drops to a growl as he says, "I think I'll call this one 'My Scarlet Work of Art.'"

And here in my brand-new studio, where I can paint and sketch and create to my heart's content, I feel like a work of art. Because I see myself through his eyes.

I reach for him. "Want to get messy with me?"

"I really fucking do," he says.

His clothes vanish, and soon, we're breaking in the studio. He sets me on the workbench, and he fucks me with paint all over my body. And soon, it's all over him as the handprints he left on me turn into smudges on his chest, his arms, his thighs. My legs wrap around him, and he drives deeper, filling me completely, taking me apart, like we're creating something entirely new together.

Maybe that's what we've been doing since we said I do.

* * *

"Well, this blouse is toast," I say, sliding my arms back into it. I grab my panties and jeans, figuring we only have to cross the yard to get back to the house, and this shirt covers enough. Asher's back in his slacks, shirt in hand, as

LAUREN BLAKELY

we slide open the door, glancing down at the drop cloths scattered with our handprints.

"I'll clean it up tomorrow," he says, flashing me a grin. "We should probably...shower."

"You think?" I tease, eyeing the red mess all over us. I love it. I love his shower, spending time with him, and—most of all—I love his big, generous heart for giving me this studio. The thought and care behind it touches me more than I can say.

But I swallow those feelings as we leave the studio, ready to hustle across the yard when a faint whimper catches my ear.

"What was that?" I ask, stopping mid-step. "Did you hear that?"

"Yeah," Asher replies, his brow furrowing.

I tilt my head, listening. Another soft whine comes from the bushes nearby. My senses go on high alert. "Is it a baby deer? A raccoon?" I wonder aloud as we move closer to the sound.

The grass rustles, and I jump as an animal emerges from the bushes—a black-and-white dog, with cool blue eyes, trembling slightly.

"Oh my god, baby, are you okay?" I crouch down instantly, reaching for her. But, of course, I'm still covered in red paint, and now her black and white fur is too, as I pull her close. She lets me hold her, the scared sweetheart. I gently run my hands over her thin frame, checking for a collar and tag. She's shaking but doesn't pull away, her tail tucked between her legs.

"No tag," I say, glancing up at Asher, who's now kneeling beside me, frowning. "She wasn't here when we went into the studio."

"Or maybe she was," he says thoughtfully. "I bet she

slipped in when the contractors were here earlier and hid." His hand rests on her head, fingers gentle as he scratches behind her ears. "Let's get her inside, clean her up."

"And take her to the vet tomorrow to see if she's chipped," I add, standing and carefully lifting the dog into my arms. She's way too light. "Come on, cutie-pie. Let's get you cleaned and fed."

The dog whimpers softly, pressing her head against my chest. All at once, I'm in love—it's instant and irrepressible. We walk to the terrace and Asher opens the door. Once inside, we head upstairs to the bedroom, both of us still covered in paint.

"Group shower?" I suggest with a grin.

He laughs. "Obviously."

A few minutes later, the three of us are in the rainfall shower, rinsing off paint and dirt.

Once I'm clean, I step out, wrap a towel around myself, and grab one for the dog. Asher hands the wet critter to me. She's thirty pounds, maybe forty, a cross between a Border Collie and probably a Husky based on her pointy ears, her silky collie fur, and her ice-blue eyes that are somehow big and hopeful.

Asher finishes up and wraps a towel around his waist, grinning as he kneels beside her. "Look at you," he says, drying her off some more. "You're a whole new dog."

"It's okay, sweet girl," I say softly. "No more paint; no more dirt. But do you have a home?"

She licks my face, and my heart melts. I glance up at Asher, my eyes silently asking—*can we keep her?*

He strokes her head, noticing her slight shiver. "We'll check Petfinder and call the rescues, get her scanned..."

"And then?" I ask, hopeful but nervous. I just want her to be okay.

"We'll see what we find out," he says, though I can tell from the way he rubs the towel over her head that he's hoping we find out she needs us.

Me too.

We pull on clothes and head to the kitchen, where we find some rice for her. She gobbles it down, tail wagging. I get it. I like it here too. And I'm starting to think it feels possible to be friends and lovers.

50

COCK-A-DOODLE-DOO

Asher

Maeve isn't just secretly pleased five days later when a local rescue tells us no one has claimed the pup. We've scoured Petfinder, lost and found boards, and nearby shelters, even after the vet confirmed the little cutie has no microchip.

Maeve's outwardly thrilled. She calls while I'm in Vancouver, right as I'm leaving the hotel to head to the arena for tonight's game. After giving me the "cutie update," as she calls the dog, she launches into how well-behaved the stray has been at the arena. She'd planned to bring her to a nearby dog daycare but decided to take her to work instead. Eleanor insisted on it when she learned Maeve had found a dog. No surprise there—this is the same woman who dresses her own dog up for portraits.

"She stays in a dog bed or sometimes a crate, and she's practically perfect in every way. She was even pretty good when I took her in the Lyft to work. Sooo...can we keep her?"

Can we?

The two-word question tugs on my heart. Like it's a we thing. Like it's up to us.

"Maeve, I'm not in charge of this," I say.

"Oh please, you love being in charge," she teases.

"In bed," I point out.

She scoffs. "Asher, you love control in general."

I bristle a little—maybe because it's true. "Fine, but that has nothing to do with keeping a dog."

But deep down, I'm secretly thrilled she's asking me if *we* can. Every time she says *we*, this romance feels more real, more permanent. A life with her. Like we're inching closer to the moment when I'll finally tell her I love her. But I hold back. I won't scare her away.

Adopting a dog feels like a commitment, even though I know it's Maeve's dog—she's the one taking care of her while I'm on the road, arranging vet visits, and walking her. Still, that *we* is pulling me closer to what I've wanted for a while now. To find that perfect moment to tell her she's the love of my life. I've been trying to show her for the last several weeks. Maybe she's finally ready to hear it.

"I can't say no to you," I admit.

She cheers. "You can stay, girl," she says to the dog, who makes an unusual sound in response—one that sounds strangely like a rooster's crow.

"What was that?" I ask.

"Oh, she has a weird bark." There's a pause, then an excited gasp. "That's it! Her name is Rooster." I laugh as Maeve continues, "She cocked her head—yup, it's her new name. Actually, hold on. I'm getting a message from the goddess of dog names...wait for it...Her name is Ruby Rooster! Since she was red–thanks to our paint–when we found her, and she barks like a rooster."

The Vancouver arena comes into view as I say, "Or maybe it's because you really like...roosters."

She snort-laughs. "I really like *your* rooster."

I grin, then ask about the mural. She updates me, telling me more about the love lessons mirrors, the night market, and she suddenly brightens. "Oh! And this coffee shop called. It's called High Kick Coffee—they have an art gallery run by a former Vegas showgirl. She saw the piece in *California Style* earlier this week, and she loves to support women artists and wants some of my paintings on the walls. They sell a lot of art there."

I think about that for a beat. "You know, now that you mention it, you do see a lot of art in coffee shops these days."

"Exactly! I think they've become the new galleries, making art more accessible," she says. I can picture her sinking into the couch, feet tucked under her, wearing one of her signature T-shirts, hair in a messy bun, and the image nearly makes me blurt out, *I love you.*

"Funny thing is," Maeve continues, "once upon a time, I really wanted my art in galleries like the Frieda Claiborne or Julien Aldridge galleries—you know, the really fancy ones I used to cater for."

I like where this is going. "And now that's changing?"

"I think so. The idea of my mirrors being in stores, my paintings at coffee shops—it just feels right. I finished that tree mural at the vegan café, and I'm working on the moon and stars at the yoga studio. Maybe this is what it was supposed to be all along. Maybe it was never about fancy galleries. Maybe it was about getting my art in front of people every day, where they can enjoy it. It doesn't have to sell for five thousand dollars to make me happy. If regular people get to see it, that makes my dream come true."

"And you're making art for, well, everyone. Not just rich people."

Her voice catches. "Yeah, I am. And I think that's really what matters to me."

I smile to myself. *She's finally finding her footing, figuring things out.* Selfishly, I wonder if this newfound certainty about her career might help my cause. *Maybe if she's sorting out these parts of her life, she'll be more open to the biggest question of all: Do you think you could love me too?*

I'm nearly at the arena when she adds one more thing. "Oh, my aunt wants to take us out again when you're back in town. She said she has exciting news for us. I have no idea what that means, but is that okay?"

"Of course," I say, though a small knot of suspicion forms in my gut. With Vivian, "exciting news" could mean anything—from a surprise dinner to something far more complicated—like she's giving Maeve her catering business and needs her to take it over right now.

But it's a good thing I'll be there—I can protect Maeve from whatever curveball Vivian throws.

I'm walking up to the arena now, and the noise of the city fades into the background as the game looms closer. I should be focusing on the matchup, running through plays in my mind, but the conversation with Maeve lingers. Balancing hockey and this thing with Maeve—it's getting more complicated. And soon, really soon, I'm going to have to tell her I'm madly in love with her.

It's on the tip of my tongue. I'm just waiting for the

right moment. I've been romancing her slowly so I wouldn't scare her away. So I wouldn't lose her.

And maybe, just maybe, she's finally ready to hear that I love her.

But for tonight, I have a game to win. I shake off the thoughts of the woman of my dreams as I near the doors.

* * *

It's early in the afternoon the next day, and I'm in the deadlifts zone at Beckett's gym, when he hops off the elliptical and strides over, motioning for me to take out my AirPods. I set down the weights and turn off the music. "What's up?"

We already lifted together earlier. I'm just doing extra sets now.

"When are you going to, you know, tell my sister you're madly in love with her?"

I blink, stepping back. He's more direct than I'd expected. I'm not entirely sure what to say to him about Maeve. I guess I figured I'd be risking our friendship if I ever did anything about the way I felt, but I also never truly thought he'd have an issue with it. That's just not his style. He trusts me. "How long have you known?" I finally say.

"Dude, you've had it bad for her for years."

Okay. So before I did. Great.

"Now's your chance. Figure it out. Treat her well. And don't forget about me. Got it?"

I swallow. Nod. "I won't. And thanks," I say, wondering if it's as obvious to the world as it is to him.

Or, more importantly, to her.

* * *

About a week later, we're getting ready for Vivian's dinner, and Maeve's twisting her hair into a clip while Ruby Rooster sits at her feet, thumping her tail as she watches Maeve get dressed.

I understand this dog so much.

Maeve checks her reflection in the bathroom mirror, and I notice it again—the twist of her wrists.

My brow furrows. "You okay?"

"Totally," she says with a bright smile, but I can't take my eyes off her wrist as she grabs the ibuprofen. She tosses back three pills this time. I count.

"You're not okay," I say, sharper than I'd intended.

"I am," she insists, her smile dimming a little. "They're just a little sore. Like I said, it's normal. That's why I do the stretches."

I draw a deep breath, trying to keep calm. "How is that normal?"

"I work with my hands, Asher," she says, then looks me up and down. "Don't you ever get sore?"

All the time. But I'm an athlete. It's literally part of the job, and I fucking deal with it. I handle it. "Yes, but it's not the same."

"How is it not the same?" she counters, already leaving the bathroom and sweeping through the bedroom where she grabs her bag.

Ruby Rooster trots after her, and Maeve coos at the dog, scratching her chin.

She stops and gives me a thoughtful look, then sets a hand on my chest. "Asher, it is. You work with your body. So do I. It happens."

I open my mouth to argue, but the words stick in my

throat. *I can handle it when it happens to me, but what if it gets worse for you? What if you can't heal quickly? Your hands are your livelihood.*

"We could look into it," I suggest, a knot in my chest tightening.

She tugs me closer. "Let's just go to dinner. Seeing my aunt is stressful enough."

I inhale, trying to just focus on the night ahead. When the dog rubs her head against me, the tightness loosens for a minute, and I lean down to give Ruby Rooster a kiss on the head, catching a whiff of something floral. "Why does the dog smell so...fancy?"

Maeve grins, then says offhand, "Oh, that's paw-fume."

I blink. "Paw-fume? Did you just say paw-fume? What the hell is that?"

She nods seriously. "Yes, I got it at the pet supply store. It's cruelty-free, and it makes her smell so pretty." She bends to the pup, cupping her snout. "Such a pretty girl. And you love your paw-fume, don't you?" Maeve asks, stroking the dog's face.

I can't help it—I start laughing. Only Maeve would get something like paw-fume. It's so *her*—a little quirky, a little over-the-top, but absolutely charming. And in that moment, I know. *Tonight. I'll tell her tonight that I am absolutely, wildly in love with her.* How could I not when everything she does melts my heart?

We say goodbye to the dog, but as we drive to the restaurant, I can't stop thinking about her wrists. *I should do something to help her. I should fix this.*

At the restaurant, I slip off to the men's room to wash my hands—and to Google *wrist pain for artists*. Tendonitis. That's it. Could be tendonitis. Wrist braces...splints... strengthening exercises. I'll order her some wrist braces tonight and find better exercises. I'll look up more later. I can fix this.

A little less tense, I join Maeve and her aunt at the table, pushing my worries aside. "How's everything going, Vivian?" I ask, trying to focus.

"Great! You had a fantastic game against Vancouver. In fact, I like the way your whole season is going."

This is a good sign—maybe she'll just chat about hockey. Maybe she won't get into Maeve's art career.

But then Vivian turns to Maeve. "How's everything going with you, Miss *California Style*?"

Maeve squares her shoulders and smiles. "Really well, actually. The mural's almost done, and I've gotten a few more jobs from it—and from the piece, of course. I can still probably cater for you now and then, but I've had so much going on with commissions that I don't know if I can take on more catering work."

Oh my god, she's doing it. She's moving forward. She's making a living as an artist. This is her dream. I squeeze her hand, letting her know I'm so fucking proud of her.

But the thought comes crashing down when I remember her wrist pain. *What if it gets worse? Will she still be able to paint? Will she still be able to make the mirrors and lamps for the night market? Will she be able to have a career?*

We order, but my mind is stuck on the same loop. *She's too young to worry about tendonitis.* I need to figure out a long-term plan for her.

I push back in my chair, and just as I'm about to excuse myself again to do some more research because that's what I should be doing right now, Maeve shoots me a funny look. Right. Vivian had news for us. I settle back in, focusing once more on the dinner.

Vivian flashes a pleased smile. "I'm going to throw you a wedding party."

What? I blink. "A wedding party?"

"Yes. I didn't get to throw an engagement party because you got married right away without family. We didn't have a reception. I really want to do this for you." She turns to Maeve, her eyes softening. "I always promised your mother I'd be here for you. Whatever you need."

Oh no. There's no way Maeve can turn her down now.

Maeve's eyes shine with unshed tears. She's clearly touched, but she says, "You really don't have to do that."

Vivian thinks this is real. Maeve must be freaking out that the truth might unfold. How much longer can we keep pretending?

Maybe this isn't simply a sign. Maybe this is the opportunity I've been wanting. This is my chance to tell Maeve we don't have to pretend.

"I'll handle the catering free of charge," Vivian adds. "I have friends who own a venue." She turns to Maeve. "We can invite your brother and Reina, of course, and any of your friends. Just give me some dates that work for you."

"I appreciate that, Vivian, really," I say, cutting in before Maeve can answer. "It's an incredibly generous offer. Maeve and I will need to take a look at our schedules though. We've both been swamped with work." I glance at Maeve, offering her what I hope is a reassuring smile. "But I promise, we'll figure something out that works for everyone."

"We will," Maeve says, sounding relieved, then stretches her hand once more, like she did earlier.

Vivian's eyes flick to her wrist. "You're doing that

again? You used to do that all the time when you were younger, back when you'd spend hours painting."

What the fuck? She's been doing this for years? My jaw ticks.

"I'm fine. I took ibuprofen, and I do my wrist stretches..."

Vivian cuts in, "You're overworking yourself, Maeve. Maybe you should consider catering full-time."

Whiplash. The way Vivian switches gears grates on me. I hate that Maeve's overworking herself to the point of pain, but I hate even more that she's being told to give up her art. "When your passion has physical effects on your body, you find ways to mitigate the effects," I say. "You don't give up your passion." The words come out strong, and I meet Vivian's eyes. "Don't worry. I can help her."

Vivian's face softens. "That's so sweet of you. I feel better knowing you're looking after her. I can tell you're in love with her."

I can't hold back completely. "I am," I say to Vivian before I can stop myself. The truth feels good. And it's good practice for when I say it to Maeve, just Maeve. When I tell Maeve this romance isn't for show. It's for real.

Vivian beams. "I knew it."

Maybe Maeve knows it too. Maybe she won't run. Especially if I can help her. And I need more info. I waggle my phone. "Sorry, I've got to make a call. My agent's been texting."

I excuse myself and rush back to the restroom, pulling up more websites for wrist exercises. There's so much that can be done—stress balls, finger stretches, therapy options. *I can help her. I can tell her I love her, and I can fix this for her.*

I return to the table, feeling a little more in control, until Maeve looks up. "What did your agent say?"

Shit. "Uh...just a new CheekyBeast campaign. Nothing big."

Then I keep my ass in the chair until dinner ends.

* * *

"You seemed a little...all over the place at dinner," Maeve says on the drive home. "Everything okay?"

Well, shit. I was hoping she wouldn't notice. "All good," I say, trying to sound confident. "Just thinking about the next game. Seattle's always a tough opponent." It's a fair excuse since we travel tomorrow with the game the next day. "But hey, a wedding party sounds fun."

It sounds great to me—celebrating this marriage would be perfect. And isn't that a step in letting her know my feelings are real? Not simply when I claim I'm in love in front of her aunt—I know Maeve could think that's for show.

"Sure," she says, and it's almost too easy. She glances over at me again. "Are you sure you're okay? You really seemed distracted."

I can't have her thinking I'm not all in. And there's one surefire way to get Maeve's mind off this: sex. Because my girl loves sex. "Sorry, honey. I was just thinking...about how much I want you to sit on my face when we get home. Will you forgive me for being horny?"

When she laughs and says, "Fair enough. Me too," I feel like I've pulled off the heist of the century.

Especially since, fifteen minutes later, we're in bed, and she's riding my mouth, grabbing the headboard like she's a cowgirl riding a bucking bronco. She's grinding down on me and groaning. "Fuck, Asher. Why are you so good at this?"

Because I fucking love you.

She rocks faster against my mouth, using me to chase her pleasure. "It's never been like this," she cries out.

It can always be like this.

"Yes. Just like that," she moans, and she's close, so close to losing control, and hell, so am I. My dick is aching, leaking at the tip, but my wife is hosting a slip-and-slide party on my face. Hell, she's trying to smother me, and what a way to go.

But I focus on my one job.

Make. Her. Scream.

I devour her sweet pussy, flick my tongue against her clit, and yank her down impossibly closer to my face till she comes in the loudest, longest orgasm in the history of San Francisco.

When she finally climbs off me, she looks like she's about to collapse, and that's fine by me. I'll straddle her waist and come on her tits like she likes. Only, she's faster than I am. She slides down between my thighs and covers my dick with her lips.

I unleash a feral groan from the unholy pleasure of her wicked mouth, but there's something I want more. Tugging her off me, I say, "Get on your back. Legs over my shoulders. Need to fuck you till you're dripping with my come," I say.

She scrambles off me.

Soon I'm balls deep in her, fucking hard and ruthlessly. "I love fucking you, Maeve," I bite out, getting closer to what I mean.

"I love it too," she murmurs.

"I love it when you come," I grunt as I drive in.

"Same here," she pants out.

"I just fucking love it all," I rasp out.

I could confess everything right now, but that's crass, even for me. Instead, I thrust deep until she cries out.

I follow her there, filling her up. When I ease out, I stare at the come dripping down her thighs before I run my fingers through it and push it inside her once more till she's arching and asking me to finger fuck her. Well, I'm not turning that down. I finger fuck her with my come till she cries out my name again.

After a quick shower, I say, "I'll walk Ruby Roo one more time."

"Ruby Roo," she repeats, like she enjoys the way the new nickname sounds.

All these things are bringing us together for real. All I have to do now is say it. As I walk the dog in the dark, letting her sniff to her heart's content, I make a plan. I'll tell Maeve when I return. I'll tell her I love her and that I want to go on a real date with her, then on another, then on many, many more.

But once I'm back in the house, Maeve's asleep, lights off to the world. The dog jumps up on the bed and curls into a tight dog ball at the foot of it, sighing as she settles in, close to Maeve. Always close to Maeve. I sit next to the two of them and practice. "I love you," I say to my sleeping wife.

Something eases inside me. I feel a peace I didn't expect. A hope for the future. My shoulders relax. I breathe out, then breathe in, imagining the days unfolding with her. Without the worry of them ending. Without an expiration date. With just...*more.*

But the second I think that, something nags at me.

Like a fly buzzing around my head. Like a hum that won't go away. A fear I've been afraid to face.

What if I lose her?

The thought grips me for most of the night, and I toss and turn until nearly five in the morning when I'm wide awake, staring at the ceiling.

Fuck it.

I get out of bed, get dressed, and go downstairs. When I turn on the laptop, I'm ready to fix this problem for my wife.

51

WHEN I AM TOO MUCH

Maeve

I pad quietly down the steps, looking for Asher. It's nearly six in the morning, and my eyelids are heavy, but once again, I woke to an empty bed after a restless night's sleep thanks to Asher's tossing and turning. Ruby Rooster was curled up at the foot of it, sleeping soundly, but Asher wasn't there. And when I turn the corner of the hallway and see the soft glow of the kitchen light, my heart sinks.

There he is at the counter again, bent over his laptop, his back to me, sipping coffee and scrolling through whatever's holding his attention this time.

A knot tightens in my stomach. If I didn't know better, I might be worried he was cheating. But that's not Asher. I know exactly what's consuming him. And that's the problem.

I step into the kitchen, and he still doesn't notice me. His gaze is glued to the screen.

I stop in my tracks, my jaw dropping as I catch sight of

the browser. Easily seventy-two tabs are open. *Carpal tunnel syndrome. Wrist therapy. Arthritis. Muscle weakness. Chronic pain. Surgery for carpal tunnel. Permanent nerve damage. Disability. Neuroma. Wrist X-rays. Electromyography. Can this turn into MS? Can this become ALS?* The list goes on.

I had no idea his googling was this bad. I knew he was worried, but not *this* worried.

"Asher," I say, my voice thin with a fresh wave of concern. My best friend is spiraling into something dark.

He jerks around, snapping the laptop shut in one swift move.

For a second, guilt flashes in his eyes. Then he shifts to his easygoing self. "What's going on? You having trouble sleeping?"

He sounds casual, too casual—like he's trying to cover it up. Because he is.

"I sleep fine. But you? You don't." My voice cracks.

"I was looking something up, you know, some exercises like we talked about last night," he says, at least partially telling the truth.

But I think he was lying to me last night. He has that same look in his eyes as he did when he left the table, part guarded, part concern. My throat tightens, but I push past it, asking, "Your agent didn't call during dinner, did he?"

His expression falters. "Why do you ask?"

I press on. "Were you googling in the restroom?"

He gulps, swallowing hard, and I see him mentally cycling through excuses as he asks, "Why are you asking?"

I don't back down. He's hurting and I can help. "You're traveling today. You have a game tomorrow afternoon. You need your sleep, Asher. You can't be up all night, googling worst-case scenarios," I say, my voice trembling, fighting to stay steady. I'm swimming in my own emotions, but I push through them and take a step closer, reaching for his hand.

He pulls his hand back.

That's so unlike him. This whole thing is so unlike him. And that's exactly why I don't back down. "Were you up all night, looking at everything that could go wrong? Because it's okay if you were. I just want to help."

"I wasn't up all night."

Emphasis on *all*.

Like that makes this okay. Like he's fine, just fine.

"You hardly slept. You have to have been awake for a while," I say, gentle but firm too.

His jaw tightens. He glances away, shame written across his face. There's so much denial in the way he avoids my eyes. But when he finally looks back, his voice is sharp. "Fine, you want to know? Here you go."

He flips the laptop open again, showing me the dozens of tabs filled with his fears. My chest tightens, and a lump forms in my throat. But this isn't about me right now. It's about him. I scan the tabs in more detail, and it's more of what I saw earlier—worries, solutions, worst-case scenarios, repeated over and over. Rinse, lather, repeat. When I caught him looking up his dad's medicine's side effects, I'd thought it was only concern, but now I see a pattern. When he obsessively researched my neck pain during a show, I'd thought it was borderline cute. But now, I see it all differently.

My laidback best friend is anything but. He's hurting, and he's managing it by trying to protect the people he loves from being hurt. Like me. By trying to "fix" some minor wrist soreness. Yes, I know about wrist pain for artists. Yes, I do exercises to stretch and strengthen my

wrists. Yes, I take breaks from painting. And yes, sometimes I pop ibuprofen.

I take a breath, trying to steady the sudden pounding
in my chest. "This feels obsessive. I'm worried about you.
Seems like you're anxious about something bad
happening to the people you care about?"

"No," he scoffs, without hesitation. The refusal is
instant and ironclad.

"Asher," I say, more worry seeping into my voice than I
want, "you're not sleeping. Or when you do, it's poor.
You're a pro athlete—you *need* rest, but instead, you're
googling health issues. I know it's hard to talk about, but...
do you think this is because you almost lost your dad?"

His eye twitches, and for a second, his face flickers
with something raw—fear. But it's gone as quickly as it
appeared. "I don't know why you think that," he snaps, his
voice rough and defensive, and so unlike him. "There's
nothing wrong with this. This is how I help. I've always
helped. People come to me for this, and I fix things. Let
me just do this, okay? You didn't mind when we were
friends, but now you want me to change?"

The sharpness in his voice stings. That's not the
answer I'd hoped for. He's so defensive. I raise my hands
in a gesture of peace. "I'm not asking you to change, Asher.
I'm saying I want to help you. I think...I think maybe you
have some obsessive tendencies."

"I'm just trying to help!" He drags a hand through his
hair, clearly agitated. His hands shake slightly as they
drop to the counter. "Let me do this. Just give me the space
to do this. Give me some fucking space."

The words hit me hard—*give me space*—and for a
second, it feels like a punch to the gut. But they don't sting
the way they might have before. This isn't about me. I'm

strong, and right now, I need to be strong for him. I dig in. This is one of those moments where I *have* to be too much. It's not about wanting his attention—it's about wanting him to feel better.

"You can't push me away," I say, my voice steady. "You're my best friend. We're going to deal with this."

He exhales hard, his frustration palpable, radiating off him in waves. "Fine. What do you want me to deal with?"

I take a moment. I need to get this right. After I collect my thoughts, I say in a calm, caring voice: "Asher, listen to me. I wonder if you feel like the more you know, the more control you have. You seem to be compelled to research every health thing—when we watch TV, when we're out to dinner with family, and most of all...when you should be sleeping. Your team needs you. You need them. And you can't be there the way you want to if you're up doing this. Your focus should be on hockey, but also...you deserve to have some peace. You deserve to feel better. You shouldn't have to carry these worries."

"I'm having a good season," he points out, and he's not wrong, but he's also fixating on the practical impact on his profession rather than the impact on his mind and his heart.

"I know, but somehow, sometime, this could catch up with you. You can't get by on caffeine and little sleep forever," I say, waving my hand toward the laptop, pleading with him to hear me. "*This* isn't helping you. All this googling seems to be stressing you out and is consuming so much of your time. You're filling your mind with information that's feeding this anxiety," I say, and he winces at that word, like it's pricked him. "You think learning more gives you control, but it's actually *controlling you*."

Asher stares at me, his face blank for several long

seconds. Then his lips part, but no words come out. My best friend, who always has a solution, who loves helping, who relishes fixing things for his friends, is left speechless.

I'm not though. I have something else to say. I haven't researched his brand of anxiety, but I know *this* to be true: "You could talk to someone. You could get help," I say.

He takes a quiet breath, and for the first time this morning, his eyes soften. It's small, a flicker of recognition, but I hope it's a start.

52

OUT OF CONTROL

Asher

She can't be right.

Can she?

No. There's no way. I glance at the computer, at all the information in front of me. Info I didn't have when I was a teenager. Info I couldn't access when I was driving my dad to the hospital. This isn't about control—it's about helping. These articles, these studies, these plans—they're good. They're useful.

This is what I do. I drove my dad to the hospital without a license. Got him there in time. Saved his life, they said. With Maeve, I helped with her neck pain. Surely, I can help with her wrists.

Right?

In the dark, before dawn, it doesn't feel like control. It feels like helping. She's wrong. I don't need to control everything.

But how did this conversation go so off the rails? I was

supposed to slip downstairs, find some info to make sure she's safe, cook her breakfast, and ask her to stay. For real. Tell her I'm madly, truly, deeply in love with her.

But instead? She finds me here—a strung-out mess before the sun even rises. This isn't her falling for me. This is how friends stage an intervention.

I close my eyes, dragging a hand down my face. "I'm not trying to control everything," I mutter, more to myself than to her. If I were trying to control things, I would've done a better job than this.

I look up, and she's nodding, but it's like she's accepting my answer rather than believing it. "Okay. Maybe you're not ready yet."

Fuck ready.

This is not how things were supposed to go. I push away from the counter, pacing, my hand scrubbing the back of my neck. "I'm sorry, Maeve," I say, but I don't know what I'm apologizing for.

What was I thinking, letting her see these habits? Why wasn't I more careful? I knew this might happen when we lived together. I knew she might see the real me. And now she has—and she's trying to help me instead of falling for me. How could anyone fall for a guy...who needs help?

"This isn't how it's supposed to work," I say, my voice tight with frustration. "I'm supposed to help you. That's what I do. I help people. I fix things."

I don't need to be fixed. That's not how my world works.

"You don't have to be perfect," she says softly. "You don't have to be amazing every second. You're allowed to be human, Asher." Her words are careful, like she's trying to ease me into something. "I just want you to see what it's doing to you."

What it's doing is breaking my heart. Because there's no way these words are coming from a woman who's falling in love with me. My chest tightens. I need to get a grip. I need to pull myself together before I can even think about saying anything to her. "I'm fine. I'm totally fine."

She's quiet for several seconds, clearly thinking. "It's six in the morning," she says, her voice steady. "I know you need some space. Why don't I take the dog for a long walk? I can go back to my apartment, too, if you need that. I can stay with Leighton. The couch spring doesn't scare me."

Sweat beads on the back of my neck and my pulse spikes. "Okay," I say distantly, taking the out she's offering for now.

She nods, spinning around and heading upstairs, probably to get ready to walk the dog.

I shove both hands into my hair, pressing my palms hard against my scalp. She'll be ready in five minutes. Five minutes to figure out how to fix this mess so she doesn't leave. Maybe I can make her eggs the way she likes, brew her a chai latte, drive her to work. Then google how to pull this back from the brink. There has to be something—someone who knows what to say or do to stop her from walking out of my life before I go on the road.

I can get this...under control.

I freeze mid-thought. *Control.* There it is again. I want to control her reaction to my control problem.

The realization slams into me, harder than any hit I've taken on the ice. I drop my face into my hands, frustration brewing inside me as she comes back downstairs. And when I look up, she's already heading for the door, about to walk away. I can't be both a hot mess and a jerk. I can't let her actually take me up on the offer for space—it's not fair to her.

This is uncharted territory, but I take a deep breath and step into it.

"You don't need to go," I say, my voice rougher than I'd intended. "Because you're right. I'm trying to control everything—even us." I look away, the admission burning through my whole body, hurting my lungs, my bones, my breath. But I have to say it. "I've been pushing this into romantic territory, and I haven't been listening to you. That's not how best friends treat each other. And I'm sorry for that." I'm shaking my head, amazed at the absolute mess I've made of...everything. This is like blowing every play in a game. Another breath. She watches patiently, waiting. "Maeve...I need to figure out what the hell is going on in my head. So, maybe I should leave instead."

Her eyes widen. Her lips part. But after a few seconds, she says, "This is your place though."

I glance around, flapping my arms in a half-hearted gesture at the kitchen. It's never just been mine. For years I've been putting up artwork that reminds me of her. I've been learning how to make the drinks she likes. I've been making space for her before I even realized how I felt. But especially lately. "This place that I designed to make you stay. Hung your art. Encouraged you to move everything in here for appearances. Then, encouraged you to sublease your place. I even built you a studio so you'd like it better." I shake my head, feeling the weight of every decision I've made in the name of helping, of *controlling*. "I wasn't giving you a choice. I was controlling everything."

"Asher, I wanted all that too. All that was lovely. The studio is amazing. There's nothing wrong with *that*." Her voice cracks, like something inside her is breaking, and the sound guts me.

Maybe there was nothing wrong with *that*, but it sure as shit feels like there's something wrong with me.

I remember what she said nearly two months ago, the day she agreed to stay until the end of the season. *I don't want to lose our friendship.*

I remember, too, when she said *Sex is complicated.*

And then I replay what she said just a few minutes ago: *You're my best friend.*

And I didn't listen.

I figured if I loved her hard enough, if I cooked for her, made the house feel like a home, created a space for her art, she'd love me back. If I showered her in the support she deserves, in praise and words, she'd fall just as hard.

But you can't love someone into loving you back.

I've made promises, though—to her brother, to myself—to protect her. And maybe that means stepping back. Honoring the boundaries she's tried to set, even if it breaks me. "You've said all along that our friendship is important to you, and Maeve, I don't want to screw that up more than I have."

"You're not screwing it up. I swear you're not," she pleads, and she sounds desperate now, terribly worried. I step closer and hope she knows this isn't her fault. "You're amazing. You're incredible. You're...everything," I choke out and that's the closest I've come to voicing my feelings, even though now is not the time. "But I'm the problem. My head is a mess right now, and I need to figure this out before I lose more than I can handle."

She swallows hard, closing her eyes, like pain's passing through her, hitting her, but not knocking her down. But when she opens them, she says, "I get it."

And of course she does.

Ironic, how she thought she'd be too much for someone like me. But the truth is—it's me. I'm the one who's too much.

Fifteen minutes later, my travel bag is packed—hours before our afternoon flight to Seattle for tomorrow's game—and I go out the front door, stepping into the blue light of dawn, leaving my car behind. Maeve doesn't have one—they're expensive, of course, but she also doesn't love driving in the city. Duffel in hand, I walk down the block toward Beckett's gym. But he might be there, and I can't face him like this.

He'll know something's wrong, and he's too close to the situation. The arena's not open for another couple hours.

I could go to a coffee shop of course. But as my feet take me toward Doctor Insomnia's, I groan. No way do I want to go there, with that name, right after Maeve suggested that that's my issue.

Besides, my fingers have a mind of their own, and they're scrolling for Miles's number.

It rings. Long and foreboding. His phone's probably on silent. But he answers on the fourth ring, with a groggy, "How much bail do you need?"

And that, right there, tells me everything.

This is bad.

"I need to crash at your place for a few hours."

There's only silence for three seconds, then he says, "Just texted you the address in case you need it."

I remember it, but even so, gratitude for his friendship floods me. "Thanks."

I call a Lyft, and after ten minutes of cruising through the quiet city streets as fog snakes along the hilly roads, and over the shrouded bridge along the horizon, we're pulling up to his home in the Marina.

I thank the driver.

"No problem. And good luck in Seattle," he says.

"Thanks, man," I say, but it feels too surreal to talk to a fan right now.

It feels too surreal to talk to anyone. When I knock on Miles's door, he opens it immediately. He's dressed in sweatpants and his black glasses. Yawning, he gives me a quick once-over, shaking his head before he says, "You look like shit."

Guy code for *what the fuck is wrong*?

But I barely know where to start. I sink down on the couch, drag a hand through my hair, and say, "I feel like it too."

At least I'm being honest.

53

THE REST IS JUST UNFINISHED

Maeve

It's early—barely seven, maybe eight in the morning. The house feels too quiet, like it's holding its breath. I wander through the living room, unsettled, and Ruby Rooster follows close behind, trotting along, head tilted as if she's waiting for me to decide something.

For someone who worships at the altar of pillows and beds, I'm now the one who can't sleep. I don't even try. My mind keeps replaying the morning, trying to figure out if I could have done something differently. Is it weird to stay while he's on the road, given what just happened between us? But what did happen between us? What are we even doing? I don't know.

I stop in the kitchen, grab some dog treats, and offer one to Ruby Rooster. She sits obediently. "Should I have said something else?" I ask her. She waits, tail wagging slightly.

"Shake," I say, taking her paw and making her shake.

"Good girl." I give her the treat, and she hoovers it down, her tail thumping harder.

"Should I go? Stay with Leighton? Or Josie? Or Everly?" I know they'd open their doors to this beautiful dog and me without a second thought.

I pause, and Ruby Rooster looks at me expectantly. "Should I stay?"

She wags her tail harder but doesn't move.

Hmm. That feels like her answer.

I give her another treat and head toward the terrace. She follows, skidding to a stop when I reach the stone railing, eyes on the sunroom.

My studio. The one he converted just for me.

He meant it when he said this place was mine. He's thoughtful. He built this for me—so I can create, be inspired.

My mind drifts back to last night, to the way he looked at me when we came together. His words. The way everything felt like more than a physical connection. It felt like friendship on fire, a love that was deeper than anything I could have painted. Like we were on the edge of something that could change everything.

And now, look at us. Apart.

But even though I miss him, even though I ache to help him, I know one thing for sure: I'm not running just because this got hard. Just because it got real faster than either of us expected. Wherever this takes us—whether back to friendship or to something more—I'm staying. He needs to know this friendship isn't something he can get rid of. It's here for good.

I pat Ruby Rooster's soft head and say, "Let's go to work."

But reality hits as I grab my things. I don't have a car.

I'll need a ride. As I'm opening my Lyft app to search for a pet-friendly option, my phone buzzes, and I see a message.

> Asher: My car's in the garage. The dog's car seat is still in the back. I know you don't love driving in the city, but even so I put the car's app on your phone last week in case you ever need to drive it. You should be able to use it to take Ruby Roo to the arena. Here's the code for the app in case there's any trouble.

The sobs come before I can stop them, with thick tears that cascade down my cheeks. Even while he's gone, doing whatever he's doing right now, he's thinking of me. He's taking care of me and this sweet girl who was abandoned until she found *us*.

And this time, like most other times when he's offered some advice, his help is exactly what I need. Perhaps it wasn't early this morning with the seventy-two tabs. Maybe it wasn't either when he was so distracted during a TV show that he let himself get caught up in doctor googling. Looking back, I'm not sure his dads wanted the help with the vitamins, even if it was well intentioned.

But right now—this message gives me hope. Because I needed *this*. An easy way to get to work with the dog. And while I don't love driving, I also don't love putting the dog in a Lyft since it's safer for her to be buckled in. Maybe Asher is starting to realize there's a difference between control and help since I don't think he's trying to control a damn thing right now.

This is pure.

I head to the garage with my dog bestie and open the back seat door. She hops in, parking her fluffy butt in the car seat he neatly installed for her. I buckle her in, securing the straps gently. "Your dad got you this," I whisper, even though she's already looking out the window, curious about the drive before we've even left the garage.

Then I rewind my words, rolling my eyes at myself. Did I really just say *your dad*? Oh my god, I did. Well, when in Rome. I snap a picture of Ruby Rooster, all pretty in her seat, then go to one of my apps and fiddle around with it for a couple minutes before sending a digital badge to Asher with the dog inside it and the words: *World's Safest Dog.*

As I drive toward the arena, a sense of resolve settles over me. A sense of strength. I'm not the same girl I was at the auction—frazzled and chaotic. I'm no longer the hot mess who didn't have a clue what to do next. I'm not saying I've got my act together, but I've found something inside myself that was there all along, waiting to surface. A real strength. A solid foundation. I can be the person someone leans on. I can be the one someone depends on. I've learned that from Asher over the last few months, from his words and the way he's lifted me up. But really, I've been learning it for years, thanks to him.

And that's who I need to be right now—the person he's been for me.

When I arrive, I park in the employees' lot, but before getting out, I pull out my phone and google how to help someone with obsessive behavior. Because that's what his actions feel like—obsession. I make some notes, bookmark a few things to share with him later, and then finally step out of the car, Ruby Rooster on her leash by my side, heading toward the employee entrance.

Inside, the mural waits, half-finished, just like everything between us.

I take a deep breath and get to work, but I can't stop wondering: Did we break up? Or are we pretending we never crossed that line?

I don't know. But I'll have to live with this uncertainty —for now.

54

GOOGLE MIRROR

Asher

That lucky fucker goes back to sleep. Miles offered me the guest room, but I said no thanks. So while he sleeps some more, here I am, slumped on his couch, tapping my phone against my thigh, feeling the pull of it. A nagging sensation to do something, fix something.

"Goddammit," I mutter into the silence of my friend's home. I grip the phone harder, trying to resist the desire to search for what's wrong with me as I look around his living room—a picture of him and his younger brother in their game-day uniforms, a shot of a platinum blonde grandma type wearing a feather boa outside High Kick Coffee, one of his sister—I think—behind the counter at a bar, and another of his parents with four small dogs.

My mind flashes to the picture of Ruby Roo Maeve sent moments ago. If we break up, and she moves back home, she'll need to make the apartment more dog-friendly. In fact, really, it'd be good to make the place more human-friendly too. I sit up straight, feeling that spark of purpose. I can fix that for her. Make it better.

"You motherfucking genius," I mutter, already visualizing her apartment—the creaky steps up to the fourth floor, the wobbly second-to-last step, the purple door, the couch with the bad spring, the sideways toilet, the short shower.

All of it. Fixable.

I might not be able to convince her to see someone about the wrist pain, but I can definitely do this. I start to google "best handyman in Hayes Valley," but after I type out the word best, the first search suggestion is "best health news sites."

My chest tightens. I stare at the screen, my brow pinching.

How to fix a short shower, I try next, but the first suggestion is "how to fix a sore neck."

It's like looking into a mirror, seeing all my fears reflected back.

Just to be sure, I type one more thing: "How likely is your wife/girlfriend to leave you after one fight," but as soon as I type "how likely is," the autosuggestions hit me.

How likely is carpal tunnel. How likely are you to develop an illness from paint fumes. How likely is exhaustion to harm your brain health.

Holy shit.

Google knows me better than I know myself. This is what I do. This is what I was doing last night when I sneaked into the restroom at dinner with Maeve and Vivian, searching for answers.

The truth hits me like a slap. This is not normal. This is...a problem.

I swallow, blow out a breath, and think back to

Maeve's comments. *You could talk to someone. You could get help.*

I thought knowing more would keep her—and everyone I care about—safe. But this? This is not fine. I didn't even tell her I loved her last night because I was too focused on preventing the next disaster. Carpal tunnel, MS, ALS—anything. Everything.

I am not okay.

I think about the picnic, the conversation with Marcus about his work, the sheer and utter irony of the fact that I'm starting a charity for sports and support, and I've completely ignored not only my own mental health, but this one deep and terrible fear that I didn't even admit I had.

I thought because I went to a grief support group when I was twenty-two I was on top of things. But I didn't dig far enough into my own past. Because the truth I've been denying is that I've been feeling this way since I was fourteen when my father almost died.

Since the day I faced that absolute terror, I've tried to insulate myself from ever experiencing it again by thinking I could stop anything bad from ever happening again with more knowledge, like I stopped the worst case for him by knowing how to drive before I was supposed to. My knowledge saved him then, but all this information isn't saving anyone now.

Least of all, me.

My eyes sting, my throat tightens, but I breathe through it.

I look down at my phone, my thumb hovering over the screen. For a second, I think about putting it away, convincing myself I don't need help. I can fix this on my own, like I always do.

But the truth keeps staring me in the face—this isn't something I can fix with a toolset or a few Google searches. It's bigger than that.

I swallow hard as I swipe to my contacts. Marcus's name blurs on the screen, and for a moment, I hesitate. Calling him feels like admitting that I can't keep everything together.

But I can't keep running from this. I drag in a breath, finally pressing the call button.

He doesn't answer. But when his voicemail clicks on, I say the hard thing for the first time in my life.

I ask for help.

"Hey, it's Asher Callahan. I would like to book a session to see you. For me. Ideally, this coming week. I need it."

* * *

That night, I lean back against the headboard in my Seattle hotel room, alone, phone in hand, scrolling through my messages. A notification pops up—appointment confirmed with Marcus for Monday. A step in the right direction. I want to tell Maeve. I'm dying to tell Maeve.

But that feels like something you say in person.

Still, I can't not contact her while I'm on the road. Even if my head's a mess. Even if I'm trying to figure things out. Even if we're stuck in this limbo.

I can still do something though.

I swipe to another screen, pulling up an online delivery service in San Francisco. A few clicks, and I've arranged for a package to be sent to Maeve tonight. Something small—but something she'll love.

I pause, my fingers hovering over the phone. Am I trying to get her to love me?

No. I exhale slowly. I just like making her happy. And that's okay too. Maybe it's more than okay.

I press send and close my eyes. For now, that's enough.

55

PROPER CARE AND FEEDING

Maeve

Some bartender dude on *First Dates* is debating whether to see a customer again—convinced she's catfished him—when the doorbell rings. I tense. Doorbells don't sit well with me, especially when I'm home alone. My girl doesn't like them either. She growls, fur prickling as I set a hand on her back. Lifting her snout, she barks again. *That rooster crow.*

"It's okay," I murmur, pausing the show. "It's probably UPS."

Ruby Rooster side-eyes me.

I pop up from the couch and head for the door. I peer through the window slat—no one's there. I look down.

Oh.

There's a food delivery bag on the porch. From Ding and Dine.

I didn't order anything. I grab it and lock the door behind me. Peeking inside, I find a warm takeout box.

Intrigued, I pull open the flaps—and burst into laughter. Asher sent me a box of warm nuts. The smile on my face is too big, and I'm still not sure if we're friends or lovers or somewhere in between.

But maybe that's okay.

I open the box and read the note:

Tips for the proper care and feeding of your best friend— keep snacks handy, especially if you're working on conspiracy theories.

At least I know this: we'll always be friends. Like we've been for the last ten years. Through all our big adventures —hot sauce taste tests, ice hotels, tree tents, lavender farms. And now to studios, pole-dancing crawls, tofu curry, flamingo underwear, napkin-folding at dinners with board members, impromptu proposals at jewelry stores, hockey games with custom jerseys, and late-night painting sessions where I felt like the women in all my pop art paintings. We've shared so many kisses that made me feel like love is worth chasing.

And auctions too. Where I bid on him to save him from a woman spinning lies. Then a night in Vegas, where he saved me from my own sadness and made good on a marriage pact inked one night as we danced to Frank Sinatra.

I flop back onto the couch, cashews in hand, reality dating show playing again. I go through the nuts quickly, but I'm still not satisfied.

I can't wait, even though I said I'd give him space.

I reach for Tatiana, the tarot deck I left on the coffee table, shuffling it, wondering if I should ask her what happens next.

But it's not like a deck of cards will know. Someone might though. Or several someones, really.

* * *

The next morning, I'm at High Kick Coffee with Josie, Fable, and Leighton for a hastily called meeting of The Padlockers. Everly's in Seattle—she traveled with the team. Said she has fond memories of the last time she was there.

The café hums with the buzz of morning chatter, and we huddle in the back, lattes and teas in hand as I give them the SparkNotes. I don't tell them about Asher's obsessive tendencies—that's personal—but I tell them enough: we've hit a rough patch.

"I did what I said I would—I didn't cling. I gave him space, even though it felt like dying. And it still does. How can doing the right thing feel so wrong?" I ask, since I'm nothing if not dramatic. But this moment calls for drama, dammit.

Josie snorts. "Maeve."

"What?"

Leighton gives me a *be so fucking for real* look too. "What she said."

"What do you mean?" I ask, turning to Fable. "You get me, right?"

My redheaded friend hedges with a "Yes and no."

"Fine, fine. Tell me what I did wrong," I say, exasperated. "I'm trying to give him space to figure things out. Remember, I'm the girl who clings."

"Maeve, you gave him space, sure," Josie says. "But did you actually tell him how you feel? Or are you expecting him to magically guess?"

I blink. "What do you mean?"

Josie sets her cup down. "We mean, you're waiting for

him to read your mind. That's not how this works. You're not clingy—you're just not saying what matters."

"Right." Josie nods. "It's not clingy to tell someone how you feel. That's called 'honesty.' It's a useful tool."

"Well, tell me what you really think," I say with a laugh, but her words hit harder than I let on. "Okay, fine. You make a point. But I told him I'd give him space."

"But did you give him information?" Leighton presses. "I know he's dealing with stuff, but does he know you're madly in love with him?"

I stare at her like she's lost it. "No, it wasn't the time or place."

Fable scoffs. "It never is," she says. "That's why it's called...taking a chance."

My phone buzzes. I grab it, hoping it's Asher, but it's Angelina with details about another job. I stare at the text, and it hits me. I didn't wait for my career to fall into place. I chased it with everything I had, gave it my whole heart, and fought like hell for it.

And if there's one thing I know how to do, it's to follow my dreams.

56

A LOVE LESSON

Asher

I sit in the visitors' locker room, tightening the laces on my skates. It's quiet—just Miles and me. He claps me on the shoulder as he walks by.

"You doing okay?" he asks.

I take a breath and nod. "Better than yesterday."

"Good." His voice is steady. "If you need anything, let me know."

I turn his offer over in my head, grateful for it, even though he doesn't know the details of what went down yesterday morning. But still, he's there if I need him. And the truth is...I think I might. More than that, I think it'd be helpful to talk. In sports, the more you practice, the better you get. So I try it first with him, taking the chance to practice.

"I'm going to see a therapist," I say. The words feel heavier than I'd expected. But in a good way.

Miles's eyebrows shoot up as he grabs his pads from the stall. "Yeah?"

"Yeah. Appointment's tomorrow when we're back. There's some stuff I need to work through."

"Proud of you, man," he says, offering a fist-bump.

Sometimes you bump fists to celebrate a win. Maybe this is one too. But more than that, it feels like genuine support. Like the kind I've been working to make accessible for young athletes. The kind I should have taken advantage of myself.

But I will tomorrow.

And that's a start too.

A little later, we hit the ice for the face-off. The game starts fast and aggressive—players crashing into each other, sticks clashing, the puck snapping between us. I shove everything else away and focus. Hockey hasn't changed—it's always been my escape. But maybe I didn't realize what I was escaping from: the way I tried to control everything off the ice.

On the ice, I know I can't control the outcome, but I can give it my all. Charging down the rink, weaving past defenders, I fire the puck at the net with everything I've got, just like I always have.

Sometimes it works out. Sometimes it doesn't.

But I do it anyway.

And that's exactly what I'll need to do with Maeve.

No wonder I haven't told her I love her. I've been trying to control the outcome of our romance, waiting for the perfect moment. But love's like hockey—you can't guarantee a win, but you can give it your best shot.

When we end the game in Seattle with the W, I change quickly into my travel clothes. On the way to the airport, I make a call to a store in San Francisco, place a rush order, then I count down the hours till we land.

* * *

By the time the plane taxies down the runway in San Francisco in the early evening, I have everything in place. I don't head into the arena with the other guys. Instead, I grab a Lyft and swing by the store. Then I call Maeve.

"You home?" I ask.

She sounds breathless. "No, I'm at the arena, just finishing up."

"Stay there," I tell her.

"Bossy," she says with a laugh.

"Sometimes I am," I reply, smiling. *I hope she likes this.*

I'm back at the arena in ten minutes, heading through the players' entrance. I didn't plan a big speech. I just go straight to where she's working.

I find Maeve, without the dog, climbing down from her ladder at the Sea Dogs mural, her painting T-shirt streaked with color, a daub of red on her cheek. My heart swells at the sight of her, and it hits me: I can't believe I waited this long to tell her. But at the same time, I know exactly why I did—and knowing that makes all the difference.

She watches me, her eyebrows lifting in curiosity as I approach.

"Question for you," I say, our familiar line.

A twitch of her lips follows. "Hit me."

"Would you like to go on a date with me? A real date. Tonight. Tomorrow. The weekend. And every weekend after that. When the season ends, during the summer too, and beyond. Because you were right."

Her lips part, but her brows furrow in confusion. "Right about what?"

I take a breath, ready to show her the real me—the parts I was afraid to show when she moved in but wound up showing her anyway. The parts I tried to hide, but now, in retrospect, I'm glad she discovered in the kitchen when I was lost in my obsession. She pulled me out. She spoke the truth to me. She helped me to see who I could become. "About me. I am trying to control everything, I do have obsessive tendencies, and I need help. So, I made an appointment with Marcus for tomorrow. I know it won't happen overnight and it won't be easy—but I'm doing this. I'm going to work on myself because I don't want to hurt you—or myself. I want to sleep better. I want to stop researching everything, learn how to be proactive in smart ways, and figure out how to chill the fuck out."

She brings a hand to her mouth, covering her trembling lip before she lets her hand fall away—the hand with that brilliant ruby I hope she always wears. "I'm so happy," she says.

I laugh. "That makes you happy?"

"Yes. More than anything. Even more than the dog."

"That's saying something," I reply, stepping closer. "But I'm not done."

"Okay," she says, breathless and maybe excited.

I cup her cheek, my thumb grazing a red streak of paint that I love on her. She shudders, and I love that too. "And part of me being so controlling is that I didn't let myself see what was happening when we first met."

"What do you mean?"

"I fell in love with you ten years ago," I say, no safety net, no guarantee, no idea if she'll love me back. I let go of her face and reach into my bag, pulling out the framed picture. "And I fell in love with you all over again when you said, 'I do.'"

I show her the picture I had printed and framed today at the same shop where I had the others made when she moved in. This one, though? It's not just of her. It's of us, in Las Vegas, at the concert, before the singer launched into the new tune about promises made and kept. The selfie I snapped impulsively.

"All those pictures I took? I was taking them for me. Because I was falling in love with you every day. And when you married me, I finally admitted to myself that it's you. It's always been you. And I don't know if you feel the same or even want me, but I'm wildly in love with you. I don't want to just take pictures of you. I want them of us. And I want *this* to be our next big adventure," I say, referring to the picture and the words I photoshopped onto it this afternoon—*Love lesson: Tell her you love her often. Tell her every day. Tell her as soon as you can.*

Her eyes shine as she looks at the words, then back at me, and I swear I can see forever in her gaze.

"And if you can handle an obsessed, obsessive, bossy guy who thinks you're the greatest thing in the world and who's trying to be a little less anxious, I'll give you the world. Because you mean the world to me, Maeve Hartley Callahan."

She takes a breath, her shoulders rising and falling with the movement. "I have the answer."

I furrow my brow. "To what?"

"Your real date question."

"Yeah?"

She reaches for my hand and squeezes it, never looking away. "I love you too. That's my answer. You're my best friend and my lover, and I want us to stay together. I want us to hold on tight to each other. Because you're my new dream."

I never knew this was possible—to fall in love with her even more. But it's happened.

57

LIKE A BARNACLE

Asher

I need to get her alone, fast. Grabbing her hand, I take two steps before stopping. "Where's the dog? You usually bring her. Is she at home?" Home. The place I want Maeve and Ruby to stay with me. Forever.

"She's with Eleanor. She and Holmes are becoming dog friends."

That's adorable on too many levels, but I have one mission right now—get Maeve naked and in bed. "Can we swing by and get her, then go? Because I need to show you just how much I've missed the woman I love."

She laughs, rising on her tiptoes and giving me a quick, firm kiss. "You horn dog."

"Pot, kettle."

She grins proudly, tugging at my hand. "Let's go."

Before we can head down the corridor to the executive suite, Eleanor appears, walking toward us with a dog leash in each hand. Her Maltipoo mix leads the way, with

Ruby Rooster scurrying alongside her. I can't help but smile, amazed. "The owner of the team is dog-sitting our dog," I say, still wrapping my head around how this is my life, especially after where I was just yesterday morning.

"Dog people," Maeve says with a shrug.

Eleanor hands off Ruby, who immediately showers Maeve with kisses, favoring her even though I've been out of town. But, yeah, I get it.

"You two seem happy to see each other," Eleanor says, clearly pleased. "I guess you've been following those love lessons."

"We have," Maeve says, her tone warm.

"Every single lesson," I agree, squeezing her hand.

"Oh good," Eleanor says, beaming.

With Ruby Rooster back with us, we head out. On the way, I pull Maeve in for another kiss. When I break it, I whisper, "I have one question."

Maeve's cheeks are red, her tits are bouncing, and her hair is a wild mess, but she answers me with a breathless, "I can take another one."

"How many, Maeve?" I ask sternly, gripping her hips hard and stilling my pace for a beat. "The question was how many orgasms can you take?"

"Four, sir," she says, then smiles wickedly. "So give me my fourth."

"Such a good wife," I say, calling for battery-operated backup in the form of the Finger Puppet, sliding it over her clit until she cries out in beautiful, filthy bliss as she comes on me. *Again.*

This time, I don't hold back. This time, I fuck her and

fill her. And this time, after I come so fucking hard inside my wife, I pull her close, cup her cheeks, and say, "I love you. That's why it's so good with us. Because I love you."

Her sigh is dreamy, content. "Because we love each other."

I hold her close, but in a way that feels new. I've stopped hiding who I really am. The vulnerable parts, the messy parts, the unfinished parts. And she's still here, loving me right back.

Later, after we're lying under the covers with Ruby curled up on top, I run my fingers through Maeve's hair, one of my favorite things to do.

"So, you really love me?" she asks.

"Have you seen my walls?"

"What do you mean?"

"The peaches, the wildflowers, the artwork you made over the years. I think all along, before we even got married, I was just...making a home for you," I admit, even if it makes me sound like a besotted fool.

She looks at me with so much love and affection, I wonder how I ever doubted this could be. But that's the thing—you don't see it when you're in the thick of it. I need to get comfortable with the unknown, because getting to the other side is worth it.

"I really like being here," she says, snuggling closer. "It's funny though. I don't think we've gone on many dates. We mostly stay in."

"Yeah, we do." And I'm more than okay with that.

"It just feels like home," she murmurs, before hopping out of bed. "And I got something for you."

I prop myself up on one elbow. "You did?"

"Well, I made it. Earlier today." She rustles through her purse and pulls out a small mirror decorated with ruby-red rhinestones. In the center is a sketch of a couple kissing, with the words *Just love me*.

"Don't drop it," she warns with mock seriousness as she hands it over. "It's got ruby rhinestones. Basically, it's priceless."

And it is priceless to me. I run my fingers over it, tracing the words. Finally, I'm free to just love her, which is all she wants. "I will. I promise." I set the mirror down on the nightstand, then pull her back into bed and kiss her softly before turning serious. "Maeve, I'm not going to change overnight. Are you okay with that?"

"Very okay," she says.

"You sure?"

"I'm positive. Besides, I liked you before I fell in love with you. And I like you even more now. Don't worry—I'm like a barnacle. You can't get rid of me."

I laugh, holding her tighter. I'd never thought it could be this easy—but then I suppose that's the joy of falling in love with your best friend. "Good, because I won't."

* * *

I'm not going to say I sleep through the night. I'm not cured. I haven't even seen the therapist yet. But I sleep better than I have in a long time. I only wake once, and I resist the urge to go downstairs and flip open my laptop. Maybe it's because I don't have anything to look up right now. Or maybe this is the start of a new, healthier habit. Either way, it feels good.

When I wake up for good around seven—late for me —my phone is already buzzing. It's a message from Everly saying, *Call me*.

Every muscle tightens. Instinctively, I check social media, and it doesn't take long to find the problem.

The woman who bid on me at the auction and lost has posted about us. *"Pay it forward, indeed—their marriage is fake."*

58

CONNECTING THE DOTS

Maeve

Maybe I sense a disturbance in the Force. That's the only explanation for why I'm awake at this god-awful hour of... oh. It's seven. I guess I should be getting out of bed. I have a mural to finish. But when I turn toward Asher, my chest seizes up.

He's clutching his phone. Shit. Is he going there again? Already?

But before I start spiraling, I remind myself that it's not the phone that's the issue—it's how he uses it.

"What's going on?" I ask, trying to stay calm. Focus on communication.

He sighs, dragging a hand over his stubble, momentarily distracting me because, damn, he looks good with it. "Miranda Blush is saying our romance is fake. She just posted a whole video laying out her 'evidence.' She told her half a million followers that our marriage is all a PR stunt."

I sit up straight, ready to march into battle. I fought her off once. I'll do it again. Quickly, I run through every event in my head—brunch with the Greers, dinner with the board, the picnic. She wasn't there for any of it. "What the hell? How does she know how it started? It's not like either of us slipped up in public."

His lips twitch slightly at my words—*how it started*. Like he's still delighting in the fact that I'm acknowledging how it started one way but shifted into something else entirely. I hope he stays in that delight for a long, long time.

But then he schools his expression. "Honestly, I think she's just taking a good guess. Her video is like, 'Does this seem off to you?' Then she lists how the first public photo of us kissing was at the auction, and how we happened to get married in Vegas right as the photo from Jen and Hal went viral. Then she points out how we posted more photos after that—photos that seemed *staged*. She's connecting dots that maybe were fake at the time."

I want to rip out her extensions. "What is she, a forensic social media-ologist?"

"I guess," he mutters, his jaw tight. "But that's all she's doing—guessing."

"Well, she's wrong. So fuck her," I say, crossing my arms. "She can't hurt us because we're together for real."

But Asher doesn't relax this time. He turns toward me, his expression still grim.

That's when it hits me—there's fallout. When you lie, there's always a price to pay. "Oh god, what is it? Is it going to affect your charity?"

"No," he says, shaking his head. "Well, yes, but I'm not really worried about that."

"You're not worried about it?"

He shakes his head again. "Soraya messaged me. Some of the donors reached out too, asking if it's true. But I'm not worried because the truth is simple—I'm with you, and it's real," he says, grasping my hand, holding it tight. "I'll happily say that to anyone. I'll tell the board, the donors, the team. I'll tell them we got married for fun, and stayed married because I wanted to make you fall in love with me. That's the only truth that matters. Whatever happens happens."

God, that's sexy. "How are you so hot when you say stuff like that?"

His serious expression softens as he leans over, cupping my cheek. "Maybe this started as a ruse, but the truth is I've been falling for you for years, like I said last night. And I will tell anyone the truth of the way I feel. Because I knew at Mr. Vincenzo's party, which was less than twenty-four hours after we were married, I wanted to explore how I really felt. I wanted to win your heart. And that desire's only gotten stronger."

I want to grab him and kiss him right now. I love how he's solved this problem, how confident he is about us, but something still isn't adding up. "So...what's the issue?"

He sighs again. "Everly's been texting me. She said Eleanor's kind of freaking out. She feels like you deceived her."

My heart plummets, and it's like all the air's been sucked from the room. Eleanor thinks I'm a liar? Eleanor, who's been so kind to me?

I gulp, panic setting in. I don't have the same protection Asher does. The charity is his passion, but it's not his job.

His job is safe.

Mine might not be.

59

HOLD MY BEER

Asher

This is exactly what Beckett warned me about. He said it that morning at the gym, right to my face.

I get up and start pacing. "Beckett was right."

"About what?" Maeve asks, watching me closely.

"He said, 'She's trying to make her way in the world, dealing with an overbearing aunt, while you're already a successful hockey player. If this goes south, you'll be fine. But if this blows up, she might not be.'"

Maeve's eyes widen, but she stays quiet, blowing out a breath.

"And he told me to protect you," I add.

She moves around the bed, stepping closer. "And you did. You have."

"Yeah, but not enough," I mutter, tension knotting up inside me—not the same kind I get over health worries, but a real fear for the woman I love. She's worked too hard to lose everything. "I want to protect you. I love you. I hate seeing you hurt."

"I love that you feel that way," she says quietly, then her tone shifts, more playful. "But you know what my brother said to me about you at the picnic?"

I scoff. "Was he doling out advice all around?"

"He pulled me aside and told me, 'Don't break his heart.'"

I shake my head, amused at Beckett's behind-the-scenes machinations with both of us, even though I have no right to be lighthearted at this moment. "So, he was onto us?"

"He was onto *you* clearly," she says, and of course that's true. "And you know what that tells me?" Maeve asks, her eyes gleaming with mischief. That's my Maeve. Always up for an adventure.

"What?"

"It tells me that everyone else could probably see it in you too."

I flash back to the day I left for Vegas, to the DickNose board and all the ridiculous advice my friends gave me. Especially the list of all the 'cute things' I'd said about Maeve. But that's it. That'll help. "The DickNose board," I say, snapping my fingers.

Maeve's understandably confused. "Um, what's a DickNose board?"

I shake my head, half-laughing. "I'm pretty sure Hugo has a picture of it. He snapped a shot of the board so he could give me shit about it forever.'"

"What are you talking about?"

As I explain the DickNose board, I grab my phone and send my teammate a text. *You still got that pic under 'cute couple shit,' right? I need it now. Do me a solid.*

As Hugo replies in seconds that he's tracking the pic down, an idea forms. "Why don't I show this to Eleanor? I can explain everything to her, just like I—"

Maeve cuts me off, shaking her head as she crosses the room to me. She gently curls her hand over mine, pushing my phone down onto the bed. "Asher, hold my beer."

I blink at her, confused but also a little turned on by the way she's taking charge. "What does that mean?"

She smirks. "You've got that appointment with Marcus in a couple hours. You need to focus on that. I'll handle Eleanor. I can tell her the truth, but...I do want that photo, so send it to me later."

Before I can say anything, she's already on the move, heading for the bathroom, nodding to the dog, who's been watching us like we're a game of tennis. "I'm going to shower so I can get to work. Can you take care of our dog? She needs a walk and a potty break."

Our dog.

And just like that, she's off, giving me orders.

I stand there, phone on the bed, our dog needing me, and I realize—I kind of like following Maeve's lead.

It's nice to have a partner who's got your back. I leash up the dog and leave right as the photo arrives.

60

THE PLAY

Maeve

I leave Ruby Rooster at home. It feels too presumptuous to bring her to this...possible execution.

I lift my hand to knock on the office door. I've already made it past Eleanor's assistant, Rodney, who told me she was expecting me. Before I knock, I pause, taking a moment to calm my nerves.

I can do this. If I bid one hundred thousand dollars to save Asher from that influencer's lies, I can use my voice to save myself.

I knock. "It's Maeve Hartley."

There's silence for a long beat. Finally, Eleanor calls out, "Come in."

I push open the door. She's sitting at her desk, Holmes on the floor beside her, and neither dog nor woman look happy. Eleanor's lips are pressed into a tight line, her blue eyes cold. Normally, she's the upbeat, go-go-go team owner who slays the business world with a smile. But right now, she's ice. I deserve that.

"Not Maeve Callahan, I see," she says, arching a brow.

"I'm both," I say. "Can I come in?"

"I already said you could."

Holmes barks at me. I take a seat and cut to the chase. "I got the job under false pretenses. That's true."

"So, Miranda was right?"

"Partially," I say. "She was right about some things, but wrong about a lot. Because nobody outside a relationship truly knows what's going on inside it. No one knows the challenges people in a couple face unless they're living it."

Eleanor narrows her eyes. "That sounds philosophical, but it's not easing any of my concerns. I put my trust in you—not just as an artist, but as a person. Frankly, I'm disappointed."

That stings, but I brought it on myself.

I take a deep breath to make sure this comes from the heart. "Asher is my best friend. He has been for a long time. That's true. We got married in Vegas as part of a pact. It was for fun. When the photo went viral, it seemed easier to stay married for a little while. We were pretending at brunch." Though in retrospect, it hardly felt that way.

She shakes her head, her jaw ticking like she's hurt. "I knew something was off, but I wanted to believe in it anyway. I guess that makes me a fool."

"I'm sorry. But the truth is—somewhere along the way, that lie became the best thing that ever happened to me."

She sits up straighter, perhaps intrigued but still not fully trusting me. "Explain."

"It was a marriage of convenience—partly for his

charity, partly for this job. But while I was married to him, I fell in love with my husband. And I'm staying with him because I want to."

Saying that out loud feels good—like, really good. And it hits me that Asher and I haven't talked about what will happen next. Yes, we're dating, yes, we're living together, but we haven't really addressed what that means for our marriage. Now I know what I want though.

Still, I focus on Eleanor and the matter at hand. "But it was a ruse to keep this job, so I understand you might not want to keep working with me. If you don't want to pay me for the mural, I'd understand that too."

Eleanor rolls her eyes. "I'm not in the business of not paying contractors, but I don't relish being lied to. I'm also not the kind of woman who hires someone for their partner's last name. I hired you for your talent. I believed in your love story. That's why it hurt." She sighs, sad and resigned. "I was going to tell my friends about you."

I take that blow on the chin. The loss of referrals stings, but I expected it, so I nod and accept it.

"And honestly, why would I believe you now?"

I suppose I can't truly prove it to her. But I know our love is real, and so I try to convey that as best I can. "I want to show you something," I say, pulling out a photo of the famous DickNose board on my phone. "This might not prove everything to you, but this is how Asher felt about me before we were even married. It was all real."

My heart squeezes as I read the things his teammates had written. The top five cute things he said about me, like how much I love night markets, how everyone should buy my artwork, how cute it was that I watched videos of people painting.

"This is real too," I say, showing her more photos I took this morning at our home. The lavender farm. The ice hotel. The double-loop roller coaster. The shot of us at the concert before we said, "I do."

"You believed in our love story because it's been happening for a decade. Well before I bid on him at the auction, before we went to Vegas. Our love story started as a friendship ten years ago, and if you believed in it, like his teammates did before we got married, it's because all of that is true. This is us. This is who we are. We go on big adventures together, and we're going to keep going on them."

Eleanor sighs, but I sense her relenting. "I appreciate you showing me this. And thank you for explaining things. But I don't like being lied to, even if it turned out to be true. You should finish the mural."

I hear the unsaid part of her message—this job won't lead to anything more. She probably won't recommend me to others, and I'm going to have to be okay with that.

You don't get everything in life. But the things I do have? A friend, a lover, a dog, my girlfriends, my brother, and a career that's starting to take off? Those are mine, and no one can take them away from me.

I leave, knowing I can move forward as I finish the job.

* * *

A week later, I'm making the final adjustments to the mural, brightening up the suspension lines on the Golden Gate Bridge when my favorite voice calls out to me.

"Hey, Mrs. Callahan."

I climb down from the ladder, beaming at my

husband, who's growing a trim beard that makes him even hotter. "Hey, Number Twenty-Nine."

"You're wearing my jersey tonight." It's a statement, not a question. He knows I'll be wearing my *Mrs. Callahan* jersey for his game. Puck drop is in a couple hours.

"Always," I say, and I hope he knows I mean it—*always*. But we haven't talked about that yet. Sure, we're living together, yes, we're staying together, but we haven't really dealt with the marriage part of our relationship. There's been no need to.

For the last week, though, I've enjoyed dating my husband—we went to his dads' thirty-fifth wedding anniversary party, stopped by a plant shop to pick up more plants for our house, and broke in a tube of pink paint in the studio. My husband is quite the finger painter, though he only has one trick up his sleeve—painting my tits.

Works for me.

We've also posted some pics of us doing life on social. Not his new painting hobby—that's just for us—but pics of us walking the dog, buying plants, and toasting to his family are absolutely online, and they're not a publicity stunt. They're not to impress donors. And they're not to win a job. They're simply us, having little adventures in this big adventure of love.

What we haven't done? Explained ourselves to the world. We decided to ignore Miranda. There's no need to say anything. Haters are gonna hate, liars are gonna lie. And we know this love is real. Asher talked to the board members and the donors—he lost a few smaller ones but they've gained more support since then in new ones. And many of the existing ones liked that he reached out one-on-one.

The one who really likes my husband? CheekyBeast. They re-upped him, and I kind of can't believe this, but it fits with their brand—they want him and Ruby Rooster in a campaign for boxer briefs with cheeky dogs on them. You bet your ass I'll be buying a lot of those. Well, my husband does have the best ass in the NHL.

I haven't heard from Eleanor though. She went out of town right after our meeting to a yoga retreat with some of the other team owners, like Jessie Rose from the Golden State Foxes, and Geeta Diwali, who owns the Las Vegas Sabers.

I don't know if she's forgiven me, but right now, I'm focused on the man striding over to me, already dressed in a sharp dark brown suit since it's game night.

"Did you nap?" I ask, dusting off my hands before I touch his tie, tap dancing my fingers down it.

"I did. With Ruby Roo," he says.

"Aren't you just the cutest dog dad," I tease.

He loops an arm around my waist. "You doing okay?"

I look around at the long and, honestly, impressive mural. I told him I was sad this morning about not hearing from Eleanor, but that I'd deal. "I'm okay. I'll be thrilled to be done, but I'll miss this too," I say. But Angelina has new work for me.

And so does Everly. She hired me to paint a mural of hot-pink silhouettes of women of all shapes and sizes dancing on poles at her studio. I can't wait.

"How about you? How was Marcus?" I ask. He had another session today, before his game-day nap.

"It's good. We've been working on cognitive behavioral therapy techniques. I'm cured," he adds dryly.

"Yay, therapy! Also, I have no idea what that is, but it sounds good."

"It is. It helps you recognize patterns in your thinking," he explains.

"Sounds hot," I say, tugging on his tie and running a hand along his stubble. "I love a man in therapy. Who also happens to be growing a beard."

"Because you like the beard for when you sit on my face."

"You got me there. And I will tonight after you win."

"Talk about an incentive," he says, then nods in the direction of the locker room. "I should go." He pauses, his lips quirking up in a hint of a grin. "Also, it's going to be a good game."

"Of course it is."

"Hell yeah," he says with even more than his usual hockey confidence.

I give him a kiss and watch him leave.

Then I finish the mural for good.

Later, when I'm putting everything away so I can head down to the ice, I spot Eleanor at the far end of the corridor with her husband, laughing at something he's said. Then she must catch sight of me because she lifts a hand and waves.

It's friendly, warm, forgiving.

At least, I hope so.

I wave back, then put my things in Asher's car before returning to the arena to change my clothes. I pull on my Mrs. Callahan jersey, a short skirt and high boots then make my way to join Josie for the game. But as I'm walking down the hall, I hear footsteps behind me, quickening. It's Eleanor, and she catches up fast.

"The mural is amazing," she says, her eyes warm, her expression maternal again. "It's everything I wanted and more."

"I'm so glad."

"And I passed on your name to lots of friends. You'll be hearing from them soon."

A weight lifts. "Thank you, Eleanor."

"I believed in your love story," she says. "And I still do."

"So do I."

* * *

With that belief, I head into the rink toward my seats at center ice, joining Josie, who's here to cheer on her guy too.

"All right, Mrs. Callahan. Let's be the loudest," Josie says, and as the lights dim and the guys take to the ice, we are.

It's a tight, tense, scoreless game that's killing me. Josie and I are on the edge of our seats, ready to cheer any time the guys get closer, but mostly sitting with our butts down, holding our breath.

No one gets the puck past any net, but the Sea Dogs are relentless, and they keep trying, with Asher creating more scoring opportunities than I've ever seen him do.

To no avail.

With the game still tied as the third period begins, he battles for the puck, then snags it, charging down the ice. Defenders swarm him, but he passes it to Wesley, who flies around them, then slips it back to Asher. I swear I've never seen Asher more focused—he's a man on a mission. He lifts his stick and sends the puck flying into the net. His arms shoot up in victory.

He turns to his teammates, triumphant, then points to me.

I'm giddy, cheering the loudest I ever have, and the funny thing is—it feels like everyone around me is cheering just as wildly. The crowd is noisier than ever. I let their cheers carry me as I shriek and shout and holler.

When the game ends a little later with "Tick Tick Boom" playing, the crowd is elated. I jump up, ready to make my way to the locker room to wait for Asher outside it, but Josie sets a hand on my arm.

"Hold on a second," she says, rifling through her bag.

I pause, waiting, looking around, but the team isn't leaving the rink. Most of the players are hanging out at the bench, including Asher, who's casually grabbing his water bottle.

That's odd. They usually take off through the tunnel immediately.

The emcee steps onto the ice as well, microphone in hand. That's unusual too. She's usually gone by now.

Then the music shifts from "Tick Tick Boom" to...I gasp.

Asher hops over the boards as "The Way You Look Tonight" plays loudly through the entire arena.

Our wedding song. My heart climbs up my throat.

And then, across the rink, fans lift up signs that spell out *Marry Him Again*.

The emcee hands Asher the mic and then leaves him alone on the ice.

I'm giddy as my husband, the man I'm already married to, my best friend, my big love, gets down on one knee, looks up at me, a few rows above him, and says into the mic, his voice filling the arena, "Maeve Hartley, you're the love of my life and my best friend. Will you marry me again and continue being Maeve Callahan as well?"

"Yes," I shout. Then I shout it again as I race down to the players' bench, and the guys help me so I can join them. I rush to where my husband stands on the other side of the boards, and he kisses me over them as I say yes to his second proposal play.

EPILOGUE: TAKE TWO

Asher

One thing I will say about Maeve's aunt Vivian is that she sure knows how to throw a party. And the food is absolutely fantastic at our wedding celebration at the end of the summer. Since, well, Maeve and I got married again last week. It was a low-key affair, just friends and close family at my dads' home in Sausalito, with the Golden Gate Bridge in the background. Beckett served as the best man.

Now, we're at a coffee shop in Hayes Valley for the party. The shop is perfect since it just started carrying Maeve's artwork. It's called MainLine, and Vivian rented it out for the night. Servers swing by with figs stuffed with goat cheese, mini mango tacos with Carlos's cilantro, and a trio of bruschetta options among other bites. And of course there are warm nuts.

It's the perfect setting—casual but fun—and somehow Vivian has managed to get the whole team, all our families, and all our friends into this space. Even Coach is here.

Vivian's busy chatting with Carlos in the corner by the front of the shop, and she looks relaxed and happy. When Vivian finally accepted that Maeve wasn't going to take over the catering business, she gave us her blessing, so to speak. And then I introduced her to Carlos, since he works in restaurant finance. He's helping her look for a buyer so she can retire, and judging from the smiles and laughter, everything is going to work out just fine for Maeve's aunt.

My gaze drifts to my wife, who's wearing *my vest*—fine, it's now hers—and a pair of jeans, and the whole look makes me want to do bad things to her. But I did those before, and I'll do them after. That won't ever change, I know it. What has changed in a handful of months is this—I've started to *chill the fuck out*. Maeve still does her wrists exercises, but thanks to my work in therapy I'm seeing them now as proactive rather than a harbinger of doom. I also stopped sending J-dad articles on the side effects of his medication. He knows them already.

Maeve's with her group of friends, but chatting specifically with Leighton, and I'd be willing to bet it's about the apartment. Maeve's sub-lease ran out finally, so the weird pigeon place is out of her hands now, and Leighton is moving back in with her roommates in a couple weeks.

Music sounds over the speakers, and it sounds like one of Wesley's playlists. That feels fitting too.

Wesley and I are standing by the coffee bar, outfitted to serve champagne and wine tonight, while Josie shows off her ring to her friends. My teammate proposed to her a few days ago, and Josie's very much enjoying her moment with the bling.

"Beat you to it," I say to my teammate.

"Didn't know it was a contest to propose first," he says.

"One, everything is, and two, I beat you to marriage as well," I reply, as Miles meanders through the crowd, making his way toward us while once again looking like he's fighting to keep his gaze off Leighton. I'm going to have to warn him that he's getting seriously see-through.

When he joins us, he gives a chin nod and a lift of his beer glass. "Finally, we can celebrate the fact that you wouldn't be here without us," he says to me.

"Oh, I'm sorry, I'm here *because* of you fuckers?"

"Dude, we're your wingmen," he says with a crisp nod.

"The DickNose board agrees," Wesley chimes in.

"Fair enough. The DickNose board gave great tips. A toast to the DickNose board and the best damn wingmen ever," I say, raising my glass.

"Best? Did I hear something about the best?" Max asks. "You must be talking about me. And if it's summer poker league, you guys are toast."

"Yes, yes, we know. You like to win at poker," Wesley says to our goalie.

"Can't help it if I'm the GOAT," Max remarks.

A throat clears. "Maybe I'll have to take you on someday."

I straighten at the sound of Coach McBride, but I don't go as ruler-straight as Miles does. Dude looks like the principal just walked in. Well, he kind of did.

"Hey, Coach," I say to the guy we all look up to. He's a former player and one of the best coaches in the league. "You want in on our poker games?"

It's not the first time he's joked about it. But it's become a running gag.

"Actually, I have another player for your games instead. And it's someone Miles knows well." He turns to Miles and says, "Did you hear the news?"

Miles swallows, looking a little uncomfortable. "No, sir."

"Your brother is joining the Sea Dogs. Eleanor Greer just traded for Tyler," he says, then looks at his watch, "about an hour ago. I've been looking for a player like him."

Damn, he'll be a great addition to the team, and my dads had been betting on this trade to happen for some time.

Coach McBride claps Miles on the shoulder. "It'll be great to have you two on the same team. Especially if you become co-captain this season."

Then he walks away on that mic drop, and we all turn to Miles.

"Co-captain," I whisper. The coach has talked about mixing up the leadership group from a captain and alternates to a co-captain. And this could be huge for my friend. "You're going to be co-captain."

Miles just blinks, then his gaze drifts once more to Leighton, and I laugh. "Dude, you are so fucked."

"Tell me about it," he mutters.

But I'll be there for him no matter what he has to deal with, just like he was there for me—just like all these guys are here for each other.

Right now, though, I need to see Maeve. I just do. I make my way through the crowd and find her with her friends, who are like her family. I cut in, saying, "Excuse me. May I have this dance with my wife?"

"Yes, you may," Leighton says with a grin.

Then I take Mrs. Callahan's hand and lead her onto the makeshift dance floor amongst the artwork. "We never had a dance as husband and wife in Vegas."

"Lucky us," she says. "We get to do all these things now. I guess that's the benefit of falling in love with your best friend and having two weddings."

"So many benefits and I love all of them."

I kiss my wife in front of everyone as "The Way You Look Tonight" plays. And tomorrow, I'll take her on our honeymoon in Paris—like I promised I would.

* * *

Want to see how generous, filthy-mouthed hockey star Wesley falls hard for his teammate's little sister? Get the roomies-to-lovers romance The Boyfriend Goal Here!

Have you met grumpy goalie Max who's a little obsessed with team publicist Everly? Get their enemies-to-lovers forbidden romance The Romance Line here!

Turn the page for a sneak peek of Miles's and Leighton's forbidden romance with the coach's daughter in The Girlfriend Zone!

Want to be the first to know of sales, new releases, special deals and giveaways? Sign up for my newsletter today!

EXCERPT - THE GIRLFRIEND ZONE

Chapter One

Miles

I didn't expect to meet her today—my future wife.

I had other plans. But as she heads toward me in the coffee shop's doorway, I just know that's who she is.

Maybe it's the ink on her arms that does it—the stenciled flowers cascading down her right forearm—or possibly the mesmerizing sea-blue shade of her eyes. But honestly? It's probably the smirk she sends my way.

Of course she's smirking. I'd smirk at me right now given what's in my arms.

And since I'm holding a life size glittery mannequin, there's no way my future wife realizes I'm her future husband. The sequined headdress with feathers wider than the doorway probably isn't helping. Nor is the espresso cup glued to the life-size doll's hand. But I'm not the kind of guy to let a six-foot-tall showgirl prop get in the way of fate.

I've got a gut feeling about her—the inked brunette beauty, not the dummy I'm lugging—and I'm the type of guy who listens to his gut. So, I don't let this little scene stop me from greeting the woman who's holding the door open for me to enter the shop.

That won't do. "I've got this. Since, well, chivalry isn't dead," I say, managing to grab the door with my free hand and yank it open further so she can exit first. Birdie—aka Grandma—watches with eagle eyes from behind the counter.

The brunette's gaze slides down to the object in my arms. "And I'm sure your date appreciates what a gentleman you are," she teases as she slips past me—or rather, past Dolly and me—out onto Fillmore Street.

And just like that, it's official. She's the one.

"Honestly, she doesn't say much," I stage-whisper, glancing down at the mannequin Birdie insisted I bring her today, saying *I need a greeter for the shop. Be a dear and grab Dolly from the foyer.*

"Occupational hazard for her, I presume," the woman deadpans without missing a beat.

"True," I agree, furrowing my brow at Dolly, then meeting the brunette's eyes again. "I don't really know her opinions on most things. Anything really."

"But maybe that's what you want in a date?" It's asked like a leading question, like she's enjoying the volley too, but is maybe also a touch skeptical of the guy lugging the doll.

"Nope. A good date needs opinions."

"Is that so? You like lots of opinions?" She sounds doubtful as she adjusts the sweater she's carrying, since it's September in San Francisco, which means you never know if it's going to be warm or breezy.

"Love them," I say definitively, matching her raised brow. "The more the merrier."

"Noted." Her tone is playful, the kind of playful that says *keep talking*.

"In fact, here's one for you. An opinion that is," I say, leaning in just slightly as I lay the groundwork to ask her out. "The chocolate mocha here is excellent."

"You're gallant, and you give out free hot beverage tips too? Is it my lucky day or what?"

"Or mine. That is, if you want to share some of your opinions with me."

She takes a beat, likely assessing me with those curious eyes. Then she nods toward the neon menu behind the counter. "Here you go. The chocolate mocha is good, even with oat milk."

And we're getting somewhere. "Good to know. That's what I'll order on my next date."

Her lips—her pretty pink lips—curve into a challenging grin. "Is that so?"

Ah hell. You only live once. I want to ask her out right now—it's pre-season but there's no hockey practice tomorrow, so why not lock in the chance right fucking now? Her smile makes me want to dive in, no hesitations. But before I can suggest a time to meet again – like *tomorrow same time* – she dips her face and checks her phone screen.

It's in her hand, and from the looks of it, someone's calling, but I didn't hear it ring.

Odd. I'd think it was a *save me* tactic, but her phone flashes with *Dad.*

The playful atmosphere shifts when she raises her face, her smile fading. Before she answers though, she looks my way once more. "I hope you get to enjoy that mocha on your next date," she says, her voice softening to the most fantastical flirty whisper. "But just so you know, I prefer tea."

"I'm filing that away," I say.

"You do that."

"Saving it for my next date. Tea," I say tapping my temple.

She shakes her head, amused. "Better not forget."

"It's in the vault."

Then, with maybe some reluctance in her expression, she turns away and answers her phone in a warm voice, "Hi, Dad."

She walks up the street. Away from me.

I stand there for a second, weighing what just went down. Did she actually turn me down or did she leave the door open? I'd like to think that was a breadcrumb – *I prefer tea* – but she could just be phenomenally smooth. I'm not sure. But then, I remind myself this wasn't going to be as easy as asking her out right here, right now. Nothing good comes easily. I watch her go, admiring her attitude, her sass, her banter, and, well, let's be blunt—her ass.

But what gets me most is when she reaches the corner. It's almost imperceptible—just a quick glance over her shoulder—but I see it. She steals a final glance at me.

Yes. Fuck yes.

It was a breadcrumb, and I will take it. Follow it. And devise a plan.

I pump a virtual fist, then haul Dolly inside High Kick Coffee, past chattering customers camped out at tables, and a handful of people waiting to place their orders. Birdie has plenty of employees here to tend to them, but she opened a coffee shop because she likes people as much as she likes bling. In typical Birdie fashion, everything in High Kick Coffee sparkles, from the countertops to the mirrors on the walls to the clock with a woman's leg kicking back and forth to keep time.

I prop Dolly behind the far end of the counter as my grandmother starts an espresso for me. "Tell me the brunette with the flower tattoos is a regular," I say, unable to shake the thought of the woman who got away for now. But not for good.

"Why? Are you in love already?" Birdie teases with a knowing grin.

"More like insta-infatuation," I admit, leaning on the counter. "But sure, call it love."

Birdie's smile widens. "Ah, young people." She gestures to her old showgirl photos hanging behind the counter—pictures of her kicking her leg high while wearing spangled bikinis and feathered headdresses. "The one with the flower tattoos? She's a photographer."

"We're working together soon," Birdie adds. "Time to update the pics, don't you think?"

I blink, trying to imagine Grandma's glory days in Vegas on stage, and now her dusting off her sequins and feathers for a photo shoot. Would she really do one now? Then again, she did insist I drag Dolly all the way from her home to her coffee shop after this morning's practice ended, so I wouldn't put anything past her.

Besides, this is the breadcrumb I wanted. "New photos sound great. Especially if you let me know when you're doing them," I say, already plotting my return. Like, say, the day when Grandma gets her new pics done.

"We haven't picked a date yet."

"But you will."

"I will," she says, then adds with a small smile. "Eager much."

"I know what I like. What's her name?"

"Leighton," Birdie says. "She comes in about once a week."

"Leighton," I say, liking the way it sounds. "Perfect. But just to make sure I don't miss her, I guess I'll be stopping by every day till I ask her out."

Birdie laughs, shaking her head. "You were always my most determined one. Now, be a dear and put Dolly by the door. She's my greeter."

"Right." I carry the mannequin easily to the front of High Kick Coffee, where the caffeine comes with an extra kick, letting Dolly greet customers, but not before sneaking one last look up the street. I can barely make out her silhouette disappearing in the distance, but that's fine.

I'll be back, Leighton. I'll be back.

I return to the counter as Birdie gets a break from the morning rush.

"How was practice?" she asks, eyeing me over the steaming espresso she slides my way.

"Great," I say, feeling a surge of pride. "Playing better than ever. It's all thanks to Coach." I owe him everything. I'm still grateful for the chance he gave me a couple years ago when my career was circling the drain. My last team let me go and for a while there I was sure my hockey days were done.

Now, everything's looking up—and has been for my last couple of seasons with the Sea Dogs.

Especially with my future wife coming back next week.

So I can buy her a cup of tea and hear some of her opinions.

Preorder Miles's and Leighton's coach's daughter forbidden romance coming soon to Kindle Unlimited in The Girlfriend Zone!

P.S. If you're looking for Fable and Wilder's fake dating the single dad billionaire boss office romance you'll find it in **My Favorite Holidate!**

BE A LOVELY

Want to be the first to know of sales, new releases, special deals and giveaways? Sign up for my newsletter today!

Want to be part of a fun, feel-good place to talk about books and romance, and get sneak peeks of covers and advance copies of my books? Be a Lovely!

ACKNOWLEDGMENTS

Thank you to Jill for the amazing insight into mental health, anxiety and obsessive tendencies. Your insight is invaluable, and I am so grateful for all of the ways that you helped shape the story.

Thank you to Lo for you guidance on the story and your insight. Thank you Kayti for brainstorming. Thank you KP for seeing the whole thing through.

I am so appreciative of Sharon for checking all the hockey and guiding me through the sport. Thank you to Rae and Kim for helping me fine tune details.

With deep gratitude to my editor Lauren who always knows exactly what a story needs.

Big love to my author friends who I rely on daily — Corinne, Laura, AL, Natasha, Lili, Laurelin, CD, K, Helena, and Nadia, among others.

Thank you to my family for making it all worthwhile. Thank you to Dylan for the paw-fume.

Most of all, I am so amazingly grateful to you — the readers — for picking this up! I hope you love Maeve and Asher like I do!

MORE BOOKS BY LAUREN

I've written more than 100 books! **All of these titles below are FREE in Kindle Unlimited!**

The Love and Hockey Series

The Boyfriend Goal

A roommates-to-lovers, teammate's little sister hockey romance!

The Romance Line

An enemies-to-lovers, player and the publicist, forbidden romance!

The Proposal Play

A best friends-to-lovers romance!

The Girlfriend Zone

A coach's daughter romance!

My Favorite Holidate

A spinoff from this series! Fake dating the billionaire boss!

The My Hockey Romance Series

Hockey, spice, shenanigans and cute dogs in this series of standalones! Because when you get screwed over, make it a double or even a triple!

Karma is two hockey boyfriends and sometimes three!

Double Pucked

A sexy, outrageous MFM hockey romantic comedy!

Puck Yes

A fake marriage, spicy MFM hockey rom com!

Thoroughly Pucked!

A brother's best friends +runaway bride, spicy MFM hockey rom com!

Well and Truly Pucked

A friends-to-lovers forced proximity why-choose hockey rom com!

The Virgin Society Series

Meet the Virgin Society – great friends who'd do anything for each other. Indulge in these forbidden, emotionally-charged, and wildly sexy age-gap romances!

The RSVP

The Tryst

The Tease

The Dating Games Series

A fun, sexy romantic comedy series about friends in the city and their dating mishaps!

The Virgin Next Door

Two A Day

The Good Guy Challenge

How To Date Series (New and ongoing)

Friends who are like family. Chances to learn how to date again. Standalone romantic comedies full of love, sex and meet-cute shenanigans.

My So-Called Love Life

Plays Well With Others

The Almost Romantic

The Accidental Dating Experiment

A romantic comedy adventure standalone

A Real Good Bad Thing

Boyfriend Material

Four fabulous heroines. Four outrageous proposals. Four
chances at love in this sexy rom-com series!

Asking For a Friend

Sex and Other Shiny Objects

One Night Stand-In

Overnight Service

Big Rock Series

My #1 New York Times Bestselling sexy as sin, irreverent, male-
POV romantic comedy!

Big Rock

Mister O

Well Hung

Full Package

Joy Ride

Hard Wood

Happy Endings Series

Romance starts with a bang in this series of standalones
following a group of friends seeking and avoiding love!

Come Again

Shut Up and Kiss Me

Kismet

My Single-Versary

Ballers And Babes

Sexy sports romance standalones guaranteed to make you hot!

Most Valuable Playboy

Most Likely to Score

A Wild Card Kiss

Rules of Love Series

Athlete, virgins and weddings!

The Virgin Rule Book

The Virgin Game Plan

The Virgin Replay

The Virgin Scorecard

The Extravagant Series

Bodyguards, billionaires and hoteliers in this sexy, high-stakes series of standalones!

One Night Only

One Exquisite Touch

My One-Week Husband

The Guys Who Got Away Series

Friends in New York City and California fall in love in this fun and hot rom-com series!

Birthday Suit

Dear Sexy Ex-Boyfriend

The What If Guy

Thanks for Last Night

The Dream Guy Next Door

Always Satisfied Series

A group of friends in New York City find love and laughter in this series of sexy standalones!

Satisfaction Guaranteed

Never Have I Ever

Instant Gratification

PS It's Always Been You

The Gift Series

An after dark series of standalones! Explore your fantasies!

The Engagement Gift

The Virgin Gift

The Decadent Gift

The Heartbreakers Series

Three brothers. Three rockers. Three standalone sexy romantic comedies.

Once Upon a Real Good Time

Once Upon a Sure Thing

Once Upon a Wild Fling

Sinful Men

A high-stakes, high-octane, sexy-as-sin romantic suspense series!

My Sinful Nights

My Sinful Desire

My Sinful Longing

My Sinful Love

My Sinful Temptation

From Paris With Love

Swoony, sweeping romances set in Paris!

Wanderlust

Part-Time Lover

One Love Series

A group of friends in New York falls in love one by one in this sexy rom-com series!

The Sexy One

The Hot One

The Knocked Up Plan

Come As You Are

Lucky In Love Series

A small town romance full of heat and blue collar heroes and sexy heroines!

Best Laid Plans

The Feel Good Factor

Nobody Does It Better

Unzipped

No Regrets

An angsty, sexy, emotional, new adult trilogy about one young couple fighting to break free of their pasts!

The Start of Us

The Thrill of It

Every Second With You

The Caught Up in Love Series

A group of friends finds love!

The Pretending Plot

The Dating Proposal

The Second Chance Plan

The Private Rehearsal

Seductive Nights Series

A high heat series full of danger and spice!

Night After Night

After This Night

One More Night

A Wildly Seductive Night

Joy Delivered Duet

A high-heat, wickedly sexy series of standalones that will set your sheets on fire!

Nights With Him

Forbidden Nights

Unbreak My Heart

A standalone second chance emotional roller coaster of a romance

The Muse

A magical realism romance set in Paris

Good Love Series of sexy rom-coms co-written with Lili Valente!

I also write MM romance under the name L. Blakely!

Hopelessly Bromantic Duet (MM)

Roomies to lovers to enemies to fake boyfriends

Hopelessly Bromantic

Here Comes My Man

Men of Summer Series (MM)

Two baseball players on the same team fall in love in a forbidden romance spanning five epic years

Scoring With Him

Winning With Him

All In With Him

MM Standalone Novels

A Guy Walks Into My Bar

The Bromance Zone

One Time Only

The Best Men (Co-written with Sarina Bowen)

Winner Takes All Series (MM)

A series of emotionally-charged and irresistibly sexy standalone MM sports romances!

The Boyfriend Comeback

Turn Me On

A Very Filthy Game

Limited Edition Husband

Manhandled

If you want a personalized recommendation, email me at laurenblakelybooks@gmail.com!

CONTACT

I love hearing from readers! You can find me on TikTok at LaurenBlakelyBooks, Instagram at LaurenBlakelyBooks, Facebook at LaurenBlakelyBooks, or online at Lauren-Blakely.com. You can also email me at laurenblakely books@gmail.com